Remarkable Praise for

"No one does it better than Nicci French."

—Lee Child

"Immensely satisfying."

—*The New York Times Book Review*

"Genuine chills and page-turning suspense."

—*Entertainment Weekly*

"Razor-sharp writing by French expertly amps the tension."

—*People*

"Will leave readers questioning everything they think they know."

—PopSugar

"Fabulous, unsettling, and riveting."

—Louise Penny

"Nicci French has become synonymous with suspense."

—*Daily News* (New York)

"Psychological suspense at its brightest and most blazing."

—A. J. Finn

"Unforgettable. Psychological dynamite."

—Alan Bradley

"French continues to impress."

—*Publishers Weekly*

Also by Nicci French

Frieda Klein Novels
Blue Monday
Tuesday's Gone
Waiting for Wednesday
Thursday's Child
Friday on My Mind
Dark Saturday
Sunday Silence
Day of the Dead

Other Novels by Nicci French
The Memory Game
The Safe House
Killing Me Softly
Beneath the Skin
The Red Room
Land of the Living
Secret Smile
Catch Me When I Fall
Losing You
Until It's Over
The Other Side of the Door
What to Do When Someone Dies
The Lying Room
House of Correction
The Unheard
The Favor

HAS ANYONE SEEN CHARLOTTE SALTER?

A Novel

NICCI FRENCH

wm

WILLIAM MORROW

An Imprint of HarperCollins*Publishers*

HarperCollins books may be purchased for educational, business, or sales promotional use. For information, please email the Special Markets Department at SPsales@harpercollins.com.

Published by Simon & Schuster in the United Kingdom in 2023.

FIRST US EDITION

Library of Congress Cataloging-in-Publication Data has been applied for.

ISBN 978-0-06-329835-4 (paperback)
ISBN 978-0-06-329834-7 (library hardcover edition)

24 25 26 27 28 LBC 5 4 3 2 1

To Caleb and Esther

Thirty years ago, in a village in East Anglia where the land is swallowed up by mudflats and marshes and a hard wind blows in from the sea, a woman went missing.

It was midwinter, sleety and dark, but Christmas was coming. There were festive lights in the high street, decorated trees in the windows, smoke curling from the chimneys of the houses. And in a barn on the edge of the village, people were gathering for a party.

But one person never arrived, and life was changed forever in that ordinary little village. Her disappearance was the start of a chain of terrible events that for more than three decades blighted the lives of two families.

This is a story of dark secrets that were buried a lifetime ago, but which never lost their power, and of the grip that the past has upon the present.

It is the story of the people whose lives unravelled from that winter day: sons and daughters, brothers and sisters, partners and friends.

It is the story of a woman. She is a wife, a mother, a confidante. She is impulsive and warm-hearted and full of life. When people describe her, they use words like "radiant," "vital," "generous," "optimistic." She is a woman of appetites: she loves food, red wine, long hot baths. She loves dancing. Walking in all weathers.

Jigsaw puzzles. Gossip. Weepy films. Nice clothes. Crumpets. Marmalade. Chance encounters. Peonies and sweet peas. Candles. Mangy dogs. Lost causes.

She loves life. She loves people. Above all, she loves her four children.

Her name is Charlotte Salter.

He looked up.

"Does that seem all right?"

"It was fine. More than fine. It was good."

"Then it's a wrap."

PART ONE

1990

ONE

"Where's Charlie?"

Etty couldn't make out the words. The party had only just started, but there was already the bustle of voices and Neil Young on the sound system. She pulled her curly hair away from her face and leaned in towards Greg Ackerley.

"What?" she said, smiling into his troubled face.

She was happy and light-hearted, a sense of excitement running through her. It was the end of term. The excitement of Christmas was on her, parties and outings and mornings lying in bed heavy with sleep. Greg smiled back. She was so close to him she could smell his scent and see the sweat glistening on his forehead. He'd been working hard, preparing all of this.

Etty had enough brothers already. Maybe too many. But he'd always been a bit like another brother to her. She looked at his prominent cheekbones, his blue eyes, his air of being preoccupied. He was attractive, sweet, a bit shy. If he hadn't been like a brother. If he hadn't been three years older than her. It was all rather confusing. Anyway, she had another boy on her mind this evening.

"What?" she said.

"Where's your mother?" he said, speaking more clearly and slowly, as if to a deaf person. "I want her to see how beautiful it all looks. Before it gets trashed."

Etty looked around the barn. It had taken all of yesterday for Greg and his father, Duncan, to clear out the rubbish and then sweep and clean it. Now it was decorated with flowers and garlands and ribbons and coloured lights. The long trestle table Greg was standing behind was crowded with bottles, glasses and a vast bowl of punch with a spray of greenery around it. At the other end was an array of quiches and dips and finger food.

"Isn't she here?"

"No."

Etty gave a snort of irritation.

"She tells me to get here early and then doesn't bother to turn up herself. She probably wants to make a grand entrance."

Greg, looking at her flushed and vivid face, thought that Etty didn't understand how special her mother was; how lucky she was to be Charlie's daughter rather than, say, the daughter of his own mother, Frances, who sometime lay in bed most of the day, or sat hunched in a chair with a vacant expression. Etty took her mother's vivacity and warmth for granted, was even embarrassed by it, not understanding it was like a fire to warm yourself on.

Etty saw the surprise on Greg's face and felt a flicker of betrayal towards her mother. But she pushed it away. Her friends were waiting for her at the entrance of the barn. Kim and Rosa were there, and Robbie, who was in the year above them and who Etty knew had come because of her.

A flash made her blink. Her brother Niall was squinting through the lens of a Polaroid camera.

"It's Keith's" he said, aiming again. "It won't really capture it."

"My mouth was full," said Etty. "You shouldn't take pictures of people when they're eating."

Niall looked at the table and pointed an accusing finger at the greenery around the punchbowl.

"Isn't that a wreath? The kind you have for funerals?"

"They delivered it by mistake," said Greg. "It's for Doris Winters. She died last week, aged ninety-seven. They'll probably come for it tomorrow. I thought she wouldn't mind if we used it first."

"Is that really what you're wearing?" Niall asked Etty.

Etty glanced down as if she was seeing her clothes for the first time: a short black dress with a flannel shirt over the top of it and her Doc Martens.

"Looks like it." She didn't feel she had anything to apologise for. Niall was dressed in a grey suit that looked a couple of sizes too small for him and a purple silk tie with a large chunky knot; Greg wore paint-spattered jeans, an old shirt rolled up to the elbows and, on his head, a shabby flat cap that his father often wore.

7

She saw her other two brothers standing a few yards away, deep in conversation. She spoke in a tone that was almost a shout.

"Paul. Ollie. Get over here."

The two of them slouched towards her. Ollie raised a hand to Greg, who had been in his year group all the way through school but who had never been his particular friend. Greg lifted his beer bottle in response then took a hefty swig.

"Niall thinks I'm inappropriately dressed," said Etty.

"What does that even mean?" said Paul.

Ollie grinned. "Nice tie, Niall."

"I came straight from work," Niall said, as if this was some kind of rebuke to all three of them.

Seeing her three brothers in this strange social setting, Etty felt there was something comic about how different they were. Niall was tall, solid, heavy-footed. His sandy hair was cut short. Even though Ollie and Etty were still at home, Niall already had the resigned, resentful air of the child who had stayed, the son who had entered the family business.

Paul seemed not just different, but a different race. He was small and thin, with a soft, round face that made him look younger than his twenty-one years. He was the child who had left, gone to college. He never talked about it, but Etty had a feeling that it wasn't working out, that there was bad news somewhere, but Paul hadn't told them about it. Paul didn't tell people things.

Ollie was the brother who was like her. At least that's what people said. They were the fun ones, the partygoers, the sex and drugs and rock'n'roll ones. Of course, it wasn't as simple as that. Nothing is. But Etty felt that that was how people saw them. People got irritated by Niall and alarmed by Paul. But things would always be fine for Etty and Ollie.

"We should get a photo," said Etty, making a gesture to her group of friends to say she would be with them soon.

"Why?" said Niall.

"We're all together. It's Dad's fiftieth birthday."

She took the camera from Niall and gave it to a middle-aged man she didn't know and asked him to take the picture. They formed themselves into a group.

"Smile," said the man.

"Smile like we're at a party we want to be at," said Ollie.

"Oh, for God's sake," said Niall.

And when the Polaroid image emerged, it showed Niall glaring at Ollie, Paul looking blank and only Etty smiling at the camera. In the background was a fuzzy Greg, chugging beer.

"Perfect," said Ollie, "and now I'm going to meet some people outside and get out of my head enough to deal with the rest of the evening."

As he moved away, Etty turned to Paul.

"You OK?"

"I'm not really in the mood."

Etty thought to herself that nowadays he was never really in the mood, but she answered as cheerfully as she could.

"I don't think any of us are really."

"I thought you had another party to go to?"

She jerked her head towards her friends.

"Yeah, we're going to sneak off when we can."

Paul mumbled something indistinct, picked up a bottle of beer and drifted away. He was six years older than her, but he still looked young and unformed. When she was a child, she'd been close to him, but nowadays she felt oppressed by him. He was so quiet, solitary and watchful. He made her feel guilty for having friends and boyfriends and fun, and the guilt made her angry.

Kim came up to her and put a hand on her arm.

"Let's go," she whispered.

"Hang on one minute." Etty turned to Niall. "Have you seen Mum?"

Niall frowned. "Didn't she come with you?"

"I didn't come from home. I came straight from Kim's. Is Penny here?"

Penny was Niall's girlfriend and at the mention of her name his frown deepened.

"I'm not sure she's coming."

"Why?"

"I don't want to have a big discussion about Penny just at this moment."

"Fine by me."

"If Mum doesn't get here soon, she'll miss Dad's speech."

"He's not making a speech, is he?" said Etty. "He can't."

"He can."

Just a few minutes earlier, the barn had felt awkwardly empty, with scattered groups and large spaces between them. Now there were enough people that she had to force her way through them to get at her father.

Alec Salter was wearing a suit, almost flamboyant, in brown with white pinstripes, and a blue tie with a red swirling pattern. As Etty got closer, she saw he was talking to Greg's father, Duncan Ackerley, and another man she didn't know. Alec put an arm round her shoulders. He looked like he'd come straight in from the open air, his face flushed, his pale brown hair a bit frizzy. There was a strong smell of lavender and of cigarettes.

"How's my favourite daughter?" he said.

She was his only daughter, and it was a joke that had worn thin long ago. She shrugged off his arm.

"Have you seen Mum?"

"I came straight from work," he said without any sign of concern.

"She should be here by now."

His expression was slightly amused and slightly contemptuous.

"It's a woman's prerogative, isn't it?"

"You mean, being late?" said Etty. "I thought the sexist saying was about changing your mind."

"You're not going to be boring, are you?"

"Niall said you were going to make a speech. You can't make a speech before Mum gets here."

"Why not? She's probably heard it all before." Alec looked at his watch. "If she's not here in fifteen minutes,

11

I'm going ahead. If she misses it, then you can describe it to her."

Alec ended the conversation by turning back to his friends, but Duncan stepped aside. He was blond and big-boned, and when he bent down towards Etty she could see her face in his horn-rimmed glasses.

"Hi, Etty. OK?"

"Have you seen Mum?"

"Not since just after lunch. She came to collect some extra bowls and a ladle. Have you tried ringing her?"

"This is a barn," said Etty. "It doesn't exactly have a phone."

There were two large wooden doors at one end of the barn. Once, many years earlier, it would have been where the cows were brought in and out. At the other end was a smaller door which led out into a field at the back. Etty held up her hand in another waiting gesture to her friends and took that exit into the darkness. She was hit by the December cold. From here she could see the shine of the broad river.

The smell of weed wafted into her face from further in the darkness and she saw a group and the tell-tale glow.

"Ollie," she said.

One of the silhouetted figures turned towards her.

"What are you doing here?" he asked, as if she was a little girl intruding on the big kids' game.

That felt cruel. Usually they were so close, but some-times, when he was with his friends, he pushed her away. Ollie was nineteen, three-and-a-bit years older than she was, and they'd always been a gang of two in the family. He had left school in June and gone travelling for several months. Next year, he'd be going to university, and not just any university but Newcastle, almost as far from Suffolk as it was possible to get. Etty was dreading it because then it would just be her left at home.

"I was wondering where Mum was."

"How should I know?"

She looked at the boys with Ollie. She recognised two from his year, and also Morgan Ackerley, Duncan's second son. He was younger than the others. In fact he was in Etty's year, although they weren't particular friends. He was clever, nerdy and painfully self-conscious.

"I don't think she's here," Etty said. "And Dad's about to give his speech."

Ollie smiled slowly. "That's probably why she's not here." He held up the spliff. "A bit more of this and it'll be like I'm not here."

"Can I have some?"

"You're too young."

"It's not like I haven't had it before."

"Then get it from someone else."

His tone made Etty furious and ashamed, but she forced herself not to reply.

"It's just weird," she said instead. "She's been talking about it for days and she's done so much for it. She wouldn't miss this."

She heard the clink of a glass and someone shouting something inside. A shape appeared in the doorway.

"You need to come in," called a voice. "Alec's making a speech."

"He can't be," groaned Etty. "He said he was going to wait for a few minutes."

"It's his big moment," said Ollie. "He's not going to wait for anybody."

Etty went into the barn with Ollie, but they didn't push their way through the crowd, instead standing just inside with their backs to the wall. Robbie slouched across and stood close beside her, in the shadows. She could feel his heat and smell the nicotine and beer. Her body tingled. She felt another presence close to her and looked round. It was Greg again. He was holding a bottle of beer.

"Have you seen her?"

"What?" said Greg.

"My mum."

"No." He took a gulp from the beer. "She's probably here somewhere. Probably organising some special surprise for Alec. That would be just like her, doing something special that nobody else would think of."

"Jump out of a cake?"

He smiled and took another swig from the bottle. Ollie was getting stoned; Greg was getting steadily and quietly drunk, while she felt horribly sober. She felt she was at the wrong party. It was time to leave.

"You could try ringing her at home," said Greg.

Etty shook her head.

"You're probably right. I'm sure she's here somewhere."

She stepped a bit closer to Robbie and he took her hand.

Her father began to talk but she couldn't make out what he was saying and she couldn't see him. Someone shouted and he stopped and then appeared above the heads of the crowd, swaying slightly. He was standing precariously on a chair.

Etty knew that her father wasn't nervous. He didn't worry the way most people worried about a speech going wrong. He knew that it probably wouldn't go wrong and, if it did, he wouldn't care about that either.

"I thought someone should say something at an occasion like this," he began, "and if someone is going to do it, then it had better be me. Apparently, this is a birthday party ..." There was laughter from the crowd, but Alec didn't smile. He just waited for the noise to die down and then continued. "My darling wife hasn't arrived yet. At least, not as far as I know. If you're here, please make yourself known in some way or other."

He paused and there was almost a silence. Etty could feel Robbie's hand caressing hers.

"Answer came there none," said Alec finally. "But I have reason to believe that the rest of my family is here. My children. My brood. My jewels. I mean, what can I say? There's Niall, the one who has entered the family business and is waiting for me to retire. Put your hand up, Niall." This had the form of a joke of some kind, but Alec was still entirely unsmiling. Niall looked uncomfortable as the partygoers turned to him.

"And then, counting down, there's Paul who does ...

15

what do you do, Paul? Studying something somewhere. Where are you, Paul?"

Etty could see Paul, over to one side, also by the wall. She couldn't make out his expression, but she knew what it would be. Wretched.

"And then there's young Oliver. How can I describe him? Artistic. Creative."

"He says it like it's a bad thing," Ollie muttered in Etty's ear.

"Ollie, make yourself known."

Ollie raised his hand, his face flaming almost as red as his hair.

"All right, Oliver, you can put your hand down now. And then finally, last and least, or do I mean last but not least, there's my little flower, the comfort of my old age, who brings all the charming feminine graces to the Salter household, my daughter Elizabeth. Where is she? Where are you? Make yourself known."

Etty was, briefly, glad that her mother wasn't there to witness this. She would have hated it. She stepped away from Robbie and folded her arms defiantly across her chest, turning away from her father. Across the room, she saw Rosa and Kim grinning and rolling their eyes theatrically. She made a grimace at them.

"Look at her," Alec continued. Etty felt her cheeks burn as some of the partygoers actually did look at her. She wasn't sure if they were burning with embarrassment or just simple anger. "Isn't she a picture? But don't look too closely. She's only fifteen and, remember, she has three older brothers." He paused. "Where was

16

I? Oh, yes, I'm fifty. Fifty. Half a century. Why did anyone think that was worth celebrating? Anyway, thanks for coming."

The speech came to a sudden end. Alec climbed down from his chair. There was a little ripple of applause, and someone started to sing "Happy Birthday," but it didn't catch.

"Arsehole," said Ollie in Etty's ear.

"Where is she?"

"Can we go yet?" asked Robbie.

The dancing started. Etty could hardly bear to watch. Duncan was gallantly trying to encourage guests on to the floor. He swung Mary Thorne round in a circle and then tried to twist her under his arm, but it went wrong and they ended in a tangle. He roared with laughter, while she adjusted her dress and her husband, Gerry, sat by himself at the side of the barn and stared sulkily at them over his beer.

Her father seemed to have disappeared.

"Let's go," said Rosa. "The other gig will be in full swing by now. This is seriously boring."

There was an end-of-term party at a house on the outskirts of Glensted. The parents were away and everyone would be there. Etty had persuaded Kim and Rosa to drop in on her parents' celebrations on their way.

"Give it a few minutes," she said. "Until Mum gets here, sees I've turned up. Then we'll go."

For a few minutes, she and her group danced

ironically to Abba. Etty loved dancing, but not here, with the uncomfortable sense that her father and his friends were watching them and they were putting on a performance of being teenagers, showing the middle-aged and the old what it was to be young and carefree.

Duncan galloped past, waving his arms wildly above his head.

"I've got a tape," said Robbie. "Shall we shake things up a bit? What do you think? My Bloody Valentine? Let's make their ears bleed."

"I'd prefer just to go," said Kim. "You said just an hour. We'll be missing the fun."

Etty hesitated. She caught a glimpse of Paul, who looked wretched, and a spurt of anger went through her.

"You go," she said. "I'll join as soon as I can."

She half expected them to protest, but they didn't, just shrugged and nodded. Kim put her arms round her and hugged her too tightly.

"You'll be OK?"

"Sure."

"See you very soon." She nudged Etty and glanced meaningfully towards Robbie. "It's going to be a great evening."

Etty watched as they left, and then made her way along the edge of the room, her eyes stinging from the cigarette smoke. She kept thinking her mother would suddenly be there, with her cascade of dark blonde hair piled on her head, wearing the red dress that made her look like a film star, smelling of Chanel and smiling so the dimples in her cheeks deepened.

Where was she? Etty looked at her watch. It was half past nine. Charlie was often late but not like this.

"Your mother," said Alec—who must have been drunk, because Etty had seen him empty glass after glass of punch, but who only seemed more sneeringly precise than ever—"your beloved mother likes to be the centre of attention. She wants everyone to be asking where she is."

"That's not true."

"Really?" Alec brought his face very close to hers. "Quite the mummy's girl nowadays."

Etty went looking for Niall and found him at the side of the barn, an oblong of light from the window illuminating him and Penny. She was sobbing and punching him in the chest. He kept saying, "Whoa, whoa!" as if he was calming a skittish horse.

She looked for Paul but she couldn't find him.

Ollie was sitting slumped on a chair near the makeshift bar with his eyes closed, rocking slightly, making a humming sound. She shook his shoulder and he opened one eye, nodded at her, then closed it.

"Sorry I was a shit," he said, barely audible. "Some fucking party, eh?"

Quarter to ten. Ten o'clock. Five past.

She thought of the party she wanted to go to, the boy she fancied.

The dancing continued. The candles Greg had put on the food table guttered.

Etty collected her jacket. She would call home to see if Charlie was there, and then she'd go on to the other party—although the fizzing excitement had gone out of her, leaving her tired and dispirited. Outside it was damply cold, with a wind coming in gusts, whipping her hair against her face. The track to the road was quickly swallowed up into a thick darkness. She had to walk slowly, trying to make out which way it went, her boots scuffling on the rutted surface, massy trees on either side like sentinels.

She thought she heard an owl, but maybe it wasn't an owl. Maybe it was Penny crying, or someone having sex in the bushes. As she reached the phone box, a figure loomed up at her.

"Morgan! You gave me a fright."

She could see his face now: so different from Duncan or Greg. He was thin and pale, glasses glinting, a shock of dark hair. He was holding a cigarette, whose tip glowed when he lifted it to his mouth and inhaled.

"I'm going to ring home," she said. "Mum's still not turned up."

The booth smelled of urine and tobacco and the receiver was greasy so she held it slightly away from her. She dialled the number and there was a ringing tone, then a static hiss on the line. Etty pushed in the coins.

"Hello?" she said.

"Mum?" The voice at the other end crackled into her ear.

"Paul?"

"Etty? Is that you? I thought it was Mum calling."

"She's not there then?"

"No."

"Where is she?"

There was a silence at the other end. She could hear him breathing and she could hear the emptiness of the house, with no Charlie in it.

It had started to rain. Morgan was waiting, his hands thrust deep into his pockets. Why was he even here, at a party for old people, when all his schoolmates were out celebrating the start of the holiday?

"She's not there," Etty said. "Why is nobody else worried?"

"You could dial 999," he said, quite casually.

"What?"

"You could call the police."

She stared at him. The police: that would make it scarily real. He looked back unblinking.

She pulled open the door of the booth again and stepped inside, lifted the greasy receiver once again and dialled three times.

"It's my mother," she said. Her voice came out high and childish. "Charlie—or rather, Charlotte Salter. I don't know where she's gone."

When she came out of the phone box, Morgan had gone. She walked back to the party alone.

Two

The back exit of the barn was like the grim underside of the party. People were doing things in the dark they couldn't do inside. Etty saw a couple against the wall to the side, entangled in each other. She smelled the reek of weed and then recognised Ollie, of course, among the group and then saw that Morgan was once more with him. She felt a stab of resentment. Apparently fifteen-year-olds were all right if they weren't his sister. She bumped against Greg, who murmured something unintelligible. She recognised the glassy expression of the very drunk and the sweaty pallor of someone who had just vomited or was just about to vomit. She murmured something unintelligible back to him and moved quickly away from him.

Someone had lit a fire in a brazier outside. As she moved towards its flickering light, she heard a familiar raised voice. Her father was jabbing the narrow chest of Victor Pearce. He was the owner of the village café and he was Charlie's friend, not Alec's. She made the scones and chocolate-and-walnut cake that were always on the counter, and sometimes Etty worked there on a Saturday. He was shorter than Alec and slight. His hair was tied back in a knot and he wore a tie-dyed T-shirt and velvet trousers.

"Hey, cool it," he was saying as he inched backwards.

Etty touched her father's shoulder and he looked round at her.

"I called the police."

Alec's face was blank as he stared at her but somehow it set her heart thudding furiously.

"And why did you do that?" His voice was suddenly quite pleasant.

"Nobody else was doing anything."

"Nothing's happened. She just hasn't bothered to turn up to my fiftieth birthday party."

"They're sending someone to our house in about half an hour."

His face was still expressionless, but Etty could feel his anger. He moved away from Victor Pearce, spun around and walked back into the barn. He disappeared into the crowd. After a moment the music suddenly stopped. The dancing faltered and there was a sudden silence.

Etty couldn't see her father but she could hear his voice, announcing that the party was over.

"At least, it is for the Salter family. Thanks for coming and all that. Turn off the lights when you leave."

"You can't drive," said Ollie to his father. "Not after all you've drunk."

"And you can? After smoking whatever it is you've been smoking?"

"I wasn't planning to drive."

Alec yanked open the door of his car.

"Get in."

"No way."

"Suit yourself. Etty?"

She thought of the other party. People would be dancing, drinking, making out. She pushed her hands deep into her pockets.

"I'll walk back with Ollie."

"Where's Paul then?"

"He's already at home," said Etty. "And Niall's going to come in his car."

"Right. Just me then. Enjoy your walk."

He climbed into the car, pulled the door shut and turned on the ignition. Ollie and Etty watched the car speeding up the track, its red taillights disappearing into the night.

It was only a fifteen-minute walk, but the rain was turning to a soft sleet that the wind flung into their faces.

They didn't say anything as they reached the main road just before it crossed the river, trudged past the phone booth, the bus stop where Etty got the bus to school in Hemingford every day and where a group of young teenagers were drinking from cans, past the new estate with its row of identical bungalows, and into the winding roads of Glensted, with its red-bricked, gabled houses. Christmas trees sparkled through windows. There was a reek of wood fires.

Etty was trying to feel irritated with Charlie for ruining the beginning of her holidays, but she couldn't push away the rising anxiety and would have run if she'd been alone. She strode along with Ollie ambling in her wake, her heavy shoes clattering on the pavements. The town dwindled to a few houses, then they were at the small, disused petrol station and the cluster of mobile homes that stood empty for most of the year. From here, they could see the outline of the farmhouse, with squares of light from the downstairs windows.

Paul opened the door, standing like a cut-out figure in its rectangle of yellow. His eyes were the colour of walnuts. His hair, the same rich chestnut-brown as Etty's, was long; Alec said it made him look even more like a sissy. Behind him in the hall, the Salter Christmas tree was a splash of gaudy colour. Charlie didn't believe in tasteful decoration. She had hung the branches with red, gold and purple baubles, strings of lights and silver tinsel. Presents were already heaped underneath it including, Etty saw, a small square one with a ribbon tied around it, meant for her.

"No sign of her?" asked Etty.

Paul shook his head.

They went into the house, taking off their wet jackets. Ollie bent down and pulled off his sodden trainers and then his socks, saving himself from toppling by a hand on the banister. His feet looked very pink and, when he stood up again, Etty saw how large his pupils were. Etty's hair dripped down her neck and her cheeks stung from the cold.

"I called the police," she said to Paul. "Was it stupid of me?"

She wanted him to say yes.

"No."

The door to the living room on their left opened and Alec came out, a full glass of whisky in his hand.

"A thoroughly memorable fiftieth birthday," he said. "Thank you all."

Headlights were coming up the drive. There were two cars: Niall's old Honda and, behind him, a police car.

"I'm pretty wasted," said Ollie in a carrying whisper, and gave a small, scared giggle. "Do you think he'll notice?"

"Shut up," said Paul. "This isn't about you."

When Niall came in, Etty felt relieved. With his brown and reproachful eyes and his fair skin that flushed up when he was embarrassed or annoyed, he was reassuringly down-to-earth and literal and it seemed unimaginable that anything awful had happened to Charlie when he was in the room.

The police officer looked no older than Ollie, and he reminded Etty of some of the boys in her class, awkward in their height and bulk. His body strained uncomfortably against the uniform and he kept easing a finger inside his collar. He came in smiling, and he didn't stop smiling. Even when he was trying to look serious the grin broke through, creasing his broad, boyish face.

"Geoffrey Bealing," he said, bobbing his head to them each in turn.

They led him through into the living room, where he sat on the armchair with a broken spring. Etty and Niall sat opposite him on the sofa, Paul took the little chair, and Ollie propped himself up by the fireplace, where cold ash lay in a heap. The heating hadn't been turned on and the room felt spiritless and grim.

Alec remained in the doorway, holding his glass which was almost empty.

"You're concerned about your wife?" Bealing said to Alec.

"No."

Bealing shifted awkwardly in his seat.

Etty jumped up from the sofa and stood in front of him, her fists bunched.

"She's gone missing," she said, her voice pitched high. "We don't know where she is. You have to find her."

"It's only been a few hours," said Niall.

Bealing looked from one face to another. His gaze came to rest on Alec.

"Is it unusual for your wife to go walkabout?"

"Walkabout," said Ollie. "For fuck's sake."

"Stop it, Oliver," said Alec. He turned to the police officer and spoke in a soothing tone. "Not at all. My wife is an impulsive woman. She will be back soon."

"How do you know that?" asked Etty. "Did she tell you?"

27

"I know because I know Charlie."

Bealing struggled to his feet.

"As you say, sir, it's only been a few hours. I'm sure there's nothing to worry about. If she hasn't come back in twenty-four hours, then contact us."

"I'm sorry you were called out. I apologise on behalf of my daughter. She's only fifteen."

"Don't treat me like a baby. Something's happened to her. She might have fallen. She might have . . ."

She didn't know how to finish the sentence.

THREE

When Bealing got back to the police station in Hemingford, the duty sergeant was drinking tea and reading the paper. He was called Guy Lock and he was a widower. He liked the all-night shift. He looked up.

"Anything?"

"Woman didn't turn up at a party."

"What do you make of it?"

Bealing grinned.

"I liked the daughter. I reckon she needs keeping an eye on. Schoolgirl but, you know, all grown up and with a bit of a temper on her."

Lock shook his head. "I used to warn my daughters about men like you. Seriously, though, watch yourself. What is she, fourteen?"

"No, boss, she's legal. Or near enough, anyway."

"This mum, though, should we be worried?"

Bealing pulled a face.

"She most likely had a tiff with the husband. She's probably safely home and making the tea by now."

*

The three brothers were sitting around the kitchen table. Etty was walking back and forward, as if she were looking for a resting place and not finding one. It was the first time they had all been together since the previous Christmas. Then, Alec had got drunk and Ollie had retreated to his room. Etty and her mother had escaped it all and gone for a long walk along the estuary in the cold and the wind and the sunshine. They hadn't talked about what they had left behind but Charlie had asked her daughter if she was all right and they had held hands as they walked. That had been enough.

"I've been dreading this party for weeks," said Ollie. "But it managed to be even worse than my worst nightmares." He looked around. "Was there anything good about it? The flowers looked nice." He looked at Niall. "How are things with you and Penny?"

"Not so good."

"Did you break up with her?"

"I said that I thought we should spend some time apart."

"So you didn't?"

"I wanted to let her down gently."

"So what did she say?"

"She wasn't happy. She left early."

"I'm going to my room," said Ollie. "Unless someone has a plan."

"You can't just walk away," said Etty. "Mum's not here. She's out there somewhere in that." She gestured at the darkness outside the window. "I'm going to stay here until she comes home."

"She's probably with a friend somewhere, moaning about Dad," said Niall.

"Which friend?" said Etty. "Give me some names and I'll start phoning around."

"You've already called the police," said Niall. "They know about those sort of things. Did that police officer seem worried?"

"He didn't seem to care very much, if that's what you mean."

"I could do with a drink," Niall said. "If Dad's left any."

"She probably felt the same way we did," said Ollie. "She couldn't face this party, so she found something better to do. Which was anything at all, just as long as it wasn't here. I mean, most of us were pretending we weren't there, even though we were, so she just took it to the next level by actually not being there. To the right level."

"Are you still stoned?" said Etty.

"Not enough. I was trying to use chemical means to get me into a space where I was relaxed and blissful, and I didn't really achieve it."

Niall was wandering around the kitchen, opening and shutting cupboard doors. Finally he found what he was looking for and half filled a tumbler with whisky.

"You've got to hand it to Mum," he said, and took a gulp. "If you're going to leave your husband, you might as well do it properly and leave him on his fiftieth birthday."

"This is our mother you're talking about." Paul sounded as if he was struggling to get the words out. "She's the kindest person in the world. Why would she do this without telling anyone? It doesn't make sense."

"It does make sense," said Ollie. "She's married to Alec Salter. When she comes back ..."

"She will come back," said Etty urgently. "You'll promise me that, won't you?"

"Of course, she'll come back," said Niall. Etty thought he was saying it in the soothing tone he might have used if he were saying, of course Father Christmas is real.

"Anyway," Ollie continued, "when she comes back, things can't just go on the way they've been going."

"It's all right for you to say that," said Etty. "You're about to go away. It'll just be me left."

Etty was sure that whatever her three brothers were saying, they all felt the same way. Something huge had happened, as if war had been declared, and they didn't know how to express it or what to do about it. She knew how they would each react. Niall always felt that he was the man of the family. He would try to carry on as if nothing had really happened. Paul would just retreat into himself, into his own darkness. Ollie was the most like her. He would talk about it. Talk and talk. But she couldn't just talk. She had to do something.

"I'll call the Ackerleys," she said. "That's where Mum would go."

"Duncan will be asleep," said Niall.

"I don't care."

There was a phone on a table in the hall just outside the kitchen. Etty picked up the phone and was about to dial when she heard voices on the other line. She instantly recognised one as her father's. She knew she should replace the receiver, but then she heard the other voice. It sounded familiar. She put her hand over the mouthpiece and continued listening. Yes, it was Mary. Mary Thorne.

She hardly took in what they were saying. It was as if they were talking in a foreign language. What she was struck by was the tone, the murmuring intimacy of it. It reminded her of conversations she'd had with boys. It would be the day after a party where they had been kissing, in the corner of a sofa or outside in the garden, and he would ring up and ask to speak to her and they would have long, strange discussions, talking in near whispers as if they might be overheard. Her father had spent the evening being sarcastic and loud and now he was talking in this strange tone she'd never heard from him before.

She replaced the phone as gently as she could. She took a deep breath and then another before going back into the kitchen.

"What did they say?"

"I didn't ring them. Dad was on the line."

"At this time of night?" Niall said.

"He was talking to Mary Thorne."

There was a long silence. Etty thought this was worse than anything. It would be better if someone got angry.

33

Footsteps sounded on the stairs and Alec came into the room with a bulging bin bag in his hand, which he left at the door. He picked up the bottle of whisky on the sideboard, took a tumbler from the cupboard and filled it, then took a sip. How was he not falling-over drunk? He looked at the four hostile faces of his children and half smiled.

"I was talking to Mary Thorne," he said in a neutral tone. "She was concerned about Charlie."

"You rang Mary Thorne at one in the morning because she might be worried about Mum."

It was Paul who had spoken, though his voice was uncharacteristically harsh.

"Who said I was the one to ring her?"

"If she had rung you," Paul said slowly, "we'd have heard the phone ring. But we didn't."

Alec downed his drink and put the empty glass into the sink.

"Don't talk to me like that," he said. "It's my birthday."

"It's not your birthday," said Paul. "Your birthday ended an hour ago."

"All right," said Alec. "Don't talk to me like that. I'm your father."

"You've got a fucking nerve," said Paul.

There was a silence that Etty could feel as if it were something physical, cold and hard against her skin.

"What did you say?" asked Alec in a low voice.

"I said you've got a fucking nerve." Paul spoke more

loudly this time. "We know about you. We know all about you. You did this. You drove her to do whatever she's done."

He stood up, kicking his chair aside so that it fell back on the floor with a clatter.

"Get out," Alec said.

"What are you talking about?" Paul shouted, and walked out of the room. There was the thumping of his tread on the stairs so heavy that the house seemed to shake with it. A door slammed.

Alec looked around. He didn't look flushed or distressed by what had happened.

"Is there anything else?" he asked. "Anything else someone wants to get off their chest?"

"How can you talk like that?" said Ollie.

"Mum's missing," said Etty, "and we're just sitting here."

"Your mother is not missing."

"Has she come back?" Etty asked with a desperate flash of hope.

"She's not here. But you know what she's like: if she has an idea, she acts on it."

"What idea?" asked Ollie.

"I don't know," said Alec. "Any more than you do. She may have been angry. She may not have felt like going to a party. God knows, I didn't."

"Angry about what?" asked Ollie.

"Did you have a row?" asked Etty. "Is that why she's gone?"

"No, we didn't have a row," said Alec irritably. "I was just giving an example. I was speaking hypothetically."

"That's it," said Niall, standing up. "I can't do this. I can't be here any more. I'm going to go and look for her."

"Where?" said Alec.

"Anywhere. I'll drive around, I'll ask people. It's better than doing nothing."

"I don't think it's really that much better," said Alec.

Niall flinched at this and Etty thought he might shout at his father too, or even hit him. But he just walked out of the room. Nobody spoke and the silence was only broken by the sound of Niall's car starting and then driving into the darkness.

It was three in the morning and the house was quiet, except for the creaks and heaves of an old building, as if it were settling itself after the events of the day.

Only one person was asleep: Alec Salter in his pyjamas, in the centre of the double bed, slowly breathing.

Since Paul had gone to university, his room had become a dumping ground for cardboard boxes and displaced items of furniture. He was sitting on his bed, fully clothed, with his headphones on. Cocteau Twins was all he listened to these days, that and Talk Talk. Music to make him swoon and lose himself. Each time it finished, he put the needle back to the beginning of the disc. *When you come to me, you come to broke.*

Ollie was also in bed, in his own room. He had been

watching television with the sound turned down. When broadcast shut down for the night, he left it on, a grey fuzziness which he hoped would send him to sleep. It didn't.

A couple of miles away, on the road to Hemingford, Niall was sitting in his car, parked at the side of the road. He was halfway through a pack of cigarettes and was feeling nauseous. He knew that there was no reason not to go back to his rented flat where he lived alone and go to bed, but when he finished one cigarette, he lit another one. Going home would be an acknowledgement that life was going to continue and that whatever was going to happen would happen. He wanted to put that moment off.

Etty was still sitting at the kitchen table. She was beyond exhaustion. Her eyes were stinging and she felt scoured by the harsh kitchen lights. But she didn't go to bed and she didn't switch the lights off.

If the house were dark, her mother wouldn't be able to see them and she wouldn't be able to find her way home.

Four

Dawn came as a grey, dull light staining the east and brought with it a sleet that melted as soon as it touched the ground. Etty lifted her head from the kitchen table. Her cheek was creased, her eyes stung, she had pins and needles in her left hand. She was still wearing her short black dress and flannel shirt and she felt grimy and very cold. Cold to her bones. She didn't know if she had slept at all but if she had, then it was only in tiny snatches because whenever she had looked at the clock on the wall above the oven the hands had barely moved.

She looked at the clock now and the minute hand quivered forward. It was ten to seven on Sunday 23rd December: two days before Christmas. The house was quiet, except for the clank of the old radiator and the unsteady drip from the broken gutter outside.

She stood up.

Nothing had changed since yesterday. The mugs they had been drinking from last night were by the sink; the bottle of whisky, nearly empty, was on the window sill. Paul's jacket was hung over a chair.

Etty went into the hall. Everything was the same there as well. Her mother's boots weren't in the hall, nor was her coat slung over the banisters. The lights on the Christmas tree were still on, a mockery. Etty crouched down and looked at the presents stacked under it: they were all from her mother, wrapped in green paper and labelled in her flamboyant hand. The one to her was small and square. She held the box against her cold cheek for a moment, then replaced it among the other presents. She switched the tree lights off.

She went quietly up the stairs to the first floor, where her parents' bedroom was. She put her ear to the door and listened but could hear nothing. She pushed open the door and stepped inside, holding her breath. The room was quite dark. She tiptoed to the side of the bed and put a hand on to the shape beneath the covers. She could still smell the lavender, sweet and insistent.

She went along the corridor, past the room which had been Niall's but was now a study and junk room. Music was coming from Paul's room. She knocked and pushed at the door. He was sitting on his bed, staring at her, or through her. His expression scared her. She closed the door again.

Ollie's room was up the next flight of shallow stairs, next to the bathroom. She banged on the door several times.

"What?"

"It's Etty," she said, entering. "You've got to come with me."

He was lying on top of his bed in joggers and a

sweatshirt. His skin was chalky and his eyes red-rimmed. His bright hair stood up in peaks.

"Come where?"

"She's not home."

"I know."

"We've got to go and look."

"Where?"

"Anywhere. Everywhere. Get up."

Her own room was at the top of the house, in the attic. It was small, with a low ceiling and a window that looked out of the back of the house across the fields. They had once belonged to the house, when Alec's father and grandfather had owned it and it had been a working farm. They'd long since been sold off. There were rumours that a developer had his eye on them for housing.

Etty cleaned her teeth in the tiny basin under the window, took off her dirty clothes and pulled on jeans, a long-sleeved T-shirt and a thick jumper that had moth holes in the sleeves. She looked out at the muddy fields, the tall poplars that marked so many boundaries in this area of East Anglia, and beyond them, the broadening river where it curved towards the bridge. Was her mother out there somewhere? She pictured her, injured, calling for help and words being snatched by the wind, freezing cold and in pain and waiting for someone to find her.

This wasn't how her holiday was meant to begin. Today she and Kim had planned to go shopping in Hemingford, because neither of them had bought

Christmas presents for their family yet, and then to the movies. Kim wanted to see *Home Alone*.

Everything felt wrong. Her hair was matted and her head banged with tiredness and her throat ached. She had a pain in her lower back, which meant her period was coming. She felt full of helpless urgency, but Ollie insisted on toast and coffee before they left, and then Niall phoned—the sound of the phone making them both startle with hope—and asked if there was any news. Paul came into the kitchen. He looked boneless and scared.

"We're going to look for her," said Etty.

He didn't ask where; he nodded several times and said he would stay at home in case she rang or turned up.

Etty's Doc Martens were still wet so she put on wellington boots and an old jacket that belonged to Charlie. She slid her hand into the pocket and found a shopping list and a pair of gloves, which she put on.

"Aren't you freezing?" she said to Ollie as they set out.

He hadn't changed from his joggers and sweatshirt. He shrugged.

"I like it," he said.

"Where shall we go?"

"I don't know."

Etty understood then that he didn't believe they were going to find Charlie like this: they were looking because they had to; there was nothing else to do.

But she felt that if she put her whole heart and will into it, she would surely know where Charlie was. She strained her eyes, searching the horizon, waiting to see her mother's familiar figure come over the hill, long blonde hair in a twist, old coat flapping, her lovely warm smile breaking out when she saw them. She turned her head from side to side as she walked, because maybe her mother had fallen and was lying in the trees lining the narrow track that led to the road.

Etty's socks kept sliding down inside her boots and she could feel a blister forming on her heel. Ollie had his head lowered and his hands thrust into his pockets and he walked very fast, as if he was angry.

The café in the square was just opening. Victor Pearce was cleaning the coffee machine as they entered. He turned as the door closing set the wind chimes tinkling and when he saw who it was he laid down his cloth and wiped his hands down his apron with the yellow sun embroidered on its bib. He was wearing a flowery shirt and orange trainers and had a silver stud in one ear. His shoulder-length hair needed brushing and his narrow face was pasty, as if he had slept badly.

"Is Mum here?"

He seemed confused by the question.

"Charlie? No. Did she say she was coming here?"

"We don't know where she is."

"You mean, she never came home?"

"No."

"That's weird."

Etty stared around her as if Charlie would suddenly materialise, at the chairs still upturned on the tables, at the windows with the metal grille still down, at the bare counter. Her eye came to rest on one of the paintings that Victor hung on the walls to sell. He said he wanted to encourage local creativity. This one was in swirly greens and blues and yellows, like a garish pastiche of van Gogh. It made Etty's head bang even more.

"You really haven't seen her?"

"I've only just opened up. Is Alec worried?"

"No," said Ollie. "He's having a lie-in."

"Perhaps they're having a cooling-off period."

"What do you mean?" Etty's voice was high. "What's she said to you?"

"Nothing. I just ..." He stopped. "I didn't mean anything really. I spoke out of turn."

"She wouldn't just go off," said Etty hotly. "She's got us. And it's Christmas the day after tomorrow and everyone's come home, all her children. She was so happy. There are presents under the tree."

"When did you last see her?" Ollie asked brusquely.

"Thursday, I think. Yes, Thursday. She brought a batch of scones round, and we had coffee." Victor pulled his hair back into a ponytail and tied it. His face looked sharper than ever, like a weasel's. "She'll be all right. She's a wise soul."

"He's a creep," said Ollie as they went back into the sleety wind. " 'Wise soul.' What's that about?"

"Mum likes him."

"She likes everyone," said Ollie. "She thinks every-one's nice underneath."

He took a squashed pack of cigarettes from his

pocket, shook one out, bent over his lighter and flicked a blue flame from it. Smoke came from his mouth in a thin column.

"Can I have one?"

He pulled out the pack and she removed one. Her fingers were trembling. Ollie put a hand round the flame of his lighter and she leaned forward and inhaled, welcoming the acrid smoke burning her throat. She felt slightly dizzy.

"We have to go to the Thornes," she said.

"Why? Because of Dad and Mary?"

He looked at Etty as he said this, almost daring her to be offended or angry.

"I don't know. Just because," replied Etty.

Her skin felt raw in the wind, and Ollie's ears and nose were red.

The Thornes' bungalow was near the main road. It was a new-build with a car porch to one side and a gravel front garden. Etty pushed the doorbell several times, hearing its answering tune inside.

The door was opened by Gemma Thorne, who was in Etty's class. The two girls had never hit if off. Etty thought Gemma was two-faced and Gemma thought Etty was hot-tempered.

"Etty! What happened to you last night? You missed a great party."

Etty shrugged.

"Everyone was there. Hello, Ollie." A smile slid across her face.

"We need to speak to your mother," said Etty.

"She's cooking."

"It's important," said Ollie.

Gemma didn't ask them to step inside, just raised her eyebrows and went down the hall, leaving them standing in the porch.

Mary Thorne came to the door with a brisk click-clack of patent leather shoes. She was quite short and she had compact, neat features: bright small eyes, a little rosebud mouth, shapely ears pressed back against her head, a miniature tilted nose. Her hair was a shiny brown bob.

"This is a surprise," she said. "What can I do for you two?"

"We're looking for Charlie," said Ollie. His eyes were watering. "Have you seen her?"

"You mean, this morning?"

"Whenever."

"Is she still missing?"

"You know she is," said Ollie.

There was a movement behind Mary, and Etty realised Gemma was sitting on the stairs and listening to them.

Mary glanced at her daughter and then back at them, her face tense. She took a step towards them.

"Perhaps you should be asking Duncan Ackerley where your mother is," she said quietly, so her daughter couldn't hear.

There was a moment of silence.

"What do you mean?" Etty said at last. "Why would you even say that?"

Mary Thorne gave a tiny shrug. "Just a thought. Since they're so close these days."

"He's our friend," said Etty fiercely.

"Look, you're obviously worried, and I realise it must be horrible for you, but I don't know anything about where your mother is."

"What about our father?" asked Ollie. His damp sweatshirt clung to his body, and his wet hair was plastered against his skull, making his face look thin and pinched, with dark circles under his eyes. "You know things about him."

"Mary," came a man's voice from inside the house. "Who is it?"

"Nobody," she called back. "Now I really do need to get on with lunch." She sounded brisk, but her face was tense. "I really hope your mother turns up soon."

And the door clicked shut.

"As if Mum's a dog," said Ollie furiously.

FIVE

As they rounded the corner, they met Duncan Ackerley.

"I was on my way to see if Charlie's come home," he said.

"No," they both said.

"We're looking for her," added Etty. "Asking people if they've seen her."

Duncan's face was weathered and he smelled of wood smoke and wet earth. He was a tree surgeon and Etty was used to seeing him in his helmet and stout boots, roped high up in the branches, a chainsaw in one hand, or throwing logs into the open back of his van as easily as if they were twigs. He often worked with Alec on landscaping projects and over the years the two families had become close, with Charlie and Duncan as the linchpins. Duncan's sons had gone to the same primary and secondary schools as the Salter children. Greg had been in Ollie's year, but they were too different to be close: Ollie so wild and intemperate, Greg quiet, inward. Morgan and Etty were in the same year too, and Etty sometimes felt guilty that she hadn't protected him more from the school bullies. It was like not looking after a member of her family.

Duncan's wife, Frances, was rarely present. She spent much of her time in bed, and had done so for many years now. When Etty was younger she had believed Frances was slowly dying, but gradually she had come to understand that she was depressed. She lay in bed because she couldn't bring herself to get up and face the world. When she did manage to go out, it was clearly a painful effort. She would look at people blankly, a frown on her face, as if they were speaking a language she was struggling to comprehend. Etty couldn't forget the school concert last year, when Morgan had played a solo piece on his clarinet. Frances had been there; she had sat hunched in the front row, her thick dark hair falling forward and something so desperately sad in her face that it was embarrassing to look at her, like looking at someone naked.

Etty sometimes wondered what it was like to have her as a mother. Maybe that was why Greg was so often silent and withdrawn, and why he often came to their house, to sit in the warmth and chatter of their kitchen and experience being in a family? Or why Morgan was so tense all the time, like a dog waiting to be scolded and kicked. She was certain it was why they often came to the Salter farmhouse with their father. Charlie was everything Frances wasn't. She was full of energy and light. She laughed a lot, throwing her head back and giving full-throated guffaws. She smiled and nodded when someone spoke, leaning forward to listen to them, making appreciative noises. She flattered people, made them feel special and recognised, touched their shoulder.

Duncan's kind face was screwed up in a frown. He looked at his watch.

"Ten-fifty," he said. "Wait till this afternoon and then call the police again."

Ollie kicked at a stone in the road and they watched as it skittered away.

"You both look a bit rough," Duncan said. "Did you get any sleep last night?"

"Not really," said Etty.

"You need to sleep." He looked at Ollie. "And you need to put warm, dry clothes on."

"She'll come home soon, won't she?" Etty knew he couldn't tell her this: she would hate him if he said yes, and she would hate him if he didn't.

"Call me when you hear anything," was all that he answered.

They walked past the farm that grew turf. In the early summer, the fields were an unnatural, manicured green, and in autumn the turf was cut and folded into giant rolls that were driven away to be laid out in gardens like carpets. Now the fields were bare and the sandy soil looked thin and sick.

In the distance stood the church with its stubby spire. In front of them was the playing fields. A man was kicking a ball to a little boy. A couple were walking their dog. A mother was pushing her tiny child on the swing.

A hearse passed by on its way to the church, followed by two cars.

"I thought they didn't bury people on Sunday," said Ollie, morosely. "They probably have to get it done before Christmas."

Christmas coming, presents wrapped, a turkey ordered, and no Charlie.

They turned northwards until they came to the main road that led to Hemingford, past the bus stop and the phone box where yesterday evening Etty had rung the police, over the giant bridge that crossed the Heming before it widened into a broad estuary. They didn't speak to each other until they reached the train station.

The man behind the glass partition hadn't been on duty yesterday. That had been Bernie.

"What time train do you think she might have been on?" he asked.

They didn't know. Afternoon. Evening. The last slow train out, trundling between small stations on its way to London.

He shook his head at them.

"Bernie's not working now till after Christmas," he said.

"She might be home by now."

They walked back over the bridge, then turned down the lane that ran alongside the river, past the track to the barn, past the big new houses with their mock-Tudor facades and lawns that stretched to the river. It was muddy and swollen today, strewn with branches that were being carried to the sea. They twitched and danced in the water like drowning things.

We haven't looked in the woods yet, thought Etty. We haven't looked in the lane to the Ackerleys' house, where the ditches on either side are deep and full of water in the winter, and where she might have fallen. Or the old mill, abandoned and full of rats. Or on the hill that looks out over the river, where Charlie loves to walk. We haven't even looked in our own garden. She might be there, just beyond the front door, just out of sight among the shrubs and weeds. She quickened her pace.

As they came towards their own house, standing alone surrounded by muddy fields, bare trees and tumbledown sheds with corrugated iron roofs, Etty stopped dead and held on to Ollie's arm.

It looked so bleak: the sleet turning to rain, the windows unlit, the chimney unsmoking. She knew her mother wasn't there.

Six

Hemingford police station was in an annex of a red-brick Edwardian building with turrets and gothic windows. Some local people had called for it to be demolished and replaced with a modern, functional construction with adequate security and parking. Other people had called for it to be demolished and not replaced. After all, what did the Hemingford police really do? Sometimes there were fights outside the King's Head on Friday and Saturday nights. There were occasional thefts of garden tools. There was a deceptive bend in the road going inland from Hemingford. Speeding cars would occasionally come off the road until a series of warning signs had been installed.

The day had been quiet, even by Hemingford standards. Nobody had come through the door. The Christmas decorations had been put up back in November. The only urgent problem was that the heating was even more unreliable than usual. When Geoff Bealing walked into the back office, Ted Vardy was lying on his back struggling with a valve on the radiator. The sergeant looked up.

"Is the radiator in the office still cold?"

"I'll check," said Bealing. "They called again. That family from Glensted. The Salters."

"What about?"

"The mum's gone missing."

With a sigh of effort, Vardy raised himself to a sitting position.

"How do you mean, missing?"

"There was a family party yesterday evening at the barn that belongs to Mason's Farm. She didn't turn up."

"That's what you expect at Christmas. When my uncle was in the force, they didn't even interfere. They just left them to it."

"The daughter was saying they're really worried. Maybe we should start looking."

Vardy gestured with the spanner he was holding. "What do you want to do? Get a search party? Start dragging the river?"

"I don't know. Make inquiries. Ask around. It's been a night and all day today."

The sergeant shook his head. "She's on a friend's sofa somewhere. But all right, if you want to go the extra mile, ring around the hospitals, see if they've got a middle-aged lady without an owner."

"And if they haven't?"

"Then we've done our duty and we can go ahead and enjoy our Christmas and hope there aren't too many drunk drivers."

"I'll do it before I clock off."

*

"I've called the police again," said Etty to Paul.

"What did they say?"

"Not much. It was that young man who came to the house. He looks about thirteen. If Dad made a fuss, I bet they'd listen."

The doorbell rang.

"I'll go," said Etty.

A young woman with short brown hair, tortoiseshell glasses and a determined expression on her face stood at the door. She was wearing a thick coat and scarf but still looked cold.

"Yes?"

"My name's Alice Clayton. I was hoping to talk to Alec Salter."

"He's not in."

"Are you his daughter?"

"Why? Who are you?"

"I'm from *The Herald*. I heard that your mother's gone missing. I wondered if I could have a—"

Etty banged the door shut.

She stood in the cold hall with her arms wrapped round her body and her heart thumping.

Why had she slammed the door on her? Perhaps she could help them: after all, nobody else was doing anything. She yanked open the door again to see a small car disappearing up the lane.

SEVEN

Etty woke when it was still pitch black, no moon or stars, no sound except the sound of rain dripping from the gutters. Her tongue felt furry and her eyes scorched with tiredness. For a moment, she couldn't remember where she was or what was wrong, though dread pressed down on her.

She was in her room at the top of the house. She had finally gone upstairs at two in the morning, after a grimly wretched evening with her three brothers. They had all wanted to do something, but there was nothing to do, no one they could think of left to ring, no place they could think of looking. Time was a nightmare; there was no way to get through it and yet, with agonising slowness, it ticked on.

The phone had rung repeatedly. Kim, full of gossip about the party Etty had missed, had wanted to come over, but Etty said no, not now. Neighbours asked questions, offered help, speculated. Penny had called twice: the first time, she had asked to speak to Niall and Niall had said to tell her he wasn't there. The second time, she left a message with Paul that he needed her at a time like this and it was no use him avoiding her.

Eventually Paul had made cheese on toast for everyone. Etty had stared at the yellow greasy sludge on the blackened toast and hadn't been able to eat, though she knew she must be hungry. There was an odd ringing in her ears, and when she closed her eyes, lights shimmered behind her lids. The ash lay in a sooty grey heap in the fireplace, the radiators were cold, nobody had cleared away empty cans and bottles, washed dishes or swept up the leaves and mud that had been trodden through the hall. The Christmas tree was shedding needles over the little group of presents Charlie had left there. The house felt abandoned.

Alec had come in late and said he didn't want anything to eat. Etty couldn't decipher his mood: he was morose, but every so often anger flared up in him then died down again, leaving him more sullen.

When Niall suggested they go through Charlie's things to see if anything obvious was missing, Etty jumped eagerly to her feet. She couldn't understand why they hadn't thought of this before. But Alec had said sharply that he was going to bed and it could wait until the morning. Etty couldn't remember what order things had happened in after that. It was a nightmarish jumble of her bursting into a storm of tears; Ollie putting his hands over his eyes and loudly, repetitively groaning in a way that sounded ghastly; Paul getting to his feet and standing over Alec; Alec raising his hand and hitting Paul on the side of his face.

It wasn't a sharp blow, more a derisive flick of his hand, but everyone fell instantly silent. The silence was almost worse than the chaos that had preceded it.

Then Niall said in a blustering tone, "Now look, I think we should all just calm down." Alec had stared from face to face and then gone upstairs. They heard the key turn in the lock.

"We'll look through her things tomorrow," said Niall.

Nobody had answered.

Etty had sat at the kitchen table, doing nothing but unable to leave, until very late. When she eventually went to her bedroom, she didn't change into nightclothes. Any intention to sleep had seemed like a betrayal. She told herself she would just lie down for an hour or so. But somehow sleep had grabbed her and pulled her into a world of nasty, incoherent dreams. When she lurched awake and looked at her alarm clock, it was nearly six o'clock.

She dragged herself out of bed. Her head thumped dully. Her eyes were sticky with exhaustion. She stood in the middle of her small room and waited for something to happen. She pressed her face to the window and peered into the wet darkness and pressed her fist to her thumping, thumping heart.

It was Christmas Eve.

When Kevin Lofthouse had been diagnosed with type 2 diabetes, the nurse had said he should cut down on fried food, do more exercise, get a dog. He hadn't cut down on fried food but he had gone to a shelter in Ipswich and come away with a mongrel who had the size and the sad eyes of a Labrador and the curly brown fur of a poodle. Every morning of the year he would be woken shortly before seven by a whimpering from the kitchen. He would make a cup of tea for himself and fill the bowl for Dennis and then they would set off for their walk, a regular circuit that would take just over an hour before they were back for breakfast.

This morning was the same as any other, leaving his home on the new estate and walking along the high street. Lofthouse slowed to take a look at the decorations. They had been officially switched on a month earlier by a minor character from a sitcom in the 1970s but now, on Christmas Eve, they somehow looked real to him for the first time. He walked to the edge of the village and then turned down to the right. As he reached the river, he let Dennis off the lead and turned right once more to follow the Heming as it widened towards the sea.

There were no sailing boats this morning and it was full and swollen after the rains of the last few weeks. When he turned to see Dennis scampering towards him, the dog had something in his mouth. It was only when he was right in front of him that he saw it was some kind of heavy material, almost like a blanket, dragging on the ground, sodden.

*

As usual, he turned back into the town just before the bridge and met Jenny Dean coming towards him with her little Jack Russell, who immediately started yapping at Dennis.

"Dennis picked this up by the river," Lofthouse said, holding up the shapeless, dripping bundle.

"What is it?"

With some difficulty, because he had the dog lead in his left hand, he shook the garment so that it unfolded.

"By the river, did you say?"

"Dennis was dragging it."

The old woman examined it more closely.

"Take it to the dry-cleaners and this might be a bit special."

"I was going to just throw it in the bin."

"I think they've got a lost-property department in the police station. If I'd left that somewhere, I'd want it back. It's on your way home anyway."

EIGHT

"What do we do?" said Bealing. There was a note of panic in his voice.

"Where exactly did he find it?"

"I didn't ask him. He just said by the river."

"Get someone to look at it," said Vardy. "The daughter, probably. She's more likely to know." He frowned. "Is she up to it?"

"She seemed pretty smart to me."

"What's this about?" Etty said, as her father reluctantly left her in the living room with Bealing. Her voice wavered.

"We want you to look at something."

"Why me? Why not my dad?"

"You'll see."

"Has something happened? Do you know where she is?"

"Sorry, we don't know anything. We've got something we want you to look at."

First, Bealing told her about Kevin Lofthouse and his

dog finding something, but Etty found it hard to make sense of what he was saying, as if he was speaking in a foreign language that she didn't properly understand.

"What?" she said, when he had finished speaking.

"We'd like you to take a look at it. If that's all right."

He opened the bag by his feet and pulled something out that Etty didn't immediately recognise. He held it out to her, but she stepped back instinctively.

"It was wet. It was almost certainly in the river. We wondered if you might recognise it."

He took out his pen and notebook expectantly.

It was as if the world had changed for her. Everything was shifting and rippling and she felt that a lead weight had been put on her chest. She had to struggle to take a breath. She sat down heavily in one of the armchairs.

"Do you recognise it?" repeated Bealing.

It took a huge effort to answer. She wanted to cry. She wanted to run home and pull the sheets over her head and pretend all of this wasn't happening.

"It's my mother's," she said, almost in a whisper.

"Are you sure?" He was writing what she said on his notepad, partly so he didn't have to meet her gaze.

"Yes. She loves it. She wears it for best . . ."

She was about to say how her mother had bought it in London when she was visiting friends. Charlie had summoned Etty up to her bedroom and taken it out of the large bag and held it up, asking: "What do you think?" Etty had made her put it on and turn round, like a model on a catwalk. It was a soft tweed coat with a little belt at the back to give it shape, large brown buttons and a purple lining. Charlie asked if it made her look fat. Etty told her not to be stupid: she looked classy and beautiful. Her mother had worn it that autumn and winter, a patterned scarf tucked in at the neck and gloves at the ready in the deep pockets. She would walk down the road in her ankle boots and this coat, with her hair piled up on top of her head, smiling at everyone, at the ready for friendships.

Etty couldn't bear the sight of it, soaked and streaked with mud. Something terrible was stirring within her, a violent sickness.

Bealing carefully replaced the coat into the bag. He looked at his damp hands and took a handkerchief from his pocket and dried them. He nodded at Etty and she stared at him in horror.

"That's very helpful," he said awkwardly.

Bealing related what Etty had said to Vardy.

"So what do you think?"

"It doesn't look good."

"Suicide, do you think?"

"You mean, she takes the coat off, walks into the river." Vardy considered this for a moment. "It's possible."

"The coat wasn't ripped. I couldn't see any bloodstains."

"They could have been washed off in the water."

"Wouldn't the body have come ashore somewhere?"

"It would have just been swept out to sea with the tide. It might never be found."

Bealing pulled a questioning face. "Do you really think she could have done that? She's got four children."

"Anyway, it's not up to us now."

"So what do we do?"

"Call the big boys in. I'll get on to the CID at Westlow. And we need to get that old geezer to show us exactly where it was found."

Bealing looked round at the closed door. "What do we do about her?"

"Tell her our inquiry is proceeding. We're not ruling anything in or out."

NINE

The house was chilly and the wind rattled its sash windows. Everything had changed. Everything had got deeper, darker, colder.

Etty could see the fear in the faces of her brothers and hear it in their voices. Charlie's coat, her beautiful new coat, had been found by the river. Nobody was saying now that there was nothing to worry about and she was sure to come home soon.

In spite of the chill, Detective Inspector Brian Cobbett was sweating as he sat with the Salter family in their living room. He was a tall, bulky man with a high forehead and hair brushed over his bald patch. He wore thick glasses that were smeary under the lights and a black jacket straining at its buttons. His red tie was knotted tightly and his black shoes shone.

"I just need to take down a few details," he said. "About Mrs. Salter."

Name. Charlotte Emily Salter.

Age. Forty-seven.

Date of birth. May 11, 1943.

Occupation. They looked at each other.

"She used to work on the pages of a fashion magazine in London," said Paul.

"That was years ago. Decades. And she was very junior," said Alec from the doorway. "Now she doesn't really have anything you could call a profession."

"She does all your admin," said Paul. His usually tentative voice was sharp. "Isn't that work?"

Alec took a mouthful of whisky and shrugged.

"She makes scones and cakes for the café," said Etty. "And she still does bits of journalism. To keep her hand in."

That was Charlie's term for it: keeping her hand in. Etty could see her now, crouched over the Amstrad in her wire-rimmed reading glasses, the tip of her tongue on her upper lip, her painted fingernails tapping on the keys.

"And then she cooks and cleans and helps Dad with his business and looks after all of us," said Paul. "She's never not working."

Etty watched Cobbett as he wrote things down. He was so slow and ponderous. He nodded a lot and pursed his lips. She sat on the edge of her chair as if she would at any minute jump up and run from the room: it was already the afternoon and soon the brief day would turn to twilight. They needed to find her before night fell. But still Detective Cobbett rumbled and hummed and nodded and slowly wrote things down.

He gave a small cough and nudged his glasses back on to the bridge of his nose.

"I need to establish as far as possible what Mrs. Salter was doing the day she disappeared. Perhaps you could each in turn tell me when and where you last saw her, and your own movements."

"Starting from when?" asked Niall. "And finishing when?"

"Just talk me through your days." Cobbett moved his gaze slowly from face to face. His eyes, enlarged by the thick glasses, settled on Paul. "Why don't you begin?"

Paul cleared his throat a few times.

His full name was Paul Owen Salter. He was twenty-one years old and a Biology student at Bath University. "I'm supposed to be doing my finals next summer," he said.

He had been in his room studying all that day, he said, and he hadn't paid much attention to the time. He knew that Charlie had brought him tea in bed at about ten, and they'd had lunch together. "Leek and potato soup," he added, "with bread."

He couldn't remember what they talked about, he said, then after a pause he corrected himself: actually, they'd talked about his upcoming finals and how he couldn't get down to revising, it was like a phobia. He sat in his room and played Tetris on his Game Boy, listened to music, or just sat in front of his books without taking anything in.

"I'm thinking of dropping out."

"Oh, for God's sake," muttered Alec.

"And you told your mother this?" Cobbett asked.

"She asked me. She knew things weren't great. She knows everything without being told. She says it's the curse of being a mother, that you have a sixth sense."

Suddenly his face seemed to shrink and his eyes to grow darker. *He's going to cry,* thought Etty. But he didn't cry; he said: "She didn't say anything about herself, if that's what you're wondering. She seemed OK." He frowned. It was as if he was talking to himself now. "Maybe I didn't notice anything because I was all wrapped up in myself and my stupid little problems."

"When did you last see her?"

Paul chewed the side of his fingernail.

"She called through the door to remind me about the party."

"What time?"

"After lunch? I don't know really. The day's a bit of a blur. I heard her downstairs in the afternoon, I think. She wasn't there when I left the house."

"So you went to the party alone?"

Paul nodded.

"Can anyone corroborate this?"

"I told you, I went alone."

Ollie was next. His full name was Oliver Malcolm Salter, and he was nineteen.

"And what is your occupation?"

"Gap year," said Ollie. "Is that an occupation?"

"He's going to uni next year and he's been away

travelling since September," said Etty. "He's come back for Christmas."

When Cobbett asked Ollie when he had last seen Charlie, his face took on a pinched, furtive look.

"Maybe late morning," he said. "I was with friends after that."

"In Glensted?"

"Glensted and around."

"Doing what?"

"Just hanging out," said Ollie.

Cobbett next turned to Alec, smiling encouragingly.

He said he was fifty years old, and the chief executive of Salter Landscapes.

"Chief executive," said Ollie, with a derisive laugh. He took out his pack of cigarettes.

"Not in here," said Alec.

Ollie rose to his feet and strode from the room, banging the door hard behind him.

"This must be particularly hard for you, Mr. Salter," Cobbett said.

Alec seemed to think for a moment, as if he was trying to remember something.

"Do you know Ralph Chettle?" he said.

This wasn't what Cobbett had been expecting and he took a moment to reply.

"What do you mean?"

"He's someone I play golf with over at the Ditton club. He's a detective."

"Yes, I know," said Cobbett.

"Some kind of inspector, I think."

"Chief inspector."

"Something important, anyway. Is he your boss?"

"He's one of my superiors."

Alec laughed. "It's a small world, isn't it? If you talk to him, give him my best. Tell him I've been working on my swing."

"I'll try to remember that."

Cobbett looked down at his notebook. He thought he ought to write some sort of note about what Alec Salter had just said. The mention of Chettle—who, as it happened, was one of his bosses—sounded like a sort of warning. Alec Salter was a well-connected man.

"I think we need to get back to when you last saw your wife."

Once more, Alec wasn't like a normal witness. Usually people found the experience of being questioned by police officers stressful. But Alec spoke in a clipped, pedantic manner, as if he was impatient with the proceedings. He told the detective that he had seen Charlie last at about nine in the morning.

"We had breakfast together," he said. "Then I went to work."

"On a Saturday."

"Yes, on a Saturday. We're a small, family-run company and we don't do regular hours. I needed to tidy things up before the Christmas break."

"What do you actually do, in your work?"

"I told you. I run a landscaping business," he replied. "We have an office on the edge of town. Gardens, community projects, corporate ones. Sometimes local, sometimes far afield. You name it. Nothing's too big for us and nothing's too small. Ornamental ponds, golf courses, roundabouts . . ."

He sounded, thought Etty, as if he was giving a sales pitch. How could he talk about ornamental ponds when Charlie's coat had been found by the river?

"Lots of people can only see you at the weekend," continued Alec. "I went to a house north of Hemingford to discuss their plans."

"Were you there all day?"

"No. I left at about midday and drove straight to the office, and then I went to my somewhat blighted birthday party."

"Just you there in the office?"

"I was with my son," said Alec. He nodded in the direction of Niall. "He works for me in a junior capacity."

Niall's face was stiff.

"Did you talk to your wife on the phone during the day?"

"No."

"So you had no contact after you left in the morning."

"No."

"And there was nothing unusual in her manner?"

"No."

"Nothing you can think of to throw a light on her disappearance?"

"No."

"Had you ... um. Well now, Mr. Salter, I have to ask you this. Had you had any kind of argument?"

"No."

"So she wasn't upset about anything? You know how women can get very emotional about small things."

Paul muttered something angrily under his breath. There was a silence. Cobbett's heavy face flushed.

"My wife is a very impulsive woman," said Alec. "She tends to be ruled by her heart not her head."

Etty let out a croak but nobody noticed her.

"It is true that she gets easily upset. She might very well have been very upset about her son taking drugs, for example. In case you hadn't drawn that conclusion about what Oliver was doing on the afternoon of the party. Or"—he turned and looked at Paul—"about another son thinking of dropping out of university. I can see that would make her extremely distressed, yes."

Paul jolted back in his chair.

"What's wrong with you?" cried Etty.

"But I can't help you. I noticed nothing out of the ordinary."

He sat back and folded his arms.

Niall spoke too loudly, maybe to drown out the sound of the little noises Etty couldn't stop herself from making, or Ollie outside, stamping furiously up and down the path. He was Niall Peter Salter, twenty-four and the eldest Salter son. He was a project manager at Salter Landscapes. "Just for the time being, while I

71

look for other things. I have a degree in engineering," he added.

He didn't live in the Salter farmhouse, but in a small flat on the other side of town. He hadn't seen his mother for several days. He had been at work all day, making calls to clients and chasing up payments.

"And did you go out at all?"

"No."

"And did anyone come to the office?"

"My father was there in the afternoon."

"What did you do before the party?"

"I went to my flat, had a shower, changed."

"Do you live alone?"

"Yes." He hesitated. "I mean, until recently my girl-friend usually stayed over."

"But not now?"

"We've recently separated."

Etty remembered Penny outside the barn, weeping and punching Niall's chest.

"I'm sorry to hear that," said Cobbett.

"It doesn't matter." Niall's loudness dropped away. He spoke drearily. "Nothing really matters now, does it? Except this."

"I'm Elizabeth Amy Salter, and I'm fifteen. I'm still at school."

Etty couldn't make her voice come out evenly. She felt nauseous. She told Cobbett that she hadn't seen or talked to her mother since Friday morning. After school broke up for the holidays, she had gone straight to her friend Kim's house and had stayed the night. They had gone shopping in Hemingford on Saturday with a group of other girls and she had gone straight from Kim's to the party, with Kim and two other friends.

"So the latest anyone saw Mrs. Salter was around Saturday lunchtime," said Cobbett. "And you think she called up to you after lunch," he added, glancing at Paul. "Maybe two?"

"Duncan said he saw her in the afternoon," said Etty, remembering. "She borrowed things for the party, a ladle and bowls. I'm not sure what time."

Cobbett wrote it down, then stared for a long time at his notepad.

"Perhaps we can have a photo of Mrs. Salter," he said at last.

Niall pointed a finger to the mantelpiece. Between a photo of the four children when Etty was just two, and one of Alec standing with their dog who had died last year, was a head-and-shoulders shot of Charlie. She was smiling at them all, a deep dimple in one cheek and her eyes bright.

"And," he said, suddenly remembering, "I will need samples for DNA. I will send one of my officers round. Something like your wife's toothbrush or hairbrush will probably do the trick, or a razor."

Forty minutes later Cobbett settled himself comfortably behind his desk. He took a sip of milky tea from his polystyrene cup before addressing his two colleagues.

"If I was a betting man," he said, "I'd lay good odds on the wife being dead."

"Suicide?"

Cobbett circled his head ambiguously. "Maybe," he said. "Or maybe not. Any news on where that coat was actually found?"

"The old bloke can't remember."

"It probably doesn't matter. And we need to find out what was going on in the marriage."

"Bad timing for us," said the officer with the bony face, looking resentful. "In eight hours it will be Christmas. I don't want to be out in the marshes instead of pulling crackers and eating turkey."

"Do you want to hang out with me and my mates for a bit?"

Robbie was standing at the door, his easy smile fading when he saw how Etty looked.

"I can't," she said.

"OK," he said lightly, wanting her to know he didn't really care one way or another. "Are you all right? You look a bit . . ."

"A bit what?"

"A bit rough."

She saw how he was examining her critically, his mouth slightly pursed in displeasure.

"Yeah, well, sorry about that, but I'm not exactly thinking about how I look. My mum's still missing."

Still missing and her coat's been found in the river

and I'm so very scared. She looked at him as he tried to think what to say.

"Really?" Robbie gave a low whistle, incredulous and almost admiring, and she flinched away from him. "Well, sorry about that, but I'm sure it'll be OK. And you can't just sit around waiting."

She wanted to scream at him. She wanted to punch his stupid, complacent face.

"Another time," he said, turning to go.

"Probably not."

He was shrugging as he walked away. Fury pulled at her, a riptide. Hot tears stood in her eyes.

"Wanker," she said under her breath.

After he had gone, Etty dragged herself up the two flights of stairs to her bedroom under the eaves. She lay on her bed and pulled the pillow over her face. Her throat ached and her skin itched; she felt toxic to herself.

There were two Ettys, two alternative beings. There was the Etty who was carefree and popular and no longer a child. She was waiting for life to unfold for her, for things that she wanted but hardly dared name, even to herself. They were going to happen, and soon, like a new season coming.

And then there was the Etty whose mother had been erased and who had been thrown into a harsh world, where she was naked and afraid. She was a sexless, terrified child and a prematurely adult woman, whose friends suddenly seemed unfamiliar in a life she was shut out from.

The two Ettys did not connect. They streamed away from each other. The one who was heading towards happiness was like a ghost, someone she might have been, and she was trapped in this other self, and she had no idea how to escape.

TEN

Etty was in her parents' bedroom, going through Charlie's wardrobe. She had already checked that her mother's passport was in the top drawer of the bedside table, where it lay alongside hand cream, face cream, a hairbrush with a web of Charlie's dark blonde hair in its bristles, tissues and a pair of nail scissors.

Now she was trying to work out if any of her mother's clothes were missing, because if they were that would mean she hadn't taken off her coat and waded into the muddy river. She pulled the dresses off their hangers one by one and let them fall to the floor. She took out the shirts and laid them on the bed. She slid the T-shirts and trousers off the shelves. When she pushed her face into the folds of a jersey, she could smell her mother: citrus and spice. She rummaged in the underwear drawer and took the shoes one by one from the bottom of the wardrobe.

She was searching for what wasn't there. She tried to remember her mother's clothes and to do that she had to recall her mother, like a slide show playing in her mind. Charlie standing by the bonfire they'd had in November, wearing a rough, striped shirt and old jeans: check. Charlie on her birthday, in an ivory-coloured silk shirt and tapered black trousers she'd had for years and wore when she wanted to look smart: check. Charlie by the beach in her green sundress: check (but of course she wouldn't take something like that; it was the middle of winter). Charlie in a sky-blue skirt: it was there. Charlie outside in her shabby everyday coat. Etty knew it was hanging downstairs. Charlie in an Italian restaurant, sitting opposite Etty, her red lipstick a bit smudged and her hair awry, muzzy with booze and lifting her glass to the company. What had she been wearing? A black dress with a high neck.

Etty tried to imagine what her mother would wear if she was going on a journey: comfy trousers, she thought, and the black leather jacket that she'd had since she was in her early twenties and living in London. Not the lovely tweed coat, she told herself, trying to believe it, trying to push the terrible fact of the coat that had been found by the river out of her mind.

And she would take a case. Etty stood on tiptoes and opened the high cupboard above the wardrobe. Both the overnight case and the larger canvas bag were there.

The sound of footsteps coming up the stairs: she waited for the door to open and Alec to stand there with a stony face as he looked at the chaos she had created. But he went into the little room next door, which served as his study. She quietly closed the top cupboard, and then saw with a lurch of disappointment that the black leather jacket was slung over the chair by the window, underneath Charlie's dressing gown. Her shoulder bag was beside it.

She subsided in the drift of her mother's clothes. Sitting there, she heard more footsteps, heavier. Niall called out Alec's name and banged on the study door.

She went to the bedroom door and opened it quietly, stepping out into the hall.

"Please calm down," said her father, sounding disdainful. He hated emotional mess.

"You told a lie to that detective."

Etty stood frozen.

"You wouldn't understand," said Alec.

"You weren't at the office all afternoon. You were barely there at all. Why did you say you were?"

"I had my reasons ..."

"You insulted me like that, and then you expect me to back you up."

"I'm sorry I wounded your pride."

"I should just go to the police and tell them what I know."

The handle of the study door rattled and Etty stepped back into the bedroom.

"Wait, Niall," she heard her father say. "Let's just be sensible about this. I am grateful you didn't contradict me. I didn't want to complicate things, that's all. Charlie will come home and it's better if we just leave things as they are. OK?"

"It's not OK. You don't seem to grasp that this is turning into a nightmare."

He started to say something else but he was interrupted by a banging at the front door.

Etty bolted downstairs and flung it open. She felt a wave of disappointment.

"Sorry," said Duncan Ackerley, seeing the expression on her face. "Only me."

He held out his arms and she let herself be briefly enfolded by him, and then stepped back before his kindness undid her.

"Her coat," she said on a sob. "Her coat was by the river, Duncan."

"I know, my dear." He didn't say anything else. What was there to say?

"What shall we do? We have to find her. Will you help?"

"I'll do anything I can," he said. "You know I will."

She registered how weary and anxious he looked and fresh terror flooded her so she tottered where she stood.

Ollie came out of the kitchen and stood beside her. He took her hand and held it in his own, which was very cold. He smelled sour, like milk on the turn.

"I want you all to come to our house tomorrow," said Duncan. "For Christmas lunch. Frances and I both agree that you mustn't be here."

His gaze took in the cold muddy hall, the moulting Christmas tree, the scattered shoes, the way that life had so quickly drained away from the house.

"But we have to wait here," said Etty. "We can't all go out. When she comes back, she'll wonder where we are."

"You can leave a note."

"Thank you, Duncan," said Alec, coming down the stairs. "We would appreciate that."

"Good. Early afternoon be all right?"

ELEVEN

"Merry Christmas."

Etty, standing in the kitchen among the debris of last night, looked round at Ollie. Red-eyed, bleary, everything askew. Was he being sarcastic or did he really mean it?

"You know what the worst thing is?" she said. "When they showed me Mum's coat, I almost wished it was her body. Then at least I'd know. Because this ..." Her throat closed up. She put her hand on her neck.

Ollie's eyes opened wide. He had lost his cool, his detachment. He suddenly seemed younger, almost like a child.

"That's rubbish. She's alive somewhere."

Etty had always felt closest to Ollie, as if they were twins, not just brother and sister. They had shared secrets. Sometimes they went to parties together. She'd fancied his friends and his best friend had been her first kiss, his hands under her shirt, under her bra, his lips cool and tasting of coffee. Now, for what felt like the first time in her life, she didn't tell him what she felt, what she had been intending to say: that their mother might never be found, that every day might be like today, with just an absence and no answers.

"You're probably right," she said dully.

"Do you want to hear something stupid?"

"What?"

"I wish Mum was here. She'd know what to do. She always knows."

Both of them looked round, hearing footsteps on the staircase. They recognised their father's deliberate tread on the wooden stairs, and when he appeared in the doorway of the kitchen, he was not only dressed, but wearing a heavy Barbour jacket and a hat and gloves.

"I thought you all might be having a lie-in," he said.

"Have you heard anything?" Etty asked.

"How would I have heard anything?"

"Lots of ways," Ollie said.

"Well, I haven't. Have you started opening your presents?"

"Presents?" said Etty.

"You know, the Christmas presents. Round the tree."

"Is that a sick joke?"

"Do I look like I'm having fun?"

Etty rubbed her face violently with the heel of both palms.

"Shall we have breakfast together?" she said at last.

"That's a kind suggestion." Alec spoke as if he were talking to someone he knew very slightly. "But I'm going out for a walk."

"A walk?"

"Yes." He gestured at what he was wearing. "Hence all of this. Outdoor jacket. Outdoor shoes."

"Where are you going?"

"I'm simply going for a walk."

"Do you want us to come with you?"

Alec gave a faint smile and looked at Ollie.

"I don't think he looks ready to stride out across the countryside." Then he shook his head. "No. Sometimes you need to be on your own. Clear your head."

He left the kitchen and they heard the door slam. Etty looked out of the window and saw her father heading for the road. He stopped and gazed up. There was a huge V of geese slowly crossing the sky. He stood staring for a long time, then progressed out of the gate and out of sight.

Etty looked at Ollie.

"Do you think Dad hates having children and being married?"

Ollie was lighting a cigarette. He took a deep drag and instantly looked more alive.

"No," he said. "I think he hates having these particular children and this particular wife." He took another drag. "Apart from you. I think he'd swap us all for another family but he'd want to keep you. Don't you think that's why there are four children even though he hates having children so much? He kept trying until he got one he liked."

"That's not funny."

"I'm not being funny."

"So what do we do now?"

"What do you mean?"

Etty gestured to the clock.

"We're meant to go to the Ackerleys' early afternoon. That gives us four or five hours. So what do we do?"

"Nothing," said Ollie. "How about we do nothing?"

TWELVE

It was one o'clock and Etty couldn't bear it any more. She had phoned Niall and he hadn't answered. She phoned every twenty minutes until finally he picked up, sounding distracted. He said he would make his own way to the Ackerleys'.

"What time?" said Etty.

"I'll get there when I can."

She hadn't seen Paul yet. She went up the stairs to his bedroom and knocked. There was no answer so she opened the door and went in. He was lying on his bed with headphones on and his eyes shut. She stepped forward and shook him.

"You can't just barge in," he said.

"I knocked. You didn't answer. What have you been doing?"

"Listening to music."

"You've been out. You've got muddy shoes."

"I went out for a bit."

"Where to?"

He stared at her, his eyes glassy, and didn't bother answering.

"I think we should go now," Etty said.

Paul kicked first one muddy shoe off, then the other one. They left smears of mud on the pale blanket.

"I'm not going."

"But we said we'd go."

"I can't put on an act. I can't pretend that everything's all right. Who are we doing it for?"

"Mum would want us to be together."

"Don't say what she would have said or what she would have done. Just don't dare."

He looked as if he might cry or fly at her, so she left him and walked downstairs.

She felt entirely alone. Alec was still out, which was a relief, but Ollie had also left the house. He said he was going to meet someone and didn't know when he'd be back. He told her they'd meet at the Ackerleys'.

Etty put on her long blue coat, wrapped a woollen scarf round her neck and stepped outside. She instinctively turned towards the river. That was the beautiful route to the Ackerleys', along the river path, under the bridge. But she remembered the sight of her mother's coat, wet and discoloured, and so instead she walked straight into Glensted, along Church Street and into the main square. To get to the Ackerley house, she had to turn left down towards the post office and then, just before reaching the river, she turned right as Glensted became scrubby countryside in a few steps. At the end of the narrow track was the Ackerleys'.

Morgan opened the door. Etty could see his face working with the effort of thinking of words that weren't crass or distressing.

"Hello. Happy Christmas, I guess." She gave a twisted kind of smile.

"Sorry about everything," he said, looking at her and then looking away. "It's shit."

"Is anyone else here yet? Dad, or my brothers?"

"No."

"Paul's not coming."

"Sure," he said. "Dad's not here at the moment, but Greg and Mum are in the kitchen."

Etty followed Morgan in the direction of the clattering and the smell of cooking. Greg was standing at the hob, stirring something. He was still wearing his oilskin jacket and a beanie and she saw that the bottoms of his trousers were damp. He looked intent on his task, the tip of his tongue on his upper lip, slightly frowning. Frances was sitting at the table with a bowl of sprouts in front of her, but she was doing nothing.

Greg raised a wooden spoon in silent greeting.

"Sorry. Am I early?"

"Someone has to be first," said Morgan.

"No news?" Greg asked.

"Is it all right if I don't talk about it?"

"Everything's a bit late, I'm afraid," Frances said, looking from Etty to the unpeeled sprouts and back. "Things have got a bit behind but Greg's stepped in now."

Then she seemed to remember herself. "You poor

thing, you poor thing." She got up from the stool and took Etty in her arms. "I haven't slept since it all happened. I just lie awake and go over and over it in my mind. I think what could have happened and then I think about you. You poor, poor children."

Etty stood there stiff and unresponsive and at last Frances dropped her arms.

Greg led Etty into the living room. There was a fire blazing in the hearth and the Christmas tree lights were on. The window gave on to a view of marshes and, beyond them, the river as it widened towards the sea. The tide was at the full. Soon it would start going out and the mudflat and rivulets would appear.

Etty sank into one of the sofas, suddenly conscious of her enormous weariness, which was like a crushing weight. Her eyes ached and her throat felt raw, as if she'd been yelling. She looked down at her hands lying in her lap, and saw she had tracked dirt over the carpets.

"It's OK," said Greg before she could say anything. "It's just mud."

She stared at him, but words wouldn't come. He bit his lip.

"I'm sorry about everything, Etty," he said at last, and for a moment he looked and sounded like his father. "Really sorry. And I should have been more help at the party, when she didn't come, but I reacted by getting insanely drunk."

Etty wanted to tell him to stop talking, to just go

away, but she knew that they were all just trying to help. She looked up at his handsome, troubled face. People didn't know how to behave around her.

"Your mum was lovely," he said, then realised the horrible mistake of that past tense. His face flushed to the roots of his hair.

They both started to say something at the same time and then stopped.

"Can I have some tea?" she asked.

He left her and she sat alone, watching the flames dance and crackle.

The front door opened and closed. She heard Niall's voice. Too loud and hearty, trying to be normal.

He came into the living room and sat beside her. He'd put on a tweed jacket that was too small for him and a pink shirt that was too large for him, and had combed his hair so it lay flat. He patted her hand and she stared fixedly at the fire and tried not to cry.

Morgan came in with milky tea for Etty. He gave Niall a glass of sparkling wine, which Niall drank all in one go as if he was thirsty.

"Something smells good," he said with forced cheerfulness.

"I'm sure Dad'll be here soon," Morgan said. "He's in charge of the turkey."

When Ollie arrived, he was very obviously out of it. He sat cross-legged on the floor and gazed around him. His nose was red from the cold and he blew on his hands to warm them.

"So where are the fathers?" he asked.

"Dad's probably lost track of time," said Morgan.

"I'll find him," said Greg.

"I'll come with you." Etty stood up. She needed to be outside, in the cold, under the great skies.

She pulled on her blue coat and they stepped out together, into the whip of the wind. Her scarf flapped and her hair blew against her face. It was foggy and already the light was starting to fade. The tops of the poplars were barely visible and to the left the massive bridge that ran over the Heming was a spectral shape.

"He was going to build up the bonfire, so we could light it when it got dark," said Greg.

Etty followed him down the garden. The bonfire was there, ready to be lit, but Duncan was nowhere to be seen. Greg called his name but the sound was swallowed up by the wind.

Small drops of rain stung Etty's cheeks. Greg zipped up his jacket and walked on.

"Where are you going?"

"The river," said Greg. "I think he said something about pulling the boat further up. There's going to be a very high tide later tonight."

He walked to the wooden gate at the end of the garden. It opened on to the marshes, where a rough track led down to the river. You could walk to the sea from there when it wasn't high tide, and in the other direction the path led inland along the river as it narrowed and wound its way through villages, fields and woods. Etty trailed after him, on to the swampy ground. They walked down to the banks of the river. The tide was quite low and there was a broad strip of mud separating them from the water. The wooden boat was pulled up into the coarse grass and turned turtle, but Duncan was nowhere in sight.

Etty gazed out across the mudflats, down to the water's edge.

"What's that?" She pointed.

"What?"

"There. By the orange buoy."

Greg squinted. Then Etty saw him go quite still, like an effigy planted in the salty earth, staring out at the shape in the river.

"Greg, what is it?"

"Go back to the house, Etty."

"No."

"Please."

"No."

He was turning the wooden boat over and dragging it down towards the water, his feet squelching in the mud. An oar toppled out and Etty picked it up and ran after him with difficulty, sinking into the dark silt, her eyes straining to make out the shape. The rickety little landing stage that Duncan had built stood stranded in the mud, the water feet away.

"Go back, Etty. I'm telling you."

"No."

They pushed the boat into the icy river, up to their knees, scrambling in, slipping on the slimy wood, wind whipping across them, seagulls and water birds crying, every movement clumsy. Greg fixed the oars into the rowlocks. His face was smeared with dark mud. He wasn't wearing gloves.

He rowed badly, the oars catching at choppy waves; his hands looked raw in the cold. Etty sat in the bow and peered out as they laboured towards the orange buoy and the shape beside it.

Greg stopped rowing so the boat was tugged by the tide.

"No," she said. "No no no no."

"We should go back. Call the police."

But he kept rowing.

She had to look. She couldn't look. Her body rocked to and fro. A keening noise came from her.

"You mustn't look," said Greg. "A body that's been in the water."

With an effort that hurt, she forced herself to gaze at the shape that was caught on the chin of the buoy and was twitching with the movement of the river. She gazed and the breath left her body and she thought she would pitch into the water.

"It's not her. It's not Mummy."

He said something but his words were snatched away by the wind.

"It's not her clothes. It's not."

"Oh, Jesus."

"Greg, who is it?"

Thirteen

Duncan Ackerley stared up at them with his open eyes. His right temple was bruised and his face swollen and shockingly white. His mouth was slightly open; he almost looked as if he was trying to smile at them. Etty thought she must be sick.

"He might be alive," said Greg. "Quick. We have to get him out of the water. Help me, Etty."

Etty knew Duncan wasn't alive but she took the oars from Greg as he ordered and tried to keep the boat still. Greg leaned out from its stern and reached for his father. The gulls screamed and the river slurped and gurgled beneath them.

He took hold of Duncan's waterproof jacket and pulled. At first, the body wouldn't shift, but at last, with a wrench, Greg dislodged it from the thick chain it had caught on and pulled it towards the little boat. At last he was able to put his hands under his father's armpits and try to get him aboard. The boat lurched and water washed into it. Etty felt a surge of panic at the idea of the boat tipping, of them being in the water, with him.

"I can't do it," he said at last. "He's too heavy. You have to row us back to the bank. I'll keep hold of him."

Etty tried to row against the tide, leaning against the oars with each stroke and putting all her strength into it. The little boat barely responded.

"It's too heavy," she said at last.

"OK. You have to hold on to him and I'll row."

So she slithered to the stern and took hold of Duncan while Greg took up the oars. They inched towards the shore, the waterlogged mass bobbing and dragging behind them. Etty wanted to shut her eyes or look away, but somehow she couldn't. She stared down into Duncan's face, his sightless, staring eyes. She wasn't used to seeing him without his glasses. She saw that he hadn't shaved that morning.

At last, they could go no further and Greg jumped into the water up to his thighs. He took the body into his arms and with a harsh sob started to tow it the last few yards. Etty clambered out as well, and pulled the boat behind her.

Greg laid his father on the mud.

"Run and get help," he said fiercely, and then started to pump at Duncan's chest.

"Come on," he was saying as Etty laboured through the mud towards firmer ground. "Come on, Dad."

Etty ran up the garden shouting and waving her arms. She burst into the house and saw faces staring at her. Frances was there, and Morgan too, gawping at her.

"Call the ambulance! Get help. It's Duncan."

"What's wrong with Duncan?" asked Frances in a wavering voice.

Alec was there, calling 999. Ollie had dropped his cigarette on to the rug and it was smouldering. She could smell the turkey, the high note of brandy, the thick rank mud that was all over her.

"Where's Dad?" Morgan was pulling at her arm. She saw his eyes, large and terrified behind their glasses, his narrow boy's face.

"Oh, Morgan," she said.

"Take me to him."

"She's not fit to go out again," said Alec.

But she turned at once from the door and from the sight of Frances, and was running back to the river with Morgan, Niall and Ollie behind her, her sopping trousers chafing her thighs and her face raw with cold. No one spoke; she could hear their footsteps thudding on the path in her wake, and their laboured breathing.

Down the garden, through the gate, on to the path. The river was sucking at the mud, making obscene, gloopy sounds. The gulls were still calling.

So they came to Duncan, lying stretched out on the mud. His head was in Greg's lap, and Greg was stroking his hair as if to comfort him.

"He's dead," he said, lifting his eyes to them. "Our dad's dead."

The rain spat down and dusk was closing in. Morgan knelt in the mud beside his father and started to shout incomprehensible words in a high, hoarse voice. Greg continued to stroke his father's hair, looking down at him as if Duncan was his child.

Frances was there now as well and was standing apart, hunched, whimpering.

Etty saw the blue lights first. Men came running down to them, their feet squelching and slipping in the mud. She stood hunched over with Niall's arm around her, and watched as figures bent over Duncan's body. One of them helped Greg to his feet. His mud-splattered face was bewildered.

The tide was on the turn again, the water creeping back up the bank towards them. Soon it would reach Duncan.

She watched them lift the body on to a stretcher. Someone put a blanket round her. Alec had his hand on her arm: she hadn't even known he was there.

"Come on," he said. "We're no use here."

They trudged back to the house in a line. Greg had his arm around his younger brother and it looked to Etty like he was holding him up. Frances tried to stay with her husband and at last they had to pull her away.

There were officers still down by the river. It was almost dark and Etty could see lights flickering and sometimes the beam of a torch swung across the water in an arc.

Etty went home in a police car. Alec followed in his own car. Her hands were caked with mud and her clothes were sodden. She could feel the mud harden in her hair and on her face, clods and scabs of dark silt. She tried to describe how they had found the body, but after all, there was little she could say. They had been looking for Duncan. They had gone down to the river and seen a shape in the water. They had rowed out and found Duncan's body.

The house was dark and cold and dirty. Paul was nowhere to be seen.

Christmas was over.

Fourteen

Cobbett looked round as he heard the laboratory door swing open. The pathologist, Mike Stackpole, was still in his green scrubs. Bald, bearded, rotund, florid-faced, he smiled cheerfully.

"Merry Christmas for yesterday," he said.

"Sorry," Cobbett said. "Your day's been spoiled."

"My sister-in-law and her family are staying with us. Party games. Charades. Yesterday's leftovers. I'm much happier here. You want to take a look?"

"Can't you just tell me about it?"

Stackpole laughed. "Squeamish? You'll get the report in a day or two, but I can give you the short version."

"So how did he die?"

"That's easy. He drowned. But you knew that. All the details will be in the report. Distended lungs, water in the stomach and oesophagus. I've taken blood tests and I know what they'll show."

"Anything else?"

Stackpole put a hand up to his head, above his right ear.

"He had a laceration wound here, on the right side of his head. Quite a severe one, involving skin and tissue and blood vessels impacted in the bone."

"So he could have fallen and hit his head on the way into the water?"

Stackpole shrugged. "It's consistent with the evidence."

"Can you tell if he would have been unconscious when he hit the water, or if he might have hit his head on a rock or something in the river?"

"I can tell you that he wasn't in a good way when he entered the water, which implies the injury was caused before that." Stackpole held up his hands, as if demonstrating. "People who are drowning tend to grab things, like weeds or stones or mud, and the grip carries on even after death. There was nothing like that, nothing under the nails."

"Could the injury have been caused by a blow from someone else?"

"It's possible."

"Can't you tell what caused the injury?"

Stackpole shook his head slowly.

"If someone is struck by a wooden object, you can sometimes find splinters in the wood. But if there was anything like that, the water washed it away."

"What about the time of death?"

"Being in the cold water messes with all of that. He could have died an hour before he was found or just a matter of minutes."

"So it could be an accident."

"Yes."

"It could be murder."

"Or manslaughter. Yes."

Cobbett stood up. He felt he'd learned nothing.

FIFTEEN

Chief Inspector Ralph Chettle was sitting in front of a log fire in the lounge of a country house hotel in Yorkshire when he was called to the phone. As Cobbett started to apologise for contacting him during the holidays, Chettle interrupted him.

"Just get on with it."

Cobbett started describing the events in Glensted.

"Yes, yes, I know all of this. What do you need me for?"

"I'm giving a press conference later today," Cobbett said. "I was hoping to announce that we're starting a full investigation into the disappearance of Mrs. Salter and subsequent death of Mr. Ackerley, and are forming an incident room."

"Hang on, Brian. Don't get ahead of yourself. Let's take these two incidents one at a time. The woman that's gone missing. Is there any evidence that there's a crime involved?"

"There's the coat that was found."

"Precisely where was that? It seems unclear."

Cobbett could feel sweat bubbling on his forehead and his armpits were soaked.

"Unfortunately, it was dealt with by a junior officer and we can't be sure exactly where it was found." He tried desperately to remember what Bealing had told him. "Beyond the bridge at any rate."

"What does the person who found it say?"

"Unfortunately there was an oversight and—um—his name wasn't taken at the time. But we'll find him."

"So you're currently engaged in a manhunt for the person who found your one apparent piece of evidence."

"It's not our one piece. There are some others."

There was a silence. Cobbett cleared this throat a few times but said nothing.

"So," Chettle said at last, "you have a missing woman and her coat in the river. That might be suggestive but you can't build a case on it."

"I wouldn't . . ."

"And Mr. Ackerley? On Christmas Day, people all over the country get pissed and fall and bang their heads, and if they happen to fall into water, they die. What was the cause of death?"

"The autopsy shows he drowned but there's a nasty knock on his head which was very likely inflicted before he entered the water."

"Mm. Have you established where it actually was that he entered the water?"

"Not as such."

"What about the scene where he was found? Anything from that?"

103

"There was a bit of a problem here, sir. The two young people found him and they went for help and more people came down from the house and then the ambulance came and there may have been a couple of passers-by. Anyway, it was already muddy and it was pissing down with rain."

"So the answer to my question is no?" said Chettle.

"Not as yet, sir."

Chettle left another silence.

"We are obviously pursuing lots of avenues," said Cobbett in a strangled voice. "It's early days."

"The early days are the important days. Charlotte Salter has been missing for five days. That's a long time. And the other case: this man was found in the river with a head injury on Christmas Day. Forty-eight hours, and you've got nothing."

"What we have is an unexplained disappearance and an unexplained death."

"With nothing tangible to point to their being connected."

"A woman goes missing and a couple of days later a man who knew her is found dead. Is that just a coincidence?"

"I don't know, Brian, you tell me. I'm going to need more than this if you want me to allocate money from a budget that we've already overspent and allocate officers we don't have in the middle of the holidays. What was the relationship between Charlotte Salter and Duncan Ackerley? Why would Charlotte Salter leave home or, worst-case scenario, why would someone want to kill her? Why would someone want to murder Duncan Ack-erley, if that's what happened? Or why would he take his own life? Who were their enemies? What steps are you taking to find out the answers to those questions?"

"That's why I want to set up an incident room," said Cobbett miserably. "I need men and resources."

There was a pause.

"I know the Hemingford police station," Chettle said. "There was talk of relocating. I'm sure they've got a spare desk or a spare room where you can do your stuff."

"I was hoping for something more."

"No, look, Brian, I'm trusting you with this. You don't need a big team. Not yet. Not until I'm convinced there's even a crime. If something else turns up, we can talk again."

"What about the press conference? Do you want me to cancel it?"

"No, you go ahead. Just be careful what you say. Am I right in thinking you've never headed a murder inquiry, if this even is a murder?"

"No, sir." Cobbett spoke stiffly. "I mean, yes, you're right. I've never headed a murder inquiry.

Cobbett was aware that Chettle already knew that before he asked. In fact, in his current rank Cobbett didn't have much experience of murder inquiries of any kind. There'd been the O'Malley case the previous year, where the husband had killed his wife and then himself. And before that there was the Dunn case that hadn't been much more than a brawl in a pub car park.

"If that's even what this is," Chettle added. "Anything else I should know?"

"The woman's husband, Alec Salter. I think you know him. He said to give you his regards and to tell you he'd been working on his swing. Or something like that."

"Working on his swing? What are you doing talking about golf?"

"He was the one who brought it up, sir."

"Just keep your mind on the job, Brian, and don't make fools of us."

When Chettle had hung up, Cobbett continued to look at the phone before slowly replacing it in the cradle.

Sixteen

At the rear of Hemingford police station, there was indeed a room that was unused, except as a storage area.

"You know how it is," said Ben Jukes when he showed the room to Cobbett. "They probably thought these things might come in useful some day."

Cobbett contemplated the discarded office furniture, the coils of cables, the broken fax machine, electric lights without bulbs.

"Can someone take this lot to the dump?" he said.

"The dump's closed until New Year."

"Or at least outside?"

"Is there any rush?" Jukes asked.

Cobbett looked across at the detective sergeant. He was a solemn, well-meaning young man with bouncy hair parted in the middle and a perpetual look of anxiety on his face.

"Get it done."

An hour later, everything was outside except for a desk, a table and some chairs that were—after some hammering—just about usable. There was a phone outlet in one wall and Cobbett sent one of the uniformed officers out to buy a phone to plug into it.

"And give me the receipt," he shouted after him.

Eight men and one woman crowded into the incident room that afternoon for Cobbett's first briefing. He looked uneasily at them, shuffled his papers around, and pushed his glasses further up his nose before beginning.

"We're investigating two things. The disappearance of Charlotte Salter on 22nd December, and the death of Duncan Ackerley on Christmas Day. We don't yet know if either of these events are actually even crimes, or if one of them is and the other isn't, or if—well, anyway, you get the picture."

He paused, trying to remember what he had planned to say. He had written it down on one of the sheets of paper he had in his hand but now he couldn't find it.

"We need to find out everything we can about these two individuals," he said.

There was a free-standing easel with several large sheets of paper clipped to it, but he couldn't see the felt-tip marker pen he had put there. He would have to write it all down later.

"I'm going to divide you into two teams," he continued. "His 'n' hers. You lot—one-two-three-four-five. You're with her. Find out about her hubby, her kids, her friends, her habits. Was the marriage good or bad? Pin down her movements. That's the key."

He swivelled to his right. "The rest of you, you're looking into him. We need to know about that morning—where he went, when. Witnesses. Look at bank statements, phone calls, talk to neighbours."

He came to a halt and shuffled through his papers again, then looked at the figures in front of him.

"Any questions?"

A young man jammed into a corner of the room put up his hand.

"If he might have taken his own life, should we be finding out about his mood over the last months?"

"What? Yes, yes. I was going to say that."

"And," piped up another voice, "if it's not just coincidence they both died, shouldn't we be looking for things that connect them?"

Cobbett flushed. "Well, obviously we should. That goes without saying." He looked at his watch. "Got to go," he said.

The press conference was held in the function room of the Anchor. There was a Christmas tree in the corner and tinsel draped around the picture frames. Cobbett was surprised by the turnout. There were local news reporters from across the region and even a local television news team. A woman missing, a dead man: there had never been anything like it in Glensted. Sitting next to Jukes, Cobbett made a brief statement describing the events and the investigation. Thinking of his boss, he tried to mix urgency with caution. He asked for questions.

"Is this a murder inquiry?"

Cobbett coughed. "We're keeping an open mind at this stage. We're not ruling anything in or anything out. We are seriously concerned for the safety of Mrs. Salter."

"David Field from Anglia News," said a man, clutching a microphone. "Are the cases connected?"

"I don't want to leap to conclusions. But if any member of the public has any information to offer, they should contact us at Hemingford police station."

"Alice Clayton," said a young woman near the front. "Is it true that there have been mistakes made by the police? We have heard that the sites were not properly secured."

"I don't know who you've been talking to. As I said, members of the public should contact us if they have any information."

SEVENTEEN

It was dark by the time Cobbett and Jukes arrived at the Ackerleys' house. From the distance, it looked hospitable: there was smoke coming from the chimney and the lights were on downstairs, making warm squares of yellow in the chilly night. But when Greg showed them through into the living room, Cobbett saw that there were still streaks of mud on the carpet and a heap of sodden clothes lay in the corner. Frances Ackerley sat hunched in an armchair near the fire, a heavy blanket around her shoulders and her dark hair falling across her face.

"Good evening, Detective," she said. Her voice was slurred.

"The doctor's given Mum some Valium," said Greg.

Cobbett nodded and took one end of the baggy sofa, while Jukes hovered by the door.

"Do you want anything to drink?" asked Greg.

"No, we're all right." He was trying to hold in his head all the things he needed to find out but the crouched figure opposite him was unnerving.

"Shall I fetch Morgan?" said Greg. "I don't know how this works."

"I need to talk to him," said Cobbett. "I need to talk to all of you. It won't take long."

Greg went from the room and Cobbett opened his notebook and cleared his throat.

"I know how painful this is, Mrs. Ackerley," he said.

She raised her head. "Do you?"

Morgan slouched in clutching a Game Boy and sat on the floor under the window. His face was swollen, his shoulder-length hair greasy. Greg followed and sat on the other end of the sofa. He looked tired, rumpled, bewildered. His brown jumper was unravelling at the hem. He kept rubbing his knuckles into his eyes.

"Why are you here?" asked Morgan, not looking up but jabbing away at his Game Boy.

"We need to establish how your father died," said Cobbett.

"It was just a stupid accident."

"That's what we need to find out. Mrs. Ackerley, can you tell me when you last saw your husband?"

Frances Ackerley didn't look at him but down at her hands, which she was kneading together.

"I don't know."

"Did you see him in the morning?"

She spoke in a detached, dreamy tone.

"I was in bed. He told me to get up. He said it was Christmas. He'd been up for hours."

"And then?"

"I got up." She made a visible effort. "I got up and went downstairs and he made me toast and marma-lade. He said I should start cooking dinner."

"What time was this?"

"I don't know."

"It was about nine-thirty," said Morgan from the floor.

"Were you there?" Cobbett asked.

"I was in my room, but I could hear them."

"So he made you breakfast," said Cobbett. "What time did he leave the house?"

"I don't know." She twisted her hands. "He put the turkey in the oven and told me to do the potatoes and sprouts. Then he went out."

"Did he say where he was going?"

"He was taking a ready-meal to Mrs. Williams."

"Mrs. Williams?"

"She lives in that tumbledown old cottage near the bridge," said Greg. "She's got no one to be with at Christmas. She used to come to ours but she's almost bed-bound now."

"How long would that have taken?"

"Not long. Fifteen minutes, maybe."

"And he wanted to pull the boat up before the high tide," said Morgan. "That's what he said the night before. And build up the bonfire in the garden, for after lunch."

There was silence. Cobbett looked down at his notepad. Jukes was scribbling busily.

"Did you see your father that morning?"

113

Morgan's eyes filled with tears. He took off his glasses and wiped them away with the palm of his hand. "No. I heard him downstairs with Mum, and I heard him go out and the door shutting. But I never saw him."

"What did you do after that?"

"Nothing much." Morgan shrugged and held up his Game Boy. "This, I guess. I might have gone back to sleep for a bit."

"And you?" asked Cobbett, turning to Greg.

"We had coffee together."

"You and your father?"

"And Mum."

"Then?"

"I don't know. I left before he did."

"Left for where?"

"A walk. I wanted to have some fresh air before everyone arrived."

"So what time did you last see your father?"

"That would have been a bit before ten, I suppose. I didn't notice the time, but I heard church bells ringing out for the service. I went up the path towards the coast, away from town. I walked for almost an hour." He shivered as if he was still out there in the filthy weather. "Then I just came back the same way."

"Did you meet anyone?"

"Meet? No. I did see the Bowden family, all six of them and their dog, coming in the other direction. They can tell you."

"And then?"

"Then I went back and helped Mum with the meal."

"You never saw your father again?"

"No," Greg said. "Until I saw him dead."

Next Cobbett and Jukes went to the Salters' house. The family were all there, though Alec had shut himself into his study and Paul was in his room, with the curtains closed and music playing. Niall was frying bacon and eggs. He said that they needed to keep their strength up.

Alec came down the stairs as Etty was opening the door to the detectives. He must have seen the car from his window. Niall came out of the kitchen in his apron, his face pink. Before anyone had a chance to speak, he blurted out in a loud voice.

"He lied."

"I'm sorry?"

Niall pointed at Alec, who had halted on the stairs.

"My father lied. He was not at the office on the afternoon my mother disappeared. I hardly saw him at all."

Cobbett rubbed his cheek energetically.

"These are serious allegations," he said finally. "Perhaps we can have a private talk, Mr. Salter."

"I admit that I wasn't at the office," said Alec. "I was meeting a friend. I should have told you earlier but I didn't want to put her in an awkward position."

"Mary Thorne." Ollie spoke in a jeering tone. "That'll be her name."

"She will confirm this?"

"Yes," said Alec. "Though she won't be happy."

"Excuse me, sir," said Jukes and, drawing Cobbett aside, whispered something to him.

Cobbett turned back to Alec.

"Do we have your permission to search the house and grounds?"

"Search away," said Alec. "You'll excuse me if I don't stay to see you poking around in all my things."

Eighteen

Early the next morning, DS Jukes came back to the house with four uniformed officers.

The officers put on gloves and green disposable over-shoes. Paul, Morgan and Etty sat in the kitchen and listened to the sounds they made as they moved from room to room.

"Look," said Paul, pointing out of the window. There were men in the garden holding poles.

"What are they doing?"

"They're going to drag the pond."

"I can't bear this," said Ollie. "I'm going out."

"Where?"

"Anywhere."

Etty stood up.

"I'll come with you."

When they returned a few hours later, the police were still in the house. Niall had also arrived. He had supplies with him: bread, eggs, pasta and jars of pesto, a large bag of potatoes that were already beginning to sprout.

"You've got to eat," he said as he put them away in the kitchen.

Ollie came into the room.

"Just thought you should know, Penny's coming down the drive."

"Tell her I'm not here," said Niall from the fridge.

"No."

"I don't want to see her."

"You've got to say that to her," said Ollie. "Not me."

"Etty," said Niall. "Will you? I'll talk to her, but not right now. I just can't."

Etty saw the patches of stubble on Niall's cheek that he'd missed when shaving, and the grubby cuffs of his shirt, and reluctantly went to the door. She watched Penny stride towards the house, her bobbed hair bouncing as she walked, her arms swinging, her chin up.

"Niall's not here," she said.

"He's in there hiding from me," Penny said calmly. She had strong white teeth and clear brown eyes, and carried an air of competence and reliability about her.

"I think that he just can't . . ."

"At a moment like this, he needs me," said Penny, and marched past Etty and into the house.

Etty stood in the hall and watched Niall and Penny head out into the garden. Niall cast her an accusatory look as he went, but she just shrugged at him. One of the police officers appeared at the top of the stairs and beckoned to Etty.

"The boss says you should come and look at this," he said. "Being a girl and that."

He led her to her parents' bedroom. Her mother's canvas case was on the floor and the officer bent down and unzipped it.

"We found these," he said. "Do you recognise them?"

Etty squatted to look. The bag was neatly packed with underwear, T-shirts, a pair of black jeans and a pair of flannel pyjamas, all of which looked brand new. There was a toilet bag as well and, at the officer's nod of permission, she opened it to find deodorant, a toothbrush and toothpaste, sanitary towels and a tab of soap.

"I don't understand," she said.

"It looks like she was making plans to leave." The officer coughed several times. "But then she didn't," he added.

Etty lifted out the cotton knickers, the striped socks. Under them were two bras. She looked at them, put them back, took out the black jeans, then the pyjamas which still had a price tag on them.

She had a sudden memory of trying on new clothes she'd bought and Charlie putting a hand on her shoulder, scrutinising her in a way that made her feel uncomfortable. "I think you've stopped growing," she had said, and Etty hadn't understood why she suddenly looked serious and almost sad. "I think you've arrived at who you are."

"These aren't her size," she said.

"Pardon?"

"These aren't her size. They're my size."

*

119

"Don't you see?" Etty said to her brothers, sick with longing. "She was definitely leaving Dad. And she was going to take me with her."

They were sitting in the café because Niall had insisted they leave the house. Victor was behind the counter drying glasses and there were three mothers with their babies in buggies, sitting at the large table by the window.

"Why just you? What about us?"

Etty stared at Ollie. "What are you talking about? You've all pretty much left home. You're adults. I'm only fifteen." She blinked back tears. "She wouldn't have gone and left me with Dad. When you say the word 'home,' it's not him you think of, is it? It's her. Wherever Mum is, that's home."

She could feel tears rolling down her cheeks now and she didn't bother to wipe them away.

Victor came over and put three coffees and one tea on the table.

"And the carrot cake's on me," he said in a low, sympathetic voice, bending over with the plate. He smelled of patchouli, and his hair wasn't tied in a ponytail today but fell newly washed to his shoulders.

"Thanks," said Niall.

"How are you?"

"How do you think?" asked Ollie rudely.

Victor stepped back, palms up. "Hey," he said. "She's my friend. I was only asking."

"Sorry," said Niall.

Victor nodded and left them.

"So," said Paul quietly, leaning across the table so they could hear him. "She was planning to leave, but why didn't she just tell us all?"

They looked at each other. Etty could feel her heart thudding, thudding, thudding.

"She was scared," Paul continued. "So scared she was going to do it in secret. Make her escape."

"Scared of what and escape from who?" Ollie gnawed at his thumbnail. "Or is that a dumb question?"

The back area of Hemingford police station had started to feel something like an incident room. There was a filing cabinet. There was a fax machine. Calls had started to come in and PC Sally Peck had been assigned to answer the phone and take a record. She had a special file for sightings of Charlotte Salter.

There was a single phone and it rang constantly, filling the room with its shrill peal. Sally Peck felt that she was losing control of it all. There were too many strands, a mess of false leads and disconnected fragments, and no one was keeping an eye on the big picture.

Now Cobbett sipped some stewed coffee from the machine in the main office. He was addressing his officers, citing off points on his fingers.

"We know that the cause of Duncan Ackerley's death was drowning, but that he was probably unconscious when he went into the water. He suffered a significant head injury. He was last seen by Mrs. Williams at about ten on Christmas morning, when he brought her a meal, though she couldn't be sure of the exact time. He didn't

121

stop; apparently he seemed in a hurry. We know that Charlotte Salter has not been seen since the afternoon of Saturday 22nd December, and an item of her clothing—which we are assuming she was wearing when she left the house—was recovered by the river."

He took a sip of his coffee and flinched.

"We need to get ourselves a coffee machine if we're going to be here any longer. Back to the case. We know there were problems in the Salter marriage. We can reasonably assume from the case of packed clothes for her daughter that she was secretly planning to leave him, taking Elizabeth with her. We also know that Alec Salter lied about where he was on the day his wife went missing, and now claims he was with Mary Thorne, who we are trying to contact so that we can check his alibi."

"So it's him," said an officer at the back of the room.

Cobbett frowned disapprovingly. "Let's not jump the gun," he said. Then he relented: "But certainly, yes, Mr. Salter is suspect number one. Now we just have to prove it." He smiled at the men. "Let's try and get this wrapped up before New Year."

NINETEEN

"What do you think?" said Paul.

He'd summoned Etty and Ollie to his bedroom. He picked up a piece of A4-sized paper and showed it to them. Etty took it and read the large Letraset print: "Has Anyone Seen Charlotte Salter?" Below was a space, then, in smaller type: "Missing 22 December." Below that was the Salters' home phone number.

"In the space I'll stick a photo of Mum," said Paul. "I'll go to the shop on the high street and do a hundred photocopies. We can stick them up on walls and lampposts."

"This?" said Ollie.

Etty looked at Paul, who had flushed red, with anger or humiliation.

"I think it's a good idea," she said. "Well done."

"What about you?" said Paul to Ollie.

"What do you want me to say?"

"I just want you to say what you think."

"All right," said Ollie. "I think something like this is a good idea for a dog or a cat because they could still be wandering around after a couple of days. Someone could be feeding them. They could have taken them in. But this is a human being. What do you expect? Do you think someone will look at this poster and say, oh yes, I've been wondering about that woman who's been suddenly living in our back room."

Etty wanted Paul to get angry and argue or just do something, but he just looked defeated.

"I think it's great," she said. "It might just remind someone of something. All it takes is one person."

Gerry Thorne answered the door. He didn't seem surprised to see the two detectives. He ushered them in and there was a moment's awkwardness as the three of them stood in the hall. Thorne was dressed in slippers, green corduroy trousers and a brown cardigan. They seemed the clothes of an older man. He had a pouchy, shapeless face, thinning hair, and his eyes were small and dark, like two currants pressed into dough.

"We're conducting interviews with people who know Charlotte Salter," Cobbett said. "As part of the inquiry."

"Of course," said Thorne. "Come through."

He led them into a living room. The television was on. Gemma was sitting on the sofa watching *The Wizard of Oz*.

"Have you got some homework or something?" Thorne asked his daughter.

She rolled her eyes at him and muttered something about it being Christmas holidays as she left the room.

"She's distressed about all this," Gerry Thorne said. "She's quite a friend of the daughter."

"Is your wife here?" Jukes asked.

"She's in the kitchen, I think." There was a pause. "Do you want to talk to her as well?"

"We do."

He shuffled out of the room and returned with his wife. They seemed incongruous together: he in his old-fashioned clothes and his air of defeat; she brisk and neat, wearing a yellow shirt tucked into tight jeans, with gold hoop earrings and discreet make-up. She looked at them warily.

"Has anything happened? Is there any news?"

"We're just here to ask some questions."

"I don't think we can be much help."

Gerry Thorne steered the detectives towards two arm-chairs and then switched the television off. He sat close to his wife on the sofa. She inched away from him. He put a hand on her knee. They both stared straight ahead.

"We like to conduct interviews individually," said Jukes.

"I just thought it would save time to talk to us both."

"It makes things simpler."

Gerry Thorne considered this. "Would you like to talk to me first?"

"Your wife first. If that's all right."

Gerry Thorne didn't move. His hand was still on his wife's knee, and at last she lifted it off as if it was an old glove she'd just noticed.

"Just me," she hissed at him.

Now he did look at her. His black eyes seemed smaller than ever. Then he stood up and moved towards the door.

"Tea? Coffee? Or maybe something stronger?"

"No, thank you," said Cobbett.

"Just give me a shout when you want me," he said.

"If you could close the door," Jukes said.

When he was gone, the two detectives turned to Mary Thorne. She didn't meet their eyes but just stared straight ahead.

"As part of this inquiry, we need to establish where everyone was in the period where Mrs. Salter went missing," Cobbett said. "Obviously, we've been talking to Alec Salter."

She didn't reply.

"He has had some difficulty recalling where he was, but he has now said that he was with you on the afternoon of 22nd December."

Mary Thorne seemed to grow slightly paler, but gave no other response.

Cobbett frowned. "Mrs. Thorne?"

"Yes?"

"Would you care to comment?"

"What do you mean?"

Cobbett gave a sigh. "Was Alec Salter with you on the afternoon or early evening of the 22nd of December?"

"I don't know why he'd say that."

"We can talk about that later. First, did you meet him on that day?"

She took a deep breath as if she were steeling herself.

126

Her face was still pale apart from two little bursts of red on her cheeks.

"No," she said.

"You're absolutely sure?" asked Jukes. "This is very important. You are telling us that you weren't with Alec Salter at any point before the party."

"I'm sure."

"And you will provide us with a statement to that effect?"

She licked her lips, then gave a reluctant nod. "All right. But not here."

"You can come to the station."

"Is that all?"

Cobbett was flicking through his notebook as if he might have forgotten something crucial, so Jukes asked the next question for him.

"Why did Alec Salter pick on you for an alibi?"

"I don't know."

Jukes looked at Cobbett, who scratched his cheek and then said, "Mrs. Thorne, are you in a relationship with Alec Salter?"

"I don't want to answer a question like that. Why should I? You don't even know if there's been a crime and you're poking your noses into people's affairs. It's not right. It's none of your business. And anyway, it's not relevant."

"That's for us to decide," said Cobbett.

"Even you being here like this, asking me questions—in a place like this, everyone will know about it."

"We can be discreet," said Cobbett. "But I'm afraid

you need to answer our questions. Otherwise we'll need to find out from other people."

And he looked towards the closed door. They could hear a clattering of plates from the kitchen.

"All right, then," said Mary Thorne, sitting back, the battle suddenly going out of her. "If you have to know, I'm not in a relationship with Alec. We've had a ..." She gestured with her hands. "Just a few times. I'm not proud of it. We were both going through a difficult time. It felt like a comfort."

"You've slept together."

"I hate that phrase."

"Did Charlotte Salter know about it?"

"No," she said sharply, and then swallowed. "I don't think so."

"Why don't you think so?"

"Because I imagine that Alec is careful about his ..." Her face screwed up in a grimace of disdain. "Peccadillos."

"She could have found out some other way. Wives do."

"I don't think that Charlotte was a woman who would have suffered in silence."

"She didn't suffer in silence," Cobbett said. "She disappeared."

He stood up, ready to go, and then remembered something.

"Did Alec Salter phone you?"

"What do you mean?"

"You're saying that he gave us a false alibi."

"I'm not exactly ..." she began, and then stopped.

She patted her hair and fiddled with the collar of her yellow shirt.

"If he wanted you to back him up in a lie, he would have needed to warn you. So, did he?"

There was a silence.

"No," she said.

Cobbett gave a little laugh.

"Think it over. If you change your mind about that, or think of anything you haven't told us, let us know. This is a possible murder investigation, Mrs. Thorne."

As he opened the living room door, Gerry Thorne immediately appeared.

"Everything all right?" he said, looking at the detectives and then at his wife.

"Yes," said Mary Thorne brightly. "All done."

"Just asking a few routine questions," said Cobbett.

"Is it me now?"

"What?"

"Are you interviewing me? You've asked my wife questions, now it's my turn."

"Is there anything you'd like to tell us?"

"Isn't that your job? What do you want to know?"

"Just at the moment, we're interested in where people were on the day of Alec Salter's party."

"I was here. I was wrapping presents, getting things ready for Christmas. Sorting things out. Doing some chores."

"And were you alone?"

Gerry Thorne looked at Cobbett and then at his wife. She stared back at him.

"I was with Mary," he said eventually.

"She was with you while you were wrapping presents?"

"Yes," he said. "She was."

The two detectives climbed into the car, and Jukes started the engine.

"So what do you think?" said Cobbett, buckling his belt.

"Poor sod."

"What?"

"Thorne. His wife making a fool of him like this?"

"I don't care about that. What about the case?"

"It seems obvious. Alec Salter lied about where he was the afternoon his wife disappeared. Lied twice. Charlotte Salter was planning in secret to leave Alec Salter; she was obviously scared of him. Then she disappears. He's killed her."

"It looks like it."

"But what about Duncan Ackerley? Where does he fit into it?"

"Let's see what Mr. Salter says about that."

TWENTY

There was a festive atmosphere in the incident room. People were passing round cans of beer and taking bets on when there'd be charges. There was talk of where the celebrations were going to be held. Cobbett arranged for Alec Salter to be brought in through a side entrance so he would avoid the reporters who had mysteriously started to gather.

Cobbett was perched on the edge of his desk chatting with a group of younger uniformed officers when Jukes came through the room and whispered in his ear that Salter was in the interview room with his solicitor.

"Which one is it?"

"Tony Fry."

"Oh, him. He'll be OK. Where's Sally?"

Sally Peck was answering the phone and she looked stressed.

"Four teas, love," he shouted boisterously. "Down in IR1."

"Any biscuits?" she asked, scowling at him.

"It's not bloody Butlin's."

Halfway down the stairs, Cobbett motioned to Jukes to halt.

"We've got him where we want him," Cobbett said. "We know that his alibi is fake. We'll play it casual and friendly and then I'll hit him with it when he's not expecting it. If we handle it right, he'll probably crack and tell us everything."

"Nice cop, nice cop."

Cobbett gave him a disapproving look.

"You just leave it to me, Ben. Don't try and be too clever about it."

They entered the interview room. Alec Salter and Tony Fry were sitting behind the table. Salter was wearing a checked shirt and a Barbour jacket. He looked like he had been interrupted on a country walk. Fry was dressed for business in a grey suit and a sober dark blue tie. His thinning strands of hair were combed across his bald head. Cobbett and Jukes sat down opposite them.

"I thought we could just have a chat," said Cobbett. He turned to Alec Salter. "You've had a chance to consult with your solicitor?"

"Yes," said Salter. He seemed calmer than when Cobbett had last seen him.

"I assume that your legal advisor has told you that you're not under arrest and that you're free to leave at any time."

"Yes."

"And he probably told you about being cautioned. It sounds worse than it is but I've got to say it. Here goes." He cleared his throat portentously. "You have the right to remain silent, but anything you do say may be given in evidence—"

There was a knock on the door and Sally Peck came in with four teas on a tray. She distributed them along with sachets of sugar and little plastic cartons of milk.

"See?" Cobbett said. "It's just a friendly chat."

"We'd like to say something," Tony Fry said. "Just to straighten things out."

"What's that?"

"Alec has told me that when he was interviewed by you he got flustered. I think he may have given the misleading impression that on the afternoon of the party he was with a friend, a Mrs. Thorne."

"He didn't give the impression," said Cobbett. "He told us that he was with her. A woman he was in a relationship with."

"Mr. Salter would now like to say that he had misremembered."

"Misremembered? In what way?"

"He was not with Mrs. Thorne on that afternoon."

Cobbett turned to Alec. "If you weren't with Mary Thorne, who were you with?"

"I think I just went for a walk."

"You think."

"Yes."

"You seem to be going for a lot of walks."

Alec Salter didn't answer, just gave a slight smile.

"Did you go for a walk with anyone?"

"No."

"Did you meet anyone on your walk?"

"I can't remember. I might have done. It's hard to tell one walk from another."

"Did you recently talk to Mrs. Thorne?"

"You will have to be more specific. Obviously I have had conversations with Mary." He said everything in a monotone, as if reading from a script.

"Did you ask her to back up your false alibi? And did she tell you that she wasn't going to?"

Alec Salter looked at his solicitor, who gave a very faint nod.

"I had a friendly conversation with Mary and I realised that I had been confused about the day of our meeting. I think that's understandable in the circumstances."

"Were you sexually involved with Mrs. Thorne?"

Cobbett slightly stressed the "Mrs." Alec seemed to consider this as if it was an interesting question.

"I think you already know the answer to this. We've had a kind of relationship, I suppose."

"Did your wife know about it?"

Again he seemed to consider. "No. But she might have suspected."

"Do you think there might have been a connection between your affair and her disappearance?"

"Is it important what I think might have happened?"

"Yes."

Alec shrugged. "I don't know. That's all I can say."

Jukes intervened. "Look, Mr. Salter, you don't seem to realise you're in a nasty position here. You were having an affair. You gave us two false alibis. You now say you can't remember what you were doing on the day your wife disappeared. Your marriage was unhappy—"

"How do you know my marriage was unhappy?"

"You were cheating on her," said Cobbett.

"And she was planning to leave you," Jukes added.

"What do you mean?" It was the first time that Alec Salter's composure slipped.

"You didn't know?"

"Know what?"

Tony Fry laid a warning hand on his arm, but he shook if off impatiently.

"I thought you'd know," said Cobbett. "She'd packed a case with clothes. Clothes for your daughter, that is."

"For Etty?"

"Yes."

Alec's face darkened. "She wouldn't have dared."

"You're saying you didn't know she was planning to leave?"

"I didn't know," he replied slowly. "She wouldn't have taken Etty away from me."

There was a silence in the room. Cobbett sipped at his tea noisily.

"So you see why we are questioning you under caution. You have problems in your marriage. You're having an affair. You lie to the police."

"I've explained all of that."

"Only because you were found out," said Jukes.

"You killed your wife," said Cobbett.

"No."

"You killed her and disposed of her body."

"I did not."

"It's better to tell us. Think of what your children are going through."

"I did not kill Charlie."

"Do you think a jury would believe you?"

"I didn't kill her and you have no evidence to say I did."

Cobbett opened his mouth and then closed it again. He cast a look at Jukes.

"What were your relations like with Duncan Ackerley?" Jukes asked.

"Duncan? Fine."

What about your wife's relations with him?"

"They were friends."

"Just friends?"

"Yes."

"Like you were with Mrs. Thorne."

"Not like that, as far as I know. Charlie was friendly with everyone. You never met my wife: she could persuade anyone they were the most important person in the world. She'd stare up at them and put her hand on theirs and winkle out their secrets and sympathise with them. Everyone loved Charlie."

"You sound bitter," said Jukes.

"Where were you on Christmas morning?" Cobbett asked.

"Out," said Alec. "From about nine in the morning. I suppose. Until I went home and changed."

"On one of your walks?"

"That's it."

"Where?"

Alec Salter shrugged. "Up towards the church, I think. I just wandered."

"Did you go near Duncan Ackerley's house?"

"Not until I arrived there for lunch."

"Did you see him?"

"No."

"Did you see anyone else?"

"Not that I recall."

"Did you kill him?"

Alec gave a sour smile at this.

"You haven't got anything, have you? Well, I'm not going to help you out."

Twenty-one

The phone kept ringing and Cobbett had to raise his voice to be heard in the incident room, which was crammed with officers.

"Just take it off the bloody hook," he shouted.

"It might be important," said Sally Peck.

"I'm trying to hold my daily briefing, for fuck's sake. Where are we? What have we got on Alec Salter?"

He went round the room, pointing his finger at each officer. His head ached. He'd had too much to drink the previous evening, after Alec Salter had left, and then he'd spent half the night lying awake, thinking of all the questions he hadn't asked.

It was because there were two cases to investigate, and he didn't even know if they were connected and he didn't even know if they were crimes: the woman who'd disappeared and probably she was dead, surely she must be, and the man who had died and maybe he had taken his own life or maybe it was just a stupid accident, or maybe he'd been killed by Salter as well. Everything was tangled up, all the dates and times and alibis. He should have a spreadsheet or something visual that would make it clear, instead of which people kept bringing him more irrelevant information.

He knew he had his man, that Alec Salter was guilty, but now he needed evidence, not just superfluous information that was only clogging up the process.

"Where did Duncan Ackerley go into the water, eh? Anyone done anything on that?"

The room was silent.

"For God's sake, I'm not your nanny," Cobbett said. "Comb the area up the river from where he was found. There must be something. Yes," he said irritably to Jukes, who had raised his hand. "What?"

"Well, I just wondered what you wanted to do about the old woman?"

"What old woman?"

Jukes waved a sheet of paper at him. "Gwyneth Mayhew, in the bungalow on Hazelwood Avenue."

"What about her?"

"I was trying to help Sally sort out the witness statements. This one has Mrs. Mayhew seeing Charlotte Salter early on the evening she disappeared."

"What? Evening? That can't be right. Why don't I know about this?"

"You do, sir."

The voice was Sally Peck's, sitting squashed up in the corner with papers spread out all round her. Her face was pink.

"I've never heard of this woman."

"I did tell you, sir. Yesterday morning, but you were

quite busy so ..." She saw the look on his face and trailed off.

"Well?"

"She telephoned to say she's certain she saw Mrs. Salter early on the evening of Saturday 22nd December."

"What do you mean?"

"She wasn't sure of the time. But after six, she says, and before quarter to seven, when she has her evening meal."

"That's impossible."

The room was silent, except for the phone ringing incessantly.

"How old's this woman? And take that bloody phone off the hook."

"Yes, sir; sorry. Ninety-one."

"There you are, then. How can a ninety-one-year-old woman be believed? She's probably half-blind. Anyway, what was she doing?"

"Sitting at the window. She said she spends her day sitting at the window watching the world pass by."

"I've never been informed of this," insisted Cobbett. He felt like a furnace. Everyone was staring at him, waiting. "She's not exactly a reliable witness, is she? If she spends her time staring out of the window, one day's just like the next. We all know what these old women are like. She may well be soft in the head."

"But if," said Jukes apologetically, "if she is right, then, well, all the alibis we've gathered are irrelevant and ..." He fell silent.

"If she's right," said Cobbett viciously, "then someone"—he glared at Sally Peck—"is going to have to explain their conduct."

"But I did—"

"I've no time for excuses. We've got to get new fucking alibis. Pronto."

Twenty-two

People in Glensted had become used to the sight of police officers, knocking at doors, standing on corners in groups, or in their hi-vis jackets down by the river, with walkie-talkies and sniffer dogs.

Two of them were on the bridge that ran over the Heming. They had walked all the way across it towards Hemingford, stooping down to look at objects, picking up any item that might turn out to be helpful—a Biro lid, cigarette stubs, an empty Coke bottle, a paper mug still containing coffee that was balanced on the parapet. Now they were returning slowly in the opposite direction.

"What's this?" said one of them as he swept his hand along the parapet, feeling for anything out of sight.

"Show me?"

The officer held out a pair of horn-rimmed glasses.

"Put it in the evidence bag. Let's get this lot back to the boss."

Five of Etty's girlfriends came to the house. They wore serious expressions and kept glancing at each other.

"Come out with us," they said.

"Not just now."

"Let us in then." Rosa held up an album Etty didn't recognise. "We can listen to it in your room, and you don't even need to say anything."

"I can't."

"We're worried about you."

"Is this a—what do you call it? Intervention?"

"We're your friends. We're here for you."

Etty looked from face to face.

"I can't," she repeated. She stepped back from them. "I just can't."

She went back inside. There was music throbbing from Ollie's room, and when she pushed the door open he was there with two of his friends, smoking and drinking from cans.

"Hi," she said, feeling like an intruder.

"We're talking about Thailand," said Rick, the first boy she'd ever kissed.

She stared at him uncomprehendingly.

"We're going there in the New Year," said Ollie. "You know that."

"I forgot. What if ... ?"

"What if what?"

"Never mind."

She backed out of the room.

TWENTY-THREE

Etty sat at the kitchen table with Morgan while Greg bustled around making tea for them. She had called round because she needed to escape the house and couldn't think of anywhere else to go. But as soon as she arrived, she wanted to leave again. Morgan squinted at her through his smudged glasses and shrugged his thin shoulders whenever she spoke. Greg was making an obvious effort to be kind to her, but he seemed miles away, tired and abstracted. And upstairs she could hear the heavy shuffle of Frances pacing her room.

Then Greg heard something and went to the window and looked out. He was silhouetted in the headlights of an approaching car.

"What now?" he said.

When they came into the kitchen, Etty felt hope that quickly became dread. Jukes, who was with a female officer she had not seen before, was shifting from foot to foot. Whatever it was, it wasn't good news.

"Have you discovered anything?" asked Morgan.

"We don't know," said Jukes. "We want you to look at something we found."

"What?" Greg took a step towards them. "Found where?"

Jukes didn't answer. He drew the glasses out of the case he was carrying and laid them, still in their transparent evidence bag, on the kitchen table.

Etty could hear Greg taking short, rasping breaths. She didn't want to look at him or Morgan; it felt indecent.

"Well?"

"Where did you find them?"

"Do you recognise them?"

"They look like Dad's old glasses," said Morgan with painful slowness.

"Yes," said Greg. "Maybe. But most glasses are like other glasses, aren't they?"

"But they do look like your father's?"

"Yes," said Morgan. "Exactly like."

"Perhaps your mother would be able to identify them."

"Identify what?" said Frances from the door. Nobody had heard her enter.

"Mrs. Ackerley," said Jukes. "Do you recognise these glasses?"

Frances Ackerley came to the table. She was wearing a thick dressing gown and her face was puffy. She bent down and peered at the glasses. Then she straightened up.

"They're Duncan's," she said.

"You're certain."

"Yes. He'd had them for years."

"Thank you."

"Where were they?" asked Greg.

"They were found on the bridge," said Jukes. "On the parapet."

Etty didn't know how long the silence lasted. She held her breath.

Frances gave a choked wail and put her head to the wall.

"No," said Morgan. "If that's what you're thinking, no."

Greg didn't speak, just stared at the glasses.

Etty could picture it and she could feel it in the pit of her stomach, a griping pain. The walk up to the bridge and then along it to the middle. Of course Duncan would have removed his glasses so that he didn't have to see the brown churning waters far beneath him. He would have climbed on to the parapet and jumped, breath pushed out of his lungs and eyes full of rushing air, and the river would have taken him, carrying his big, strong body just as it carried branches and litter, towards the sea. If he had not snagged on the buoy's chain, perhaps he would never have been found. But why? Why would Duncan take his life?

"Obviously this is significant. I am sure Inspector Cobbett would like to ask you some questions," said Jukes. "If I could use your phone."

"Now?" said Morgan.

"Does it have to be at once?" Greg gestured towards Frances.

"Can't you leave them be?" said Etty furiously. "For tonight at least. If what you're suggesting is true, what does twelve hours' difference make?"

"We'll come back tomorrow morning," said Jukes wretchedly.

Greg was steering Frances out of the kitchen. Morgan was still sitting at the table, his head in the cradle of his arms. Etty touched him timidly on the shoulder but he didn't react. She put on her coat and left them there.

Twenty-four

"Mrs. Ackerley." Cobbett gave a dry, hard cough. "Can you think of any reason that your husband would have taken his own life?"

She shook her head slowly.

"He wasn't anxious or depressed?"

"I don't understand." She put her arms round her body, cradling herself. "I don't understand," she repeated. "I'll never understand."

"Did you suspect that your husband was having an affair with Mrs. Salter?"

She gave a harsh laugh. "And killed himself because she was gone?"

"It's just that there are rumours ..."

"Who'd live in a small town?"

"Is that a no?"

"I have no idea," she said. "I wouldn't blame him. What was he supposed to do? I mean, look at me."

Cobbett looked at her. She was a big-boned woman but unnaturally thin. Her clothes hung off her and her eyes looked too large in her gaunt face. There was an unkempt look to her, as if she'd long ago given up on herself.

"I'm ill," she said impatiently.

"I'm sorry to hear that."

"Ill in the head."

Cobbett murmured something. He wished he'd brought Sally Peck with him. She was a contrary woman but she would have known what to say.

"I wouldn't have blamed her either," she said. "Anyone could see it was a bad marriage. He's a nasty, cruel man," she added with a burst of loathing.

"You mean Mr. Salter?"

"Of course I mean Mr. Salter. Do you know what his last words to me were?"

"Mr. Salter's?"

"Duncan's."

"No."

"He said, 'Maybe you should at least brush your hair, Frances, and make a bit of an effort with yourself for once, before our guests arrive, for the boys' sake if not for mine.' That was the last thing he said to me. That's how I'll always remember him, telling me to pull myself together."

"I know this must be painful," said Ben Jukes to Greg. "Had your father been depressed lately?"

"Dad loved life. It doesn't make sense."

"And was your father involved with Charlotte Salter?"

"How can you ask that?"

Jukes waited. Outside, gulls squawked raucously. It was a grey, wet day; the sky was like a sheet of metal.

"They were close friends, that's all. Can't people just be friends?"

"You're sure about that?"

Greg frowned, looking past Jukes and out of the window, down to the river where he had found his father's body. He looked suddenly young and unsure.

"The thing is," he said at last, "they were alike, Dad and Charlie."

"Alike?"

Greg was speaking slowly, struggling for words.

"They were sociable. They liked having fun. Laughing. They cheered each other up." He lowered his voice, as though his mother, who had retreated to her bedroom, might be able to hear him. "I think they helped each other."

"Helped each other in what way?"

"I mean." He faltered. "They were both going through tough times."

"Tough times?"

"You know, in their marriages."

Again, Jukes waited. At last Greg filled the silence.

"Mum—she isn't very well. Dad is, he was, like her carer." He looked down at his callused hands. "I've seen that more than ever in the past few months. I've been working with him, while I wait to go to university. Cutting down trees, mowing the playing fields and things like that." Words spilled out of him at last. "It's tiring and can be monotonous. But he works . . ." He stopped and gulped and corrected himself. "Worked—all day and then he would come back and look after

Mum. He was always so cheery with her but it must have taken a—"

"No!" Morgan Ackerley cut in.

His glasses were so smeared it was hard for Jukes to see his eyes. His clothes were muddy. His hair was unbrushed. He looked awful.

"I know it's a painful thing to contemplate."

"No way. No. That's a horrible thing to say. I don't care if his glasses were on the bridge. My dad never cheated on Mum and he never killed himself. That's not who he was. It was just a stupid accident. Anyone who says different is just talking crap."

"A letter came yesterday, addressed to Mum," said Etty to Paul.

She held up the rectangular envelope with Charlie's name and address typed in the centre.

"Have you opened it?"

"I didn't like to."

"Give it here."

She handed it across and he ran his finger under the gummed flap and pulled out the folded sheet of thick white paper.

"What is it?" asked Etty, watching his expression.

"It's a job interview."

"What job?"

"It's a trade magazine. *Hair and Beauty*. In London. They are pleased to inform her that she's got an interview on Tuesday, 8th January, at 11.30 in the morning."

"She was looking for work," said Etty, almost dreamily. "In London. She never said anything."

She left Paul and walked into the garden without bothering to put on a jacket. The wind caught at her, slapping her hair round her face and making her eyes water.

She tramped past the outhouses, past the little pond covered in duckweed that the police officers had dragged, past the apple trees and the wooden swing. She thought of the canvas case in Charlie's wardrobe neatly packed with clothes in Etty's size. She thought of the interview. Charlie had been going to leave Alec, and she had been going to take Etty with her. She'd been planning it all in secret, putting arrangements in place for a new life away from Alec and from Glensted—and then she had disappeared without trace.

Etty's heart ached with the knowledge that she and her mother had been just days away from a different life.

Twenty-five

Cobbett put down his mug on the edge of his desk. Too near the edge. It tipped off and shattered on the floor.

"Well," said Cobbett. "Is nobody going to clear that up? Sally?"

"Sir."

"Sweep that up, will you?"

"Me, sir?"

"Yes, Sally, you. Chop, chop, we want to get this meeting under way."

Sally Peck stood with her head lowered. "Why?"

"I beg your pardon?"

"Why me, sir?"

"Because I told you to."

"I know, but ..." She stopped. Everyone looked at her. One of the men sniggered. She walked out of the room, feet banging on the boards.

"Right," said Cobbett.

He stood propped up on his desk, facing the room. Behind him was a large-scale map of the area. He jabbed his glasses further up his nose and his gaze darted round the room.

He's out of his depth, thought Sally Peck with satisfaction, coming back into the room with a dustpan and brush. She set about noisily sweeping up the broken china.

"It now seems likely that Duncan Ackerley took his own life, for reasons unknown. Maybe it was connected to Charlotte Salter's disappearance and maybe it wasn't, but it doesn't look like we are looking for anyone else in connection with his death." He scowled at Ben Jukes's nervously raised hand. "What?"

"What about the head wound, sir? Surely that—"

"Never mind that," said Cobbett airily. "The head wound could well be a red herring. He could have hit his head on the bridge as he jumped, or smashed it on a rock or whatever when he entered the water."

There was a silence in the room. Cobbett looked from face to face, displeased.

"We still have a suspicious disappearance," he said, "and we still have a prime suspect."

He stopped and glowered at the crouched figure of Sally Peck.

"Unfortunately, due to some ..." He searched for the right phrase. "Problems with assembling the case, we have had to start again with gathering alibis. Jim is responsible for drawing up a timeline of the day; everything you find out he will enter, so we should be able to have a comprehensive picture of what was going on in Glensted on the evening Charlotte Salter disappeared."

He folded his arms and leaned back.

"Let's start with you, Ben, and the Salter family."

Ben Jukes read out the statements he had gathered.

Alec Salter had arrived at the barn at about six-thirty. He admitted to leaving for about twenty minutes and driving to Victor Pearce's place because he thought his wife might be there. But no one answered the door and the windows were dark. Niall Salter had also arrived at six-thirty. He had had a row with his girlfriend—now his ex-girlfriend—and had gone out at about nine to get some fresh air. He was vague about whether he had been with anyone. Paul Salter had arrived at about the same time but had left early, at nine-fifteen, and gone straight home, while Ollie Salter came half an hour later, and was there until the party ended, though he spent some time outside with friends.

"And the girl?" asked Cobbett.

"She got there early, with a group of friends, and apart from walking to the phone box at the end of the track, had been there all the time."

"Right. Moving on: Trev, what have you got?"

Trevor Gilchrist rose to his feet, clutching his notebook.

First of all he had been to Hazelwood Avenue. The old woman remained convinced she had seen Charlotte Salter in the early evening. From there, he'd gone to interview Victor Pearce. He had confirmed that he was friendly with Mrs. Salter: she baked cakes for his café.

"Yeah, yeah," someone said, and a ripple of laughter ran round the room.

But he denied being in a relationship with her, Gilchrist continued, though he knew there were rumours. He said that he thought Charlotte Salter was lonely and anxious, and although she hadn't told him in so many words, he had gathered she was unhappy in her marriage. He claimed that he had last seen her on Friday 21st December, when she had said there was a misunderstanding she needed to sort out, but hadn't said what. He had assumed she was alluding to her relationship with her husband. He had been at home the evening of the party the following day, until he left at about half past nine to make an appearance.

"Alec Salter said the lights were out when he went round," said Ben Jukes.

"Pearce was very insistent he was there, so he's either lying or Alec Salter never went round there. He also said Alec Salter picked an argument with him at the party and pushed him out of the barn."

"And Christmas Day?" asked Cobbett.

On Christmas Eve, Victor Pearce had gone to Reading, where his elderly parents lived. He had returned on Boxing Day. His mother had confirmed this.

"I thought it no longer mattered about Christmas Day," muttered Sally Peck under her breath.

Next, Simon Foxall rose to his feet, grinning nervously. He had been back to the Thornes' house, he said, and he'd heard them shouting at each other before he rang the bell. He had not had a friendly reception. They had both said they were together in the hours leading up to the party, and then at the party itself. And they had been together all of Christmas Day.

Cobbett frowned, looking dissatisfied. "Anyone else got anything to say?"

"Yes." Sally Peck, dustpan and brush still in her hand, was standing by the door.

"Go on."

"I did a door-to-door, like you asked. A few things came up."

"Such as?"

"Such as Niall Salter was snogging one of his sister's friends at the party. She's only fifteen. I reckon that's why he was being a bit evasive about what he was up to that evening. Plus I spoke to his ex, Penny Anderson. He broke up with her the day before the party. She says he's been behaving oddly. He wasn't at his workplace all afternoon, like he claimed, because she went there to see him."

"It no longer matters what he was doing then."

"It matters he lied," Sally Peck said stubbornly. "Also, I talked to a man called Keith Palmer who was at the party. He had a Polaroid camera and lots of people took photos. There are loads of them and he gave them all to me. I haven't looked at them yet, but they might show us something."

"What?"

"I don't know."

"You have been busy."

He said it like it was a bad thing and she blushed.

"It's difficult," she said. "Because the phone keeps ringing and we've no time to speak to everyone who thinks they may have relevant information. I've been trying to keep up with the statements that we've gathered so far and put them in some kind of order so we can make sense of them, but to be honest everything's a bit all over the place, and you've told us we have a prime suspect, but isn't it a worry that we could be going in the wrong direction? And if we do that, we miss . . ."

She stopped dead. Cobbett's face had turned an ominous, mottled purple.

"Are you telling me how to run my investigation?"

"No, sir. Not at all. I just—"

"If you can't manage to keep up with things, then you know what you can do."

And he marched from the room.

TWENTY-SIX

Sally Peck and Simon Foxall tacked the Polaroid photos on the cork board, next to the timeline and the giant map. There were dozens of them, some badly over-exposed or out of focus: the barn seen from the outside, a dark mass in a splurge of blurred lights; small groups posing for the camera; Alec Salter caught from the side, not smiling; Alec Salter, caught from behind, his hand on the small of a woman's back; people drinking or dancing; faces taken from too close so that their features seemed over-large and their eyes were red from the flash. Duncan was grinning broadly. There was one of the Salter siblings, only Etty obediently smiling. Apart from that, Etty seemed unaware she was being photographed. In one, she was talking to an older man and was wrinkling her nose; in another, she was dancing with three other young people; in the third, she was looking strained and anxious.

It was easy to work out which had been taken early in the evening and which later. There was a drunken randomness about some of them, people's feet or their midriffs, half a face, a handbag lying on the floor. Sally Peck even wondered if a child might have got hold of the camera at some point, because there were pictures of an out-of-focus green wreath, a large ladle with cigarettes stubbed out in it, a blurred shot of the ceiling and several which were impossible to decipher.

She tacked them all up anyway, and then she and Foxall stood back to look at the unpromising collage.

"Can't see how they'll help much," said Foxall. "It's just pictures of middle-aged people getting rat-arsed."

"You're probably right."

"Sorry you got it in the neck."

She shrugged and tried to sound unconcerned. "It's OK," she said, although of course it wasn't.

TWENTY-SEVEN

The day before New Year's Eve, Etty opened the door to Alice Clayton.

"Yes?" She had stopped expecting to see her mother standing on the threshold.

"We met before. Alice Clayton from *The Herald*. I wondered if you had changed your mind about speaking to me. Or perhaps your brothers would like the chance to put their side of the story."

"Why would we want to talk to you? What good would it do? It wouldn't bring her back."

"Maybe not. But it would bring her disappearance to public attention. We could show photos of her. It might jog people's memories."

Etty nodded, uncertain.

"Plus, it's not as if the police have got very far, is it?"

"No," said Etty drearily. "It isn't."

"So how about it?"

"How would it work?"

"We just have a chat. You tell me about your mother, about what you're feeling, about the investigation. I won't print anything you don't want me to."

Etty chewed her lower lip in indecision. She was wearing ripped baggy jeans and a flannel shirt over a turtleneck top. Her hair was tied back in a single clumsy plait. Alice Clayton saw that she had bitten her nails to the quick.

'I can't do it here."

"That's fine. We'll go somewhere else."

Etty nodded.

"Maybe my friend Kim's," she said uncertainly.

But no, she remembered: Kim had called that morning and said she was going into town. She had asked Etty to come with her and Etty, unable to bear the thought of bright lights and crowded streets, had refused.

"Or the café," she said. "In the centre of town. There's an overflow room at the back that Victor will let us use."

They sat at the table and Victor, eyes bright with curiosity, offered them a hot drink, but they both just wanted a glass of water. When he was gone and the door closed, Alice Clayton laid her little cassette recorder on the table. Etty looked at it nervously.

"It's easier. Then I don't have to keep stopping you while I write things down. My shorthand's not the best."

"OK."

"And as I said, nothing will be published that you don't want."

She pressed two buttons on the machine and leaned forward to make sure it was working.

"Right," she said. "We can forget about it. Why don't you start off by telling me about your mother and your relationship with her."

It was stilted at first, like Etty was describing a stranger to the journalist: Charlie's family, her work, her interests, her beauty. But bit by bit the awkwardness fell away and words poured from her. She realised she had been desperate to talk about her mother to someone like this young woman with a smart, sympathetic face, who listened with her head slightly to one side and made occasional encouraging sounds.

She told Alice Clayton things she hadn't known she remembered: Charlie in a yellow bikini teaching her to swim one summer in Cornwall; Charlie and her sister Caroline, who had died when Etty was nine, getting tipsy together while Alec looked on disapprovingly; Charlie weeping every time they watched *Dumbo* together; Charlie marching Etty to a friend's house to make her apologise for ganging up on her at primary school; Charlie playing football with the boys and tackling Paul so fiercely he had ended up in A&E; Charlie in a monumental rage with them all for expecting her to clear up after them; Charlie putting make-up on in front of the bathroom mirror while Etty sat on the edge of the bath and watched her; Charlie holding Etty's forehead while she leaned over the toilet bowl and vomited that first time she had ever got drunk; Charlie flirting with her friend's father and Etty hadn't spoken to her for days; Charlie standing at the school gates with the other mothers and Etty could have burst with pride that she was her daughter. She recalled coming into the house one evening and finding Charlie sitting at the kitchen table, looking so sad that Etty barely recognised her.

She told Alice Clayton about the night of the party, about the awful days after, the police searching the house and dragging the pond, about her and Greg hauling Duncan's body out of the swirling water on Christmas Day, about the case packed with Etty's clothes, about Charlie's job interview in London, about how she knew she was still alive, about how she knew she was dead, about how she hated going to sleep because when she woke she had to remember all over again that Charlie had gone; about the dreams that came and how some of them were nightmares that she lurched awake from sweating, but in others her mother was vividly and even monstrously alive. In one, Etty had been holding her under the water to drown her; even now she could see Charlie's submerged face gazing up at her.

She hadn't realised she was crying but when she at last stopped speaking her face was sticky with tears.

"God, Etty," said Alice Clayton. "That was amazing."

"Is that what you needed?"

"And some."

"I hope my brothers don't mind me talking to you."

"What about your father?"

"I don't care about him. I hate him. You can put that in if you want."

"It might be best not to." Alice Clayton hesitated, then said: "It must be doubly awful for you with him being a prime suspect."

"Shall I tell you the thing that would be most awful? That Mum never gets found and I spend the next two years with Dad, me and him alone in the house. And we never get to know if she's alive or dead, and every day for the rest of my life I'll be missing her. I don't think I could bear it."

Alice Clayton didn't say anything. They sat in silence for several moments, hearing the hum of the café beyond the closed door.

"I just need to take down a few facts," the journalist said at last. "I take it your actual name is Elizabeth?"

Etty nodded.

"And how old are you?"

"Fifteen."

"What? Oh, shit."

"What's the matter?"

"It said in the papers you were sixteen."

Yeah. One paper got it wrong and then they all did."

"I can't print this. You're a minor."

"What's that got to do with anything? I chose to talk to you."

"Etty, I'm really sorry. I could get into terrible trouble. I just can't."

165

"So I said all of those things for nothing?"

"Look, if I could get permission from your—"

"Forget it," said Etty, standing up and pushing the table away so the water slopped on to its surface. "Just forget it. Leave us alone."

The photo of Charlie that Paul had chosen for the poster was quite recent. She wasn't wearing make-up or posing for the camera the way she often did. She wasn't even smiling. She was looking off to one side with an enquiring expression. Her dark blonde hair was pulled loosely back and she was wearing her tweed coat—the one that had been found by the river.

Etty and Paul walked round Glensted with their bundle of posters. It was early on Sunday evening, the day before New Year's Eve, and the little town centre was quite busy. People were standing outside the pub smoking, and the restaurant's tables were full. Etty, seeing a group of her schoolfriends on the other side of the street, pulled Paul down the side road.

"I can't meet anyone," she said urgently.

Kim was there. She was wearing dark eyeshadow and her lashes were spiky with mascara. She was laughing. Etty stared at her as if she was a stranger.

They had masking tape, some tacks and a hammer and a torch. They taped the sheets of paper on to lampposts and hammered them on to trees and the sides of fences. Over and over again, Etty stared through the darkness at her mother's face in the frail pool of light, under the question *Has Anyone Seen Charlotte Salter?*, until the words stopped making sense and the face became somehow mysterious to her.

"What if it rains again? It feels like it might—or snow even."

Paul shrugged. "We can put more up."

They finished their round of Glensted, ending at the bus stop.

"We can do Hemingford tomorrow," Paul said.

Walking home, they passed the posters again, their mother's face gazing past them as if she could glimpse something they were all failing to see.

Etty went home and sat in the hall, under the mockery of the Christmas tree. She saw the small package with her name written on it in her mother's hand and, picking it up, she slowly unwrapped it to reveal a little blue box. She lifted the lid and there, on the plush interior, was a round golden locket. She held it in her palm for several minutes before putting it round her neck.

TWENTY-EIGHT

New Year's Eve came and went. In Glensted, a gang of drunk teenagers threw a dustbin through the restaurant window and a fourteen-year-old girl was taken to the local hospital with alcohol poisoning.

Alec drank whisky in his study and got more and more coldly sober with each mouthful. He steadily worked through the papers in his desk. He went to bed before the year turned. Paul also went to bed early—before eight o'clock. He dragged the chest of drawers in front of the door so that nobody could disturb him and crawled under the covers where he lay for hours, listening to distant music and then to fireworks.

Niall intended to go to London, where he was going to stay with friends: he couldn't stand being with his family any longer. But his car broke down on the A12 and he was sitting on a grass verge with lorries rumbling past him when the old year passed. He started to cry and was still crying when the AA man arrived.

Ollie was with a group of friends who he had been at school with. They started in a friend's house and then saw in the New Year on the bridge. Ollie was very stoned. He leaned over the parapet and looked at the brown water eddying by beneath him. A girl he had always fancied put her arm on his shoulder and asked him what he was thinking.

"I'm thinking I'll never see my mother again," he said, and she moved closer, pressed her lips to his.

Etty was at a party. She didn't want to be there but it was better than being at home with her father. Her friends were making an effort with her but their pity and concern made everything worse. She put on a green velvet shirt of Charlie's and make-up that she thought, when she stood in front of the mirror, made her look clownish. Kim tried to make her dance, but she felt heavy, uncoordinated; she couldn't make her body move to the music. Robbie was making out with Gemma Thorne in the corner. He saw her and looked away. She drank too much, and then went into the garden, where she let a boy in the year above her kiss her, but then she pushed him violently away, full of loathing. She wanted to hit him, or be sick, or curl up in a ball and let darkness enfold her. When people asked her, with that horrible sympathy, how she was, she just grunted and turned away. The truth was that she didn't know how to get through time. Minutes felt unendurable, a special kind of agony. "Take it step by step," her mother used to say when she was overwhelmed by things. "Don't look too far ahead."

But Etty couldn't stop herself looking far ahead, at a future that stretched out like a blank, glaring road.

Charlie was gone. Niall and Paul and Ollie would go. It would be her and her father in a house whose empty spaces she dreaded.

Etty drank too much but Morgan, who was also at the party, drank even more. He lay under a rose bush retching. Someone must have called his house, because just before midnight Greg arrived to take him home. He hauled Morgan up and into the house just as people started cheering in the New Year. Etty stood in a ragged circle, where people were linking hands and singing "Auld Lang Syne," and watched as Greg manoeuvred his scrawny brother towards the front door. His face was grim. He looked years older than he had looked the night of the party nine days go.

Just nine days. Charlie had disappeared and Duncan was dead and Etty didn't understand how she would be all right ever again.

Alec was interviewed again, released again.

Frances Ackerley was seen wandering along the river-bank with her hair flying wildly in the wind, shouting. People said she should be in hospital.

Gradually the biscuits and cakes and casseroles, the flowers and letters of sympathy, dried up. Gradually the media interest died away.

The incident room in Glensted was no longer as full of people. The urgency had gone out of the inquiry. Officers were taken off the case. Cobbett started smoking again. He shouted at his team more than usual, and his wife worried about him getting an ulcer.

Sally Peck, trying to keep control of the paperwork, started putting things in cardboard boxes that she kept under her desk. When everyone else had gone home, she would go through documents and witness statements, her forehead wrinkled in confusion. The Polaroid photos were beginning to curl on the cork board.

It started to snow, thin and windblown at first, but then thickly, flakes settling and covering the roofs, the hedges and fields, making the landscape pristine and unfamiliar.

The posters of Charlotte Salter became muddy, sodden, unreadable. People stuck other posters over them, for missing pets or forthcoming concerts in Hemingford. Soon nothing was left of them except for a few small shreds that remained attached to a tree or a lamppost. Half a face, a woman's mouth, a handful of words. Has anyone seen? anyone ...

Twenty-nine

It was the middle of the morning of the last Monday in January and DCI Chettle and DI Cobbett were walking along the bank of the Heming, where the river became wider as it approached the sea and the land became marshier, a maze of muddy water channels. Cobbett was wishing he had been warned about where they were going, but Chettle had arrived at the police station without warning. Chettle was wearing a heavy coat and when he parked his Jaguar in a lay-by close to the river, he had changed his shoes for wellington boots. Cobbett was in his grey suit and leather shoes.

Chettle took a deep breath. "Good to be outside, isn't it?" he said.

Cobbett looked down at his soiled shoes and the spattered lower trouser legs. "I'm not quite dressed for it."

Chettle sniffed. "I thought it would be wise to get out of the office. Nobody listening, nothing official, just a straightforward chat about where we stand."

Cobbett felt a lurch of anxiety. He had been dreading a meeting of this kind.

"I hope I've kept you in touch."

"It's been a month. Over a month."

"It's been frustrating," said Cobbett.

The path had narrowed, so they had been walking with Chettle in front. Now he stopped and turned round.

"In what way?"

Cobbett looked towards the water. There was a group of seabirds in the mud. The peninsula was famous for its birds. People came specially to look at them but Cobbett didn't know the difference between the special ones and the normal, ordinary kind.

"Our focus has been on Alec Salter."

"You still believe he killed his wife?"

"He never seemed that bothered. And then he kept changing his alibi and in the end didn't have one at all. They had problems with the marriage. She may have been thinking of leaving him."

"Seemed," said Chettle. "May have been." He sniffed. "Anything else?"

"His children think he's capable of it."

"Have they told you that?"

"They've given that impression."

"Is there any actual evidence that she's dead?"

"There's the coat we found by the river."

"I know about the coat. Anything further?"

Cobbett wished he'd had time to prepare for this inquisition. He was here without his notes and files and people to back him up.

"According to her family, she hadn't taken any clothes with her. Her passport was still in the house."

"What about her purse?"

"Her purse was missing but her family said she always carried that with her."

"What about the other case?" Chettle asked.

"It seems almost certain now that Duncan Ackerley took his own life."

"Why did he?"

"We don't know. But the fact that the death came so soon after the disappearance of Mrs. Salter seems suspicious."

"Were they having an affair?"

"There was some gossip in the village. We're keeping an open mind."

"An open mind," said Chettle. "God give me patience. Give me something to work with here. Are there any promising lines of inquiry?"

"There have been some sightings of Charlotte Salter. We're following them up."

"Yes, I heard about that. One of them was in Scotland, another was in Majorca."

"It only takes one," said Cobbett.

Chettle gestured around at the landscape.

"That's why I came out here like two spies who're worried about being overheard. We can talk freely. There are no records of what we say. We can speak frankly and bluntly. So let me say what a hostile outsider might say about this inquiry. In the case of the disappearance of Charlotte Salter, the local police were so late in beginning their inquiry that valuable opportunities for solving the case were almost certainly missed."

Cobbett started speaking in response but Chettle held up his hand to stop him. "Does that seem an unfair summary?"

"We can only deal with the evidence that we have."

"I don't think that statement of the obvious will be accepted with much enthusiasm by the boss. But we are where we are and we'd better make the best of it. I've one or two thoughts to share with you. If you'd like to hear them."

"Yes, of course I'd like to."

"There are various possibilities. It may be that Charlotte Salter simply ran away or that she went for a swim and drowned."

On a freezing December evening, with the party she had organised just beginning, thought Cobbett.

"I don't think that's likely," was all he said, his face stiff.

"There is another possibility. When I was just starting out, an old detective told me: don't complicate things if you don't need to. The simplest solution is usually the right one."

Cobbett didn't reply. He wasn't sure what that meant. And he didn't know what the simplest solution to these cases was.

"Do you follow me?" said Chettle.

"Not exactly."

"I don't want to tell you what to do. I don't want to tell you what conclusions to come to. This is your case."

That word "your," Cobbett thought bitterly. He

wouldn't be saying "your case" if Cobbett had solved it. It felt like he was being stuck with something.

"You said there was another possibility," he said.

"As we know, Charlotte Salter and Duncan Ackerley might have been having an affair."

"It's been alleged."

"You said that Charlotte Salter was making secret plans to leave."

"That's what the evidence suggests."

"She was leaving her husband. That's the way it's been portrayed. But maybe she was also leaving Ackerley. And maybe he didn't like it."

"Are you saying that he killed her?"

"I'm suggesting a line of inquiry. It's the oldest motive there is. If I can't have you, then nobody can."

Cobbett was getting cold. He wanted this meeting to end.

"If he killed Charlotte Salter, then who killed him?"

"He killed himself in a fit of remorse. I've seen it a dozen times."

Cobbett remembered Alec Salter telling him that he played golf with Chettle.

"Is this something you want us to investigate?"

"I want you to investigate everything," said Chettle. "That goes without saying. But it seems to me that this investigation is running into the sand. Your wheels are spinning and you're not getting anywhere. Now it may be that in the next week or two, some compelling piece of evidence may emerge. Perhaps Charlotte Salter will suddenly come home. But it's looking less and less likely. At a certain point, this investigation will come to an end, one way or another. And it may be that the theory I have suggested is a way of drawing a line."

Cobbett looked around as if he was concerned someone might be listening.

"How do we actually do that?"

"I'm not telling you to do this, of course."

"Of course."

"But at certain point, you can—tactfully—let it be known that you believe that Charlotte Salter is dead, presumed murdered; that you believe Duncan Ackerley died by his own hand. And that you are not looking for any further suspect. It's a simple matter of declaring victory and moving on. But it's up to you, of course. It's your inquiry."

Cobbett thought of many things he could say but one glance from Chettle stopped him from saying anything.

"This is the friendly version," Chettle continued. "We're out here, unofficial, informal. Once we go back to town, it's public, on the record. People, including me, might start to ask questions about the progress of the inquiry. Awkward questions." He clapped his hands together, as if to warm himself. "Anyway, those are my thoughts about the direction of the inquiry. We should be getting back. It's turning cold."

THIRTY

At the beginning of February, the four Salter children and the two Ackerley brothers gathered in the farmhouse.

It had been Greg's suggestion, and he arrived with cans of beer and several cartons of pizza that he had bought from the supermarket in Hemingford. Etty looked from face to face as they sat in the kitchen, swigging beer from cans and manoeuvring limp slices of pizza into their mouths.

Greg had lost weight in the last month and his blond hair was longer. He kept pushing it off his face, which in a certain light looked so uncannily like his father's that it made Etty's heart skip a beat. She couldn't forget, would never forget, her last sight of Duncan Ackerley. She avoided going down to the river and even the sight of the massive bridge felt ominous.

She had seen Morgan at school, where they were both objects of sympathy and avid curiosity, but they'd scrupulously avoided each other. She didn't want to seem like him, so obviously mangled by grief: a twitchy, blotchy, scrawny creature who looked several years younger than his age. Now he hunched over the table, his glasses smudged and his dark hair falling over his face. He had barely spoken since coming into the house.

Early tomorrow morning Paul would leave for university. His bags were already in the hall, and he himself seemed different, like he was already in transit. He was wearing a clean blue shirt rolled up to the elbows and his hair was newly washed. He had shaved. He was ready to be gone.

Ollie was subdued this evening. The wildness had gone out of him over the past week or so, and he just seemed exhausted. His glance kept sliding across to her and she knew why: he felt guilty. In two days" time he was off to Thailand with three friends. Soon Etty would be alone with Alec.

Niall was late, and he looked awkward and out of place as he took his seat among the younger people. He no longer came to the house every day and Etty hadn't seen him for almost a week. *Is this how it goes?* she wondered. Something unbearable becomes something to be endured. Life resumes.

"I thought we should meet because, well, it's better to have things out in the open," said Greg. His voice caught. He sounded nervous. "I would have asked you to ours but Mum's not well. Anyway, here we are."

He didn't seem to know how to continue. The kitchen fell silent.

Morgan lifted his head. "The police came to see us," he said with a sudden violence. "Fucking fuckers."

"They came to see us as well," said Ollie.

"They're saying that they are convinced Dad took his own life," said Greg.

"Which is stupid," said Morgan, his voice pitched high. "It was an accident."

"And they aren't looking for anyone else in connection with Charlie," continued Greg. His fists clenched and unclenched as he spoke. "They're saying they were having an affair and Dad killed Charlie and then killed himself in a fit of remorse."

"That's just rubbish," said Morgan. He glared at the Salters. "You know that, right? You know they weren't. You know Dad didn't kill Charlie. He didn't."

No one spoke for a few seconds. Niall cleared his throat, opened his mouth, closed it again.

"I guess," said Greg, "that nobody really knows anything, right? About any of this. That's what makes it even more horrible."

"I believe you," said Etty. Everyone turned to look at her. She could feel her chest open up, and she instinctively put her hand on the locket Charlie had given her and which she never took off. "I don't think they were having an affair, deceiving everyone. They weren't like that. I don't think Duncan killed Mum. He was her friend. He was *our* friend. I think the person who killed her—"

"She's not dead," cut in Paul. "She's out there somewhere."

"She's dead," said Ollie. "For God's sake."

"I think the person who killed her," said Etty, loudly

and with a sob in her voice, "is upstairs in his study, thinking he's got away with it."

Upstairs in his study, Alec Salter heard his daughter. He lifted his head from the documents he was sorting and looked out of the window. There were snowdrops in the damp grass, shimmering in the twilight. Soon it would be spring.

He smiled.

Etty stood in the hall as the Ackerley brothers put on their boots and jackets. Morgan went ahead into the darkness. His thin shoulders were bunched and his head pushed forward into the easterly wind. But Greg hesitated.

"Will you be all right?" he asked. "Being here, I mean?"

Etty stared at him for a long moment. "Are you going away too?"

"I guess so. It was always the plan."

"You can't leave as well," she blurted out. "What would I do then?"

She put her arms round him, under his thick jacket, and pressed her face against his chest. She could smell wood smoke and hear the steady tick of his heart.

"Etty," he said, stroking her hair.

She lifted her face blindly to be kissed, anything for comfort, anything to be less alone. He lowered his head but then suddenly pulled away, his face working.

"Please," she said. "Please. Don't leave."

181

"You'll come through this," he said.

He bent to lift something from the tiled floor behind Paul's cases and handed it to her: the angel that had been on top of the Christmas tree. It had pink wings, a white gauze skirt hiding the clip that fixed it to the tree's spear, and a stitched smile on its face.

"I'll see you," he said, and headed out of the door.

Etty watched him as he joined his brother and the two shapes disappeared into the night. Ollie came and stood beside her, and then Paul and Niall. Nobody spoke. Thick tears were running down Etty's cheeks and she made no effort to wipe them away.

At last she turned and went very slowly up the stairs, clutching the smiling angel, wanting to die.

PART TWO

2022

THIRTY-ONE

"What shall we do with this? Throw it away?"

Etty looked at the shabby little angel that Ollie was holding and such a jolt of memory went through her that it hurt.

"We can't," said Niall. "Mum used to put it on the top of the tree after we'd finished decorating it."

Etty pushed away the image of Charlie standing on a chair and biting her lower lip in concentration as she fixed the figure in place.

"It's a bit worse for wear," said Ollie. "But maybe we can mend it?"

"We can't keep everything that holds memories," said Etty. "Or we'll be keeping half the house."

Ollie shrugged and dropped the angel in the bin bag that was already half full.

"This is taking too long," said Etty, glancing at the time on her phone.

They were in the living room, which after three decades of neglect looked more like a railway station's waiting room, ceiling cracking, chairs standing in a row and the old sofa sagging. But the window was wide open to let in the warm spring air and, from where she stood, Etty could see the cherry tree in blossom, the old quince tree and the flawless blue sky.

Everything was the same—the same photos on the mantelpiece and pictures on the wall, the same yellow curtains that Charlie had made, the same rug, now faded and threadbare—and yet everything was jarring and strange.

Etty couldn't remember when they had last been in the same room. Twenty years ago? Twenty-five? And now they were three instead of four. Niall's hair was receding and he had put on weight, breathing heavily when he moved. Ollie's slimness was now sharp and angular.

"We need to have a system," she said.

Niall put a photograph album on the table and wiped the dust off its mock leather cover.

"I wish Paul was here," said Ollie. "It feels wrong doing it without him."

Etty started to answer him when she was interrupted by angry shouts from upstairs.

"Charlie, where are you?"

The three of them looked at each other. Nobody replied.

Etty went to the living room door and looked up the staircase. Her chest felt tight and her breathing all wrong and she instinctively put her hand up to touch the round gold locket that hung round her neck, as if it was a talisman.

Her father was coming heavily down the steps, one at a time. He gripped the banister with one large, knuckly hand. He held the other hand in front of him, as if brushing away invisible impediments. His shoelaces were undone. He was wearing a thick cardigan in spite of the balmy weather and his white hair needed cutting.

"Charlie?" he said.

She stood up straighter, lifted her chin, looked at the man she had cut out of her life for so long.

"It's Etty."

The name was unfamiliar in her mouth. She hadn't been Etty for three decades: she was Elizabeth, Lizzie to those few people she allowed close. Only here, in this life she had fled from, was she still Etty Salter.

"Etty? Etty's my little daughter."

"I'm your daughter."

He frowned. "I'm not a fool."

"It's just been a long time," said Etty. "Since you saw me."

Such a long time, she thought: I ran away from an ogre and came back to an angry, unravelling old man.

"When all's said and done," he said.

A young woman appeared at the top of the stairs, slender and dark-haired.

"Alec!" she said, hurrying towards him. "I thought you were asleep!"

"Who are you?"

She reached him on the staircase and put a hand on his arm to steady him.

"Let me tie up your laces," she said. "Or you might

trip. I didn't know you'd woken up. Do you want to go downstairs? It is time for a cup of tea."

He looked at her, almost in surprise.

"Where are you from?"

"You know, Alec. I'm from the agency."

"I don't mean that. What bloody country?"

"I'm from Spain. You know that."

"Don't be rude, Dad," said Etty.

"Couldn't they get someone from England?"

It was when Alec was at his most apparently disinhibited, his most demented, that Etty recognised her father.

"Hello," she said to the young woman, who turned to where she stood in the hall below her.

"I did not see you. You must be Alec's daughter, Etty."

"Yes."

"I am Lucia, from the care agency. I am looking after your father. Aren't I, Alec?"

"No. Will no one tell me where Charlie is?"

"I'm pleased to meet you, Etty," said Lucia. "Niall has told me about you." She guided Alec slowly down the stairs.

"Charlie is dead," said Etty to her father. "She disappeared thirty years ago and has never been seen since."

"You can let yourself out," said Alec.

Etty stood to one side and let them pass her and enter the kitchen. Instead of returning to her brothers, she went slowly upstairs. She went past Alec's old study and saw it was a junk room now, a place where everything that didn't have a place ended up: piles of magazines and books and broken furniture were crammed in there. The window was barely visible, but there was a jagged crack running across the top pane of glass and ivy was pushing its way through the frame and into the room.

She didn't look into Alec's bedroom, she couldn't bear to, but continued along the landing, past Ollie's room where he had already slung his bags, past Paul's room whose door she did not open, up the stairs to her own old room in the eaves.

The narrow iron bedstead was still there, the tiny basin, the same wardrobe, which when she opened it rattled with empty hangers. There was a pair of white plimsolls she used to wear on the floor and a crumpled flannel shirt. The poster of a lighthouse was peeling on the wall, and she saw that a strip of photos of her and Kim, taken in a booth when they were fifteen, was still tucked into the frame of the mirror. The rag rug looked like rats might have got to it. The blue-checked curtains were thin and dusty.

She looked out of the small window and blinked in surprise. Rows of new houses stood where the fields used to be. From here she could see the garden, which was a scrubby neglected wilderness. Charlie's vegetable patch and her herb beds were grown over or gone. But the roses still flowered in an untamed profusion of pinks and whites.

Far off, she could see the curve of the river. She turned away.

*

She went downstairs again and back into the living room. Ollie and Niall were still there and they didn't appear to have done much more sorting. They were stooped over a photo album, turning its stiff pages slowly.

"Come and look at you in this one, Etty," said Niall. "You and your scary frown."

"No, thank you."

"Isn't that Morgan Ackerley?" said Ollie. "I remember that day. You climbed the beech tree with him, and he got stuck."

Etty didn't move. She didn't want to look at photos of the Ackerley family any more than she wanted to look at ones of her own.

"Did you see his last series?" said Ollie. "Morgan Ackerley famous. What were the odds?"

"He sent me a WhatsApp a couple of days ago," said Niall. "I was supposed to reply."

"What about?" asked Ollie.

"He's here. Him and Greg. In Glensted. They wanted to talk to us. I didn't know what to say."

"Talk about what?"

"He said it was better face to face."

"It might be interesting," said Ollie.

"Shall we meet?" Niall asked. "Find out what it's about?"

"You can leave me out of it," said Etty. "I'm going back on Sunday."

"Then let's do this evening." Niall sounded like the big brother again, taking control. He took his mobile out and started keying in a message.

190

"I see Frances around sometimes," he said when he'd finished.

"Is she all right?" Etty remembered Frances during those terrible months after Duncan's death: the terrifying chaos of her grief.

"She remarried."

"That's not what I asked."

"She seems pretty well, actually."

His phone gave a ping and he looked down.

"That was quick. Morgan says tonight is good. He says we can go to Frances's house if we want."

"No," said Etty quickly. "Let's meet somewhere in Glensted."

"We could meet at Victor's," said Niall.

Ollie lifted his head. "You mean the café? Does that still exist?"

"It's a wine bar now. But it's still run by Victor Pearce and he still pretends to be a hippy."

"Maybe not there either," said Etty.

"There's not much else in Glensted," said Niall. "The restaurant has long closed. There's the Anchor."

Etty turned away from her brothers to stare out of the window at the wasteland that used to be a garden.

"OK, Victor's," she said at last. "Half past six?"

"Look at this one of Mum." Ollie slid a photo out of its transparent envelope and held it out.

"We're never going to get this done," said Etty, not looking.

"God, she was lovely though," said Ollie. "I think I

spent the next three decades searching for someone like her. No wonder both my marriages fell apart."

"I still dream about her," said Niall abruptly. "Do you ever do that?"

"We need to get help sorting all of this junk." Etty picked up her phone.

"I used to think I saw her on the street," Ollie said. "I'd look out of a car window and there she'd be. Just a glimpse. Sometimes I ran after her and then a stranger would turn their face and this horrible disappointment would spike through me. I don't see her any more, though. That's probably a good thing, right?"

"OK," said Etty. "I think I've found someone."

She turned from her brother and dialled the number As she left the room, they heard her introduce herself. And when she came back in a couple of minutes later, she told them that a woman called Bridget Wolfe who cleared houses and offices, no job too big or too small, was coming to the farmhouse in the morning to look round.

"Because we clearly can't do this alone. We're barely making a dent in it."

"You could have asked us first," said Niall.

"You've done too much already, all these years. It must have been awful."

Niall's cheeks turned pink. "Someone had to. And to be honest, Penny's done more than me."

"Yes," said Etty. "I'm glad you've got Penny."

THIRTY-TWO

"I'm feeling a bit nervous."

Greg Ackerley—broad-shouldered, blue-eyed, his blond hair touched with grey, and wearing round glasses—looked so like his father now that Morgan was sometimes startled back into the past at the sight of him.

"We've known them all our lives," he said. "They're not just friends. They felt more like cousins. Obviously we've lost touch, but you never lose that."

"It's still weird."

What had once been Victor Pearce's café was now a bar that served Suffolk tapas and wine, and one or two cocktails. There were still watercolours for sale on the walls and Pearce was still there, more gaunt and greyer. Morgan told him there were going to be five of them, so Pearce pulled two tables together right by the window. Morgan sat with his back to the street.

"Don't want to be spotted?" said Greg.

"Don't be silly."

"They'll be excited. A local celebrity."

Morgan laughed. "It won't be like that. They'll

come up to me and say: Who are you? And I'll say my name and they'll say: Weren't you on that cooking programme? And I'll say no and they'll say: Then what have I seen you on? And I'll say: Maybe the series I did about Russia? And they'll say no and look disappointed. So that's why I'm sitting with my back to the window."

Morgan had aged well, thought Greg ruefully. The scrawny little kid with the tumble of dark hair and woebegone eyes behind smeared spectacles had gone, and in his place was a trim man with dark, artfully tousled hair and a beard that was just a few days more than stubble. He used contact lenses now, and the jeans and cotton shirt he was wearing were clean, crisp and obviously expensive.

Greg looked over Morgan's shoulder.

"I think I can see them. Across the road. Don't look round, it'll be too obvious."

"What'll be obvious?"

"I'd never have recognised her."

"Who? Etty?"

"She's slim and smartly dressed and grown-up and serious-looking. She's middle-aged."

Morgan laughed. "What do you think *we* are?"

The door opened and the Salters stepped in, and what had felt like an empty room now was suddenly full and bustling. Greg and Morgan stood up and for a moment the two groups looked at each other, almost aghast at the strange, awkward comedy of this meeting. Then they approached each other and the men tentatively hugged. Morgan stepped towards Etty with his arms outstretched, but she moved backwards and held out a hand, which he shook.

"I guess that's something we learned from the pandemic," he said. "We don't have to hug everyone."

"I didn't hug before the pandemic," said Etty.

It sounded like a humorous comment but Etty said it without smiling.

Before they could sit down, Victor Pearce came out from behind the bar and approached them.

"I heard you were here," he said.

Etty stared at Victor with eyes which were Charlie's eyes, thought Greg. She wasn't like her mother, who'd been soft and smiling and blonde, but at the same time she was unmistakably her mother's daughter.

"How did you hear?" asked Ollie.

"I don't know. People told me." He looked at Etty and was visibly affected. "Wow. How long has it been?"

"Pretty long."

"You never said goodbye."

"Etty thinks goodbyes are overrated," said Ollie.

"You look so like . . ." Victor began, and then stopped himself.

"I don't," she said. "Not really."

"What about a bottle of white wine?" said Victor. "It's from up the road. That's something new since . . ."

"Since our time?" said Ollie.

"We'll give it a try," said Morgan. "This is all on us, by the way."

"What else do you do?" Etty asked Victor.

195

"We've got red, and our cocktail of the week is a special Glensted negroni."

"I'll have a gin and tonic," said Etty.

"Anything to eat?" Victor asked. "We've got a smoked meat platter. A cheese platter. All local."

"Fine," said Morgan. "Both of them."

"Excellent. By the way, I saw that documentary you did. It was very good."

"The Russian one?" Morgan asked.

"No, I don't think so. It was something else."

When he left them, there was some awkward small talk about when they had all arrived in town and about the new estate that was being built on the outskirts and about the bar and how long it had been going.

Niall asked Greg what he did, and Greg shrugged and looked down at the table, his broad fingers following the knot in the wood.

"This and that," he said. "Odd jobs really."

"He's being modest," said Morgan. "He rescues people from their domestic crises. Leaks and floods and electrical failures and fallen trees. Everything. He's amazing at fixing things and he's made that into his profession."

"I wouldn't really call it a profession," said Greg.

"Do you do plumbing?" asked Niall. "Because we've got a slight problem with—"

"Niall!" said Etty fiercely, and he had the grace to blush.

"Sure," said Greg. "While I'm here I'd be happy to help."

"Where do you live?" asked Ollie.

"Up the coast about fifty miles. It's pretty nice there."

"His wife's a deputy head," said Morgan. "And they have a son called Mark who's studying anthropology at university. They have a cute cottage near the sea. Greg's made it really nice."

"See?" said Greg. "Morgan may be famous but he still appreciates us little people."

"Well, I don't want to forget my humble origins."

Etty cast a glance at Greg's face. Suddenly they were like teenagers again, that joshing each other that was always on the verge of turning into a real fight. Observing Morgan's success from a distance, she'd almost forgotten that he was the younger one and Greg had been the reliable, capable one.

"What about you?" Morgan asked Ollie.

Ollie smiled in a way that was painful to see.

"You really want to know?"

"I really want to know."

"All right, I work for a company that supplies things to other companies."

"Like what?"

"Trust me, you don't want to know that."

Victor came back with the wine and the gin and tonic, and then the meat and the cheese on seasoned wooden boards. He identified the cheeses and the meats and where they had come from one by one. There was also local chutney and local chilli relish to accompany them. When he was gone, Morgan poured the wine into four glasses and took a sip from his.

"It's better than you'd expect," he said. "It's certainly better than it used to be." He picked up his glass and his expression turned serious. "It seems incredible, but I think the last time we were all together was at the funeral."

"We weren't *all* together," said Niall evenly. He didn't look at Etty, but everyone knew who he meant. She didn't respond but her face had an icily composed expression.

"I still can't believe it," said Morgan. "Paul was special. He always took things hard, I guess."

"I think we all took it hard," said Ollie.

"And now you're here for your dad," said Morgan.

"That's right," said Niall. "I mean, of course, I'm always here. But that's what Etty and Ollie are here for."

"It must be painful," said Morgan.

"Yes." Niall spoke stiffly.

Morgan ran a hand over his beard and his voice became quieter. "So much time has passed, so much water under the bridge. I feel we've got such a lot to talk about that I don't know where to start but I thought we should have some sort of toast to mark this moment. I'm not sure exactly what to toast."

Etty took a long drink from her gin and tonic and set it back on the table. She looked at Morgan.

"You contacted Niall. You said you wanted to meet."

Morgan gave a small laugh. "It's funny. You're all on that side of the table and we're on this side. It feels like an interview."

"I can't believe we all lost touch," Greg said softly. His face was troubled. "After everything that happened."

"We needed to get away," Ollie said. "And after Paul ..." He stopped. It was like he couldn't say the words. "It felt like a curse on the family." He looked round at Niall. "I felt bad about leaving Niall, though. He stayed. He was left to pick up the pieces."

Etty drained her glass and stood up.

"I need to go outside for a moment," she said.

She walked out on to the pavement and they could see her on the other side of the window, smoking a cigarette.

"I was surprised she wasn't at the funeral," said Morgan. "I always thought that she and Paul were close."

Niall and Ollie exchanged glances.

"She wasn't really in a good place at the time," said Ollie. "She wasn't in a condition to come to a public event like a funeral."

"I googled her once or twice," said Morgan. "All that came up was the law firm where she works. It looks like she's done really well."

"Well, she's clever, our Etty," said Ollie.

"I wondered if she was married and had children. It didn't say anything about that on the website."

"No, none of that." Ollie looked nervously at his sister out on the pavement. "I'm not really comfortable talking about her. We're not in touch that much nowadays. But she's been great here, arranging things for Dad. I don't think we could have managed it without her. All the legal stuff and the forms. She just got it sorted."

"We heard about Alec," said Greg. "Is he going into a home?"

"We thought we could manage with a live-in carer," said Niall. "But he's always been difficult." He smiled grimly. "As you know. Lucia's great but now he's got to a new level of being difficult."

Etty came back in, ordered another gin and tonic and sat down.

"I'm glad we're able to do this," Morgan said, resuming where he had left off. "Because we've all been affected by this. I think that your family and our family are the only people who can really understand what we've been through."

Etty didn't smile or nod in response. "You mean that we were both wondering whether our fathers were murderers? Is that what we've got in common?"

"Jeez, Etty," said Ollie. He looked across at Morgan. "Niall told us you wanted to talk, face to face. Was it just about getting in touch?"

Morgan took a sip of wine. When he next spoke, he had settled into his rhythm and was the man they had seen on television, practised and fluent.

"I'm so glad we're in touch. We've missed you. But we wanted to tell you something before you hear it from anyone else. Thirty years ago, something terrible happened, two people died and there was never a proper resolution. The police basically stopped their inquiry.

They let it be known that once our father died, they weren't looking for any further suspect. I'm not sure that Greg and I really knew how to process that. We were just numb, traumatised, whatever word you want to use, and we went our own ways, had our different lives, our different careers. But there it was, always in the back of our minds." He looked across the table. "I'm sure you must have felt the same."

Nobody spoke. Etty wasn't looking at him but out of the window.

"For years we talked about how we need some way of coming to terms with what happened," he continued. "We need closure, to use the dread word."

"And how are we going to get that?"

"We've had a thought and we'd like you to be involved, to the degree that you'd like to be. At the very least, we want you to be onside. The two of us are doing a podcast."

Niall and Ollie glanced at each other. Etty was impassive as ever.

"A podcast?" Niall said. "What do you mean? What kind of podcast?"

"We want to tell the story of what happened, but not just that. It's really about whether we can find a way to make sense of it for ourselves so that we can move on."

"You mean it's just you two talking into a mike?"

Morgan smiled. "I don't think anyone would want to listen to that. We want to interview everyone involved. This isn't just our story. It's the tragedy of two families, it's the tragedy of a village, and it's the tragedy of a system that failed us all."

For the first time, Etty gave the faintest of smiles. "So what do you want from us?"

"Because it's your story as much as it is ours. It would mean so much if you would agree to be interviewed. We want everyone to give their own perspective, to have their side of the story fairly presented."

"Are you being paid for this?" Ollie asked.

Morgan shook his head. "We're doing this for ourselves. And for you, of course. It just feels like a story that needs to be told. Perhaps it will help us all. It may be therapeutic. That's what I hope."

"When are you planning on doing this?" Etty asked.

"We've actually done a couple of interviews already. We've talked to a couple of people in the village, done some of the groundwork. But obviously one of the strands is your mother's disappearance. We'll be respectful and empathetic, and we'd love you to contribute. If you're comfortable with it."

"This is all so sudden." Niall looked confused. "Do you really want to go there?"

"We've never believed that our father really was a murderer," said Morgan. "Have we, Greg?"

Greg hesitated. Etty could see him searching for the right words, just as he'd done when he was a teenager. They all waited for him to speak.

"I have to be honest about this," he said at last. "I don't know what happened and I don't know what I believe. When Morgan told me about the idea, I was shocked at first, about digging up the past. But I decided I should be involved because I know what I feel. Dad was a good man."

"We'll have to see what we uncover," said Morgan.

"But if your father isn't the murderer," said Ollie slowly, "does that mean our father is? Is that going to be the punchline in the final episode?"

"I have no idea about the final episode."

Etty drained her drink and stood up.

"I'm done," she said. She turned to her brothers. "I'll be back at the house."

"What about the podcast?" said Greg.

"I don't want to have anything to do with it."

"We just want you to have the chance to put your perspective."

"I don't have a perspective." She pulled her coat on but just before she reached the door, she turned around. "You can't libel the dead. I suppose you've checked that. But you'd better be careful of anything you say about anyone who's alive."

"We just want the truth," said Greg.

Etty shook her head slowly.

"The truth," she said. "You people."

She opened the door and walked briskly away, her coat blowing in the wind behind her.

"She's changed," said Morgan as they were walking back to Frances's house. "She used to be so warm and ..." He hesitated, considering. "Such a bright spark."

Greg didn't answer. He was thinking of the teenage girl who had put her arms round him and lifted her face blindly to be kissed, her eyes wet with tears.

"She's suffered," said Morgan. It was as if he was rehearsing what he would say in his podcast. "She's had to learn to defend herself against the brutality of the world."

"She was just a kid," said Greg. He sounded as if he was talking to himself.

"I was just a kid too. But you and me, we've come through. It doesn't feel like any of them have."

THIRTY-THREE

Etty woke the next morning with the dawn. She hadn't closed the curtains and the small window was an unblemished square of silver-blue. For a few seconds, she lay quite still, staring out at the room she had last slept in nearly thirty years ago.

She sat up abruptly, swung her legs out of bed, stood and crossed to the window, which she opened to let the air in. It was already warm. In the distance the poplars shimmered in the morning breeze.

She dressed in jeans and a long-sleeved T-shirt, cleaned her teeth at the little basin, picked up her notebook and pen, and went downstairs. The rest of the house was quiet until, passing by Alec's room, she heard his voice.

"No," he was saying. "Scram." Etty waited, her hand on the banister. "You blart," he said, incomprehensible but obscene. He made a low guttural sound that was halfway between a laugh and a groan.

She continued down the stairs. The same step creaked. The same clock on the wall told her it was twenty-five past five. She slid her feet into the boots she'd left in the hall, quietly opened the front door and went outside.

Charlie's old garden no longer existed. Of course it didn't. Even in Etty's last eighteen months in the farmhouse, alone except for Alec, nature had taken over, weeds throttling the flower beds, the vegetable patch quite obscured by nettles and ragwort. Now it was wasteland. The apple tree was dead and brambles ran riot.

Etty went down the garden, past the rank little pond covered in duckweed, past the broken-down sheds. She found the quince tree that still had some of its floppy pink blooms and sat down under it, though the ground was still damp.

She opened her notebook, took the top off her pen, but for a long time she didn't write anything. She lit a cigarette and smoked it slowly, watching the spirals of smoke dissolve into the blue air. Thoughts and images came crowding in on her. This was why she had never come back: everything here held a memory, and every memory was a sprung trap.

She understood she had been unpleasant last night. Greg and Morgan had looked at her with bewilderment: she knew that they were seeing the old Etty, that eager creature she had put away long ago, and the new one, brisk and cool and hard. But at least she had survived.

She turned to her notebook and started going through the to-do list, written out in bullet points in her neat cursive. Contact estate agents. Finalise arrangements with the care home she had found. Settle last payments for the home-care agency. Make sure that she and her brothers all had lasting power of attorney. Cancel utility bills for the house.

She stared back at the house, slates missing from the roof, crumbling mortar, leaking gutters, blistering window frames, everything shabby and neglected. It already looked abandoned.

Back in the kitchen, Lucia was making breakfast for Alec. The young woman was wrapped in a voluminous white towelling robe and her hair was in plaits. She looked young and fresh and out of place in her dingy surroundings.

"How long have you been a carer?" asked Etty, searching through cupboards for coffee.

"Only six months. I'm saving to go travelling with my boyfriend."

"Do you enjoy it?"

Lucia shrugged. "Sometimes. It depends on who I'm looking after."

"Do you enjoy it here?"

Lucia cracked an egg into a bowl, then looked at her frankly.

"Your father is not always easy."

"No."

"Sometimes he says horrible things."

"I'm sorry."

"But I tell myself that he is ill. He has a brain condition. It is not him; it is not personal."

"He was never easy," said Etty.

"He talks about you a lot."

Etty could feel herself flinch. She turned away and spooned ancient coffee beans into the grinder that had been there when she was a teenager.

"He understands more than you think. He asks when you will come."

"Well, I'm here now."

Through the window, she saw a car come too fast down the drive and stop with a violent splatter of gravel by the porch. A young woman was crouched over the steering wheel with a mutinous expression on her face. Niall sat beside her and he seemed to be shouting. Etty saw that there was a learner plate on the car.

The two of them got out, each slamming their door loudly, and then the car door at the back opened and another figure got out. Etty would have recognised Penny anywhere: she still had bobbed hair, though it was grey now, and a determined expression on her strong face with its square jaw; and she still stood very upright as she walked, her arms swinging as if she was on an energetic hike. Etty had always liked her. She liked her now, as she strode past her angry husband and daughter and up to the front door.

"Hello, Etty," she said as she came into the kitchen, as if they had met last week. "Hi, Lucia. All OK?"

"Good," said Lucia.

"Fine," said Etty. "Coffee?"

"Please. I've had an unrelaxing journey here, to put

it mildly. And speak of the devil, this is our youngest daughter, Mia. Mia, this is your aunt, Etty."

Mia had unbrushed hair and a face full of piercings. Her cropped top showed that her belly button was also pierced. She had a thunderous expression on her face.

"The long-lost aunt."

Etty neither smiled nor put out her hand. They stared at each other, then Mia's face broke into a grin. She looked suddenly young and sweet.

"Cool," she said.

Niall came in, pink-faced and sweating. "Are we late?"

"You're early. Ollie's not down yet."

"I am," came a voice from the door.

Ollie looked half-asleep still, his stubbly face puffy, his shirt half-unbuttoned. His glance took in Penny, Mia and Lucia and he made a circling gesture with his thin hand. "Morning, everyone. Long time no see, Penny."

"Very long," she said.

"Any coffee going spare?"

"No." Etty pointed at the pot. "There are some beans left."

"I will make some more," said Lucia.

"No you won't," said Etty. "Waiting on a dysfunctional family isn't part of your job description."

"So," said Penny, "what's the plan?"

"A woman called Bridget Wolfe is coming any minute now. She does all kinds of house clearance jobs. So I assume she'll look round and see how long it would take and give us a quote."

"I thought we'd be doing most of it ourselves," said Penny.

"No. Because that would mean you and Niall doing most of it, just like you've done everything else for the last thirty years. For which we're very grateful, aren't we, Ollie?"

"Christ, yes," said Ollie thickly, through a mouthful of white bread.

"Can I have the old oil lamp for my room?" asked Mia.

"No," said Penny.

"Why not?"

"Because there are lots of people ahead of you in the queue and because it would be a fire risk."

"Just because—" began Mia.

Niall pointed at her. "Be quiet for once in your life."

"Charlie!" The voice was slurred and querulous. "Charlie, where are you? I'm getting fed up of waiting."

Bridget Wolfe arrived in a large white van with a rusty back door and no registration plates. When she swung herself down from the driver's seat, Etty saw that she was short and strong, probably in her early forties. She was dressed in a belted khaki all-in-one suit and had stout black boots with bright blue laces, and a messenger bag slung over one shoulder. Her hair was cropped and her eyes were so dark they looked black.

"Bridget?" Etty said as she approached.

"And you're Etty Salter, the youngest member of the famous Salter family. And you," she said, turning to look at Ollie who'd ambled out to join them on the drive. "You must be Ollie Salter."

"Yes."

"I always knew we'd meet. It was meant."

"Oh," said Ollie. "Really?"

"I'm here to help you," said Bridget firmly, as she went into the house. "Hello, you're Niall."

"Yes," said Niall, "yes, I am."

Penny stepped forward to join Niall.

"And I'm Penny."

"Yes," agreed Bridget. "Very good. So here we all are."

She sat herself down at the table and looked at them in turn.

"Mia," said Mia reluctantly, when Bridget's gaze settled on her. "But I'm not really here. Ignore me."

"We thought," said Etty, "that the best way to proceed would be to—"

Bridget held up her hand. Etty stopped.

"I'm going to make some suggestions and see what you think. I've worked with families a lot, so you're in safe hands with me. Think of me as your enabler."

Ollie grinned and Niall blinked several times.

"First off, there are things here that people will want. Some of you will want the same thing, so how do you reach an agreement? I'll tell you how. You each separately, and without conferring ..." Here she wagged a finger in the air reprovingly. "You each write a list of the things you most want, numbered one to ten, or actually, in this case, maybe one to twenty is safer. Then you go round in a circle, saying what you want, item by item.

211

See? It's great. You don't get to think, *oh, I wanted that,* when someone selects an object, because you didn't really. You know you didn't because you didn't choose it in the first place. I know that objects can become like avatars—do I mean avatars? Anyway, they stand for a whole lot more—which is why my job is so hard and why it is so important I get it right. You're saying goodbye. You're acknowledging the past and then you are letting it go. Letting. It. Go." She made a shooing gesture with her hand, batting the past out of the window.

Niall muttered something inaudible.

"We can put Post-it notes on everything you've written down," continued Bridget, and she put a stack of Post-it notes on the table. "What's left, I deal with. I've got paper and pens here for you all."

She pulled a handful of loose paper out of her bag and then scrabbled around in it for an assortment of pencils and pens, which she handed round.

"You want us to do this now?" asked Ollie.

"I don't want anything," said Etty.

"Oh, careful, you might find that's not true. And yes, do it now. While you're making your lists, I can go round the house to see what's what, and then we can reconvene."

Obediently, Niall, Ollie and even Etty took a sheet of paper and a pen. Niall at once began scribbling furiously. Ollie stood up and announced he needed to go from room to room to refresh his memory.

Mia gave a raucous laugh. "Look at you! You're like children at a party, not sure how to play the game."

"Penny," said Niall. "Come and help me."

"Against the rules!" cried Mia. "She said no conferring."

Etty looked out of the window. Small, mild clouds were moving across the blue sky. The poplars dipped and bent in the wind. She imagined the eddies in the river, the lap of tiny waves on the bank. She picked up her pen and wrote: *One piece of Charlie's jewellery.* Then she laid the pen down again and folded the paper in half.

She thought of the simple gold chain Charlie had loved. The moonstone ring that she would wear on her middle finger. The twisted silver bracelet, or the small drop earrings that always used to remind her of a raindrop.

"Time's up," said Bridget, re-entering the kitchen.

"I've written more than twenty," said Niall.

"Do you think you can clear the whole house?" Etty asked. "Is it just you?"

Bridget smiled. "This is nothing. I mean, there is rather a lot, and I can tell it mostly hasn't been touched for years, but that's all right. Archaeology is one of my passions; this house is full of layer upon layer of history. But of course I can do it. I have my lads to help lift and carry. It might take time."

"How much time?"

"I'd have to work flat out, but what does two to three weeks sound like?"

"Fine."

"Will your father still be in residence?"

"For the next week or so he will."

213

"That's all right with me as long as it is with him. I can work round him. But people can be difficult sometimes."

"Will you send us a quote?"

"No."

"No?"

"That's not how I do things. I don't charge a fee. I will sort everything out. Some things I will throw away, some things I put up for sale in my shop, and there are items here I would want to put up for auction. Everything that goes for less than £500 is mine. Everything that's over £500 goes to you, minus a small fee for selling it. You can trust me to tell you if I come across something especially valuable. And then, once your father has gone, I will clear the whole house of rubbish and get it ready to sell. What do you think?"

"We need to discuss it," said Niall.

"It seems fair to me," said Etty.

"But it's quite a big decision and we should confer." Niall sounded flustered.

"Yes," said Penny. "Of course we should."

"How about I go and smoke my cigarette in the garden," said Bridget cheerfully, dipping her hand into the pocket of her jumpsuit and producing a single bent cigarette. "And you do this conferring."

Fifteen minutes later, the Salters watched as the white van drove back up the drive, exhaust fumes billowing.

"I've taken to her," said Ollie. "She said it would be a healing process for us. We could do with that."

"Let's put those Post-it notes up," said Niall.

214

Thirty-four

Just before seven on Monday morning, Etty left her Clerkenwell flat and—as she always did—walked down to the office just by the Barbican. Many people didn't like this area. They said it lacked soul, it lacked history. That wasn't quite true. There was a history. This had been part of the medieval City of London. Shakespeare had lived here. But the medieval district had burned down in the fire of London and the parts that hadn't been burned had been bombed in the Blitz. They had been replaced by offices and concrete tower blocks. Etty liked them. She liked the cleanness of them, the starkness. It was a place you could live unnoticed, without being bothered.

The case she was dealing with was on the face of it quite simple: her client, a celebrity footballer, was bringing a claim for the unjustified infringement of his right to privacy, misuse of private information and breach of confidence. She had a meeting with the barrister in his chambers the next morning, so she sat at her desk with coffee and a pile of files. She knew she'd be there until eleven at night. She would go home and eat a takeaway and drink a bottle of wine and it would start again tomorrow and the day after that. There would be no time to think about the previous few days. That was good.

After Ollie's divorce, he had stayed in Bristol to be near Lindy and the two boys, who were men now, near enough, and who were the best things in a life that hadn't gone how he had planned or dreamed. He lived by the Downs but, as he always half-jokingly explained, on the wrong side. Not on the Clifton side with Georgian houses and views of the suspension bridge. He had only been able to afford a little modern maisonette, but there were walks nearby and, in any case, his work involved so much travel that he was hardly at home. In the upcoming week, he would be in Coventry, Plymouth and then back up to Birmingham. He had hoped they could continue doing all these on Zoom but they'd had a meeting. They need to trust us, his boss had told him, and you only really trust someone when you meet them face to face.

The first evening back he'd sat in his living room with his usual Mexican takeaway and a beer. After two years, he still hadn't really made his mark on the place. He thought of the Post-it notes he had put on some of the things in the farmhouse: that painting of a forest, the armchair, the small wooden dresser from the kitchen, the old oil lamp. He would have liked to have claimed the table, but it was too big. It was bigger than his kitchen. He would have to hire a van. But did he want these things from his past around him all the time?

Greg went home that evening too, just for the evening and night. He had promised Morgan he would return the next day.

His wife Katherine was sitting at the little desk in the living room when he arrived, her spectacles perched on the end of her nose, her bony, clever face intensely concentrated.

He put his canvas bag on the floor just inside the door and came up beside her, putting a hand on her shoulder. She turned and smiled, but put up one finger, telling him to wait while she got to the end of whatever it was she was working out, so he waited. She had always liked his patient stillness.

She laid down her pen and he bent to kiss her.

"Hi," he said.

"How did it go?"

"I don't know. It was strange. Meeting them all again."

"It must have been."

"It's nice to be home. It all felt so sad."

"Well," she said. "What happened to you all was sad. You don't need to do this, you know."

"I told Morgan I would."

"Oh, Morgan," she said, affectionate but faintly derisive. "He can look after himself."

*

On the same evening, Niall and Penny sat with the Campari and tonic they always had on Sundays.

"So they swanned in," said Penny, "and then they swanned out again."

"That's not fair," said Niall. "They've lives to lead."

"You're always defending them. You've got a life to lead as well. You've got a job, you've got a family and you're still the one who has to deal with Alec when there's an emergency. When he falls over in the night, you're not the one who's conveniently a hundred miles away."

Niall lifted up his drink and then put it back on the table without putting it to his lips. *I don't even like Campari,* he thought to himself. He ran his forefinger softly around the rim of the glass. He took a slow breath. He was getting better at this. A few years ago, he might have raised his voice and then they would have gone down the slippery slope into their usual argument. Instead he spoke in a voice that was almost theatrically calm. He suspected that this made Penny even angrier than when he shouted, because it was harder to respond to.

"We've been talking for a year about sorting Dad's situation. We knew he needed to move into a home and that meant selling his house and that meant dealing with all of the family stuff in the house. We just never got around to it."

"You mean *you* never got around to it."

"Yes, I mean I never got around to it," said Niall,

still in the same even tone. "There was always something else that needed doing, so I never quite got around to it. I was starting to think we'd left it too late. And then Etty and Ollie came to talk it over and five minutes later Etty picked up the phone and just got on with it and now it's done. I feel grateful to her."

"That's the easy part. The hard part is just the daily grind of being here day after day. You're the one who didn't run away. Do they feel grateful to you for that?"

Niall shook his head slowly. "You remember those years. We thought that Etty would go the way Paul did. I remember seeing her, when her life got out of hand. I thought nobody could come back from that. But she did. She made something of herself."

"She's tough as an old boot," said Penny. "I always knew she'd be fine."

"The time I visited her in that squat. I thought the next time I'd hear about her was that she'd been found dead as well."

"You keep saying that. You talk more about her than you do about your own children."

"Ollie and Etty needed to get away. Maybe to save themselves."

"And they left you to it."

Niall could have said that when he first worked in the family firm, he'd thought it was just a transitional period, and now it was thirty years later and he was still there. He could have said many things, but he didn't say any of them.

"We don't need to think about them," he said, in what was intended to be a soothing tone.

"I'm just looking out for you," Penny said. "If I don't look out for you, who will?"

"I know that," said Niall. "And I'm very grateful."

THIRTY-FIVE

"How do we do this?" said Greg, looking around.

They were standing by the river, by the jetty, right at the spot where their father's body was dragged ashore.

"This is going to be one of the key moments," said Morgan. "We want it to seem spontaneous. I mean, we want it to *be* spontaneous."

"Have you been back here?"

"You mean to this spot?"

"I come whenever I'm in Glensted," said Greg. "I had this idea that it'll stop the place having power over me."

Morgan looked up. He had taken the portable recorder out of his leather shoulder bag and was plugging the microphone cable into it.

"Stop," he said.

"What do you mean?"

"What you were saying, that was great. But you should have saved it for when we were recording. We need to capture those moments."

"Isn't it too windy?"

"This mike will be fine. It should be. It cost enough.

But when it's your turn to speak, I'll hold it really close to your mouth. Don't let it bother you."

"It's easy for you to say."

"There's nothing to it. Don't think about it. Just imagine that you and me are having a normal conversation. Don't project. Don't think of the audience." He looked down at his recorder and then back up. "Ready?"

"I think it would be better if it were just you."

"It's about the two of us," said Morgan. "It's about our journey. A journey that started here and that ends here, one way or another. Anyway, let's see what we get. If you're not happy with it, we'll do it again or do something different."

"So how do we start?"

Morgan held the mike close to his own mouth. He smiled.

"We're already going," he said. "Remember. It's just the two of us having a conversation." He gave a cough. "My brother and I are standing by the River Heming on a beautiful May day. It's a river with a history. We used to study it at school. Twelve hundred years ago, the Vikings came up in their longships and plundered and pillaged and settled here. Six hundred years ago, they used to load wool on to ships and send them over to Belgium and Holland. This was the richest part of England. It paid for the building of churches and manor houses. And thirty years ago, Greg and our friend, Etty Salter, found the body of our father, Duncan, just down there in front of us. This is where everything started and nothing was ever the same again." He turned to his brother. "Greg, so we've come back. What are your feelings?"

Morgan held the mike in front of Greg's mouth.

"Well," said Greg. "Erm—I—that is—when I come here, in fact, whenever I come back here, I try to, I mean, I try to come back here whenever I come back because, it's—um—it's hard to explain really, it's like I want this place, I want it not to have so much power over me. Do you know what I mean?" He looked despairingly at his brother. "It's like it's a cursed place and I don't want it to be cursed."

Morgan pulled the mike away from Greg's mouth and pressed a button on the recorder.

"That was a good start," he said. "Especially at the end. I thought that was good about it being a cursed place. But I think maybe we could have another go at it."

"My mind went completely blank. I was trying to remember what I'd said before but I couldn't get it straight. And then when I started talking, I had a sort of out-of-body experience. I was listening to this other person talking and then just got self-conscious."

"You were fine," said Morgan. "But don't perform and don't have an out-of-body experience. Just talk the way we're talking now." Almost casually, he restarted the recorder and started talking into the microphone once more. "It's funny, I don't believe in magical thinking. I tell myself it's just a river: it was flowing before we were born and it'll be flowing after we're gone. But I can't help myself when I'm here. It almost feels haunted."

He held the mike towards his brother.

"I want it to be a river again," said Greg. "That's why I keep returning to it. But I'm haunted by this image of my dad going into the water, and his body being carried down towards the sea and then snagging, just here."

Morgan nodded encouragingly at him and said nothing, so after a few seconds Greg continued.

"Perhaps he didn't want to be found. Perhaps he wanted to be swept out and lost forever."

Morgan stood for a moment, holding the mike in place, and then he suddenly seemed to remember where he was.

"That was great," he said. "But it was strange. While you were saying that last bit, I was suddenly thinking: Why haven't we had this conversation before? Did it have to take a podcast for us to be able to start to process this?" He pondered for a moment. "If we move things around, that thing you said about being swept out to sea, I think that could be a nice ending for the episode. You'll really get the listeners shedding tears."

THIRTY-SIX

"Glensted is just an ordinary Suffolk village. It's not a tourist destination. It's not on the way to anywhere. On one side is a small wood. On the other the River Heming, which flows into the North Sea. My name's Morgan Ackerley and I grew up there."

"And my name's Greg Ackerley. I grew up there too. We're brothers."

"It's a quiet village. Not much has happened there. And then, just before Christmas in 1990, that all changed. A woman went missing and, a few days later, a man was found dead in the river. The woman was called Charlotte Salter. She didn't turn up at her husband's fiftieth birthday party and she hasn't been seen since."

"The man was called Duncan. Duncan Ackerley. He was our father."

Etty pulled off the busy Friday evening road on to a lay-by. She'd downloaded the podcast a couple of days earlier but she hadn't been able to face listening to it. Now, driving back up to the house, she felt she should force herself, just to know what was being said about them. She had told herself that it wouldn't matter, whatever it was, yet as soon as she heard the familiar voices, her hands started to tremble and her vision to blur. She couldn't trust herself, so she sat in the car and listened to the podcast as the lorries roared past, shaking the car, feeling too close.

There was a recording from one of the police press conferences asking for information about Charlotte Salter. An old woman, whose name Etty didn't recognise, talked about what it was like during those days: *"In the old days we didn't even lock our doors. We were all friends and neighbours. Suddenly we didn't know who to trust."*

Morgan and Greg had a conversation while walking along the main street. They stopped one or two people and asked them for their memories. One of them was a teenage boy who had never even heard of the case.

"There's been a hole in both of our lives," Morgan concluded. *"We don't even know what to call it. It's a tragedy. Is it also a crime? Both of us ran away from Glensted. For this series we've come back to try and make sense of it all. Who knows what we'll find?"*

It was quite dark by the time she drew up in front of the farmhouse, just a sliver of moon above the chimneys. Ollie's car was already there. As she approached the front door, she saw a great pile of things had been heaped up by the side of the porch: chairs and buckets, rolls of carpets, a coffee table, two boxes of china, several more of kitchen appliances, a tarnished mirror, multiple overflowing bin bags.

The hall was entirely empty, aside from the grandfather clock, which Niall had claimed. Dust lay thickly on the boards. Her footsteps echoed.

"Hello," came a quavery voice.

She looked up and Alec was standing there. He was in checked pyjamas which hung loosely on him, and he was staring down at her with a frightened expression on his face.

"It's just me," she said.

"Who are you?"

"Etty."

"No," he said.

Etty went up the stairs towards him. He took a step back from her and held up a hand as if to ward off an attack.

"Shouldn't you be in bed?" she asked.

"I'm waiting for Charlie. She never does what I say. She folds over."

"Folds over?"

"Have you taken it? I know what's going on here. I want my things put back where they belong. Everything. They're taking everything away."

Etty nodded. "We're having a clear-out," she

said. "I'm sorry if it upsets you. You should go back to bed."

"It's too dark in there."

Etty looked towards the door of the room where Lucia slept. It seemed wrong to wake her. Reluctantly, she took hold of Alec's arm and tried to steer him back towards his room, but he shook her off.

"Who do you think you are?" he said.

"I'm your daughter."

His gaze wavered in and out of focus, his mouth puckered. Etty wondered if he was going to cry. She didn't know if she had ever seen Alec shed tears, and she dreaded him doing so now because then he would become just a pitiful, lonely old man, scared of the dark. She had to keep her heart hard. She put her hand out again and tugged at him.

"Something is wrong," he said. "Who else knows where she is?"

"You mean Charlie?"

"Charlie?"

"Alec!" Lucia was hastening down the corridor towards them, tying the belt of her dressing gown as she came. "Etty, I am sorry. I thought he was asleep."

"No worries," said Etty. "I'm sorry we woke you."

"I was not asleep."

"Is Ollie here?"

"I think he went out."

"OK."

She went up the next flight of stairs and into her bedroom. Nothing was left in here except the narrow iron bed and the mirror. The carpet had gone, and there were paler patches on the walls where pictures had been.

Etty took off her clothes, cleaned her teeth, climbed under the covers. It felt like being in a prison cell.

Thirty-seven

"What do you reckon then?"

Bridget Wolfe, dressed in a black singlet and khaki trousers, her strong bare arms gleaming with sweat, beamed at the Salters.

They were in the living room, which when Etty had last been here had looked like a dingy, overcrowded waiting room and was now empty except for one small armchair with a Post-it note on its seat bearing Ollie's name, and a large cardboard box that was taped shut.

"Amazing," said Ollie. "I don't know how you did so much in five days."

"When I say I'll do a job," said Bridget, "I do it. The lads I use helped with all the lifting. My shop is stuffed to the gills, so I've stored most of it in my outhouses until I have time to sort it all. Obviously I've barely started in the kitchen. Kitchens are always the most work. And I haven't touched Mr. Salter's room."

"He goes in a week," said Etty. "Can you wait till then?"

"Of course. He doesn't usually seem to notice me being here. He's mostly in his room, and the kitchen. And that nice young woman who's looking after him makes sure he has at least one walk a day. But yesterday he came to where I was working in ..." She stopped for a moment, her cheerfulness gone.

"Paul's room," said Etty.

"Yes. Your poor brother. God rest him. Anyway, your father was very agitated. He kept asking me what I was looking for."

"You told us all to meet you here," said Niall. "Mia's outside in the car, so I can't be long."

"Yes, I did." Bridget regarded them all, her face solemn. "Part of my job is like being a removal person. That's easy. Part is like being an archivist, collecting things and putting them in order, cataloguing them, giving a narrative to the objects that make up a life. And another part is like being a guardian of secrets. It can be very powerful."

"I'm sure," Etty said. She wanted a cup of coffee and a cigarette.

"What I'm saying is that there are things I have found that you need to see and decide what to do with. They might be distressing; they might open old wounds."

"Like what?" asked Ollie.

Bridget leaned down and dipped her hand into her messenger bag, drawing out a sheaf of papers. "First of all, these were written to your father. I don't think he would understand what they are any more, but it's not for me to throw away letters or personal documents."

"Letters?" asked Niall. "What kind of letters?"

"I haven't read them, but I did glance at a few. You might call them love letters."

"Charlie's?" Ollie's voice was slightly husky.

"No."

"Oh, I see." Etty gave a harsh laugh. "You've got letters from other women there."

"Yes."

"Throw them away," said Ollie. "Why should we want to see them?"

"Give them here," said Etty.

She took the letters and riffled through them.

"Different women, over the years," she said. One of them she had been to school with, but she didn't say that. She crumpled them in her fist. "I'll burn them, unless either of you two want to actually read them."

"No," said Niall.

"Fuck no," said Ollie, wrinkling his nose.

"Any other secrets?" asked Etty.

Bridget nodded. She reached down into her bag again and drew out two notebooks with dull green covers. Etty had a sick feeling.

"These belonged to your brother," said Bridget. "Again, I haven't read them, but I saw enough to know that he poured his pain out in them."

There was a silence in the room. Etty could feel the blood in her temples pounding.

"I don't want to see," said Niall at last. His voice was gratingly loud. "I don't want to know. Of course Paul was unhappy: he killed himself, for God's sake. I don't need to read about it now, when it's more than a quarter of a century too late and there's nothing we can do except feel guilty and wretched all over again. And the same goes for any other secrets you've collected. Get rid of everything."

He turned and strode from the room.

"I think I agree," said Ollie. "Some things should be kept in the dark." His face twisted. "It must be obvious to you that our family hasn't done too well. Mum disappearing, then Paul taking his life: it wrecked us all in our different ways."

He stole a glance at Etty, whose face was stony.

"But at least we're here, managing to get on with our lives in whatever way we can. It feels like coming back here, having the past dug up, could wreck us all over again. So I'm with Niall."

He too left the room. Bridget turned her dark eyes on Etty.

"Well?"

Etty bit her lower lip.

"I'll take them," she said at last.

Etty made herself a strong cup of coffee and took it outside. Both Ollie's and Niall's cars had gone and Alec and Lucia were walking slowly up the drive, Lucia's arm linked through the old man's, who walked with a shuffling gait.

She went round the back, past the wilderness that used to be Charlie's garden, and found a spot to sit. The grass was full of daisies and the warm air stirred around her.

She sipped at her coffee, lit a cigarette, stared down at the notebooks in her lap, running one finger across their covers. They felt like bombs that might suddenly go off. Only when she had finished her cigarette did she open one of them at random. She was dry-mouthed and the sight of Paul's handwriting—cramped and neat, unmistakable—made her breath stutter. For a moment she looked away, asking herself why she was doing this.

The date at the top of the page was for 18 June 1993. Two and a half years after Charlie disappeared, two and a half years before he took his own life. Everything he owned must have been brought back here after he died: she wondered if Alec had ever read these words.

She let her eyes shimmer over the words, taking in fragments only.

It's no good ... one foot in front of the other ... this is pointless ...

She flicked through the notebook.

It's back again, I was wrong to think I was through the worst ...

It was clear that Paul turned to it only when in great distress. There were weeks when he didn't write anything, and then a crowd of days when he expressed self-loathing (at one point he called himself a worm)

234

and a sense of futility. There was a person he mentioned who had left him.

She saw the word "Mum" and put her thumb on the page.

I have not lived up to her hopes for me.

Etty closed her eyes and waited for the feeling to recede.

It felt indecent to be reading words of such naked loneliness and need. Why hadn't he ever turned to her? But perhaps he had and she hadn't responded. She'd been in no state to help anyone else. She remembered one time when he'd come to see her at her university and he had been so flat and affectless that she had got angry with him and he'd left early. She felt nauseous at the thought of it and tried to push it away, deep down where it couldn't be felt except as an indefinable ache.

She lay down on the grass and watched tiny white clouds scud past. Could she have saved him? That's what people always ask themselves when somebody they love takes their own life. But could she? They'd all deserted each other, she and Ollie and Niall and Paul.

Sitting up again, she took the other notebook and flicked through its pages, determinedly not reading the entries, until she came to the day of Charlie's disappearance: 22nd December 1990. There were only a few lines.

One of my bad days. I sit in my room and look at the books spread out in front of me but the words are meaningless squiggles. I can hear Mum downstairs, moving around. She keeps trying to find out what I'm feeling. I can't bear it. I'll go mad if this continues.

Etty stared at the sentences for a long while. She was remembering Paul on that day, how grim and silent he had been, and all the while a storm of feelings inside him. So many secrets.

Thirty-eight

"It's all in the editing," said Morgan.

He was still in his pyjamas and sitting hunched over his laptop, wearing huge headphones which he took off when Greg came in.

"I'm starting to understand that," said Greg.

"You sound like you disapprove."

"I kind of assumed it would just be, you know, beginning, middle, end."

"That sounds boring."

"When I heard that first episode, I almost didn't recognise it as a story about Dad."

"We need to hook the audience from the beginning," said Morgan, sitting back in his chair and stretching his arms. "We've already got loads of material but now we have to think about structure, what to withhold. We need characters as well. This house-clearance woman looks promising. And at the same time, we need to have the emotional journey. I'm still hoping one of the Salters will come on board. Finally, we've got to have some kind of ..." He paused. "Some kind of click at

237

the ending, when the machinery fits together and the story's complete."

Greg laughed and shook his head.

"What?" said Morgan.

"I think you're getting delusions of grandeur. Do you really think we can do what the police have failed to do for thirty years?"

"It's not necessarily about solving the crime. It's about solving it emotionally."

"That sounds a bit deep for me. How long before your sabbatical ends?"

"I took six weeks off—so I've just under a month left. Can you stay that long?"

"There are some jobs I've promised to do, nothing major. I can pop back to do those—it's only an hour and a half. Obviously I'll go home every so often, and maybe Katherine can join me at the weekend. But am I actually helpful?"

"You're essential," said Morgan. "The two brothers on a quest."

"I thought I sounded a bit stilted."

"That'll get easier."

"I hope so. Coffee?"

"Great."

Greg went downstairs to the kitchen. Through the window, he saw his mother in the garden, trimming the roses with a pair of secateurs that Duncan once used. The little border terrier she and Lester had rescued was padding around beside her. She was seventy-nine now and her long hair, tied back into a knot, was almost white. But she was robust and vigorous. Greg couldn't get used to the change in her. In his mind, she was a hunched figure in a chair, her face either full of anguish or slack and defeated. Now she stood upright, and her expression was composed and peaceful. She was a woman who'd come to terms with herself.

After Duncan had died and he and Morgan had left, Frances had gone to pieces and was on antidepressants and in and out of hospital for months. Then it seemed like her life had unexpectedly turned on a hinge: she had got herself a job as a financial assistant at a firm of architects in Norfolk and then, three years later, married Lester, who apparently had been her sweetheart when she was a teenager. She was retired now. She worked in the garden, went to concerts with Lester, took their dog for walks along the river, read voraciously, did the crossword—Duncan used to proudly say that Frances had been the cleverest woman in her cohort at Cambridge, where she'd studied maths. It was hard for Greg not to compare all of this to how she had been all through his childhood years. How had Duncan stayed so steadfastly cheerful and affectionate through all that time?

As if she could see Greg looking at her, she looked towards him and waved her hand. He waved back, and they smiled at each other amiably. It was sometimes hard to think of her as his mother.

Half an hour later, she had a very different expression on her face. Morgan had asked her if she would consider being interviewed for the podcast and it was as if he had slapped her in the face. She looked at him sternly.

"And why would I want to do that?"

"It might help to talk about it," he said softly. "It's a wound in your life, and we've never talked about it."

"Don't give me your spiel." Morgan flinched in surprise. "And don't look at me with that sorrowful expression either. If I wanted to talk about it—which I don't—do you think I'd do it in public? My wound, to use your word, has healed over. Why would I want to reopen it? I don't understand why you're intent on doing this, but it's your affair and I can't stop you. Perhaps it will help you and Greg, I don't know. I hope so, of course. But just don't expect me to get involved."

THIRTY-NINE

Bridget's house was outside the village. Etty walked there, past the playing fields, past the church with its stunted spire and its mossy gravestones, on to a muddy track that wound up through the trees. When she saw it, she thought she must have made a mistake. Surrounded by tumbledown outhouses and standing among a tangle of untended shrubs and rampant weeds, it looked derelict. One of the windows was broken, several of the others were smeared with dirt of decades and uncurtained. The chimney had lost several of its bricks and seemed as if it might topple at any moment. There was a menacing crack running up the wall beside the door.

But when she knocked at the door, Bridget opened it at once and greeted Etty as if they were old friends. She led her through and poured coffee for the two of them. Etty looked around.

"I know what you're thinking," said Bridget with a smile.

"What am I thinking?"

"You're thinking that these are all the things that I've scavenged from other people's houses."

Etty didn't quite know how to respond because that was roughly what she had been thinking. The surface was decorated with a riotous collection of ceramics, knickknacks, sculptures and glass ornaments.

"It's quite a collection," she said.

"Some people are grateful," Bridget said. "And some people think I'm a criminal. They think I'm going to find hidden treasures and sell them surreptitiously for lots of money. But I've got strict rules about that. If I find something valuable, I only take a commission."

"I know."

"And I hardly ever do find anything. People have the wrong idea. They've been watching too many TV programmes. The fact is, most people now don't want old furniture, they don't want second-hand books, they don't want your old videos."

"You don't need to convince me of that. I don't think any of us have very high expectations."

"Some of those hunting prints are probably worth a bit. I'll get back to you about them."

It took some effort for Etty to recall that Bridget was referring to the pictures on the wall of her father's study. They were the sort of things you might expect to see in a newly refurbished country pub.

As they drank their coffee, Bridget showed Etty her house. It was like stepping through the looking-glass. When Etty had bought her own flat, ten years earlier, she'd had it decorated so that she couldn't see anything that she wasn't going to use. It was all bare boards and concealed cupboards. There were no plants, no decorations, no objects.

Bridget's rambling old house was crammed with the remnants of other people's lives. You could barely see the wall for the pictures. You could barely see the floor for the rugs. Every surface was covered.

"Every time I throw something away," Bridget said, "I feel I've failed. There's a home for everything somewhere and if there isn't, I find a home for it here. Or outside. Wait, I'll show you."

Bridget led her outside. Her home had been a small farm, she said, but back in the 1960s it had gone the way of all the small farms in the area.

"When I came here, it felt forgotten and unloved." Bridget gestured around her. "If it had been left another ten years, it would have been lost. There were holes in the roof. I won't even tell you about the things that were living in the house."

"What do you use the outbuildings for?" said Etty.

"It's where I sort things and store things before I bring them to the shop or into the house. I feel like I've created a museum. But I'm not quite sure what kind of museum."

"A museum of people's lives," said Etty.

"That's right. Maybe I should do tours."

Bridget walked to the largest of the outhouses, with a corrugated-iron roof and a wooden door fastened shut with a piece of rope, which she untied.

"Take a look."

Etty peered inside. It was crammed with items of furniture, old tables, chairs missing a leg or two, an old bath, a sofa disgorging its stuffing, a bed standing on its side . . .

"Wow," she said. "There's a lot of work here."

"I'm not scared of work."

"Don't you get lonely out here?"

Bridget laughed. "I'm not alone all the time. I have gentlemen friends occasionally to stay. But they usually need to be regifted in the end, just like everything else. Would you like another coffee?"

"You wanted to talk to me about something?"

"Yes, of course. Once I start, you can't stop me."

They walked back into the house and Bridget chattered while filling the kettle, grinding the coffee beans and pouring on the boiling water. Etty was barely paying attention. Bridget handed her the coffee mug, then looked at Etty more intently.

"Sometimes in my job, I feel like I'm a kind of priest or a doctor. I go into people's houses and I learn their secrets and I can provide some sort of a comfort."

Etty didn't reply. She wasn't sure if she wanted to have the sort of conversation that Bridget was embarking on.

"You're a family that has suffered a loss."

"You don't need to go through our house to know that. Our mother disappeared thirty years ago. It was a national news story. And then my brother took his own life on an anniversary of the day she went missing. So, yes, our family has experienced loss."

"I meant more than that. Sometimes a tragedy can

bring a family together. But you left and you didn't come back. And you cut off all contact with your family. And one of your brothers did much the same. I felt so much pain in that house. Not just that. I felt a pain that had been buried."

A faint ironic smile appeared on Etty's face. She couldn't quite believe it. The woman she had hired to clear out the rubbish from the family house was trying to have the kind of intimate conversation with her that she'd never even had with her own siblings. But she wasn't going to get angry with her. She wasn't going to give her the satisfaction of feeling that she "understood" her in a way that other people didn't. She wasn't going to get emotional. She spoke in as even a tone as she could manage.

"I think you're reading too much into this," she said. "When I look at my friends from school, hardly any of them have stayed in the area. They're all in Manchester or London or abroad. My brother Niall's the exception. Anyway, you rang and asked me to come over: what was it you wanted to see me about?"

"Sorry," said Bridget. "I got carried away. Wait a moment." She left the kitchen and came back with a small cardboard box. "These are letters I found in a box in that little cupboard over the stairs that led to your room. I had to hang out over the drop to look inside, but I managed. They're addressed to you. I thought you'd want them. They're rather intimate."

She removed the top of the box.

Rather intimate. Etty stepped forward and she saw immediately what they were. Her face suddenly felt both hot and cold at the same time. She hoped it didn't show, that she hadn't blushed the way she used to when she was a girl. It had been at least a quarter of a century since she had written a letter with a pen. In the last few years, she hardly sent any personal message longer than a couple of words in a text.

They were so private that Etty had hidden them where she was sure they could never be found. They were like the treasure that is buried in the hope that you can return one day to reclaim it. But you never do and gradually they are lost and forgotten.

Until they're found.

Now Etty really did need an immense effort to remain calm.

"How do you know they're intimate?"

"It's part of the job," Bridget said indifferently. "I sort things out: this is rubbish, this might be worth something and, occasionally, this is something that they might not want to be thrown away at all. There were so many bits of paper and old bills that were just waste but I needed to check. I didn't read them all."

"They're private letters."

"You hired me to do this. Don't worry, Etty. In my job, I've seen things you couldn't imagine. And not in a nice way."

Etty suddenly felt icily cold. She picked up the box.

"It's all so long ago," she said. "The person in these letters isn't me."

"Don't say that. It's always in there somewhere. Like rings in a tree."

Etty shook her head. "If you find any more of my letters, you don't need to alert me. Just get rid of them."

Bridget looked puzzled. "If it means so little to you, then why are you here?"

"You know why I'm here. My father can't look after himself any more and everything needs to be sorted out. It's just a matter of arrangements and managing bureaucracy. It's the sort of thing I know how to do."

"It sounds like a beautiful thing to do for your parent when he needs you. A real act of love."

"If you believe that, you don't understand our family at all."

"It's funny," Bridget said. "There seem to be so many people coming back to Glensted to deal with their past."

"You mean Greg and Morgan Ackerley? Have you met them?"

"Morgan contacted me. Apparently they're doing some sort of radio programme."

"It's a podcast. Why did he contact you?"

"It's a small world. They've been talking to people and I've been talking to people and they heard about me. So he came here to see me. He's just like he is on the telly."

Again, Etty had to make an effort to control herself. She could hardly bear the idea of Bridget "talking to people" in Glensted, nor the sort of private Salter family matters she might be talking about.

"I'm not sure that it would be a good idea to take part," she said.

Bridget gave a funny little laugh.

"What?"

"I've already done it."

"That ..." Penny was searching for the right word. "Bloody woman."

Etty was sitting at Niall and Penny's kitchen table. There were the remains of the lunch of bread and cheese and paté on the table.

"Penny—" Niall began.

"Don't apologise for her."

"I'm not apologising for her. Why would I apologise for her?"

"How you ever let that woman into your family, I just can't imagine."

"It was me," said Etty.

"You couldn't have known, obviously. She isn't even showing the tiniest modicum of professional behaviour. She's going around Glensted blabbing about the Salter family to anyone who'll listen. My friend Ruth met her in the street and she was saying that there were some nice pieces of furniture in the house. Nice pieces of furniture."

"I don't really care if people know about our furniture," said Niall.

"It's not just about the furniture. Honestly, if she's talking about your father's furniture, then what else is she talking about? And now Etty"—she gestured at Etty in a way that made her feel like some strange animal that had wandered into the house—"tells us that she's appearing on that frankly disgusting podcast thing talking about your family secrets."

"She's not going to be talking about our family secrets." He turned to Etty with a new look of concern. "She isn't, is she?"

Etty wasn't sure what to say. She had told them about the podcast but she hadn't told them about Bridget reading her letters.

"I don't know. I don't think she'll be indiscreet."

"How can you be so sure?" said Penny, now in a full rage. "She told Antonia in the post office that she felt really sorry for your mother, but that she couldn't say any more."

"So she didn't actually say anything?"

"But she's itching to, given the chance. God knows what she's said for that podcast."

"She's probably not said anything," said Niall, "and even if she has, it's some stupid little thing they're doing for a hobby and about four people will listen to it."

Penny turned to Etty. "You do this sort of thing, don't you?"

"What sort of thing?"

"Can't you sue them?"

"Who?"

"Morgan and Greg. And that clearance woman."

"Sue them for what?"

"For telling your family secrets in public. For . . ." She gestured wildly in the air. "Invasion of privacy. Don't you have a right to your privacy? Can't you sue them on behalf of your family?"

Etty shook her head. "I spend half my time trying to persuade people not to sue other people. It's expensive, it's a horrible process and often you just end up making things worse."

"Do they listen to you?"

"Sometimes. Sometimes not." She thought for a moment. "I don't think that we can really stop Greg and Morgan making a podcast that involves our missing mother. It's not clear that she has a right to privacy. She certainly doesn't if she's dead. And it's their story as much as ours. If we had a great deal of money and we didn't care about wasting quite a lot of it, then we could make life miserable for them but it would probably end with more people hearing about it than if we did nothing at all."

"So you're relaxed about everyone hearing about your mother and what happened to her and what it did to your family."

"I'm not really relaxed about anything at all."

"But you're going to stand by and just let it happen."

Etty stood up. "I'm not going to stand by. I'm going to go back to London and get on with my life and it's going to happen, one way or another."

Penny turned to her husband.

"What about you? Can't you go and see them at least? Try to persuade them? Or what about Ollie? Would he do it?"

Now Niall's expression changed. He looked at Etty and then back at Penny, suddenly ill at ease.

"I think Ollie's agreed to be interviewed by them."

FORTY

"A glass of white wine," said Etty.

"Large or small?"

"Large."

"Coming up."

Victor Pearce turned away to take the bottle from the fridge behind the bar, and Etty studied his back: he was thin and sinewy, with grey hair tied back into a neat ponytail and a stud in one ear. Then he faced her again, holding a glass, and she saw his narrow, lined face and slightly crooked teeth.

These jump cuts in time were disconcerting. She saw Victor as he was now, seventy or so, but looking like an aged youth with his long hair and his agile body, and she thought of the Victor she had known when she was a teenager, with his tie-dyed T-shirts and his collection of off-the-peg aphorisms about karma, spiritual awareness, how the darkest hour only has sixty minutes and real life is in the present moment. Alec had called him a charlatan; Charlie had protested that he was an idealist with a good heart.

"How are you, Etty?" he asked as he put the glass in front of her. "It's been such a while."

She sipped her wine.

"I'd say that I am not at my best. It's quite dislocating to return here and find everything's changed and yet nothing has. I went into the newsagent to buy some cigarettes and two women who I didn't recognise were whispering about me."

"You're the one who got away," he said.

"And yet here I am, Victor."

"People in this village never got over what happened."

"Poor them."

"Glensted was marked by it. Nothing had ever happened here, and then there was a double tragedy and no real resolution. Places have souls, just as people do. This place is in perplexity and mourning."

"If that's the case, what do you think of the podcast? Does it help or harm?"

"I think Greg and Morgan are doing something that might have consequences far beyond their intentions. It's a serious thing to open old wounds."

"I thought you believed in opening wounds. Shining a light, you'd say. So you disapprove?"

"Not at all. In fact, I was interviewed by them myself."

"Why am I not surprised. What about?"

"The effect on the village. But mostly about my memories of Duncan and Charlie. I loved your mother, you know. Don't look at me like that. I mean I loved her in a platonic way. I recognised her soul."

"Right."

"She used to bake things for the café, you know, so I saw a lot of her."

"Obviously I remember."

Etty used to help her at weekends and the memory of it came at her in a rush, before she had time to defend herself. Beating butter and sugar together, adding eggs one by one, dipping a finger in to taste the mix, Charlie in a voluminous apron beside her sifting flour, chatting, sun slanting in through the kitchen window, mother and daughter.

"I've got something I wanted to show you. Hang on."

He disappeared into the kitchen, and Etty went on sipping her wine. It was early evening and the room was deserted, though the tables were all set up, a little vase holding a sprig of eucalyptus in the centre of each, candles ready to be lit.

"Here."

Victor put a square, spiral-bound book in front of her. It looked like a photo album and she shrank from it.

"Look inside," said Victor.

She opened it and saw her mother's handwriting. It was a book of recipes. Coffee and walnut cakes, scones, Irish soda bread, lemon drizzle cake, brownies, ginger oat cookies ... She flicked the pages one by one, not speaking.

"She wrote things down over the years and after she disappeared—years after, actually—I collected them all up and put them in this book. It's a kind of memorial."

Etty was staring at a recipe for custard tarts without really seeing it.

"I know how much you loved your mother," said Victor in a soft voice. "You can talk about her to me. You know that, don't you? You can say anything to me, Etty. We go way back."

Etty scrutinised him: a man who didn't know how to grow old. He looked uneasy under the sharpness of her gaze, but smiled and then put a hand over hers. She jolted and pulled it away quickly.

"As a matter of fact, I've got something I wanted to show you as well," she said, only now making up her mind, but decisively, in the corrosive burn of her rage.

She put her hand into her bag, pulled out the bundle of letters Bridget had found and slapped them down on the bar.

"These," she said.

Victor didn't move. His eyes flickered from the letters to Etty and back again. He licked his top lip with the very tip of his tongue, lizard-like.

"Well?"

"What do you want me to say? It was intense. *We* were intense. And then you left without even saying goodbye and I missed you, Etty. How I missed you . . ."

Etty leaned across the bar. "I was *sixteen*," she said. "Sixteen. You were—what? Forty? Twenty-four years older than me."

"Age," he said, palms upwards in a gesture of peaceful resignation. "That wasn't the point."

"My mother had just vanished. My brothers had all left. I was in a state of ..." She stopped. For what was a word that could hold everything she had been then, full of terror and desolation and at the same time empty of all hope?

"We comforted each other."

"Is that what you call it?" She wanted to hit him, scream.

"And desire." He nodded at her. "Don't forget that. You wanted me just as much as I wanted you."

"Fuck you. I wanted my *mother* to come home," Etty almost cried. "Everything else was just—sleazy, meaningless shit."

"No," he said.

"Yes. Meaningless shit, Victor. Just like you are."

"Then why did you keep the letters I wrote so many years ago?"

"They were in a box that Bridget Wolfe found."

"I feel your anger, but—"

"Stop," said Etty. She looked down at her wine and saw there was only an inch left. "Can I have another glass of wine, please? Red this time. And large. The cheapest one will do nicely."

He looked surprised by her abrupt change of tone, but poured it for her. She picked it up and threw it over him, splashing his incredulous face, his stupid ponytail, and staining his expensive silk shirt.

"That was childish," he said.

"The eternal child inside me, Victor." She wrinkled her nose. "It doesn't make me feel as good as I thought it would. Because you're the kind of person who will never have insight, who will never face up to the truth about themselves." She saw his face darken. "My mother was wrong about you."

Etty picked up the glass of white wine and chucked what was left of it up into his face in a last futile gesture.

"Well, really!"

A high voice came from behind her, and Etty turned to see an old couple staring at her and the wine-drenched Victor with almost identical looks of gap-mouthed astonishment. Then the woman's expression changed.

"Etty? Etty Salter?"

For a moment Etty didn't recognise her. Then she did.

"Mary Thorne," said the woman.

"I know."

Time doesn't heal all wounds, she thought, whatever Victor might have to say about that. She still felt a visceral loathing for Mary Thorne, which was unfair of course. Etty had always hated the way that women blamed the other woman, rather than the man, and anyway, she was hardly in a position to judge. She had been involved with married men over the years, knowing they were married. Maybe she was drawn to them *because* they were married so it was a safe and bounded affair, one that wouldn't pierce her defences.

Yet she looked at Mary Thorne now—still slender

and groomed, beads round her neck and earrings in her lobes, her mouth painted pink, though her brown hair was steel-grey and her heart-shaped face was creased with wrinkles—and she hated her. She remembered her cool, brisk manner that horrible day she and Ollie had gone round there and wished she had left a bit of wine in her glass.

"I would offer you a drink," she said. "But I think Victor needs to wash his face and change his shirt."

Victor slid away, and Mary Thorne stared after him, her eyes bright with excitement: it would be all round the village before morning came.

"How are you?" asked Gerry.

Etty wouldn't have recognised him: he had no hair and had grown spectacularly thin. Clothes hung off sharp bones and his face sagged. Etty thought he must be ill.

"Fine," she said.

"We heard on the grapevine you were back, of course," said Mary Thorne.

"Of course."

"Your poor father."

"What about my poor father?"

A wince righted the woman's face. "I'm simply extending my sympathy."

"Thank you." Etty set her glass down with a clink and stood up. "Now I must be going."

"Are you involved with this programme?"

"Programme? Oh, you mean the podcast. No."

"That is wise." Mary Thorne was visibly relieved. "But if you see the Ackerley brothers, could you perhaps tell them Gerry and I would like to have a word."

"I don't expect to see them again. I'm only here to clear the house."

"We want," said Gerry, "to set the record straight."

"You don't want me to talk to them, but you want them to interview you?"

"Simply because there have been too many nasty rumours flying round this village," said Mary Thorne. "We thought that was all over and done with, but now they're going round talking to everyone, and your family is back as well, it's all started up once more so it feels like something terrible might happen all over again. It was thirty years ago."

"You'll have to ask them yourselves," said Etty.

"Why are you so hostile?" Gerry put a warning hand on his wife's arm, but she shook him off and continued. "All this time, and you still hate me."

"I do need to go."

"I made a mistake. One mistake. Haven't you made mistakes in your life, or are you so pure and innocent?"

"Of course I have," said Etty, struggling to be fair to this old woman with her brave make-up and her sick husband. "But the fact is that when I see you, I'm fifteen again and my mother has disappeared and I don't know how I'm going to bear it."

FORTY-ONE

Brian Cobbett laboured along the bridge to where Morgan and Greg waited. The years had not been kind to him. Where he had been stout, now he was unhealthily overweight and his face was florid. He had a few wisps of white hair left. By the time he reached them, he was sweating profusely.

"Thank you for agreeing to do this," said Greg.

Cobbett looked at him warily.

"I don't know," he said. "All this raking up the past."

"Some things can't be put behind you," said Morgan, switching on the recorder, holding out the mike. "Not only did our father take his life, he was suspected of murder. And it was you in charge of the inquiry, Inspector Cobbett."

Greg glanced at him: he was getting used to his brother's swift changes. He was going to be stern, the son seeking answers about his dead father.

Cobbett looked at the mike in panic.

"Have we started? I'm not sure I'm ready. You just said we'd have a chat."

"Take your time. We'll edit out things you're not happy with."

There was a silence. Cobbett ran a finger round the inside of his collar.

"What do you want to ask?"

"There were a lot of questions about the inquiry," said Morgan. "And about the way you closed the case down. It wasn't stated openly but there was an obvious implication that our father killed Charlotte Salter."

Cobbett rubbed his mouth with the back of his hand.

"I understood you wanted me to talk about how hard the two cases were, how upset you children were, things like that. I gave up being a detective long ago. We did our best and that's all any of us can do. I came here as a favour to you."

"I thought we were going to start by talking about the bridge," intervened Greg. "That's why we're here, after all. This is where Dad jumped from, isn't that right, Detective Cobbett?"

"Yes," said Cobbett, relieved to be on safe ground. "We found his glasses on the parapet where the bridge is at its highest above the river."

The three men all looked down towards the churning water beneath.

"It's a long drop," said Morgan. He looked at Greg.

"It is," said Greg obediently. "A long way to fall."

"Several hours later, his body was discovered further downstream, where it had been swept on to a buoy. Had it not been for that, he might never have been found," continued Cobbett. "You two don't need me to tell you that. Terrible. A terrible tragedy for your family."

The voice rumbled on. The two brothers looked down at the waters beneath them.

"Do you ever think," asked Morgan, "that you might have got it wrong?"

"I'm not going to lie," said Cobbett sententiously. "There are cases that don't work out the way you want." His expression hardened. He was visibly pulling himself together. "You asked me a straight question and I'll give you a straight answer: my belief then and now is that your father killed Charlotte Salter and then in a fit of remorse took his own life."

Forty-two

"What do you want me to say?"

"It's not about what I want you to say," said Morgan, though this wasn't strictly accurate. "It's about what *you* want to say. Or what you need to say, even."

"The question is, do I want to say anything?" Ollie grimaced. "It seemed like a good idea, but now I'm not so sure. I don't think Etty's going to be very happy."

"It doesn't seem that Etty's ever happy," said Greg. "She seems so—"

'You might find it cathartic," cut in Morgan. "I'll just ask questions and you answer them however you want. Don't worry about pauses and repetitions and making mistakes. It's all going to be edited."

"Right." Ollie ran his long thin fingers through his fading hair. "Off you go then."

"Today, a beautiful warm day, finds us outside an old barn on the edge of Glensted," said Morgan sonorously.

Ollie shifted from foot to foot, his mouth twitching as if he was going to start laughing. Morgan frowned at him and continued.

"Many years ago, cows were kept in here. Now it's being turned into a luxury residence with a view over the Heming. But for years, it stood empty, and on Friday 22nd December 1990, it was where Alec Salter celebrated his fiftieth birthday."

"Saturday," said Greg.

"What?"

"The party was on Saturday."

"No worries, I'll correct that later."

He coughed, took a breath. "About a hundred people turned up, but Alec Salter's wife never arrived, and she was never seen again."

"We don't know that," objected Greg.

"What?"

"You can't say that because it makes it sound as if she's dead. Someone might have seen her."

"Everyone knows she's dead."

"Don't mind me," said Ollie.

"Sorry. Look, I'll do the intro later, let's just jump straight in with the questions. Right?"

"Right."

"With us is Charlotte Salter's youngest son, Oliver. Hello, Oliver."

"Hi," said Ollie, grinning furtively at Greg.

"That evening must be very vivid in your memory."

"Hardly."

"Sorry?"

"It's a bit of a blur, to be honest. I was stoned." He paused. "So were you, Morgan, if I remember? Very, very stoned." He pointed at Greg. "And someone else might have got very drunk and vomited outside."

Morgan and Greg managed a smile at this. They just wanted to make sure the interview went ahead.

"That's right," Morgan said. "I was fifteen and you and your gang seemed impossibly cool. I remember trying to pretend I was an old hand and struggling not to cough."

"Yeah," said Ollie. "You were a funny kid."

"I didn't enjoy being a teenager," said Morgan. "I was too serious and nerdy."

"Does anybody enjoy being a teenager? Mostly we just pretend to be having fun."

"Shall we get back to the party?" Greg asked.

"Right, the party I don't properly recall," said Ollie. He seemed to have forgotten that he was being recorded. "I tell you what I do remember, though. I remember my father not caring Mum wasn't there. And I remember Abba playing and all these middle-aged people waving their arms in the air and jumping up and down. And I remember walking home with Etty, and the trees kept looming in and out of focus. And I remember the house being cold and dark, as if the life had gone out of it." He thought for a moment. "I think I only realised that after she was gone. When she was in the house, it was like there was a fire in the grate, giving out warmth and a beautiful light."

"Good," said Morgan. "This is good."

"But what I really remember are the days after. Jeez."

"Go on."

"Go on what?"

"What did you do during those days?"

Ollie shrugged. "Waited. Trudged round the village in the sleet with Etty. Time seemed to have stopped. Every minute took so long to get through. Me and Etty went to see the Thornes once; that was grim. Mary Thorne was so—so indifferent to what we were feeling that I wanted to throttle her. I quarrelled with Dad, of course. We all did, especially Paul. We blamed Dad for everything."

"Do you still?"

Ollie hesitated, making up his mind how far to go with this.

"He had affairs, he cheated on Mum; maybe I shouldn't be saying this but he won't hear your podcast, and anyway it's an open secret and I assume other people have been saying the same to you. He made her unhappy. But I'm the age now that he was then. I know what messes people make of their lives. Look at me. But I've never forgiven him for how he was to her. I can't stop feeling that if he'd been a better husband, she would still be alive today and if she was alive maybe we'd all be OK. Etty hasn't forgiven him either; she's worse than me. And Paul . . ." He stopped.

"Paul?"

"Actually, I don't think I want to talk about Paul. Let's leave him in peace."

"I'll ask you something else then. What was your mother like?"

Ollie's face went blank.

"You don't need to answer," said Greg. "You don't need to say anything you don't want to."

"Sometimes I can't even remember her any more," said Ollie. "I have to look at a photo to bring her face back to me. What do you want me to say? She was my mother."

"Of course," said Greg.

"You know, I'll tell you what she was like: she was *nice*. She was nice to me when I was a cross, druggy teenager. She was nice to the woman in the corner shop and that old man who used to wander round the village with his mangy dog and had something wrong with him. She was nice to everyone. She made them feel special. Sometimes people, and by people I mean men, misinterpreted that. But really she was just being kind."

"Ollie," said Greg. "What do *you* think happened to your mother thirty years ago?"

Ollie looked at him, then at Morgan who was standing motionless beside his brother, holding out the mike.

"Someone killed her," he said at last. "Maybe it was my father. Maybe it was yours. Maybe it was someone else. But she died that night. For a long time all of us waited for her, looked for her, pretended she was going to come home. Paul especially insisted she would come home. But she was always dead."

"Don't you feel the need to know who killed her?"

Ollie's face tightened. "We went through all of that thirty years ago and barely survived. One of us didn't survive. Why stir all of that up again?"

"But I guess that's what we're doing here," said Morgan serenely. "For better or worse, because we feel the past is not done with and we owe it to our father, we're stirring it all up and seeing what floats to the top."

FORTY-THREE

On the Wednesday, when Etty was in her office, just finishing a Zoom call with clients, Penny rang her.

"Is anything wrong?" Etty asked.

"Yes, there is."

"Is it Dad?" The word felt nasty in her mouth, too intimate.

"It's Lucia. She's torn a tendon in her foot and can't work."

"Presumably the agency can provide cover?"

"That's the thing, they can't find anyone at this short notice. They say by the weekend they'll be able to."

"Sorry about that."

"Is that all?"

"I don't see what I can do."

"No? So what do you think happens? I'll tell you what happens, it falls to Niall and me, which is always what it's been like."

"In a week or so, he'll be in a home."

"It's our wedding anniversary. We're supposed to be going to Lisbon for four days. We never go away together."

Etty went to the window of her office and stared out at the blue sky above the office buildings. She couldn't do this.

"Well?" said Penny.

"You're not expecting me to look after him?"

"Niall said you wouldn't. He said it was useless to call you. But Ollie's got flu."

"I've got work."

"We've all got work."

Fuck, Etty thought: *fuck fuck fuck.* She took a deep breath.

"All right," she said.

"You will?"

"I said yes, didn't I?"

"You have to get here today. We fly early tomorrow morning."

"I'll be there." She looked at her watch. "By five."

"I'm not going to say thank you."

Etty gave a smile despite herself. "Good. You shouldn't."

Driving to Glensted, Etty listened to the next episode of Morgan and Greg's podcast that had dropped a few hours ago, while London dwindled and the countryside opened up into woods and fields and peaceful rivers.

She tried to listen to it in the same way that, as a child, she had squinted at things through the lattice of her fingers, only half seeing. Or as if it had nothing to do with her life, but was a story that had ended long ago.

Victor Pearce used almost exactly the phrases he'd

repeated to her, about how places have souls, about "perplexity and mourning." *Everything's a performance,* Etty thought.

Then it was Brian Cobbett on the bridge, sounding rattled. Why had he agreed to be interviewed? He was clearly being set up as an incompetent buffoon.

There followed a brief scene in the churchyard with the local vicar. Morgan said in a low, sorrowful voice that this was where Duncan lay and where Charlie would have been buried if her body had ever been found. He read the dates of a gravestone belonging to a woman who had lived to the grand age of ninety-seven and died around the same time that Charlie had gone missing.

"I think of what Charlie would have been like if she too had lived to the ripe old age she deserved," he said. "Or my father."

The vicar spoke about the fleeting nature of life and the solace of God.

When Morgan spoke again, after a meditation on the strangeness of the passing of time, he and Greg were at Bridget's house. It was just a short clip but Bridget was in her element. She once more described herself as an archivist and a guardian of secrets, and told the brothers that the pain in the Salter house had been palpable to her. She felt that clearing away objects was also a way of healing the wounds of the past and that she could help them all.

"Oh no you can't," said Etty out loud.

Her hands gripped the steering wheel more tightly

when she heard Ollie's voice and she pulled into a parking space. She opened both windows and lit a cigarette. Her hands were trembling. She swore under her breath when Ollie spoke about Alec's affairs. Several times, he mentioned her: "me and Etty," he said. He wasn't just "I" but "we." She remembered how close they had been, how they'd accompanied each other through their childhood right up until that terrible passage of time. And then they'd abandoned each other.

That evening, Etty tried to imagine herself a robot, a programmed computer on legs. She made a dhal for her father and watched him while he ate. She wiped his mouth. She led him to the bathroom and waited outside until he'd finished in there. She took him to his bedroom and watched as he fumbled with his buttons, and eventually she helped him undress and put on his pyjamas.

As he climbed into bed, she remembered that she had asked for a piece of Charlie's jewellery—perhaps the moonstone ring or the linked gold necklace to wear next to the golden locket she never removed. She started opening the small drawers of the dressing table and found each one empty. She looked in the chest and nothing of Charlie's was there either.

"Thieving bitch," said Alec from the bed.

"Where's all her jewellery?"

He looked at her with an expression that moved between fear and a baleful resentment.

"Who did you give it all to?"

She could hardly bear the thought that he'd handed out rings and bracelets and necklaces as gifts to all those other women who'd come after Charlie.

Alec grinned. She thought of punching him and then pulled the duvet cover up a bit so he was comfortable.

"Sleep well," she said, and left the room.

That night, he called her Charlie, or Lucia, and sometimes he called her Etty. He shouted out in his sleep and she came downstairs from her threadbare little room, just the iron bedstead left, even the curtains gone, and told him it was just a dream. He put out a hand, liver-spotted and with loose skin around the swollen knuckles, and she recoiled, but then she took it.

For so long he had been a monster in her imagination: the man who had cheated on Charlie and who perhaps had killed her. She didn't want to feel pity, nor to hear him talk about his little Etty, the apple of his eye. She didn't want to remember how when she was a small child she had loved him.

On Thursday afternoon, she left him in the living room, sitting asleep in the one remaining armchair by the window, and went for a walk. Lucia always took two hours off each day and so could she. She walked into the centre of Glensted by the side roads, and the woman standing across the street had to call her several times before she heard.

"Etty? Etty Salter!"

It didn't sound like a greeting but a command. Etty crossed the road. The woman was plump, wearing a lime-green dress, and Etty had no idea who she was.

"Yes?"

"Gemma. Gemma Thorne."

"Oh. Hello."

"I heard you were here."

Etty didn't reply.

"I was surprised, I must say. You never come back. Not even with your father the way he is."

Etty didn't reply.

"Anyway, here you are."

They stood looking at each other. Etty remembered how she'd always disliked Gemma.

"I come often," said Gemma. "With my daughters and my son whenever they can make it. They're all grown up now, of course. You don't have children, do you?"

"No."

"I didn't think so."

"I'll be getting on," said Etty.

"Wait." Gemma put a hand on her arm and Etty flinched. "I wanted to say something. I followed you up here to say it."

"What?"

"Keep away from my parents."

Etty hadn't been expecting that. She moved away from Gemma and regarded her coolly.

"I don't know what you mean."

"They're old. Dad's not well. What do you think you're doing, swanning in and upsetting them like this? If he has a collapse, that'll be your fault."

"I've no intention of going anywhere near your parents."

She strode away and took the path that led away from Glensted, past the playground, which had rubberised tarmac now and brightly painted equipment, and towards the church with its stunted spire. At the gate into the churchyard, she hesitated. Somewhere in there was a gravestone with Paul's name on it. She had never visited him, though he had lain there for more than twenty-five years.

At last she pushed open the gate and went in and wandered past the graves, some old and mossy, some newer, with shiny headstones. It took her several minutes to find Paul's place of rest: just a simple grey headstone with his name and his date of birth and death. But someone had put anemones there recently. *Penny,* Etty thought. She could imagine Penny tending Niall's brother's grave, just as she looked after Niall's father. Doing what was right, putting a healing hand on the chaos of the past.

Etty stood for a while, looking at the modest stone and the bright flowers, then she hunched her shoulders together and walked out of the graveyard, up into the woods. From the top of the hill, she could see all of Glensted laid out beneath her: the old centre, the new developments, and beyond that the broad shine of the Heming. That was where her life had been for eighteen years. Now it was like a dream.

FORTY-FOUR

"It does no harm to ask," said Morgan.

He and Greg were walking up the drive towards the Salter farmhouse, carrying their recording equipment.

"I'm not sure," said Greg. "And what about his carer?"

"Let's see. It would be great to get even a few seconds of him. Just the sound of his voice. He's central to our story."

They stood at the front door. Morgan looked at his brother.

"Well? What if we got him to confess."

Greg considered.

"That would be the perfect ending," he said.

"See?" said Morgan. "You're thinking like a podcaster."

Morgan knocked at the door. There was no answer. He knocked again, longer and louder, and they waited to hear footsteps.

"He's not here." Greg was relieved.

But Morgan had turned the handle and the door swung open.

"We can't just go in!"

"Why not? We always used to. Hello? Hello, anyone home?"

His voice echoed in the bare hall.

"Let's go," said Greg.

But then they heard a querulous voice from the living room.

"Who is it? Who are you?"

Morgan strode towards the room and entered, a smile on his lips, his hand extended. Greg followed carrying the equipment.

"Hello, Mr. Salter, Alec," said Morgan. "We haven't met for years and years, but I'm Morgan Ackerley."

Alec, sitting in the chair with a light blanket over his knees, shrank back. He looked bewildered.

"Duncan's son. You remember Duncan."

"Duncan," repeated Alec. "The ash blight."

"And here's Greg."

Greg raised a hand, acutely uncomfortable. "How are you?"

"Something's very wrong," said Alec. "What's happened?"

"Nothing's wrong."

"Where's Charlie?"

"Charlie?" Morgan had turned on the recorder and was holding out the mike.

"Go away," said Alec. "Leave me in peace. I want everyone to leave me. Not Etty, though. Where's Etty gone?"

"We just wanted to ask a few questions." Morgan

was speaking slowly and loudly, as if to a deaf toddler. "About what happened here thirty years ago."

"What happened?"

"When Charlie disappeared."

"I don't know anything about that. I told them already. How many times do I have to say it?"

"Do you think your wife is dead, Mr. Salter?"

"I met her in a garden and she was wearing a yellow dress. I thought she was the prettiest girl I'd ever seen. Why did she have to do it?"

"We shouldn't have bothered you," said Greg. He cast a reproachful look at his brother. "We'll leave you now. I'm so sorry."

"Don't leave me. Everyone leaves."

"What happened to Charlie, Mr. Salter?" Morgan asked. And then: "Did you kill her?"

Etty came back to discover the front door was open. *Careless of me,* she thought. She went into the house and thought she heard voices coming from the living room. She went towards them and stood just outside, listening. She heard Morgan Ackerley ask in a loud, deliberate voice:

"What happened to Charlie, Mr. Salter? Did you kill her?"

And she heard her father answer: "Of course I did. Are you a fool like everyone else?"

She banged open the door, and the two brothers swung round.

"How dare you? How fucking dare you?"

"Etty," said Morgan.

"Out."

"He said that he—"

"I heard what he said. Get out of this room at once."

She practically pushed them out of the living room and in the hall turned on them again.

"My father has dementia and you sneak in here when he's alone."

"We didn't actually know he would be alone," said Morgan. "We expected his carer to be with him."

"That's your excuse, is it?"

"He confessed to Charlie's murder."

"He's got dementia."

"He still confessed. Don't you want to get to the truth about what happened to your mother?"

"Truth? He could have said anything."

"If he killed Charlie, then our father is innocent."

"If you broadcast any of that, then I will sue you."

"Of course we won't," said Greg shakily. His face was ashen.

"Can you do that?" asked Morgan.

"I'm a lawyer, Morgan. My father doesn't have mental capacity. You broadcast what he said and I promise I'll make you regret it."

"Etty," said Greg. "I'm so very sorry—"

"You're as bad as Morgan. Just leave."

FORTY-FIVE

While the kettle was boiling, Etty washed up some plates and mugs and glasses. She wiped the surfaces. She put one bag of Assam and one bag of Earl Grey in the pot. She was still sorting out her own feelings. After Greg and Morgan had gone, she was so angry that she felt she needed to do something about it, like punch someone or punch a wall. She seriously considered calling the police and reporting what they had done. But she knew that it was pointless. The police barely investigated actual crimes any more. A couple of years before, her flat had been broken into. She had called the police and their only response had been to give her a reference number. Your insurance company will need that for your claim, she had been told.

At the most, Greg and Morgan might be guilty of trespass, but they only had to say they had been invited and the police wouldn't do anything about it anyway. Could she scare them with a legal letter? Probably not.

She poured two mugs of tea and went into the living room.

Alec was in the same position as when she had left him, except that his blanket had slipped off.

She put it back on his lap and then gave him his mug. He looked at the tea as if he wasn't entirely sure what to make of it, then lifted the mug slowly towards his mouth, his hands shaking, and took an exploratory sip. He gave a little groan and held the mug away from him. Was it too hot? Etty took the mug from his hands and put it on the table to the side.

"When you're ready for it, just say."

"Where's everything gone? Someone's taken it all."

"I'm sorry about Greg and Morgan," she said. "Did they upset you?"

"No, they didn't upset me."

The answer seemed automatic, like a machine that had been imperfectly designed to imitate the speech patterns of a human being. Probably he had already forgotten about the interview, but he was showing signs of distress, blinking and twitching. Was it the shock from these people he no longer remembered, bursting in, pressurising him? Or, deep down, was it the sense that he had been found out?

Etty had been furious with Greg and Morgan. She had shouted at them. Even now she had the impulse to do something that would damage them in some way. But, she also understood what they were doing.

"I almost feel sorry for them," she said aloud.

"They lost their father and then he was blamed for what happened to Mum. How did you feel about that? Did you ever think that Duncan killed Mum?"

"Duncan," said Alec nastily. "A bit too bloody friendly with my wife."

"You were friends with him too."

Alec frowned as if he was trying to remember something and then making an immense effort to say something, but he didn't speak.

"You know," said Etty musingly, speaking to a man who could no longer understand her words. "For those last two years here, every day after school, every single day, I thought Mum might suddenly come back, although of course I knew she wouldn't. When I cooked dinner for us, I always made sure there was enough for her too, if she suddenly knocked at the door. I never told you and you never noticed, but it's true. Most mornings before I went to school, I'd throw the extra food away. I could never stop doing that, as long as I lived in Glensted."

"You're a good cook," said Alec. "I always like your cooking. You can do a good roast."

That was Charlie, thought Etty.

"I'm a vegetarian now," she said. "I haven't cooked a roast for twenty years. Almost thirty." She swallowed. "I think that was one of the reasons I went away. Every time the door opened, I thought it might be Mum. Every time I saw headlights on the ceiling when I was lying in bed, I thought it might be

Mum coming back. The only way of stopping that terrible, terrible longing was for Mum to return, or for me to do something stupid to myself. For a few years I did do some stupid things to myself. And then I left completely, so I was never anywhere that reminded me of Mum and then I ..." She paused. "You know you hear about soldiers volunteering for missions where they hope they'll be killed? I did things like that, except it wasn't in a war. Sometimes I think about the places I found myself at three in the morning. There was nothing anyone could do to me that was as bad as the way I felt inside."

She sniffed and wiped her face with the back of her hand.

"I want my tea," said Alec. "If you please."

She picked up the mug. It was safely cool by now. She handed it to him and he sipped at it, clumsily, like a small child. Liquid ran down from the corners of his mouth. There was a kitchen roll on the shelf and she ripped off a couple of sheets. She took the mug away from him and cleaned his face.

"I wasn't meant to be this person," Etty continued. "Remember when I was at school, before it all happened? I was the happy one. I was good at schoolwork. I had friends. I liked having fun. People wanted to be with me. Boys fancied me." She was saying words she had never said aloud before. She had, almost by mistake, drifted into the kind of conversation she had never had with her father, never could have had. "I told myself

I'd never come back here ever again. And here I am and I'm not sure it was a good idea."

She looked at him and he gave no sign of having understood what she was saying. Of course, that's why she had said it. After she left the room, he wouldn't remember she had even been there.

FORTY-SIX

On the last weekend in May, when the sky was a mild blue and Charlie's long-neglected patch of garden was a riot of wild roses and frothy peonies, the Salter siblings gathered for their final days at the farmhouse. A room had come clear, and next week, Alec was to go into the home in Hemingford. His bags had already been packed by Lucia, who had returned to work with a bandaged foot and limped heavily around the empty, echoing rooms. Niall told her to take the weekend off. Between them, they would take care of their father.

All the beds except Alec's and Lucia's had been removed. Ollie and Etty had spent Friday night on roll-up mattresses provided by Penny. Etty had lain on the floor of her bare room and watched as the sun came up and the square of window filled with the silver light of dawn. Outside was an impossibly dense chorus of birdsong.

Paul used to know the names of birds, she thought. Paul and Charlie. She remembered walks as a child, the two of them pointing out the warblers and the finches, spotting the green woodpecker and, sometimes, a kingfisher glimpsed among the rushes by the Heming. Etty remembered a night when she and Paul had sat for hours in the garden listening to the tawny owls in the trees above.

She needed to get back to her London life, she thought, before this terrible nostalgia wore away all her defences and the past flooded in.

There wasn't much left for them to do. Bridget had been amazingly efficient. She had left some things in the kitchen and said she would remove all of those once Alec had gone and they had left. The house would be put on the market the following Friday, although the estate agents from Glensted had warned that sales were sluggish and that some people might be put off by the condition of the building.

A sense of things ending gripped them all. They went from room to room, where all the paintings had gone, all the rugs taken from the floors and books from the shelves. Light slanted in through windows thrown open to let in the balmy air. A few dead bees lay on the wooden boards of the hall.

Etty was seeing the house as it was now—bare, a place of absence and what was not—and as it had been. Memories came thickly and unwanted, dashing themselves against her and hurting. Etty felt like Charlie and Paul were in the next room, round a corner, up the stairs. She half expected, when she opened the door to the living room, for both of them to turn towards her.

"Will you ever come back?" Niall asked suddenly, his voice too loud.

Ollie and Etty turned to him.

"You won't, will you?" His mouth twisted. "Why would you?"

"Why do you stay?" asked Etty softly.

"I run the business, don't I. Someone had to."

"Did they?"

"And I have a family here, my whole life."

"Did you never want to leave?" Ollie asked.

"What do you think? Every day I used to say, just a few more months, then I'll leave. Somehow it never happened. Anyway, sometimes I think it's better like this."

"What do you mean?"

"You two left, and how's that worked out? Are you happier than me? Have you got free of the past?"

With an effort, Ollie grinned. "Is it too late for us?" he asked.

Nobody answered.

FORTY-SEVEN

"Who wants more coffee?"

It was unusually crowded in the Ackerley kitchen on Sunday morning. Frances and Lester were there, as were Lester's two teenage grandchildren who had slept in his ancient camper van overnight and were now eating croissants with a steady urgency. Morgan was sitting at the table answering emails on his phone, tapping one finger against the wood like a metronome. Greg was making coffee for everyone and as he poured water on to the grounds, Katherine came into the room, creased with sleep. She smiled vaguely round the room and picked up a croissant.

"Is that really the time?"

"I wish I slept like you," said Morgan. "I've been up since half past five."

"You should meditate," she said.

"Morgan likes not sleeping," said Greg. "He works while the rest of us are snoring."

"You don't need to work today. It's Sunday."

"What time shall we have the barbecue?" Frances

was dressed in black trousers and a cream-coloured shirt, as if she was about to go to a meeting.

"Have we got everything?" asked Katherine.

"I did a big shop yesterday." Greg counted things off on his fingers. "Barbecue coal, tick. Ribs, tick. Lamb medallions, tick."

"We're vegetarian," said one of Lester's grandchildren.

Greg grinned. "Corn on the cob, tick. Haloumi, tick. Large mushrooms—"

"Please don't say tick," said Morgan."

"OK. We have large mushrooms. And ice cream."

"And enough drink?" asked Lester. "There are quite a few neighbours who might drop by."

"Of course."

"I'm going to suggest to Niall and Ollie and Etty that they join us." Greg glanced across at Morgan. "A peace offering."

"They won't come."

"Probably not. But I got plenty of beer and wine and also . . . oh shit."

"What?"

"I forgot the champagne. I bought it and said I'd collect it after the supermarket shop. I'll have to go and fetch it." He stood up. "I won't be long. Half an hour there and back, forty-five minutes at the most."

"Do you want me to go?" offered Katherine, but half-heartedly.

"No, it's fine. My mistake."

"I thought we could all listen to the latest podcast together now," said Morgan. "It went live a few hours ago."

"What latest podcast? We haven't done one."

"I did it when you were away. I thought you wouldn't mind. A lot of it is just material we've not used edited together into a kind of narrative, and I fill in the gaps. But I'm rather pleased with it, if I say so myself. It has an elegiac tone to it."

"Elegiac," said Greg. "What do you mean?"

"Looking back at the past."

"You should have said."

"I'm saying now."

"Well, the elegy will have to wait till I'm back with the champagne."

"I might pass," said Frances.

Under the table, Lester took her hand and squeezed it.

Etty made porridge for Alec, who was still in his pyjamas. She stirred the pot and thought about what Niall had asked her and Ollie yesterday—"Have you got free of the past?"—and Ollie's response. "Is it too late?" Etty believed that she had not got free of the past, and that it was too late, and she just had to live with that as best she could.

Yesterday Niall's daughter Mia had asked her if she had ever wanted to get married. She had said that she didn't have a high regard for marriage.

"Was there anyone special?" Mia said.

The truth was that there had never been anyone special in Etty's life, not the way that Mia had meant it. There had been the men Etty had fallen for because they weren't available, and the ones she had left because they were and wanted more from her than she wanted to give. There were the heady flings and the slow-burners. But Etty had always known that none of them would last.

"Didn't you want children?" Mia blushed at her own question.

"Can you imagine me as a mother?"

In fact, Etty had sometimes secretly yearned for a child, yet she had taken great care to prevent that happening. The one time she found herself pregnant, she had had a termination.

She ladled some porridge into a bowl for Alec, made sure it wasn't too hot, then put it in front of him. She put a spoon into his arthritic hand and watched as he very slowly lowered it into the porridge. He had a glassy expression on his face. She didn't know if he understood what was happening, why the house had emptied around him, or that he was shortly to leave.

Her mobile rang and she answered. It was Kim, the only person she had kept in touch with from childhood days, and that only sporadically. Kim was warm and fiercely loyal and she wouldn't let Etty slide away from their friendship.

"Etty, hi, are you OK?"

"Yes. Why? Is there any reason I shouldn't be?"

"I just listened to the latest episode of that podcast. Have you heard it yet?"

"No. I didn't even know there was a new one. Is there something in it I'm not going to like?"

"I don't know. It feels different from all the others. It's so intimate about all of you. And really sad."

She wanted to be alone when she heard it, but Ollie insisted they listen together. So after they had taken Alec to his room to get dressed and Etty had made a strong pot of coffee, he downloaded it and laid his phone flat on the table between them, pressing "Play." Etty took a sip of scalding, bitter coffee and then looked away from him, out of the window at the dog roses and the poplars in the distance, as Morgan began to speak, soft and sombre.

He began by talking about his father. It was skillfully done. He spoke of his own childhood memories of Duncan, his cheerfulness and kindness, his practicality, how he'd adored him and never felt able to live up to him. He talked of Duncan's strong hands, his singing voice, his favourite blue jumper, his sweetness to people who were in trouble.

His narrative was laced with other people's memories of Duncan: snippets Morgan had gathered from people in the village. There were also pseudo-spiritual meanderings from Victor and some revelations from Mary and Gerry Thorne that Etty could have done without, although they were hardly news to her. There were some halting sentences from Greg, who told a story about Duncan teaching him to fish and who ended by saying that not a day went by that he didn't miss him. That was his only contribution to the episode.

Then Morgan described seeing his father's body laid

out beside the river on Christmas Day. He sounded as if he were about to weep and Etty didn't know if that was genuine, theatrical, or both at the same time.

He moved on to Charlie. Etty didn't move as he spoke of his own memories of a "radiant" woman with rings on her fingers and a husky voice who always smelled nice, nor when Ollie spoke in a voice thick with tears about his beloved mother and how he missed her. She remained frozen in place when she heard Alec saying, "I met her in a garden and she was wearing a yellow dress. I thought she was the prettiest girl I'd ever seen."

Now people from the village were talking about the aftermath of Charlie's disappearance and Duncan's death. People she didn't know were talking about her family; they were talking about Ollie, his wildness, and then about her. The pretty little thing, like a waif, heartbroken, heartbreaking. They talked about Paul. Paul dying. Taking his own life. Wreckage. Etty twisted her fingers together until they hurt and she didn't look at her brother and he didn't look at her.

At last it was over, they were back in the present and Bridget Wolfe was talking Morgan through all the objects she had collected from the Salter farmhouse. She was the curator of a museum of lost happiness, she said. This chair that Charlie had sat in; this photo of Charlie half smiling; this cake tin that she put her brownies in; this pewter candlestick; this old coat that had still been hanging under all of Alec's jackets and coats, with a shopping list in its pocket: in their shabby ordinariness, they held the secrets of the past.

Etty thought she heard her father's shuffling footsteps in the hall, but he didn't come into the kitchen.

"And this diary," Bridget said. Morgan was making small, encouraging sounds. "The green soft-backed appointments diary where Charlie wrote to-do lists and reminders, where you can see what she was doing in the last weeks of her life."

"Perhaps no one has looked at this for thirty years," said Morgan. "Wow."

"We can see the woman in it," said Bridget. "So interested in the here and now, the small problems and joys that make up a life. And there are other things in there as well, things I find interesting. Very interesting. I can't say more at the moment."

Bridget came to an end. Morgan was speaking, once more from the churchyard. He said he was laying flowers on Duncan's grave.

"I feel in my bones that we will find out what happened here in Glensted thirty years ago," he said, as music started to play. "We are getting closer to the truth."

They had reached the end. Ollie pressed "Pause."

"Well," he said. "That was hard to listen to."

Etty turned to him. He had tears running down his cheeks; he looked old and sad and lonely.

She reached across the table. For the first time in three decades, they held each other's hands.

"God, I've missed you, Etty," he said.

Forty-eight

"Where's Dad?" Etty asked ten minutes later.

"Isn't he in his room?"

"No. Nor his old study, and he isn't downstairs."

They looked at each other.

"I thought there was a sound of him in the hall when we were listening to the podcast," Etty said. "Did he hear any of it?"

"He's probably in the garden."

But he wasn't in the garden.

They searched everywhere they had already looked. They called his name and he didn't reply.

"Where would he go?" asked Ollie.

"No idea, but he can't have gone far. We need to find him."

"Right. I'll go towards the village and you go to the river and along there."

"God, Ollie, I hope he hasn't gone to the river."

"Should we call Niall?"

"Not yet."

*

The shoulder of lamb that was far too big for two people was roasting in the oven when Mary and Gerry Thorne sat down in the living room to listen to the podcast. It took them some time to download it. Gerry kept jabbing buttons and complaining about the internet.

"It's disappeared," he said.

"What do you mean, disappeared?"

"It just vanished off the screen."

"Let me try."

"No. You know what you're like with computers."

"You can talk," she said acidly, watching as Gerry bent over the laptop.

At last he found it.

"Ready?"

"For goodness' sake, just play it."

They sat side by side on either end of the sofa and listened. Neither of them spoke until it came to the section where they were interviewed. Mary Thorne nodded, satisfied, as she heard herself describe Duncan as "the perfect gentleman," always ready to do a good turn, the life and soul of the village.

"He hasn't used what I said." Gerry sounded resentful.

"Shh."

Morgan had moved on to Charlie. Victor Pearce talked about her zest for life. He said something about the rumours that had run round the village after she had disappeared. Morgan asked him what he meant and he replied that not only were Charlie and Duncan said by some to have been lovers, though he for one had never believed that, but also Alec and a woman in the village, to remain nameless, had been involved at the time of Charlie's disappearance.

Then Mary Thorne's voice filled their living room again, high and self-righteous. "It meant nothing. I felt trapped in my marriage, bored wretched, and so I behaved foolishly."

Mary Thorne jerked forward.

"He promised he wouldn't use that," she hissed. "He *promised*."

Gerry Thorne stared at his wife.

"Why is it the woman who always gets the blame?" the voice on the podcast continued.

"I'm going to sue him."

Then it was her husband's turn.

"What went on between my wife and Alec Salter is a private matter. It has nothing to do with what happened to Charlie or Duncan." There was a pause. "I forgave her," he added. "It took time and it was hard, but I think I can say that I haven't ever used it against her."

"That is just rubbish," said Mary Thorne, standing up and looking down at Gerry, who sat like a cadaver on the sofa. "You've used it against me every single day. When I am having a nice time with other people, when I don't do what you want to do, whenever you're not getting your own way, when you're losing an argument, you remind me. Even if it's just the way you look at me, raising your eyebrows, giving that little smirk, making those stupid huffy sounds through your nose, reminding me that *you forgave me—*"

"Now you're just being paranoid. Do you think it's your guilty conscience speaking?"

"I know you, Gerry Thorne. Don't pretend you've not taken revenge on me over the years in a million tiny ways."

"Don't shout. You've got lipstick on your tooth, by the way."

She glared at him, her face contorted. "It's true what I said to Morgan Ackerley. I felt trapped and bored and I still do. I've spent my whole marriage feeling that."

She stopped. Her breath came in short, angry gasps. In the sudden silence they heard Bridget was talking about being a curator of the museum of lost happiness: she named the chair, the photo, the cake tin, the candlestick, the old coat and the green diary.

"Shall I turn it off?" said Gerry as it cut back to Morgan. "I think we've heard enough."

"I'm going out," said Mary. "You can deal with the lamb."

"Suit yourself."

Gerry Thorne waited until his wife had left, and then he too went out, forgetting to turn off the oven.

Half an hour later, Gerry was slowly making his way back home, feeling tired and slightly ill, when he saw Alec Salter wavering slowly along the road near the new housing development. He was wearing checked pyjamas and slippers, and with one hand he was gesturing, as if making a point.

Gerry went towards him.

"Alec, what are you doing here?"

There was something wrong with him. His eyes glittered and his mouth dragged down; he smelled odd.

"Shall I take you home?"

"It's too late."

"What do you mean?"

"Too tired. I have to sit down."

Gerry looked round helplessly for assistance but the road was empty. He was old himself; his body ached. The familiar pain in his head started up.

"I'll get my car," he said. "You wait here."

"No time."

"Wait and I'll collect you."

But when Gerry returned twenty minutes later in his car, Alec Salter was gone.

FORTY-NINE

Etty was sure her father would be found almost immediately. Someone would see him and help him, or he would come back home. When she parked her car by the river, she checked her phone. Nothing.

She started walking along the river with a gradually increasing feeling of hopelessness. How long had it been now since he had gone? Twenty minutes? Half an hour? Even at his shuffling pace, he could have gone a mile away in any direction. And if he had got to the river? What then? At what point did they need to call the police? Was a lost, helpless old man the sort of thing that the police bothered with? She could feel her heart beating more and more quickly. She decided it was time to phone Niall. She tried his mobile but it went straight to his voicemail. She tried again and the same thing happened.

She decided to try the landline, even though she dreaded the idea of talking to Penny.

"This is Etty. Is Niall there? He's not answering his phone."

"He's not in the best mood at the moment," said Penny. "He's listening to this horrible podcast. I really don't know how this sort of thing is allowed. It's indecent. There must be some way—"

Etty interrupted her.

"I need to talk to him right away."

"What shall I tell him it's about?"

"What are you, a fucking receptionist? I need to talk to my brother right now."

Penny was so taken aback by Etty's tone that she couldn't even reply. She held the receiver towards Niall, who was sitting at the kitchen table, already halfway through a bottle of wine.

"It's your sister," she said. "She says it's urgent."

Niall took a gulp of wine and then came across and took the phone.

"This bloody podcast," he said. "Have you heard it?"

"Alec's gone."

"What do you mean, he's gone?"

"I went up to the room and he wasn't there."

"He's probably locked himself in the bathroom. Or in a cupboard, thinking it's a bathroom."

"He's nowhere in the house."

"How could you let this happen?"

"Let's get to the blame game after we've found him, if that's all right. I'm looking for him right now. I'm down by the river."

"The river?" said Niall. "You think he's thrown himself in the river?"

"I don't think anything. He's wandered off and I

thought you might be interested to hear this. But you can just go back to your podcast, if you want."

Niall started to shout something back but Etty had ended the call. He looked across at Penny.

"Did you get that?"

"That's what they do," she said. "They wander."

"Thank you for that, doctor," he said, sarcastically. "That's extremely helpful at a time like this."

"What are they playing at? How could they let their own father wander off?"

Niall glared at his wife but he couldn't think of anything to say that wouldn't make things worse. He picked up the car keys from the table but then fumbled them and they fell to the floor. He had to kneel down to pick them up.

"What are you doing?" said Penny.

"What do you mean? I'm going to look for my father. He could be in a ditch somewhere. Or in the river."

"How much have you had to drink?"

"Just a glass. It's fine. This is an emergency. Where's my phone?"

"How would I know?"

He searched the pockets of his jacket.

"It's all right, I've found it." He called Etty and waited while it rang. "She's not answering."

"You've just talked to her."

"We ought to look in different places. If she calls, tell her I'm looking ..." He paused and thought for a moment. "I haven't decided yet."

"I'll be sure to pass that on."

He frowned.

"He can't have got far, can he? Someone's sure to find him."

"Do you want me to drive you? You've definitely had more than one glass."

"What? No, you need to be here in case anyone rings. Anyway, after listening to that thing I need to get out and do something and be alone. Otherwise I feel I'll just explode."

Penny started to say that he wasn't in a fit state, but he walked out without paying her any attention.

"I heard you on the podcast," said Frankie.

Frankie was in her gap year and she was earning some money in the bar before going travelling.

"I didn't know anyone listened to it who wasn't actually involved," Victor said.

"I thought you came over really well," she said. "I've never known anyone who was part of a crime investigation."

"I wasn't part of it. Not really."

"Who do you think did it?" she said.

"Did what?"

"The crimes. Have you got a theory?"

"I don't know," he said, pretending to be busy arranging glasses. "The police thought it was Duncan Ackerley."

Frankie laughed. "They wouldn't be doing the podcast if it was their own father. The whole point is that they need to prove that their father was innocent. Unless that's the twist."

"What do you mean 'the twist'?"

"He's the main suspect, so he can't have done it. But maybe it'll turn out that he really did it after all."

"I don't think they know. They're just talking to people. Asking questions."

"I bet they know. These podcasts are all a fake. They pretend that they're investigating but they've worked it out in advance. Obviously that house-clearing woman knows something. She probably found something in the diary."

"Actually, could you hold the fort for a moment?" Victor said. "I need to go out for minute. Do something."

He pulled on a jacket and stepped out on to the high street. He crossed it and walked past the old village hall and the primary school and reached the heathland where the buildings stopped. He saw a figure moving slowly along the footpath on the far side. He had to squint to recognise Alec Salter. He was surprised to see him out alone and wondered briefly whether everything was all right. But he had other things on his mind. He didn't want to meet or talk to anyone just now and he walked decisively in a different direction so that he wouldn't cross Alec's path.

As Ollie drove down the high street he almost hit Victor, who was crossing the road, apparently oblivious to his surroundings. He halted and then leaned out to ask Victor whether he had seen anything but he was already out of earshot. Ahead he saw an old couple walking along the pavement, hand in hand. He parked the car and approached them. He vaguely recognised them the way he vaguely recognised everyone in Glensted, without being able to put a name to them.

"Excuse me," he said, and they looked at him in surprise. "I'm really sorry to bother you but I'm looking for my father, Alec Salter. You don't know him, do you?"

"Alec Salter?" said the man slowly, so slowly that Ollie thought he would go mad. "I think I know the name."

"It doesn't matter. It's just that he's not well. He's got dementia and he's gone missing. He's in his pyjamas. He's not safe."

"We live just here," said the man, pointing along the road. "We're just going home."

Hopeless, thought Ollie, forcing himself to thank them. What was he to do? He didn't even know what direction his father had gone in. He'd make some calls and then he would drive out of the village and then along the road that came back on the north side. He might see something. But what if he didn't? By now Alec could be lying in a field somewhere, slowly dying.

"So, are we going to listen to the podcast?" said Greg, as he put the champagne bottles into the fridge.

"You can listen to it any time you want," said Morgan.

"I want to hear it now. I'd like to know what I've missed out on."

"Why are you angry about this? You've come in

looking furious, as if you've worked yourself into a mad rage."

"I'm not at all angry."

"Who else wants to listen?" Morgan looked around.

"I'm fine with it," said Katherine. "I'd like to hear it." She smiled at Greg. "You look nervous about it."

"I don't think I'll listen to it, if that's all right," said Frances.

"It's not really all right," said Morgan. "You haven't heard any of the others; can't you at least listen to this?"

"Very well, if that's what you want . . ." Frances folded her arms and sat back. "Can we play it through the radio?"

"No, we can't play it through the radio," said Morgan. "It's not a radio programme. I've got a speaker I can connect to my phone on Bluetooth."

"I've no idea what any of that means. Do you, Lester?"

Lester shook his head.

Greg switched on the podcast.

"I hate hearing my voice," said Morgan.

"No, you don't," said Greg.

"It's a lovely voice," said Frances.

Greg took a bottle of white wine from the fridge and opened it and poured it out.

"I don't understand why everyone is talking like this," said Frances.

"Like what?" said Morgan.

"About private things. Or rather, things that should be kept private."

"It is rather raw," Katherine agreed.

"People like it," said Morgan. "It's like being a bit of a celebrity. Just for a little bit they can be the leading character in their own story."

"That sounds a bit cynical," said Greg. "Is that what we're doing? This woman Bridget . . ." He stopped, listening more closely to what she was saying. He turned to Morgan. "Is she for real? This diary. Do you think she really has something?"

"We'll talk to her again next week," Morgan said. "Follow up on it."

His phone rang and he answered it, holding a hand to his other ear to block out the sound of the podcast. "What? . . . Do you know where he went? . . . No, I haven't. Hang on, wait a second." He moved the phone from his ear and turned to Greg. "This is Ollie. He says that Alec's gone missing."

"What do you mean?" asked Greg.

"He's wandered off. Have either of you seen him? Did you see him when you went to get the drink?"

Greg shook his head. Morgan thought for a moment.

"I'll get in the car and drive around," he said to Ollie. "I'll ring you."

"Do you want me to come with you?" said Greg.

"No, you've only just got back. You stay here." He gave a faint smile. "You can stop Mum wandering off."

*

Etty had walked half a mile along the river then turned and walked back, thinking ever more desperate thoughts. *This can't be happening,* she told herself. It can't be happening. She decided to get her car and drive to the other side of the village and then park again and just walk around and maybe she would see something, or see someone who had seen something. Then her phone rang. It was Ollie.

"I've found him."

"Oh, thank God. Where was he?"

"Walking along a footpath heading God knows where. He's confused but he's fine. I'm taking him home. I'll see you there."

Etty was trembling with something, relief, distress, anguish, she didn't know which. She felt an overwhelming need for a drink, but instead she lit a cigarette, and then sat on a fallen tree for several minutes, thinking incoherent thoughts. She was about to turn for home, when she thought, no, now she knew her father was safe, she didn't want to see him. She was almost tempted just to collect her car and drive back to London, leaving all this disorder and pain behind.

But there was one last thing she needed to do. If Bridget was saying she knew something about her mother that nobody else knew, then she wasn't going to wait to find out about it on some bloody podcast. She was going to find out from Bridget herself. Right now.

FIFTY

She walked fast, past the playing fields, past the church-yard, up the little track that led to the woods. She still felt agitated after her father's disappearance, angry with herself for taking her eye off him. Niall had been right to ask how she'd let it happen. She'd talk to him later, apologise. He'd sounded drunk. She wondered if he was all right, but perhaps none of them were all right.

Soon, she thought: very soon she would leave this mess and return to her tidy life where everything was in its right place—her neat, bare flat, her long hours of meticulous work, her regulated relationships, her sense of being always in control.

And as she was thinking this, she saw a thin dark plume rising above the trees in the distance, and at the same time she smelled something acrid. She stopped, and even as she stood there the plume billowed and spread like a stain across the sky.

Etty started to run. The steep slope made her breath come in gasps and she soon had a savage stitch in her side but she didn't pause until she rounded the corner and the garish scene lay ahead of her, dancing red and orange flames and the great smudge of black smoke against a flat blue sky. She could hear the crackle and roar. She took out her mobile and as soon as she got the ringing tone, began to run again.

"Fire," she panted. "House on fire. Glensted, in the woods beyond the church." She couldn't remember the name of the farmhouse. "Bridget Wolfe's place," she said. "Terrible. Quick."

Now she could feel the heat of the flames and could see behind them the crumbling shape of the farmhouse and its outbuildings. The awful smell in her nostrils. The air full of flung scraps, like a crowd of maddened bats.

The woods might catch, she thought. Soon the hill might be on fire.

The wind suddenly switched direction, blowing the flames backwards, and for a moment the house was clearer. It was a charred skeleton, yet it still retained its shape, though as Etty stared in horror, one of its chimneys wavered and crumpled like a piece of cloth.

Then from out of the door came a figure fringed in orange flame. It ran, and as it ran the flames danced merrily on it and grew stronger, brighter. It reached out its arms. It gave an inhuman howl.

Etty charged up the slope. It was as if she was charging into hell, the wall of unendurable heat and the ghastly brightness of fire, the woman burning.

They reached each other. Etty hurled herself on Bridget and brought her to the ground. She started dragging her away from the house and then hitting at her, trying to extinguish the flames. Her own hair hissed. Needles of vivid pain stabbed through her and she realised she too was in danger of being set alight. Her jacket was burning. Her skin was peeling. She was crying out, calling for help, choking, slapping fire off her body and Bridget's, thick smoke in her lungs and her eyes streaming so she could no longer see anything, and why did no one come?

But then the flames on the body were out. There were sirens, coming closer.

She staggered to her feet. On the ground was the scorched remains of a person. In the ruin of the face, oh God, a single eye opened.

"Help's coming," whispered Etty.

The eye closed.

FIFTY-ONE

The windows of the commissioner's dining room had a view across the capital. Chief Superintendent Craig Weller stood staring across at the huge Ferris wheel slowly turning. He felt a presence beside him.

"Bloody eyesore."

He looked around at the commissioner.

"People like it, sir. Apparently."

"They don't have to see it every day."

Weller looked around at the long table, laid for eight.

"Looks like I'm early," he said.

"The rest will be along in a few minutes. I wanted a word in private."

Weller swallowed nervously. The commissioner wouldn't fire him in the executive dining room, would he? Just before lunch? The two men were still standing side by side, looking out at the river, as if they were still discussing the view.

"There's been a fire outside a village called Glensted." The two officers looked at each other and the commissioner gave a faint smile. "Don't worry. I hadn't heard of it either. It's up near Ipswich. A woman died from burns received. The report just came in. It was arson. So it's now a murder inquiry."

Weller felt a rush of relief. He couldn't think of any way he could be held responsible for a fire in East Anglia.

"One of our friends from the Home Office has been in touch," said the commissioner. "Which is never a good sign. Someone's dug out the file and it doesn't make for happy reading."

Weller looked round, puzzled.

"What file?"

"The media attention is about to shift to the Glensted case and about five minutes after that happens, someone will notice that there were two suspicious deaths thirty years ago in the same village. And about five minutes after that they'll realise that the original inquiry was a complete botch job."

"At least it's not our botch job," Weller said.

"I don't think you're meant to say that bit out loud," said the commissioner, and the smile froze on Weller's face.

"I didn't mean anything by it."

"We've had an informal request," said the commissioner. "You may have noticed that the police have had some bad results in the last few years."

"I think it's been exaggerated in the media, sir."

"Save it, Craig. This is me you're talking to. I was told at a very high level that they don't want another high-profile fuck-up, is that clear enough?"

"But it's not actually our case, sir."

"Funny you should say that, Craig."

Weller felt a lurch in his stomach.

"Are they looking for advice?"

"We're beyond that, Craig. We're well beyond that."

"Sorry, sir, I'm probably being dense. Do you want *me* to take over the inquiry?"

The commissioner's eyes narrowed.

"We've been told to second someone to lead the inquiry, so we've got to do it. But let's be honest, we're dealing with a stalled inquiry from thirty years ago. If you go down and fail publicly, then it's our problem."

"But this only happened twenty-four hours ago! Surely it's early days."

"Early days is when it's best to act. Before it becomes a bad news story."

"But—"

"This is sensitive, Craig. I'm trusting you to deal with it, pronto. Find someone young, promising . . ."

"You mean someone disposable?"

"We're all disposable, Craig, one way or another." He turned and put his hand on Weller's shoulder. "Ready for lunch?"

PART THREE

FIFTY-TWO

Maud O'Connor only liked cooking when she had time and the kitchen to herself. This evening, she had the time and the space because Silas had gone to play five-a-side football with his mates. He had promised to be back by six, or at least well before seven, and there was a special meaning in this promise: it was the right time of the month. Her most fertile time, according to her body's calendar. They would go to bed together and make love, and she would try not to think of what it might mean, try and concentrate only on giving pleasure and taking it. Then they would eat this meal together. There were already candles on the table. Music was playing from a playlist Silas had made when they'd driven to the south of France last summer.

She squinted at the recipe book that Silas's mother had given her for Christmas. She always followed recipes meticulously, laying out the ingredients on the work surface before she began, very different from Silas, who was slapdash and flamboyant. Usually he cooked, and she cleared up the extravagant mess he left in his wake.

Today she was making asparagus tart, with a tomato salad on the side. The pastry was already chilling in the fridge; she removed it, dusted the surface with flour, and rolled it out to a satisfying evenness. She lifted the dough into the pie dish and put it in the oven. She snapped the woody bits off the asparagus stems and put them in a pan to steam.

She glanced at the clock on the wall. It was twenty to seven.

The asparagus were ready so she drained them and cut off the tops. The recipe said she needed to purée the stems, so she did this in a blender as the recipe instructed, beat the eggs and then added cream and grated Parmesan and the green mush. She made a salad dressing.

She and Silas had been together for four years, and they'd decided to try for a child four months ago. Maud—who had four siblings and had been surrounded all through her teenage years and her twenties by friends getting pregnant by mistake—had thought it would happen at once. Four months wasn't long, she told herself—but it felt horribly, significantly long, and every time she got her period she would be cast down. *What if it never happens?* she asked herself. She didn't say it out loud to Silas, but she had suggested they try in a more organised way from now on: hence the date night, for which he was late.

It was twenty past seven now and Silas hadn't come. She glanced at her phone to make sure he hadn't messaged her.

She looked on WhatsApp. He wasn't online, but she sent a message anyway: *ETA????*

The pastry was ready. She took it from the oven and tipped in the creamy mixture, laid the asparagus tips on the top, put it back in the oven and set a timer.

It was half past seven.

She picked up her mobile. His phone went to voice-mail. She poured herself half a glass of red wine and took a small sip, then another. She opened a packet of crisps and pushed a few into her mouth.

There were children playing in the little garden that belonged to the ground-floor flat. One of them fell over and began making a sound like an electric drill.

The timer went. She took the tart out of the oven.

Quarter to eight. Eight o'clock.

"Where the fuck are you, Silas Brand?" she said out loud.

She was annoyed, but she was also slightly worried. What if something had happened to him?

Eight twenty-five. He was still offline. She bit her lip, called another number.

"Jonnie?" she said, when he answered.

"Who's this?" He was jovial, sounded rather drunk.

"It's Maud."

"Maud! Of course it's Maud. Hello there, Maud."

"Is Silas with you?"

"Silas—are you here? Yes, he's here. We're all here. We're having a drink or two."

"Right," she said.

She imagined asking Jonnie to tell Silas to come

home, the sniggers of the men: that Maud O'Connor, the woman back home, making dinner, being upset, nagging.

She didn't say anything. She felt a pulse of rage in her temple and closed her eyes.

"Hang on. What? Oh, right. He says he'll be back before long. He says not to wait."

Not to wait, Maud thought, putting her mobile on the table with a thump, her chest burning with anger. Had he *forgotten*?

A minute later, her phone vibrated on the surface and she thought, it'll be Silas apologising, saying he's on his way. She took a few deep breaths to ease her anger against him and picked it up without looking at the caller ID on the screen.

"Maud."

She recognised the person from that single syllable. Not Silas. Her boss, Chief Superintendent Craig Weller. He always managed to suggest that he was on his way to something more important and that you were preventing him.

"Can you speak?"

Maud surveyed the failed preparations.

"Yes, I can speak."

"I've got a job for you."

As he talked, Maud looked around the room, a large and light-filled communal space that was the kitchen room, dining room and living room combined. It was the reason she and Silas had bought the flat for more than they could really afford, especially after Silas threw up his safe job for a start-up company with friends. All the other rooms were tiny—especially the second bedroom that was really a box room, but large enough for a cot. She pushed the thought of the cot away.

"What do you think?" Weller said.

"Sorry?"

"When can you start? The sooner the better."

"Can I let you know in a few minutes?"

Maud ended the call. It was gone nine o'clock. She tipped the pie dish upside down over the bin and let the asparagus tart fall with a gloop in among the rubbish. She dropped the unfinished packet of crisps in there as well. She tipped the rest of her wine down the sink and washed the glass. She put the plates back in the cupboard and the cutlery back in the drawer.

She called her boss.

"I can come at once."

FIFTY-THREE

"Well, lads," said DI Whitman, setting his glass heavily down on the table and dragging the back of his hand across his mouth. "And, pardon me, lady as well. I should wend my way. Got to be up bright and early."

He stood up, a heavy-set man with a florid face, swaying on his feet and looking blearily at his juniors.

"I think we can say," he pronounced, "that we've done a good job today. A very good job. No hanging about. Not a word to anyone, mind."

He tacked towards the door of the bar, bumping into chairs as he went.

"He's going to feel like something the cat dragged in tomorrow," said Micky Harrison cheerfully. "He's worse than a girl at holding his drink."

"Talking of girls." Jack Lovell turned towards the young woman on his left; she had a round face, bobbed brown hair and a pale birthmark on her forehead. "What'll you have, Heather? It's my round."

"I need to go. Like he said, we've got to be up early."

"Can't hack it?" Micky Harrison leaned towards

her. He had full red lips, slightly protuberant pale blue eyes and a mop of hair that he continually ran his hand through. "Don't be a party pooper."

"A half then," she said reluctantly.

"Jack?"

The detective sergeant, a thin, sharp-faced man with sandy hair and eyebrows, nodded. "Same again. Though I'll be up before any of you, what with the twins waking at fucking sunrise."

"Still not getting enough sleep?" Heather Dillon asked.

Lovell groaned in answer.

"Well," she said, "from what the boss said, this case will be over almost as soon as it begins."

"I'll believe that when I see it."

"Did you see the body?"

He grimaced.

"And she didn't die quickly, so they say."

"People are saying Glensted's cursed."

Harrison returned with the drinks, distributing them carelessly so that beer slopped on to the table. His eyes, slightly bloodshot, gleamed.

"Well, well," he said. "The evening's suddenly got more interesting. Get an eyeful of her."

A woman in her early thirties had come into the room, a glass of beer in one hand and a plate with a thick sandwich on it in the other. Her blonde hair was curly and half tied back from a face that was startlingly pale, with a straight nose, thick brows and a mouth that seemed slightly asymmetrical. She wore baggy black jeans, a white T-shirt, a black leather jacket, scuffed biker boots. When she put her glass and plate on the table next to theirs and took off her jacket, they could see a tattoo on her forearm.

"Where has *she* come from?" Harrison didn't bother to lower his voice. "Glensted won't know what's hit it."

The woman leaned back in her chair, half closed her eyes and lifted the glass to her lips, then with both hands she took the hefty sandwich and bit into it.

"She looks weird," whispered Heather.

"You're just jealous."

Harris rotated his chair so he was facing the woman.

"Good evening," he said. "We were just saying how we hadn't seen you before."

She looked at him with eyes that were grey and not unfriendly.

"I've just arrived," she said in a low clear voice, whose accent sounded east London.

She turned back to her sandwich.

Harrison pulled his chair closer to her table.

"I'm Micky." She didn't reply. "And this is Jack and Heather. We're celebrating. Won't you join us?"

"No, thank you."

"Aren't you going to ask what we're celebrating?"

"Watch it, Micky," said Jack. "It's a bit early to be bragging."

But Harrison ignored him. He inched his chair even closer to the woman.

"An *arrest*," he said. "That's what."

He reached back one arm to his own table, grabbed

his glass and raised it to his mouth, drinking as if he was thirsty. There was foam on his upper lip.

"I think," said Heather urgently, "that you should be a bit careful with what you say, Micky. The boss told us to keep this under wraps."

"And I think you should loosen up, darling." Dillon flushed a deep red and Harrison turned back to the woman. "A local character was burned to a crisp two days ago and we've already got our suspect. How's that for quick?"

"Shut up, Micky," said Lovell.

The woman posted the last of her sandwich into her mouth and stood up, though her glass was still half full.

"I'll leave you to your celebration."

"Where are you going?"

"To my room."

"You're staying here?" Harrison's smile stretched across his face. "That's convenient."

"Good night," she said, and picked up her jacket.

"Hang on, not so quick, love. I'm a gent and I don't let ladies walk home alone. I'll escort you to your door. You might want to invite me in for a nightcap."

He drained his glass and lurched to his feet, then took a step towards her so they were almost touching.

"Watch it," she said, and gave him a gentle push, so that he toppled back into his chair. She smiled down at him. "Micky, you said? Well, Micky, I reckon you're going to feel really rotten tomorrow."

"Good pick-up line," said Lovell, with a thin, sarcastic smile.

"Frigid bitch," said Harrison as she left them.

"Half the pub heard what you were saying," said Heather wretchedly. "What if it gets out and the boss hears?"

"Give it a rest, will you?"

"What if she's a journalist or something? They're everywhere and the boss said not to talk to them."

"Does she look like a fucking journalist?"

"Come on, Micky," said Lovell. "Time to go."

"No way. It's your round."

"The evening's over."

Maud sat in her little room, hearing the sounds of the pub beneath her. Her head ached with all the reading she'd done that day, going through documents, making notes, trying to find a shape in the mess that she had been landed with, trying to hold all the information in her head.

There were three missed calls from Silas. She waited several minutes before she picked up her phone. This time, he was the one not to answer. They had talked yesterday after she had arrived at the Anchor in Glensted, when he had been hungover and angry, and she had been sober and polite in the chilly way that drove him mad. He had accused her of storming out just because she was pissed off with him for being late for a meal, and she had corrected him. She had left because she had been called away on a case and couldn't hang around on the off-chance that he'd roll in. She told him she hoped he'd had a good time with his mates, but that they had now missed the window of opportunity.

"It was just one evening," he said. "Are we going to make this into a military campaign?"

"I thought we agreed—"

"Not like this. Not so I feel guilty for having a night out with friends."

She wanted to ask if he was having second thoughts but she didn't, because she didn't want to hear the answer.

Now she sat on the bed and pulled off her leather jacket and her boots, untied her hair and shook it loose, gazing around the strange room that she would come to know well over the next days and weeks. It had a sloping ceiling, a table under the window that looked over the high street, a lumpy mattress that reminded her of her childhood, and a large wooden chest of drawers where she put the clothes she'd brought. She wished there was a bath rather than just a shower. She liked soaking in long, hot baths, preferably with candles. It was where she did some of her best thinking.

She usually loved the start of a new case, when everything was unknown, a bit scary, and she told herself that an argument with Silas wasn't going to blight that. They would sort it out.

She called his number again; again heard his voice telling her to leave a message. Such a familiar, warm voice, and a stab of unexpected homesickness went through her.

"I miss you," she said. "Call me."

FIFTY-FOUR

At twenty to nine the next morning, there were eight men and three women in Hemingford police station's incident room. Some of them sat on chairs or perched on desks; others stood. DS Lovell had arrived early, newly shaven and wearing a freshly ironed shirt; his pale hair was combed flat across his scalp, making his face seem narrower than ever. He stood beside DC Dillon, who looked pasty and ill at ease.

"Bloody typical," grumbled a man sitting by the door. "He tells us all to get here promptly, and doesn't bother to turn up himself."

"He's probably still in bed," said DC Harrison. "With the mother of all hangovers."

"How's yours?" Lovell called over to him, and he scowled. He was unshaven and there was a bleary air to him, as if he'd struggled out of bed a few minutes ago.

At last the door opened and a woman stepped into the room.

"What the fuck," said Harrison. Then, louder: "Couldn't keep away, eh?"

The low hum of conversation died away and she stood in the silence, apparently unperturbed.

"Can I help you?" asked one of the officers.

"Lost your way, love?" called Harrison boldly.

She looked at them and didn't smile and didn't reply. She stepped forward to allow DI Whitman to follow her into the room. Beside her he looked even bulkier than usual. His face was very flushed and his eyes looked small and mean. He banged his briefcase on to his desk, then turned to face them all.

"Sorry to have kept you."

He stopped. Everyone waited.

"This was not my idea and suffice to say I'm not happy. We've made terrific progress on the inquiry into Bridget Wolfe's murder, and I know we all thought we could wrap it up quickly. But the powers that be have decided otherwise and ours is not to reason why."

He stopped again. He looked even more flushed and Lovell wondered if he was about to have a heart attack.

"I'm here to tell you that I am stepping down from the case with immediate effect." When he spoke again, it was as if every word was being held in tweezers. "It has been decided that it is appropriate to bring in an outsider." He stopped again and swallowed. "I know that whatever your individual feelings about this decision, you'll be professional."

He took a handkerchief out of his pocket and wiped his forehead.

"The detective taking over from me is Detective Inspector Maud O'Connor, from London," he added, giving the last word a jeering emphasis. "On secondment. As you can see, she's young. It's probably part of some fast-track scheme. I hope you'll help her out. She doesn't know the community, she's not used to our ways. So, make me proud."

The response of the officers in the room was oddly muted. They knew they were watching a career end in front of them. Whitman didn't look at the woman standing next to him. He just nodded at the assembled officers and stomped out of the room, closing the door behind him with a solid bang.

Maud O'Connor waited for a few seconds after Whitman had left before taking up her place behind the desk. She put both her hands on its surface and leaned slightly towards the room. This morning she was wearing grey flannel trousers and a plain white blouse; her hair was tied tightly back, no curls escaping, and the only make-up she wore was red lipstick. She was ready for business.

"I know this is a surprise," she said, letting her gaze travel round the room. "But you're professionals and so am I. I'm sure we can work together. It's true I'm an outsider. Given the history of what happened in Glensted thirty years ago, and the feelings about the way the local police force dealt with that, it was felt a fresh pair of eyes might be helpful. Now, we've got a job to do."

"It's already done," called a man from the back. "Or haven't you heard?"

"I've heard you have someone in custody. That needs

dealing with, of course. In the meantime, I think we should start the investigation again. From scratch."

There was an angry buzz around the room. She waited it out.

"We'll have another meeting tomorrow at the same time. I expect everyone to be here with reports of their progress then. In the next hour, I am going to allocate jobs to each of you and get this investigation up and running."

"You don't even know who we are," shouted someone angrily.

She looked at him, frowning slightly.

"Frank Mason," she said after a pause. "Joined the force three years ago. Do you want me to prove to you that I've read your file?"

He reddened.

"I didn't mean anything," he said.

"You're a tech person. We'll need that. I know a bit about all of you," she continued. "And a little more about a few of you." She didn't look at Harrison when he said that, but he flinched. "Of course, you're right: that was just me doing my homework and I don't know you personally. Not yet. Now, Jack." She looked straight at Lovell, her grey eyes calm and dispassionate. "You're my second-in-command, I believe. I want to see the person you're holding."

FIFTY-FIVE

The woman who was led into the interview room looked as if she was sleep-walking. Her legs were unsteady and her head drooped, but when she lifted it, Maud saw that her left cheek was raw and blistering, one eyebrow was singed and there were bald patches on her scalp where her hair had been burned.

She sat at the chair the woman officer pulled back for her and put both arms on the table. One of her hands was heavily bandaged. She was in her late forties, beautiful in an austere kind of way with her gaunt face and high cheekbones. Maud had seen photos of her, but they were from long ago when she had looked softer and sweeter, a teenager with freckles and huge eyes, her hair a tangle of curls. Her eyes were red and sore now, the skin around them puffy. She looked as if she had been weeping for days.

"Elizabeth," said Maud.

"You'd better call me Etty. That's who I am here. Different life, different name."

"All right then. Etty."

"Who are you?" Her voice was hoarse and she spoke with difficulty, as if it hurt.

"Maud O'Connor. I've just been put in charge of the inquiry."

Now the woman looked at her.

"You're young."

"Has a doctor seen you?"

"Ollie took me to the hospital. Someone bandaged my hand."

"Your cheek needs attending to. It looks nasty."

Etty shrugged.

"I want you to tell me what happened," said Maud.

"Again?" She closed her eyes briefly, then opened them and spoke almost in a whisper. "How many times do I have to go over it?"

"I need to hear from you exactly what happened on Sunday."

So Etty told Maud the story of her day. Listening to the podcast, hearing that Bridget had found her mother's diary, Alec going missing and setting out to search for him, hearing he'd been found and on an impulse going to Bridget's house.

"Because I had to know," she said.

"About the diary?"

"About my mother."

"And then?"

"Then I saw smoke. The house was on fire. It was awful. Like hell. Have you ever seen—?"

"No," said Maud. "Nothing like that."

"I called the fire brigade and I ran towards it. I don't

know why. It was so hot. My lungs were burning. Then I saw her."

There was a silence. Maud didn't speak. The woman opposite her picked at the bandage on her hand and bit her upper lip.

"She came out. On fire. Towards me. Like I could do anything for her. I tried to put it out. Her. But it was hopeless. She died. I can't begin to imagine the agony she died in."

"Did she say anything?"

"One eye opened for a moment. Looking at me. I still see it in the dark."

Maud pushed a glass of water towards her and with difficulty, wincing as she did so, Etty took several gulps.

"Everything tastes like ash," she said.

"Why haven't you asked for a lawyer? You must have been offered one."

"I *am* a lawyer."

"Why haven't you made use of the law then? You know you're suspected of murdering Bridget Wolfe."

Etty looked at her.

"Maybe I want to go to prison," she said. "Maybe it would be a relief."

"What do you mean?"

"I'm so tired. I'm so tired of keeping going. Everything hurts."

"Your mother?"

She nodded.

"My mother and my brother."

"Yes," said Maud. "I heard about Paul."

"No, you didn't. You didn't hear it all."

"What do you mean?"

Etty spoke in a dull tone.

"It was the fifth anniversary of the disappearance. And of our father's birthday. Let's not forget that. Paul rang me. He said he was in a bad way, he said he couldn't cope. I wasn't doing so well myself. I told Paul I'd get back to him. Two days later they broke down the door and found him. He'd taken all his pills. He'd been saving them up." She looked up at Maud. "I know what you're going to say. It's not your fault. But I looked it up. If you save someone from killing themselves, there's a seventy per cent chance they won't try again. Seventy per cent. So don't say it."

Maud watched as the tears ran down her cheeks and Etty didn't wipe them away.

"I haven't cried for thirty years," she said. "Dry as a desert. Now I can't stop. I'm an ocean of tears."

Maud waited a couple of beats. Then she said:

"Did you murder Bridget Wolfe?"

"Of course I didn't."

"Did you do anything to cause her harm?"

"Yes. I brought her into our family when I asked her to clear our house. She'd still be alive if I hadn't done that."

"Nothing else?"

"That's enough."

"Have you someone who can collect you?"

"What, now? I can go?"

Maud looked at her watch.

"We're not far off the moment where we have to charge you or let you go. And there isn't the evidence to justify charging you. But you're a lawyer, you knew that, right?"

An hour later, Maud accompanied Etty out of the police station. A dishevelled middle-aged man with fading red hair was leaning against his car, smoking agitatedly. He dropped the cigarette when he saw them and walked swiftly towards them. Maud watched his face change as he saw his sister, taking in her burned cheek and bandaged hand, the way she stumbled as she walked. He put an arm round her shoulder and she briefly leaned against him.

He looked at the detective. His anxious expression changed to one of anger.

"So you arrest my sister for no reason and then you just let her go. Is that how it works?"

"This is Ollie," said Etty. "My brother."

"I think she needs some rest," said Maud.

"I bet she does. After all she's been through."

"Has she got somewhere to stay?"

"She'll be fine, no thanks to you lot."

"I am here, you know," said Etty, trying to smile.

"Of course. Sorry. You need to keep me informed of your whereabouts," said Maud.

"Or what?"

"Nothing much. But I assume you want to help us." Ollie started to speak but she held up her hand and continued. "I understand that you feel angry. If you have a complaint, you can make it to the appropriate department. If you have something to say to me, then just say it."

"OK, I'll say it," said Ollie. "It's happening again. There's been a murder and we're all going through it again and nothing will be solved. Again."

"You think that the death of Bridget Wolfe is connected with the deaths thirty years ago?"

"Well, of course it is."

"Can you say any more than that?"

"How could it not be connected? If there are three deaths in a place this size, then of course they're connected."

"Two deaths, one of which was believed to have been by the person's own hand, and one disappearance, isn't that right?"

"I don't know why I'm even talking to you," said Ollie. "Who's actually in charge of this investigation?"

"As of this morning, that would be me," said Maud.

"You? You look about twelve."

Maud turned back to Etty.

"Have something to eat and get some sleep," she said. "I'll be in touch."

FIFTY-SIX

"She was our main suspect," said Jack Lovell when Maud entered the incident room.

"I know."

"We thought that we had a pretty good chance of a conviction."

"Really?" said Maud.

"She had a motive; she's an angry woman. And she didn't have an alibi."

"She was at the scene when Bridget Wolfe died, if that's what you mean by not having an alibi."

"Murderers generally are at the scene when their victims die."

"A slightly odd way of committing a murder, don't you think?"

"There's no single way," said Jack Lovell. "There aren't rules for murders. And sometimes it's simple. You arrive at the scene, there's a dead body, there's a person with the dead body. That woman Elizabeth Salter, she had every chance to show us she was innocent and she didn't say much at all and what she did say didn't make much sense."

Maud started to smile and then realised that Lovell was speaking seriously.

"Unfortunately that's not the way the legal system works," she said. "She doesn't have to prove she's innocent. We have to prove she's guilty. If she's guilty."

"All right then, boss," he said. "So what do you want to do now?"

Maud waited before replying. Lovell was several inches taller than she was and he was standing very slightly too close to her. She was aware that every word he had said to her had an element of challenge to her. Even when he said the word "boss" there was an irony to it, as if there was something slightly comic about this cheery word being applied to a woman like her.

"I think we should go to the scene," she said. "Can you give me a lift?"

"Don't you have a car?"

"Yes."

There was a pause.

"Of course," he said.

When she got into the car, she had to remove sweet wrappers from the passenger seat. She gathered them up and put them into an empty shopping bag that she found at her feet. Lovell drove away with a screech of tyres on the gravel in the police station car park.

"I googled you," he said.

Maud didn't reply. She was looking out of the window at the houses and shops they were passing.

"I saw that you were in charge of the Butler investigation. That must have been difficult."

Now Maud looked round at him.

"Why do you say that?"

"Most officers don't like the idea of investigating other coppers."

"Yes, that's what people say."

"Some people think he was badly treated."

"I know."

"I mean, the guy had resisted arrest. He had a record. I think it was ridiculous."

"I agree," said Maud.

Lovell parked just near the entrance to Bridget's drive.

"Really?" he said, sounding surprised.

"If it had been up to me, Butler would have been charged with murder, not manslaughter." She looked around the car. "This is a small thing, and I wouldn't say it in front of the rest of the team. If you had been given this as a rental car, what would you say?"

"I don't know what you mean."

"You'd take it back. You'd say it was in a disgraceful condition."

"I'm sorry," said Lovell, "but maybe we've had other things to be getting on with."

Maud sat back and gestured around her. "This car is part of the public face of this investigation. Someone might look at it and think to themselves: If they can't

340

keep their own cars clean, then what else can't they do? And the same goes for the incident room. Can I leave that to you?"

There was a pause. Lovell's mouth was closed, his jaw muscles flexing.

"Yes, of course." They got out of the car and faced each other over the roof. "One more thing."

"What?" asked Maud.

"How would you like to be addressed?"

She looked puzzled for a moment, considering this question.

"I don't give a toss," she said, "as long as it's not something stupid."

There were other cars parked along the grass verge, so that at places the road was almost blocked. Maud and Lovell stepped through the gateway into what had once been the farmyard. What Maud saw when she stepped off the road was so unexpected that it took her a few seconds to make sense of it. It was like a crime scene that had got mixed up with a garden party.

The blackened remains of the house and the sheds on the far side of the yard were still smoking. The smell of it hit Maud so forcefully that she immediately felt it was sticking to her skin and to her clothes. The yard itself was crowded. People were standing in groups. Some were talking, others just staring around them. A man in overalls was dragging a blackened fragment of machinery towards the road. Maud looked at Lovell in disbelief and then turned to the man.

341

"What are you doing?"

"What's that to you?"

Maud took out her badge and held it in front of the man's face.

"And?"

"And you put that down at once and tell me what you're doing?"

"We've been hired."

"To do what?"

"Do some clearing out."

"All right," said Maud. "You can stop that right now. Is anyone else here working with you?"

"A few of us."

"You all need to stop what you're doing this moment, don't touch anything else, leave and don't come back until you have permission. In writing. From me."

"Who's going to compensate us?"

"If you even touch anything, starting from now, you'll be charged with interfering with a crime scene."

The man mumbled something under his breath and then turned and approached two men carrying a charred piece of furniture.

Maud walked across to a group of people who were filming a news item. A woman holding a microphone was addressing a camera. Maud stepped in front of her.

"We just need a minute," said the bearded man holding the camera.

"You need to leave this property," said Maud.

"We have the right to report on a matter of public interest."

"As long as you do it outside this property. This is an active crime scene."

"Where does it say that? I don't see any signs. I don't see any tape."

"I'm in charge of this investigation and I say it."

The woman's expression changed from resentment to a sudden interest.

"Really?" she said. "Can we do a quick interview?"

"You can contact the press office, like everyone else."

She walked back to Jack Lovell, who was looking impassive.

"Well?" she said.

"What?"

"How did this happen?"

"Don't worry," he said. "We've done all the scene of crime stuff. We've done the forensics and the tyre tracks. Everything's been photographed."

Maud nodded slowly. "Everything's been done?"

"That's right."

"I thought your boss had been pushed out because he wasn't up to the job, but maybe he actually committed the murder. Because I've never seen a crime scene more effectively contaminated than this one. It's almost impressive." She clapped her hands and spoke loudly so that the remaining people in the yard looked at her. "This is a crime scene. Everyone leave. Now. Don't remove anything. Don't even touch anything."

She waited until everyone else had left the yard before she turned back to Lovell and spoke in the calmest tone she could manage.

"Two things," she said. "First, you said that the scene of crime people were here. So where's their report?"

"I don't think they've done it yet."

"Perhaps you could contact them and ask them to hurry it up. If they aren't too busy."

"I'll try."

"Trying isn't enough. Do it. And secondly, the horse has well and truly bolted, but I think we should make an attempt to close the door, just to be on the safe side. Could you phone the station and ask them to come up here and bring some of their tape with them and stretch it across the entrance ways? And perhaps they could add a sign or two. Would that be possible? And I want you to wait here until they arrive."

"What are you going to do?"

"I'll walk back."

"All the way to Hemingford?"

"Yes. It's not far."

"Do you know the way?"

"I'll do my best."

As Maud came back into the road, she saw the television crew sitting in a car. She tapped on a window and it rolled down.

"Don't even think about going back in there after I've gone," she said.

Further along the road, she took a footpath heading in the direction of Glensted. She took out her phone. No missed call from Silas, no reply to her message. He was probably busy, but no one was so busy they couldn't send a few words. Maud liked looking at things full in the face, naming them to herself and then finding ways of dealing with them. The anxiety stirring inside her made her uneasy. She didn't know what to do with it.

She stared at her mobile's screen, willing it to light up with his name. Then, against her better instincts, she called him. To her surprise, he answered on the first ringtone.

"Maud."

"Is this a bad time?"

"I'm about to go into a meeting."

"Can we talk later?"

"I've been tied up. I'll call you."

"Are we all right?"

"Of course." He spoke with a forced heartiness.

She waited a beat, then said, "Bye then. Love you," casually slipping in the last two words.

"Bye."

She sat on the grass verge, in the shade of a beech tree, and waited for her feelings to subside. She needed to concentrate on the job in hand, not get distracted by small difficulties in her private life. She gave herself a small shake, pushing her hair from her face and squaring her shoulders, then called up another number.

"Could I talk to the chief super?"

A few seconds later she heard the familiar voice.

"Well?"

"It's a beautiful part of the country, I'll give you that," she said. "I've just left the murder scene, if that's what it was. I'm looking down at Glensted and the river and the marshes."

"I thought you could do with a holiday," said Weller. "What about the inquiry? How's it going?"

"It's worse than you thought," said Maud. "Much worse."

"I don't think it can be much worse. I saw the initial report. What about the investigating team? Are they happy to have you there?"

"Not very."

She heard a grunt from the other end of the line.

"Can you manage them?"

"I'll see. All I've had so far is an innocent woman in prison and a contaminated crime scene."

Another grunt.

"If it was easy, that fool Whitman would still be running the inquiry. One day, someone from the media is going to look at this case and see that this group of clowns has made us all look like idiots. It's your job to do something about that."

"The media are already out in force. Apparently there's also a podcast about the cold case."

"Bloody hell. Have you heard it? What does it say?"

"I don't know."

"Then don't waste time talking to me. Get a move on."

Fifty-seven

When Maud returned to the Anchor she was full of a restless energy: the feeling of gathering up facts and impressions and trying to hold them in her head, of trying to see what wasn't there, the gaps and absences. She was looking for a piece of solid ground, waiting for a pattern to emerge.

She went up to her room and had a quick shower. Pulling on jeans and a jumper, for the evening was cool, she sat at the table, took the papers out of the folder and opened up her laptop. She was thinking about Etty and Ollie Salter, two middle-aged people with years of distress written into their faces. Thirty years ago, their mother had disappeared. They must know she was dead, yet in some deep part of them, they must be still waiting for her to come home.

Now a murder had triggered that intense loss, and Etty had cried for the first time in decades, cried like the child she had been. Maud's job was to solve that murder. Was it her job to solve the other crimes as well? If they were crimes.

She worked for two hours, making notes on Bridget Wolfe's murder and the police's response to it. It was entirely focused on Etty Salter, neglecting to interview anyone else, corrupting the scene of crime. It was as if the crime had been immediately solved, so nothing else mattered. She thought of the detectives she'd met in the pub. She thought of the pathologist's report that she still hadn't seen. It all made her head ache.

At nine, she went to the bar and ordered a glass of red wine and a lasagne, which she ate swiftly, avoiding the stares of other people in the bar and flicking through messages on her phone. She relished being alone, a stranger in a strange place, that sense of being vibrantly alert to new impressions.

When she went back to her room, she thought about phoning Silas. He had said he would call her as soon as he was free, so perhaps it would be better to wait. It seemed strange that she was weighing up the pros and cons like this: at any other time, she wouldn't have worried about that, but would simply have called him.

She called. He answered, sounding distracted.

"Is this still a bad time?"

"No, it's fine."

"I wanted to make sure everything was all right."

"Of course it is." He paused. She could picture his handsome face, a day or two's worth of stubble on his chin, the eyes that in some lights looked stormy grey and in others blue, rich brown hair falling in a wing over his forehead, a wide, generous smile. "Sorry I didn't come home," he said.

"Sorry I left."

"We should talk," he said.

"Yes. I guess I could drive back for an evening. Or you could come here one night?"

"I'm rather busy, Maud."

"We're both busy." He didn't say anything, so she added: "Do you want to know about the case?"

"I already know. I've seen it on the news. I've seen *you*."

"What was it like?"

"They said you'd been brought in to shake things up and that you were no stranger to controversy. They mentioned the furore over the Butler case and then they showed a clip of you shouting at some journalists and practically pushing them out of the place where your woman died."

"A bad start."

"You looked good, in control."

Maud closed her eyes. Maybe everything was all right after all.

"Maybe I could drive up tomorrow evening."

"I can't. I said I'd see my parents."

It had never been made explicit but Maud was very aware that Silas's parents were at best ambivalent about his relationship with Maud. They were both university lecturers, while her father was a roofer, and that was just the beginning of their problems. Whenever they met, Maud could feel them straining to be friendly, all the time constrained by their habitual hostility to the police, although she'd gone up in their estimation with the Butler case.

"Right," she said.

She thought of suggesting other days but bit back the words. She didn't want to plead with him. She let the silence hang between them.

"Perhaps the weekend."

"Silas," she said. "If there's something wrong, you need to tell me."

"There's nothing wrong! Don't make everything about us; I'm tired. Things are hard at work."

"I'm sorry to hear that," she said evenly. "But there are things we need to discuss."

"I'm here. You're the one who left."

Maud felt her chest tighten. Her father used to tell her to breathe through her anger. She breathed.

They said goodnight. Maud stood at the window and looked out at the street. There was no one around. The windows of the houses opposite were dark. It felt that the whole of Glensted was asleep. She longed for London, where the lights never go out, where there are always people and cars and noise.

Although she was tired she knew she wouldn't sleep. She downloaded the most recent episode of Morgan Ackerley's podcast and listened to it intently, pausing it every so often as she made notes. When she climbed into bed, her brain was still crackling.

She drifted off to sleep while composing to-do lists in her head, and she dreamed of the missing woman, though in her dream Charlotte Salter had her own mother's face and she was on fire.

*

She drove to Hemingford in the misty early morning, and sat at her desk with a cereal bar and a coffee from the pub. The other officers drifted in in ones and twos for the morning meeting and stood in groups, chatting in low voices and casting glances at her. Micky Harrison shrugged when she asked about the pathologist and the crime scene report and picked his teeth.

When Jack Lovell arrived just before the briefing was due to start, she asked him as well, but he interrupted her to ask if she was ready for the press conference.

"What press conference?"

"The one in ten minutes."

"Nobody told me about this. Who organised it?"

"Sorry," Lovell said airily, and she thought she detected the twitch of a smile. "Assumed you knew. We can't cancel it now."

"All right," she said, keeping her voice as level as she could. We'll have the meeting afterwards. Make sure everyone knows and is prepared."

"Right."

"And smarten yourself up a bit. You're coming with me."

Maud was startled by how many journalists were waiting for her when she stepped outside. She had expected a handful of local reporters. Instead there were dozens of men and women, including some from national media. She recognised some of the people she had seen yesterday outside Bridget's house. Cameras flashed and mikes were held out as she introduced herself and Jack Lovell.

"This is my second day," she told them. "There isn't a great deal to tell you about the progress of the case. I can tell you, however, that a woman in her forties—"

"Elizabeth Salter," called a voice. Maud ignored it.

"A woman in her forties has been released from custody." At the clamour of voices, she held up a hand and continued: "Because there was no reason to detain her."

"Excuse me," a voice called out. Maud saw a middle-aged woman with short grey hair and round glasses. "Alice Clayton from *The Herald*."

"Yes?"

"Can you tell us why Inspector Whitman's been replaced so quickly? It hardly seems fair to the local police force."

"It was felt that a fresh approach would be useful," said Maud.

"Is that a polite way of saying he's made mistakes?"

"Like allowing us lot to trample over your evidence," called a young man boldly.

"Is it a public rebuke, sending in the big boys from London?"

"Do I look like a boy? It's a polite way of saying a fresh approach would be useful," said Maud.

"Like your fresh approach in the Butler case."

"Each case is unique."

"Audrey Jackson." A young woman was holding out her mike. "Is this murder connected to what we in the area call the Glensted Mysteries?"

"I don't know," said Maud.

"Of course it is," said a voice she recognised. She turned towards it.

A thin, dark-haired man with a close-shaven beard was standing to her left.

"Morgan Ackerley," he said. He too was holding out a small mike.

"We're not ruling anything out."

"It's clear to me," he said in his rich, solemn tones, "that our podcast has brought the past back to life again. Someone doesn't like what we are discovering."

"I'd like to talk to you about that," Maud said, as pleasantly as she could manage. "But not right now."

Alice Clayton held up her hand. "Can you tell us about the pathologist's findings?"

"Unfortunately we haven't yet received the pathology report."

"Can I speak to that," said Jack Lovell, taking a step forward so that he stood beside her and towered above her. "The pathologist's report was very clear on the cause of death. While Bridget Wolfe had inhaled toxic gases and this would have been fatal, her actual cause of death was not that. The intensity of the fire was the cause: that means that the soft tissues contract, the skin tears, the fat and muscles and internal organs shrink." He spoke with a grim satisfaction. "In other words, Bridget Wolfe burned to death."

Beside him, Maud stood rigidly still. She forced herself not to display any emotions.

"The skeleton, however," he continued, "was not

burned. The pathologist could find no sign of other damage. Nobody, for instance, concussed her before setting fire to the house."

There was a silence. Then the questions started up again, but Maud spoke over them.

"Thank you," she said. "That's it for today."

"Do you want to explain?"

"I don't know what you mean." Lovell smiled down at her, raising his eyebrows in mock puzzlement.

"I asked to be told as soon as the report came in. Instead, I am told about it in the middle of a press conference."

"I assumed you knew."

"Stop your stupid little boys' games. I'm not interested in them. A woman has been murdered, in the cruellest way imaginable, and instead of helping to find out who did it, you want to trip me up in public. Is that why you became a police officer? Is it a game to you?"

Lovell looked taken aback. He bit his thin upper lip.

"It was just a mistake," he muttered.

"Yeah? Well, I'm having no more mistakes like that. Do you hear?"

He nodded sullenly.

"Right. In ten minutes' time we will have that briefing." Lovell turned to go but she called him back. "Jack, you either work with me or you're off this case. I'd be fine with that. I'd be fine with getting shot of the lot of you."

*

"It's me again."

Maud was standing outside the morgue, readying herself to see Bridget Wolfe's body. That morning, she had looked at recent photos of Bridget when she was alive: a short, vigorous-looking woman in her early forties, with a strong jaw, hair cropped close to her scalp and dark, bright eyes. Maud thought she would have liked her.

"Yes?" Her boss sounded curt.

"I want one of my own people."

"What's wrong with your own team?"

"They're not mine. They're either useless or down-right hostile. I'm not complaining; I can deal with them and I will and I don't need your help or anyone's with that. But I want an ally, someone I can bounce ideas off." There was a pause and Maud watched a small brown bird sitting in the lime tree across the road. She didn't know what it was: there hadn't been much nature where she had grown up and she could only recognise magpies, blackbirds and robins—and scruffy London pigeons, of course. Warm wind ruffled at her hair. She could still feel the anger inside her, flickering embers of the rage of earlier. "I'm not actually asking," she said. "I'm saying."

There was an abrupt, approving bark of laughter at the other end of the phone.

She ended the call, squared her shoulders and pushed through the doors into the morgue, to look at the terri-fying remains of what had once been the eccentric force of nature called Bridget Wolfe.

FIFTY-EIGHT

"Are you up for this?" Niall asked.

Etty nodded. Her chest felt raw, as if it was still full of acrid smoke. Her head thumped and the stinging pain in her cheeks made her wince. It felt as if her skin was shrivelling. She looked at her brother's concerned face and then hastily away. She mustn't cry, not now, but it was as if all the barriers she had erected over the decades had been washed away.

"You don't have to," he said. "Not after what you've been through."

"It's OK. I'm OK." She knew she wasn't; Ollie knew; Penny knew. Everyone treated her with a terrible kindness and concern. "We'll do this together, all right?"

They were standing by the front door of the farmhouse, waiting for Ollie to bring Alec downstairs. Niall's car was already packed with everything Alec was going to need; it seemed pathetically little. After a lifetime of accumulation, his possessions had dwindled to two suitcases and a canvas holdall. Niall had already taken his favourite armchair to the home, although apparently there was barely space for it in the compact room.

They heard Ollie's voice and shuffling footsteps, and then Alec appeared in the doorway. He seemed to have shrunk in the past few days. He was a small old man with rheumy eyes and a suspicious expression.

"Ready?" Niall asked with a forced cheerfulness.

Alec stared at him in bewilderment.

"Is it all right I'm not coming?" asked Ollie. "I mean, it doesn't need all three of us."

"Fine," said Niall.

"Right. Well, bye, Dad."

Ollie patted his father on the shoulder and Alec glared at him.

"Where are you taking me?" He addressed the question to Etty.

"To your new home," she said.

"Is Charlie there?"

"No." It was an abrupt answer but she didn't know what else to add.

"She's never there," said Alec peevishly. "I spend my life waiting. I said sorry. Women!"

Niall helped him into the front seat and buckled his safety belt. Etty climbed into the back.

"I've changed my mind," said Ollie, and squeezed in beside her, shifting some of the cases to make room for himself.

"This is just like old days," he said. "A jolly family outing."

No one said anything. Etty closed her eyes, feeling the

throb of her cheek, of her hand. She thought about Paul, about her mother. For a moment, she almost believed she could smell Charlie's perfume.

They drove over the bridge and arrived in Hemingford. Niall manoeuvred the car down side roads until they came to a square, red-brick building with a row of symmetrical windows on its top floor. It was set back from the road and had a circular driveway that Niall drove down.

"Here we are," he said.

"Where?" Alec twisted round towards his daughter. "Where are we?"

She stared at him and couldn't look away.

"This is where you're going to live now," Niall said.

Etty saw the incomprehension on his face. Then the terror.

"You're going to like it," said Niall.

"Is Charlie in there?"

"Charlie's dead," said Ollie. Then he muttered under his breath, "I shouldn't have come."

Niall got out and went round to the passenger door. Etty joined him.

"Let's go and see your room."

"Is it prison?"

"Of course not," said Niall.

He took a suitcase in one hand and hooked his other arm through his father's. Ollie reluctantly got out of the car and joined them, taking another case and not looking at anyone.

"Come on then," said Niall.

"I didn't mean to."

"What didn't you mean?" Etty asked him suddenly, urgently. "Dad?"

"I don't want to go to prison."

"It's a home, Dad. Your home." Niall looked as if he was about to cry.

"Don't let them," Alec said to Etty. "Please."

"What didn't you mean?"

"Charlie," her father said to her. "Do you forgive me?"

FIFTY-NINE

Maud left the police station before six and, instead of driving back to the pub in Glensted, she headed for the A12. Before eight o'clock, she was in east London, inching her way through traffic. This was home: potholes, fumes, lives jostling against each other, a skyline of jagged buildings. The big skies, meadows and marshes of Glensted were a different world.

She parked outside the flat and let herself into the communal hall where Silas's bike hung on its rack. Good. He was in. She hadn't rung in advance to say she was coming. She unlocked the door that led to the stairs to their flat, which she ran up two at a time.

"Hi!" she called. "It's me."

She stopped. She could hear voices. Silas appeared, holding a can of beer.

"You didn't say you were coming."

She put her arms round him and kissed him on his mouth, tasting beer.

"Are you pleased to see me?"

He wrapped an arm round her, but loosely. This

wasn't how she'd let herself picture it: she'd imagined a passionate embrace that would lead them tumbling to their bedroom where they'd fuck and whisper endearments and say sorry.

"Who's here?" she asked, taking off her jacket and entering the living room.

There were five other people there; she only knew Jonnie. Silas introduced her to them—Paula, Mica, Sophie, Robbie—and they raised their hands to her cheerfully. The room was lit by candles even though it was still bright outside, and there were several empty cans on the table and a bottle of vodka. There was music playing that she didn't recognise. It was as if she was a stranger in her own home.

The doorbell rang.

"More people," she said brightly. "It's a party."

"That'll be the pizza," said Jonnie, getting up and leaving the room.

"I'm sure there'll be plenty for you as well," said Paula. "We ordered a ridiculous amount."

"No, I'm not staying," said Maud.

"What do you mean?" Silas turned to her. His face was flushed. He was wearing a fragrance she didn't recognise.

"I'm here for work stuff. So I just wanted to say hello, make sure everything was all right."

"Everything's fine."

"Good. I'll grab a few things from our room and be on my way."

He followed her into the bedroom, which was a mess,

the bed unmade and dirty clothes lying on the floor, several mugs on the bedside table. She pulled a couple of shirts off their hangers and threw them on the bed.

"What's up?" he asked.

"You don't seem very glad I'm here."

"It was just unexpected."

Maud turned to face him.

"Can I ask you something?"

"Sure."

"Is it because you've got cold feet about having a baby?"

"What?"

"Don't do that. It's me, Maud. Things are horrible between us and I need to know why. And if you've changed your mind about trying for a baby, I really, really need to know that."

"I've just been very busy . . ."

"You've been busy before. Please. I'm driving back to Glensted tonight and I want you to tell me before I go why you're being so . . ." She paused.

"So what?"

"Evasive."

"That's just in your mind."

"You didn't come back for our date night—and I won't believe you if you say that you didn't realise it was a big deal."

"If you won't believe me, then there's no point in speaking."

"You've not called or answered messages. You don't seem wild about the idea of me coming back to London to see you and you don't seem to want to come and see me. And now, here …" Maud gestured around. "I feel I'm unwelcome in my own home."

"Of course you're not."

"So what's going on?"

"Maud," he began, but a voice called from the living room.

"The pizza's going to get cold."

He grimaced. She turned away and picked up her shirts, collected a random handful of underwear from the top drawer of the chest.

"Bye," she said.

"Don't go like this."

But it was a weak protest and she ignored it, running back down the stairs, shutting the flat door with a bang, sliding into her car, where she sat motionless for several minutes before turning the key in the ignition and driving away.

Sixty

She hadn't been lying when she had told Silas's friends that she was in London for work. She drove towards Tottenham, turned down a narrow street, and found a parking space a few doors down from the apartment block where Carrie Kessler lived. She rang the bell and waited a long time before anyone answered, but she'd called her after she had left the flat, so she knew she was there.

"Hello?" The voice was husky and breathless.

"It's me."

"I'll buzz you in."

The buzzer went. Maud pushed open the door and went up two flights of stairs. Carrie was standing at the flat's entrance.

"Blimey!" Maud said as she approached her. "You're enormous!"

Carrie grimaced.

"And I've got over four weeks before my due date."

"You're sure it's not twins?"

"It had better not be. Come in."

Maud followed her along the landing and into the little kitchen that looked out over the street. She watched a fox nose through a spilled dustbin opposite.

"Drink?" Carrie asked.

"I've brought us a bottle of sparkling elderflower, and some crisps. I'll get glasses, shall I?"

"I'm not an invalid," grumbled Carrie, but she lowered herself gratefully into an armchair.

"Is it uncomfortable?" Maud asked as she poured elderflower into two glasses and snapped open the pack of crisps.

"I pant when I walk up any stairs, my ribs hurt, my boobs ache, and sometimes when the sprog kicks me, I shriek. Apart from that, and the small issue of getting pregnant by mistake and being a single mother and having hormones all over the place so I shout at people even more than usual, all fine."

Carrie Kessler was a small woman and she had always been skinny, with dark hair that looked as if an electric shock had made it turbulent. Now she was like a cartoon version of pregnancy, her thin arms and legs, her triangular face, and the great dome of her belly. She wore jogging pants, a voluminous shirt, slippers. She sipped at her drink, pushed a handful of crisps into her mouth, sighed.

"It's nice to see you," she said.

"You too. So you've got a whole month left?"

"That's right. It was felt that my job didn't really suit a pregnant woman who couldn't get out of a chair without groaning."

Carrie was a police officer. Maud had met her years ago, when they were both starting out, and had worked several cases with her. Her male colleagues called her a spitfire, a little dragon, a firecracker and, referencing her crazy hair, toilet brush. Maud liked her dry humour, her courage and her loyalty.

"What are you going to do?" she asked Carrie.

"Sleep."

"Apart from that. I mean, I've read that babies are often a week or two late for first-time mothers. That'd be six weeks."

"See friends. Buy all the things babies are supposed to need. Get ready for this great change."

"Won't you get bored?"

Carrie eyed her curiously. "All right, Inspector, why are you here?"

"Obviously, I was going to come at some point anyway."

"Obviously."

"But it occurred to me you might have time on your hands."

"And?"

She gave Carrie a skeleton outline of the case and the hostility she had encountered among her team.

"I want an ally," she said.

"To go up there?"

"Yes."

"I can't exactly chase villains."

"This investigation has been so messed up. I want someone sane to look through it. Also, I'm badly in need of someone to talk to. I haven't got anyone there."

"You believe that the three cases are linked?"

"I think it's a useful working hypothesis."

"From what you've told me, the police believe that the 1990 cases were solved."

"I know."

"What do the local force feel about being told that their solved case wasn't actually solved?"

"They're not happy about it."

"Would I be part of the official investigation? If they're hostile to you now, what will they be like if you bring in another outsider?"

"I'm in charge. I have a budget, and I'll pay you properly."

"Where would I stay?"

"I've already reserved a room for you in the pub I'm staying in."

"When for?"

"Tomorrow, but I'm sure I can change it to tonight, if you want. It's not exactly full."

Carrie thought for a moment.

"Your working hypothesis had better be right," she said.

"It doesn't just have to be right. We have to prove that it's right."

Carrie pulled a face.

"It's 'we' now, is it?"

"Is it?"

"What else have I got to do? I'll see you tomorrow."

Sixty-one

Carrie looked around the room, unimpressed.

"There are people who like staying in hotels," she said. "I've never understood that."

"The room has a desk and a chair and a kettle and Wi-Fi that works fairly well. That's all you need. And when you want a rest there are some nice walks and lots of fresh air."

"What happens if I go into labour? Where's the nearest hospital?"

"Ipswich, I think. Then there's Norwich."

"Ipswich?" Carrie took out her phone and tapped at it and then looked up at Maud. "I hope you're good at delivering babies."

Maud gestured at the desk. There were three piles of files: red, blue, buff-coloured. "And I'll send you the links for the online files."

"Is there anything particular you want me to look for?"

"I want you to read it through and tell me what you think."

"That's a bit vague."

"I know," said Maud. "Start with Charlotte Salter, she's the key."

"Why?"

"It's the fiftieth birthday of her husband, the man she's unhappily married to. She never gets there and she's never seen again. And she's connected to all three cases."

"You think she's dead?"

"I don't know. But if she's alive, where is she? If she's dead, where's the body? Bodies are hard to hide, hard to get rid of."

"You say she was unhappily married. Maybe the fiftieth birthday was the moment where it all snapped, where she couldn't take it any more."

Maud pointed at the stack of files.

"You'll see somewhere in there that she was planning to leave."

"There you are, then. And it was easier to disappear back then. No mobile phones. No CCTV cameras."

Maud shook her head.

"I don't know. She may have hated her husband but she didn't hate her children. She would have known what she was doing to them. One of them killed himself. When I arrived, the daughter was in custody. She was not in a good way. She's nearly the same age as my mum, pretty much the same age as her own mother was when she went missing. I just wanted to rescue her, even though I knew it was too late. Yet people do strange things. Perhaps Charlotte Salter will just come back one day and explain everything."

Carrie looked down at the files. "You think the answer is somewhere in these?"

"Probably not," said Maud. "But at present it's almost all we've got."

"And meanwhile your team of detectives is out there investigating. What will they think about me being here, going through their work?"

Maud appeared unconcerned. "We're all on the same side, really. We just want to solve this case."

"I'm not sure that's how it works," said Carrie. "I mean in the real world."

Maud picked up the little electric kettle.

"Would you like some tea?"

Carrie frowned. "My grandmother told me that when she was pregnant with my mum, she smoked and drank through the whole pregnancy and my mum didn't turn out any the worse for it. Looking at my mum, I'm not sure if that was really true, but at a moment like this I could do with a cigarette and a gin and tonic."

"Really?"

Carrie laughed. "I suppose I'd better stick with a herbal tea. Just for appearance's sake."

Maud flicked through the little sachets of tea: Breakfast, Earl Grey, Fruit.

"I'll get you some from the shop," she said.

Carrie picked up the first of the files. "So this is everything?"

"Everything I could lay my hands on. Statements, forensics, some newspaper reports. And when you're finished, we can listen to the podcast about it." She saw Carrie's expression of bemusement. "No, really. It's made by Duncan Ackerley's two sons. One of them is Morgan Ackerley. You know, the one who does those documentaries."

Carrie wrinkled her nose.

"I always thought he was a bit cheesy."

"He has lots of fans."

"One other thing," said Carrie.

"What?"

"Have you got the physical evidence from 1990?"

"Not yet. It must be in storage somewhere. You've read my mind. That was the next thing on my list."

Lovell was on the phone when Maud walked into the incident room. He held up his hand, as if he were waving her away, telling her he would get back to her when this important call was over.

"Yes, I might be home a bit late," he said into the receiver.

Maud didn't back away but just stood there, waiting for him to finish. Lovell continued to talk while occasionally glancing round and becoming more and more self-conscious, and he seemed to lose the thread of what he was saying.

"Look," he said distractedly. "I'd better call you back. Something's come up." He looked round at Maud. "Sorry. A bit of a domestic emergency."

"That's all right," said Maud briskly. "Do you need to take some time off to deal with it?"

Lovell flushed red. "It's not that important. I'll deal with it later."

"Anything new to report?"

"Not really, if there was anything new I'd ..."

Lovell stopped and there was a silence. Maud smiled cheerfully.

"If there was anything new, you'd tell me," she said. "Good. Now, one thing we haven't talked about is the storage of the physical evidence. Where is it kept?"

"You mean from the fire?"

"No, I mean from the 1990 inquiry."

"That's not really our concern."

"And what is our concern?"

"We're investigating the death of Bridget Wolfe."

"And while we're investigating it, I'd also like to know where the physical evidence from 1990 is kept."

"All right," said Lovell, "I'll put someone on it."

"I think it might be simpler if you just did it yourself," said Maud. "Let's talk again in fifteen minutes."

"Fifteen minutes?"

"What's it going to take? One phone call? Two?"

It was twenty minutes later when there was a knock at Maud's office door. Lovell came in. He had put the jacket of his suit on and fastened the top button of his shirt and tightened his tie. He looked like a nervous schoolboy coming to the headmistress's study.

"You look like you're not bringing me good news," said Maud.

"It's not exactly bad news. It's just turned out to be a bit complicated."

"How can it be complicated? Either the evidence is there or it isn't."

"In a way."

"What do you mean, 'in a way'?"

He gestured helplessly.

"At the moment, old evidence is stored in a facility over near Colchester. I talked to an officer there and he told me that they only have stuff going back about eight years."

"What about older evidence?"

"It was all a bit difficult to get my head around. He was telling me that some evidence from settled cases is reviewed and then either preserved or destroyed."

"But this wasn't a settled case."

"It wasn't exactly settled because the main suspect died. But there was a general agreement that the case was closed."

"Jack, I've read the original findings. There was no general agreement. There were some leaks to the media but there was no formal finding. The case just gradually ground to a halt. But it was never officially closed."

"I don't know about that. But from what this officer was saying, the problem is that the storage was contracted out to a firm and then it went bust, so it was taken over by another firm and moved between different places. He thinks it might be in a storage facility in a farm up near Hadleigh."

"But there must be a record somewhere of their holdings."

"Kind of. But the database we use is from a new contract. The records of evidence in the eighties and nineties were done on another system and this office says that there are problems accessing it."

"What kind of problems?"

"We can't access it."

Maud sat back in her chair and breathed deeply.

"So you're saying that the evidence of an open case might have been deliberately destroyed."

"It wasn't necessarily considered an open case."

"And if it hasn't been destroyed, it might have been lost."

"There's no reason to think it's been lost."

"Well, that's good news. But if it hasn't been lost and it is actually in this storage facility on a farm somewhere, we can't check whether it's there. Aren't there any paper records?"

"Apparently they were destroyed when they shifted over to computer data."

"How big is this storage facility?"

"Quite big. I think they've got evidence from right across the region."

"You'd better send someone over there."

"To do what?"

"To find the evidence."

"It might not even be there."

"This is what we do, isn't it? We're detectives. We find things."

"Not if it's not be there to be found."

"Just give it a try. By the way, don't send Dillon."

"Why? I was thinking she would be the person to send."

Maud very nearly laughed at this. She knew why he had immediately thought of Dillon. Because it was a boring job. Because it was probably a waste of time. But she didn't say any of that. Too much of her career had depended on the things she hadn't said.

"I've got something else in mind for her," she said. "In the meantime, I want you to find out something about Bridget Wolfe. There's nothing here." She tapped the folder in front of her. "Who were her family, her friends? Was she in a relationship? Financial state of affairs. I don't have her phone records or her bank statements."

"I thought you believed her death was connected with the cases of Charlotte Salter and Duncan Ackerley."

"Belief is one thing, proof something else. It might be a waste of time—but most of what we do is a process of elimination. Let's do this properly."

When Dillon came into the room, she looked uncomfortable. Maud smiled at her and gestured at the chair.

"I want your help with something."

Dillon brightened. "Me?"

"Yes, you. The diary that Bridget Wolfe referred to in the podcast . . ." She stopped. "You have listened to the podcast, haven't you?" Dillon nodded. "It's been taken for granted the diary was destroyed in the fire."

Dillon bit her lip. "I think so," she said.

"I want you to look for it."

"Where shall I look?"

"I'm asking you to do this, not telling you how to do it. But for example, has anyone gone through her shop in Hemingford?"

"I don't know."

"Well, I do. They haven't."

Heather stood up and then hesitated.

"Yes?" Maud raised her eyebrows at her.

"Just—well, thanks."

"I'm just asking you to do a job. Don't be grateful."

SIXTY-TWO

Niall, Etty and Ollie stepped out of the house into the dazzling light. Niall locked the front door and then he pushed the key back through the letterbox, where they heard it clink on to the floor.

They looked at the dilapidated house they'd grown up in. It looked kinder in the June sunshine. There were roses growing up the porch and a blackbird was singing from the cracked gutter. Etty tipped her head, half expecting to see a face—her own? her mother's?—pressed against the glinting panes.

"I'll let you know how the sale goes," said Niall.

There was a pause.

"This is harder than I imagined." Ollie's voice wavered. "If you hadn't noticed, I'm not much good at saying goodbye."

"Thanks for being here." Niall spoke gruffly. "We did it as a family."

"Whatever that means." Ollie tried to laugh.

"Etty?"

She turned to Niall but didn't speak. Her eyes were glassy.

"Will you be OK?"

"Yes."

"You're not well yet."

"I need to go back to work."

"But if you're ill?"

"I'm not ill," she said.

"It doesn't seem right," said Niall.

But Etty lifted her bandaged hand and smiled at them.

"Goodbye, brothers," she said, and turned on her heel, walking to the car with what she hoped seemed a purposeful stride, though the ground seemed to tip under her and the landscape in front of her blurred and wavered.

Niall and Ollie watched as she fastened her belt and started the engine. The little car jumped forward, then spluttered up the gravel drive too fast. It swept through the gates and up the track towards the road, but as it rounded the corner it came to a screeching halt.

"What the fuck," said Ollie, and they both ran towards her.

Etty was slumped over the wheel, sobbing as if her heart would break. She lifted her tear-sodden face as Niall opened the door. She looked as desolate and as helpless as her fifteen-year-old self.

"Etty?" Ollie crouched by the door. "Etty, are you all right?"

"I don't know what's wrong with me," she said. "I'm not usually like this. I don't know what to do."

"I knew you weren't ready," said Niall. "Come back with me."

"I've wrecked my life," she said, and another huge sob dislodged itself from her chest.

"Don't say that!" said Ollie. "I can't bear it if you say that."

"What shall I do now?"

"It'll all be all right." Niall patted her awkwardly. "You've had a traumatic experience and you need time to recover. Come home."

"I don't have a home."

"Please, Etty." Ollie was pulling at his faded hair; his own eyes were full of tears.

"Come home to me and Penny."

"I've been homesick all my life."

Two hours later, Etty was lying in Niall and Penny's spare room. The sheets were crisp and clean, the pillow plump, the curtains half closed against the brightness outside. There was a glass of water on the table beside her that she sipped at occasionally, trying to rid herself of the foul taste of burned hair, burned clothes and burned flesh that still clung to her. Etty could hear Penny in the kitchen downstairs, clattering dishes. A radio was on somewhere; a man's voice indistinguishable but comforting.

She must have slept because when she woke the light was muted. She thought she could hear Mia talking. Doors slammed. Cars drove past. She slept again. She thought how lovely it would be to sleep for a hundred years.

Sixty-three

Just after five o'clock, Maud met Carrie on the pavement outside the pub and they walked off the high street and on to the footpath that quickly brought them out of the town. Carrie was breathing heavily as they climbed.

"This is even worse," she said. "Now I'm going to go into labour in the middle of a field. How will you deal with that?"

"I thought you might like some fresh air, some country views."

"We're not meant to live in the countryside," Carrie said dismissively. "It's not natural. We're meant to be bumping up against each other, living on top of each other. I checked online about that podcast, by the way. It's become a big deal since Bridget Wolfe died. There are people in America who are online looking at this area on Google. They've got their own theories about whether it was Alec Salter or Duncan Ackerley. I saw someone on Facebook saying they thought Charlotte Salter had killed Ackerley, then faked her own disappearance. It's like a soap opera. You'll have tourists coming here soon. Amateur detectives."

"Then we'd better get a move on," said Maud. "You've read the files?"

"I've looked through them."

"Did anything strike you?"

"It's a joke, isn't it?"

"What do you mean?"

"All of it, the old investigation, the new investigation. I've never seen anything like it. You'll need to look at the evidence all over again. When can you do that?"

"There's a problem with that," said Maud, and she told Carrie about her experience during the morning.

"So what are you going to do?" asked Carrie.

"I'd like to do what the ancient Romans did to their opponents. I'd like to get rid of the whole department, demolish the police station, plough the ground where it stood, put salt in the earth so that nothing will grow there and then start all over again."

"Great. But failing that."

Maud didn't answer for a long time.

"That podcast. I've fast-forwarded through it but I think they're doing a better investigative job than the police have done. What we'll do is we'll get some food, listen to it together properly and take some notes. Then we can make a plan."

Maud's phone rang and she took it from her pocket. She didn't recognise the number.

"Yes? … No, I'm afraid that won't be possible … How did you get this number? No, I can't do that …

Thank you, goodbye." She looked at Carrie in disbelief. "Well, that didn't take long. It's someone from Seattle. Will I be interviewed for a podcast?"

"You mean *the* podcast."

"No, another one. They're spreading."

"I can come up on Sunday afternoon if you want," said Silas.

"Do *you* want?"

"I'm the one suggesting it, aren't I?"

"Then yes, I'd like that," said Maud. "I'm staying at the Anchor. It's quite basic."

"I can't stay."

"You can't stay the night? Or Saturday night would be even better."

"No."

She pushed away disappointment and something else—something like a sense of abandonment, a fear that was blooming inside her. "Well, we can have a walk along the river. It's rather lovely here in a desolate kind of way. Marshes and big skies."

"Good."

"Silas—"

"Got to go."

Sixty-four

"Right," said Maud, early the next morning. She had been at work since seven and hadn't had breakfast yet. "What have you got for me?"

DC Harrison wasn't looking at her but slightly to her left, as if there was another, more important person in the room.

"I did what you said and drove all the way over to the storage facility in Hadleigh. It was a bloody long way to go for a—"

"I didn't ask what you had done, Micky. I asked what you've found."

"Nothing."

"Nothing?"

"There is no evidence."

"That's a pity."

Harrison shrugged. "It was thirty years ago, after all." Maud frowned, thinking hard.

"I need to speak to Sally Peck," she said, half to herself. "Who's she when she's at home?"

"She was the officer who collated most of the evidence."

"What use is she now?"

"I won't know until I've talked to her. Can you find out where she is?"

"Me?"

"Yes, please." Maud smiled into his flushed face.

"I'm quite busy."

"It shouldn't take long. I'd like you to make it a priority, please."

Half an hour later, Maud was calling the number that Harrison had tossed down on her desk.

"Is this Sally Peck?"

"That's me."

Maud explained who she was and the reason for her call.

"I realise this may be a wild goose chase and the evidence no longer exists," she said. "You probably can't help."

There was a long pause.

"Actually," said Sally Peck at last, "I think I might be able to."

Maud liked driving. She chewed gum and listened to music and the green landscape flowed by, punctuated by church spires, winding rivers and small woods. Carrie sat beside her, her hands on her belly, her eyes half closed and then fully closed. A snore escaped her.

"Here we are," said Maud, pulling up outside a small house on the outskirts of the town where Sally lived.

Carrie jerked awake.

"I wasn't asleep; I just had my eyes shut," she said.

They got out of the car and Maud rang the bell. The door opened almost before it finished its tuneful chime.

Sally Peck was in her mid-fifties. She looked strong and wiry; her brown hair was streaked with grey and there were crow marks round her eyes. She wore jeans and a sweatshirt pushed above her elbows. Her feet were bare.

"Sally? I'm Maud O'Connor."

Maud held out her hand and Sally took it. She had a firm handshake and her gaze was direct.

"And this is my colleague, Carrie Kessler. It's good of you to see us."

Sally gave an odd laugh, then turned and led them through to the kitchen.

She moved round her kitchen with a kind of neat efficiency that Maud liked. She looked out at a garden that was lush with flowers.

"You like gardening?" she asked, for something to say.

"It's what I do." She poured boiling water over the tea bag and the coffee grounds. "I mean, it really is what I do. I'm a gardener."

"Cool," said Maud.

"It's mostly weeding and chopping things back, cutting the grass for the older folk. It suits me better than being in the police."

"I hate gardening," said Carrie. "With a passion."

"When did you leave the force?" Maud asked.

"Nineteen ninety-three."

"So you weren't a police officer for long."

Sally put their drinks in front of them, and a plate with several slices of cake. She drew up a chair and sat opposite Maud.

"Help yourself. Orange, cumin and cardamom cake."

"So you're a baker too."

"My partner is."

"I haven't had breakfast," said Maud, and took a slice. "Why did you leave?"

"Why do you think?"

"You mean, being a woman?"

"Being a woman. Being gay. It was hideous. I don't know why I thought I could hack it and I don't know why I stuck it for as long as I did." She took a slice of cake and broke off a fragment, rolling it in her fingers. "You're young for a DI. Maybe things have changed since my day."

Carrie gave a particularly loud snort.

"Not enough," said Maud. "You know why we're here. You said you might be able to help." She took out a notebook and flicked over to a new page. "Can we talk about the evidence that's gone missing? I understand that you were largely in charge of collating it."

"Collating. That's one way of putting it."

"How would you put it?"

"Cobbett was out of his depth, panicking and throwing his weight around to compensate. He decided early on it was the husband, Alec Salter, and we hardly looked at anyone else. We didn't take statements properly, we didn't interview the right people or check alibis, there was a pile-up of information that no one read through. It was a nightmare. Cobbett tried to blame me for some of it."

"You? Why?"

"Why not? I was junior, a woman, a convenient scape-goat. Anyway, he told me to throw stuff away, or at least not to bother him with it. Not to cover things up exactly, just because it became clear that we'd been barking up the wrong tree: Charlotte Salter had been seen much later in the day than had at first been assumed, so we had to begin again. We had piles of documents and photos that we didn't have space for and that seemed to have become irrelevant. A lot of it was stashed in cardboard boxes under my desk. And then when Duncan Ackerley died—well, it was all a complete car crash. When the case was shelved, it was like they were just pushing all the mess out of sight and hoping no one noticed."

"And nobody did."

"If they did, they didn't care." She fiddled with the cake, still not eating it. "But I cared," she said at last.

There was something about her tone that put Maud on alert, but she didn't say anything.

"It was my first time on a case like this. I couldn't let go. I guess I got a bit obsessed, not in a healthy way," she said apologetically.

"I can understand that."

"Those young people, the Salters and the Ackerleys. I thought they deserved better."

"They did," said Maud. "They still do."

"But all the evidence was just thrown away?" Carrie put in.

"Not exactly. It's a bit awkward really."

Maud waited.

"Better come with me," said Sally, standing up.

Maud and Carrie followed her up a flight of stairs and on to the landing. Sally took a long metal pole and inserted the hooked end into a trapdoor above them. It opened and a set of metal steps unfolded.

"There's a light up there." She looked at Carrie dubiously. "You'd better wait here."

"Don't you worry," said Carrie. "I was going to."

Maud climbed up the steps after Sally and scrambled into a loft space that ran along the length of the house. There were a few cases stacked against the near wall, a roll of carpet, several pots of paint. And at the far end, several cardboard boxes.

"I thought it was better than throwing it away."

They drove back with Maud's little car laden with boxes. One of them had to go on Carrie's lap. She picked at the thick tape that was plastered across the lid and managed to make a small gap.

"I think it's photos," she said.

"Crime scene photos?"

"No." Carrie inserted a hand and pulled out a small blurred image. "It's a Polaroid."

She held it up and squinted. "It's hard to make out. But it looks like it's someone's foot."

"There may be something there. We'll check them out later."

"Do you want a sandwich?" Carrie peered into the bag at her feet. "I've got tuna and mayonnaise or cheese and pickle."

"Whichever. I'm ravenous."

"Cheese and pickle is less messy if you're driving."

Carrie passed it over and Maud took a large bite. She didn't speak until she had finished it.

"You know what Sally was saying about being in the police. How awful it was being a woman back then."

"She was bullied," said Carrie.

"Have you ever thought of leaving?"

"All the time. What about you?"

"When I said I was going into the Met, my friends all thought I was joking. Some of them were appalled. My dad didn't much like it either, for different reasons. He thought I'd have a hard time. Sometimes it's like those dreams you have where you're running in soft sand. Sometimes it's like I've walked into the men's changing room by mistake. But really, I like solving problems," said Maud. "I like days like today, when I've worked away at something and there's a sudden chink of light."

Carrie looked across at her friend, with her halo of blonde curls, her grey eyes that in a certain light looked green, her lopsided grin. Sun had brought out the freckles on her startlingly pale skin. In her cotton jumpsuit and scuffed leather sandals, she didn't look like a police officer—whatever a police officer is supposed to look like. More like a barista.

"We need more than a chink of light," she said.

Sixty-five

When they got to the Anchor, Maud said that she needed to get back to the station.

"Why don't you make a start on this? Find out what we've got, make a comprehensive list."

Carrie shook her head. "I do love a list. But no."

"What do you mean?"

"It's one thing you having me hidden away, going through notes that everyone else has access to, or discussing the case with me, thinking things through together. That's OK. But not this. You can't take newly found evidence to the pub for me to read rather than to the station."

"I can."

"Well, of course, when I said, 'you can't,' I meant you mustn't. Or at least, I don't want to be part of that. Sorry."

Maud felt a jolt of anger and clutched the steering wheel tightly, waiting for it to pass. Then she nodded.

"You're right. OK. Come and meet the team."

She tied back her hair more tightly and turned the ignition back on.

"You look like you're going into battle," said Carrie.

Maud told Lovell to get as many of the team together as possible, and then she and Carrie entered the incident room. Maud felt curious eyes on her and then a low muttering as Carrie swayed into the room behind her. Someone started laughing. Carrie, hearing it, turned and looked at him and the laugh faded away.

"I've called you together for two reasons," Maud said. "The first is that we have new evidence. I'll come to that. The second is to introduce you to Detective Sergeant Carrie Kessler."

The silence was instant.

"Carrie has come from London to help in this case," said Maud coolly. "As I've said, we all want a result and we'll take any help we can get."

The faces in front of her were angry and incredulous. A babble of sound broke out. She held up her hand.

"Is there a problem?"

Micky Harrison put up a hand.

"Yes?"

"We should be asking you that question. If you think that we're not doing a good enough job, maybe you should just tell us straight out."

Maud paused. She believed that in fact they *weren't* doing a good enough job and she was tempted to tell them. Perhaps it would do them good. She swallowed hard. She had spent too much time not saying what she really thought, or not all that she thought, and she was going to do it again.

"I can see that it's difficult having another new face. But if we can get a result here it will make us all look good. If anyone has a problem working with me, just come and see me in private and I'll arrange a transfer."

There was a silence. Finally it was broken by Heather Dillon.

"You said there was new evidence."

"Yes. Carrie, do you want to speak to this?"

Carrie nodded. "We've retrieved the physical evidence from the Salter and the Ackerley cases," she said. She was brisk and businesslike. "They're in boxes in Maud's car. There are quite a lot of them, so a few of you should fetch them. Not including me."

Maud tossed a bunch of keys to Harrison and he let them drop to the floor with a jangle. Maud raised her eyebrows at him, then turned to the man next to him.

"Frank?"

There was a silence. Then Frank bent down and picked up the keys.

"Come on, lads," he said, and three other officers followed him.

A few minutes later, there were seven boxes on the floor.

"Frank and Carrie," said Maud. "You're in charge of this. Select a couple of others and go through everything.

Make a comprehensive list of what you find. Photos up on the board. We'll review it all when I get back."

"Where are you going?" Lovell asked.

"We. I'm going to interview Mr. Salter. You're coming with me."

Sixty-six

"Mr. Salter." Maud spoke in a low, clear tone, but the old man in the armchair didn't raise his head to look at her. Although the day was mild and the room felt too hot to Maud, he was dressed in thick corduroy trousers and a cardigan with oversized buttons. "I am Detective Inspector Maud O'Connor."

"He only hears what he wants to hear," said Penny.

Maud had asked Niall to be present at her interview with Alec Salter, and he had brought his wife with him because, he said, she knew his father better than almost anyone. Lovell opened his notebook and uncapped his pen.

"Mr. Salter," repeated Maud more loudly. "I am a detective. Do you understand what I'm saying?"

"Am I in trouble?" His tone was fretful and he rubbed his hands together in an agitated way.

"Of course not," said Niall.

"I want to ask you a few questions about your wife, Mr. Salter," said Maud. "I am talking to everyone about what happened to her."

He looked at her then, with a cunning air that unsettled her.

"You won't find her," he said.

"Do you know what happened to your wife?"

"Charlie?"

"Yes. Do you know what happened to her and why she never came home?"

"She's always late," he said. "Woman's prero—" He stopped, looked confused. "Something's gone amiss."

"He means he can't remember the word," said Penny.

"My arse," said the old man.

"Dad." Niall spoke reproachfully.

"What? What do you want?"

"Mr. Salter," said Maud. "Do you remember—?"

"Everyone's gone," he said.

"I haven't gone," said Niall. "Me and Penny are still here."

Alec looked at him with such contempt that Maud almost had to look away.

"Where's Etty?"

"She's not well."

"Pretty little thing. A bit wild, but she'll get over that."

"Your wife disappeared on 22nd December 1990," said Maud. "She never came to your birthday party and she was never seen again."

"Everyone loves Charlie," said Alec angrily. "Charlie this and Charlie that. Good women make me sick. Now that Mary." He smiled at Maud and lifted his hands to gesture the outline of a woman's body, then added, "She was all right. You're not so bad yourself. Need a bit of lipstick and some heels."

"Will you tell me what happened to your wife?"

"People keep asking me that." He was irritable again, peevish.

"Did you see her that evening, Mr. Salter?"

"Are you the police?"

"Yes. I'm a detective and I'm looking into the disappearance—"

"I'm not stupid, you know. Something's going on and I'm not stupid. People talk to me as if I'm a child. A baby. I know things."

"What do you know?"

"You won't find it."

"What won't I find?"

"I'm not saying anything to you. I reserve ..." The expression of sudden and absolute bewilderment came into his face again.

"Do you mean your wife's body?"

"What?"

"Do you mean—?"

"Where's Etty?"

"Dad—"

"Go away. I'm sick of you."

Penny suddenly stood and yanked open the window. Then she turned and bent down to the old man and said, quite calmly, "Well, we're all sick of you as well."

"Penny," said Niall. He seemed, thought Maud, to

have been reduced to speaking single words. His face was pink with awkwardness.

"Niall stayed," said Penny to Alec, loud and slow. "Everyone else left, and he stayed because he thought it was the right thing to do. He saved your business. We've looked after you in your old age because there was no one else to do it. And you've never once shown gratitude."

"That's enough, Penny."

"I think this interview is over," said Maud.

Sixty-seven

Greg pulled up at Hemingford railway station and leaned over to kiss his wife on the cheek.

"I'll be home soon," he said.

Katherine put the flat of her hand against his cheek and looked at him searchingly.

"You can come home now," she said. "You don't need to be doing this, you know. I don't really understand why you are."

"I promised Morgan."

"Morgan's fine," said Katherine. "More than fine. He's like a cat that's got the cream. What's happened is beyond his wildest dreams." She raised her eyebrows. "Do you think there's a tiny part of him that's pleased Bridget Woolfe died like that? He's famous all over the world now."

"Kathy!"

"I don't like what's happening. It's like feeding time at the zoo. Journalists everywhere, other podcasters, everyone wanting a piece of the action, and Morgan's the star of the show. Glensted's famous—there'll be tours of the place soon. It feels ..." She wrinkled her nose. "A bit obscene. This is your dad we're talking about."

"I know."

"Morgan doesn't need you any more. He hasn't needed you for a long time. Why can't you accept that? He's a famous TV personality and now he's an even more famous podcaster—"

"And I do odd jobs. I know." Greg didn't seem put out. "But I think you're wrong. I think he needs me more than he knows. There's something febrile about him. It reminds me of how he was after Dad died."

"That's what I'm worried about. Everything's got stirred up again. I can see it in your face."

"What can you see?"

"Distress," she said simply.

"I'll just stay a few more days." He looked at his watch. "You'd better go or you'll miss your train."

Morgan was pacing up and down the upstairs room he had transformed into his study. Greg could almost feel the energy pulsing off him.

"Don't you see?" Morgan said. "Everything's changed. We're in charge now."

"In charge?"

"In charge of the investigation. We've set the agenda. The police are following in our footsteps."

"And that's a *good* thing?"

"It's amazing. What we need now is to interview that new detective."

"I thought she wanted to interview us."

"Exactly. She thinks she's interviewing us and all the while we're interviewing her. It's like the Larsen effect."

"What?"

"Acoustic feedback. It's the positive loop gain—"

"Enough." Greg held up his hands.

"Anyway, we need Inspector Maud O'Connor." Morgan paused in his pacing and looked out of the window at the marshlands and, beyond them, the sea. "She's quite a colourful character, don't you think?"

"She's younger than I'd have expected."

"Great clothes," said Morgan enthusiastically.

"Morgan, do you think—"

"And then someone was telling me she's got a sidekick hidden away in the pub. Maybe we should have a drink or a meal there this evening, take a look."

Sixty-eight

Returning to the Anchor that evening, Maud saw the Ackerley brothers sitting at a small table in the corner. A woman had cornered Morgan and was asking him questions, while Greg nursed a beer. Maud paused, then made up her mind. She walked across to him.

"DI O'Connor," said Morgan, standing up. Maud could see that he had a raggedy, intense charm about him, with his thin, lived-in face and dark eyes that held her gaze.

"Nice talking to you," he said to the woman, indicating she should go, and she took a last, ardent look at him and sidled away.

"We were hoping to see you," he said.

"Really?"

"We'd like to talk to you at some point. For the podcast, that is. Greg and I started it as a little project, for ourselves really. But it seems to have become something bigger. It's all gone a bit crazy." He gave a crooked, self-deprecating smile that she didn't trust at all. "And so we need to hear a voice of reason and sanity."

"This is a live investigation," said Maud. "Not an entertainment."

"Of course. I wouldn't ask you to do anything unprofessional. Just give a general sense of things from your point of view. I think that citizens have a right to know about their police force."

Maud smiled slightly at his sententious tone.

"I'll think about it."

"I'd like it to be in the next episode," said Morgan. "It might help you as well. People might come forward."

"I'll consider it. But before anything else I'd like to talk to your brother."

"Me?" said Greg.

He stood up and gestured to the chair opposite.

"I can't stop. But could you meet me down by the river tomorrow, probably early afternoon?"

He was visibly startled.

"Why?"

"I know it might be painful but I'd like you to walk me through what happened on the day you found your father's body. I'll ask Etty Salter to come as well."

"Can I come too?" It was Morgan, sounding almost plaintive.

"I don't need you but I can't stop you," she said.

He grinned.

"That's good enough for me."

Sixty-nine

"It was in the van," said DC Dillon. "In the glove compartment, with the manual and the packet of tissues." Her voice was loud with excitement, and Maud held her mobile slightly way from her ear.

"Wasn't it searched?" said Maud.

"It actually belongs to a guy who helps her out."

Maud took a breath. There was no point complaining about it yet again.

"Do you want to see it?"

"I'll meet you in the station."

"When?"

"Now, of course."

Dillon looked at Maud as she snapped on the polythene gloves.

"I probably should have worn gloves," she said.

"Yes," said Maud.

"I didn't think it was necessary. We already knew Bridget Wolfe had handled it and it was in the van she'd been using."

"The good thing about rules," said Maud, "is that you don't have to think about them every time. You just follow them."

Maud opened the humble cheap notebook and saw the words "Charlotte Salter" written on the first page, in a beautifully shaped cursive script. As she started to turn the pages, her fingers were almost trembling with excitement. This had been the Holy Grail, the key, this is what—they assumed—Bridget Wolfe had been killed for. This is what her home had been burned down to destroy.

As she turned page after page of shopping lists, appointments, jotted memos, phone numbers, her excitement gradually faded.

"Anything about leaving home?" Dillon asked.

"It's not really that kind of a diary," said Maud.

She was flicking through the pages more quickly now, looking for any longer entries, anything that might show her plans or her feelings. Finally she reached the end and closed the book.

"I can't see anything there."

"So you think Bridget Wolfe might have got a bit carried away?" Dillon asked.

"And it got her killed." She pushed the book away. "It might be worth taking a closer look at the book, checking names and numbers, things like that. But I think it's another dead end." She gave a sour laugh. "What is it with this case?"

*

An hour later Maud leaned back on the table, facing her team. "This needs to be quick, I'm afraid. I've an appointment and I'm conscious it's the weekend and you all have lives."

"Where's Micky?" came a voice.

"He's no longer on the case," she said evenly. "First off, the boxes of evidence. What've we got?"

Carrie nodded at Frank Mason and he cleared his throat, then took out a page of typed notes from a transparent folder.

"First of all, the Polaroids," he said. "You'll see they are on the board, like you said." Everyone stepped forward and looked at the curled and fading images on the cork board. "There are forty-seven of them. They were taken at Alec Salter's birthday party, the day Charlotte Salter disappeared. We've tried to put them up in some sort of order. You can see all the food nicely laid out at the beginning, there's people talking, giving speeches, bits of dancing here. And then here"—he put his finger on the bottom of the board—"there are pictures from what must be the end, someone slumped on the floor, piled-up plates, cigarettes stubbed out in some kind of ladle."

"Yes, I see," said Maud thoughtfully. "Good."

"We couldn't identify all the people," said Carrie.

"It was a long time ago." Maud looked across the range of photos. "But that's Alec Salter, giving his birthday speech I guess. And that's Duncan Ackerley. He looks just like his sons. And there are the Salter

405

siblings; I think that is Greg Ackerley in the background, drinking beer. And that's young Etty Salter." She touched one of the pictures with her forefinger. "And again ..." She touched another one. "She seems worried. I guess she was wondering where her mother was." She tapped the photo softly, thinking how Etty looked both very different from her mother, and yet so similar.

"There's all sorts of stuff," said Carrie. "It's like a little museum. There's this." She held up a handbill. "'Has anyone seen Charlotte Salter?' I suppose the children must have done that and stuck it on lampposts."

Maud took it and looked at it.

"Nice face," she said.

"There's pieces of physical evidence." Frank picked up a dirty old woollen coat wrapped in polythene. Maud noticed approvingly how he and Carrie seemed at ease with each other. "This was Charlotte Salter's coat, found by the river. Actually, there were two pieces of evidence found by the river. There's also this." He picked up a small package. "These are Duncan Ackerley's glasses. They were apparently found on a bridge upstream from where his body was found."

Maud took the package and looked at the glasses with a slightly puzzled expression.

"It feels like one too many, don't you think?"

"What do you mean?" Carrie wrinkled her nose.

"Two different crimes and a piece of evidence for each one found by the river."

"I don't understand," said Dillon.

"It's probably nothing," said Maud. "Go on."

"There's various lists and reports here," said Mason. "There's the pathologist's report on Duncan Ackerley. Drowned, but he had a wound on the side of his head."

"What kind of wound?"

"Inconclusive. There's the transcript of the Alec Salter interview. Under caution." He examined another piece of paper. "They found that Charlotte Salter had packed a bag of clothes for her daughter."

"Anything else?"

Carrie held up a bundle of paper.

"There's a stack of witness statements. The latest person I could find here who said they saw Charlotte Salter was a woman who saw her on the evening of the party."

"What was she doing?"

"Walking—in that coat Frank just showed you—in the direction of the party."

"How far away from the party was she?"

"I don't know, but the woman lived in Glensted, so it can't be very far."

"That woman sounds like someone we should talk to."

"I did the maths," said Carrie. "If she was still alive, she'd be over a hundred and twenty."

Maud groaned.

"There's plenty of gossip in here as well," continued Carrie. "Alec's alleged to have been having an affair with a local woman."

"There's no alleged about that. He did."

"And Charlotte Salter had two affairs. Allegedly."

"Yes, with Victor Pearce, the café owner, and with Duncan Ackerley." Maud pulled a face. "We should check out those rumours about Charlotte Salter." She stepped back and addressed the room. "So, thirty years ago the police started by thinking it had to be Alec Salter. They compromised the investigation because they pursued that single-mindedly. Then Duncan Ackerley dies. After a few weeks of getting nowhere, they suddenly decide it must be him and he killed himself in a fit of remorse. But Duncan Ackerley didn't kill Bridget Wolfe. At least there's one thing in this case we can be sure of."

"Could Alec Salter have done it?"

"I've met him. It doesn't seem very likely. He's old and frail and cognitively impaired. But let's not rule it out."

Maud paused, then walked back to the cork board. She gently touched one of the Polaroids: three cigarette stubs in the scoop of the ladle, lipstick marks on one of them.

"This one's interesting," she said, and no one could tell if she was talking to them or to herself.

Carrie grinned. "Yes," she said. "That's what I thought."

Maud sat back on the table, swinging her legs in their sturdy boots, leaning forward.

"Right," she said. "That's the new evidence. What about the rest of you? Has anyone found anything new. Jack?"

"Sorry," he said. "It wasn't for want of trying. I've

been trawling through Bridget Wolfe's life. It was quite colourful. Parents both dead. She's got one brother, who lives in London. He seems genuinely baffled by his sister's death—and by her life I'd say. Her cousin—the one who identified the remains—lives in Norwich and saw Bridget sometimes. He said that she had always been an outsider, an oddball. His wife thought she was on the spectrum." He shrugged. "She'd obviously been through difficult times. But he said that the last time he saw her she was cheerful, very keen on getting chickens. She hadn't lived here for more than a few years. She was a bit rootless. A few years ago she was in that group of people who chained themselves to trees to stop a motorway being built. She had plenty of money in the bank and spent almost nothing. She wasn't in a relationship and in fact hadn't been for years as far as we could find out from her brother and cousin. She had breast cancer in 2018 but it was caught early. We looked at her phone records and nothing leaped out. Frank had a bit of a trawl through social media."

"It didn't take long," said Frank. "Not much to report. She wasn't on Facebook or on Twitter. She did use Instagram occasionally, but only to put up photos of objects she'd found while clearing houses. Nothing from the Salter house, though. And she didn't have many followers."

"OK," said Maud. "Yes, Fred?"

A lanky, spoon-faced man had raised his hand. "It's not a question really. It's something I heard. It's probably not relevant."

"Go on."

"I was speaking to Mary and Gerry Thorne like you told me to, and she said something about Victor Pearce and Elizabeth Salter having been an item."

"*Elizabeth* Salter? Etty. Not Charlotte?"

"That's what she said. She said she saw Elizabeth Salter throwing a glass of wine over him."

"When? Was this thirty years ago?"

"No, now. A few days ago."

"Have you talked to Victor Pearce?"

"No, I thought—"

"What are you waiting for? Lastly, you should all know that Dillon found Charlotte Salter's diary, the one that Bridget Wolfe mentioned in the latest episode of the podcast."

There was a murmur around the room and Maud put her hand up to stop it.

"Yes, I know," she said. "We thought this was going to be the key to it all." She paused. "You can all tell that there's a 'but'" coming. It's just a collection of shopping lists and phone numbers. Dillon's going to do some cross-checking but we're not hopeful. It looks like we'll have to do some more police work."

She jumped to her feet. The room felt different this morning, the air lighter.

"Right," she said. "Here's how we're going to proceed. I believe we are looking at three cases that is also a single case: one solution to three deaths. Someone who was here thirty years ago has been triggered, presumably by hearing about the discovery of a diary, to

410

kill again. So I intend to split this team up into three working groups. You lot here." She made a sweeping motion with her hand. "You will be looking into the disappearance of Charlotte Salter. Heather, you can be in charge of that."

Heather Dillon nodded.

"You lot." She demarcated the central group. "You're looking at the death of Duncan Ackerley. Jack's in charge. And the rest will continue looking at Bridget Wolfe's murder. Frank, you can coordinate that. I want you to check the alibis of all those people who were also involved, however peripherally, with the cases of thirty years ago. That is: Victor Pearce, the Thornes, and all the Salters and Ackerleys, of course. OK? Oh—and also ask them if they've heard that podcast and, if so, what day and time they listened to it. In other words, did they hear it before Bridget's death? OK?"

There was a murmur of agreement, then Dillon raised her hand.

"Is this including old Mr. Salter?" she asked.

"He was the main suspect thirty years ago, even if they couldn't manage to pin it on him, and he remains a suspect now."

She pushed a hand through her tangle of curls.

"Jack, I want one of your team to visit Frances Ackerley this morning to ask her about these." She picked up the package lying beside her on the table and handed it over to him. "Duncan Ackerley's glasses. Find out how often he wore them. And try and get a sense of the woman, see if anything feels off."

411

Jack nodded.

"Also, take the photo of the ladle with cigarette stubs in it and show it to her. See if she remembers anything."

She turned back to DC Dillon. "Heather, an old woman called Gwyneth Mayhew saw Charlotte early in the evening on her disappearance, the last known sighting of her. One of your lot needs to go to 23 Hazelwood Avenue and walk at a moderate speed from there to the barn up near the river, and tell me how long it takes."

She pointed to the map she had taped to the wall that morning.

"Go there by this route." She ran her forefinger along the roads. "And then back by this. Oh, and check that there are streetlights on her road—it would have been pitch dark at that time of year. If there are, make sure they were there thirty years ago. Everyone feed what they've got to Carrie, who will coordinate it all. OK? Any questions before I go?"

"Yeah," called an officer standing by the door, his hands thrust deep in his pockets. "What some of us want to know is, are you actually getting anywhere with all this delving into the distant past?"

"Thanks for asking," said Maud. "I believe I am."

SEVENTY

Maud drove to Niall Salter's house and parked behind his van. As she got out of the car, he appeared round the side of the house carrying a metal ladder.

"You're early," he said.

Maud looked at her watch. "Four minutes."

"I don't know if Etty's ready."

"I can wait."

"I'm worried she's not up to this."

"She said she was when I spoke to her earlier this morning."

"There's saying and there's meaning."

Maud nodded, studying him. He was stocky, with thinning sandy hair and a round, ruddy, outdoor face. The furrows on his brow looked as if they'd had been chiselled by decades of bemusement and anxiety.

"Are you up to it yourself?" she asked him.

"Going to the barn? I've been past it dozens of times, hundreds even."

"How is your sister?"

"She's covered in burns and blisters. Penny says her body looks like she's been tortured."

"I'm sorry," said Maud. "She's lucky to be alive. She was brave to try and save Bridget."

"She cries all the time. You probably think that's normal, after what she witnessed. Let me tell you, it's not. When she came back to Glensted this time, she seemed carved out of stone."

The front door opened and Penny Salter came out. Maud introduced herself and held out her hand but Niall's wife just glared at her.

"I hope you know what you're doing," she said. "Because if you think dragging Niall and Etty down memory lane will cause anything but unnecessary pain—"

"It's OK, Penny."

Etty had joined her. She wore a white T-shirt and black cotton trousers. Her hair was still wet from the shower. The burn on her cheek was an ugly red welt.

"Shall we walk from here?" asked Maud. "We could drive."

"Walk," said Etty. She put on a pair of sunglasses.

Niall led the way until they reached the road that led to the barn, when he slowed and the two women joined him.

"Talk me through it," said Maud. "As far as you remember. Did you both arrive at the party by foot?"

"I did," said Etty. "I came from a friend's house. It was the end of term and I'd been to a sleepover the evening before and then we spent the day together. I wasn't looking forward to the party; none of us were.

Lots of drunk middle-aged people making fools of themselves." She raised her eyebrows but Maud couldn't see her expression. "The same age as I am now. I'm my mother's age. I think of that often."

"I drove," said Niall, uncomfortable at his sister's dreamy voice. "I parked there." He pointed to a field.

"What time did you get here?"

"I only know what I've said over and over again, not really what the truth is. Presumably you have a record of it."

"Yes," said Maud.

Etty looked at her and almost smiled.

"All right, I'll say it again. I got here at the beginning of the party. I thought I should, seeing as it was my father's birthday party. I stayed until the end."

"Who else was there when you arrived?"

"Who?" Etty frowned. "I'm not sure. It was so long ago. I know Dad was there. And Niall—he either came just before me or just after."

"Just before, I think," said Niall.

"You were taking photos."

"You took the photos?" asked Maud.

"I borrowed a Polaroid camera for a while. I didn't take many. Someone else took over."

"What about your other brothers?"

She saw both of them flinch at the plural.

"I think Paul got there at about the same time as us," said Etty slowly. "But you can check that. I think Ollie got there a bit later. You can ask him."

"I called him a couple of hours ago. He said he

415

thought shortly before seven, which is what he said to the police at the time. But he also said what you've said: that it's a memory of a memory of a memory."

"And yet I feel like it happened yesterday," said Etty. "Or that it was about to happen."

She was staring at the barn, which had scaffolding all round it.

"Long ago, before I was born," said Niall, "they used to keep cows here. Then it was used for storing straw and bits of machinery. It was a good party space for a while. Now it's going to be turned into a home that nobody in this area could afford in a million years. It'll be all plate glass and special oak floors and someone from London will probably buy it as their weekend retreat."

"You remember your father being there when you arrived, and also Paul. Who else are you sure was there?"

"All the Ackerleys," said Etty.

"Definitely?"

"I think so anyway. Though I'm not sure when Morgan arrived. He was hanging out with Ollie and his gang, smoking weed."

"Not Frances," said Niall. "She wasn't there."

"She never came to parties," said Etty. "You probably know all of this but she suffered from severe depression for years."

"For some reason," added Niall, "she recovered remarkably, after the first couple of years. Shock, I expect," he said vaguely. "Maybe it did something to her system. Shook her up, like a reboot."

Etty made a small, exasperated sound.

"Mary Thorne came early," she said next. "I know she was there. I remember seeing my father put his hand on her back."

She gave a small shiver.

"There are two entrances," said Maud, looking at the barn. "So people could have come and gone without being noticed."

"I guess."

"And nobody saw your mother?"

"You know that. Why are you even asking?"

"Did she say what time she was going to arrive?"

"She would have been there at the start," said Etty. "She'd organised most of it."

"When did you start worrying?"

"By eight," said Niall. "Or nine."

"Earlier than that," said Etty. "I knew something was wrong. She would never have turned up that late. Dad kept talking about her being unreliable but she wasn't."

"You say you were there until the end," Maud said to Etty. "But you left the party to make the phone call."

"That's right. Morgan came with me," she remembered. "Or at least, he was there when I phoned."

She could remember it: pressing the coins into the slot, waiting to hear her mother's voice though knowing she wouldn't. Then Morgan telling her she should call the emergency services.

"And you?" Maud turned to Niall. "Did you leave at all?"

He cleared his throat.

"I was outside with my wife. My wife to be. As a

matter of fact, we'd split up. She came to find me and was quite upset."

"Nothing else?"

"I think I went for a little walk with someone."

"Someone?"

"Why does it matter?"

His face was flaming.

'Just say it," said Etty. "Whatever you're feeling embarrassed about thirty years on, spit it out, Niall."

"I was with another girl."

"A girl."

"That friend of yours, Etty."

"What friend?"

"You know. Gemma."

"You and Gemma Thorne? No!"

"Just a little stroll. To clear my head."

"She was my age. Fifteen."

"I was feeling upset."

"And your brother Paul: was he there all evening as well?"

Maud knew all the answers, of course, but hearing them remember that evening was helping her to feel it as well, turning the abstract into the real and solid.

"He went home early," said Etty. "He hated parties like that. He was at home when I called to see if Charlie was there."

"You didn't see him go?"

"That doesn't mean anything. He would just have taken himself quietly off, the way he often did. Quietly, not wanting to make a fuss."

"Why are you asking all of this?" Niall asked. "It's ancient history. The police went over and over things. We said everything then."

"Let's have a quick look inside, shall we?"

She walked over to the barn's double doors. They were held shut by a long piece of timber which she lifted. She and Niall creaked open the doors, and they all stepped into the cavernous space. Light slanted through the high windows and came in spears from the broken slats in the roof.

"This will be a big job," said Niall, staring around him.

"How changed is it?" asked Maud.

"It's virtually as it was. I know they've laid the drainage pipes and electric cables outside, things like that. But inside, it's much as it has been for decades. More dilapidated, that's all."

Etty didn't speak, but she took off her sunglasses and walked slowly round the room, trailing a hand against the rough wood.

"It was all lit up," said Niall. "Duncan and Greg did that. And there were two long trestle tables there." He pointed. "For drinks and food. There was a sound system over there. People danced. And then, all of a sudden, it ended."

'You all went back to the farmhouse at the same time?" Maud asked.

"Me and Ollie walked back because Dad was well over the limit," said Etty. "He drove."

"And I had my car there so I drove myself," said

Niall. "I remember arriving at the same time as that young police officer."

"Who was useless," added Etty.

"And your brother Paul was there when you arrived?"

"Yes."

"So who was left at the party?"

"Everyone," said Niall. "Though I think they all went home pretty quickly after we'd made our dramatic exit."

"What did the five of you do after the police officer had left?"

"We waited up quite a long time." Etty started to walk back towards the doors and they followed. "Dad argued with Paul. It was ugly, awful."

"Then I think Ollie and Paul went to their separate rooms. I know Dad did."

"After he'd called Mary Thorne and whispered intimate things down the phone," said Etty. She touched her raw and puffy cheek with the tips of her fingers. "God, I sound about fifteen again, don't I?"

"And you two?"

"I drove around," answered Niall. Maud thought he looked suddenly ill.

"Where to?"

"Hemingford. At one point I stopped and smoked several cigarettes, one after the other. A way of killing time, I guess."

"And I sat in the kitchen and waited for her to come home," said Etty. "And then it was the next day and she hadn't."

SEVENTY-ONE

Outside in the dazzle of sunlight, Niall looked at his watch.

"I'm late for a client," he said.

The two women watched as he jogged away. Maud took a surreptitious look at her watch. It was midday. In four hours she would see Silas.

"I've another request," she said to Etty.

Etty put her sunglasses back on.

"What?"

"I want you and Greg Ackerley to go through the same process down by the river, tell me everything you remember from when you found Duncan Ackerley's body."

"When?"

"Now. Greg has already agreed and I think Morgan wants to come too."

"I bet he does."

"So?"

Etty shrugged her thin shoulders. Maud could see the sharpness of her collarbone.

"Let me call Greg and tell him we're on our way then."

She made the call. Then she turned to a yellow sign attached to the wall by the barn entrance: J. FLYNN AND SONS, BUILDING COMPANY. QUALITY BY DESIGN. At the bottom was a phone number. Maud dialled it. When a woman answered, Maud identified herself.

"I'm calling from the barn at Mason's Farm. You're doing the renovation, right? Well, you need to stop." The woman started to protest but Maud continued speaking. "No, no, listen. You need to stop right now. It's a crime scene. You'll receive a letter of confirmation."

The woman continued to protest. Maud held the phone away from her ear and looked at Etty with a slightly amused expression.

"Then tell your boss," she said finally. "He can ring me on this number, if he wants, and then I'll tell him what I've told you."

She ended the call and the two women started to walk towards the river.

"You really think you can solve all three cases at once?" Etty asked.

"I think it's all three or none."

"And I'm not a suspect?"

"Can I ask you something?"

"You mean, instead of answering my question. Go ahead."

"What happened between you and Victor Pearce?"

Etty's pace didn't slow and Maud couldn't make out her expression behind her sunglasses, but she could feel Etty shrink into herself. For several long seconds she didn't reply.

"Don't you hate your job?" she said at last. "Poking into people's private lives, making them look at things they've kept hidden away for years, forcing them back into their self-loathing and shame?"

"Are you ashamed?"

"I was then and I am now—though he's the one who should feel ashamed and instead I think he feels complacent and wisely sorrowful. For nearly a year we had a—a thing. We had sex, that is. I was sixteen so it wasn't actually illegal. He waited a few weeks till I was over that particular line. He was in love with my mother, I think, or at least had a crush on her. So when she disappeared I was like this weird substitute."

"And you?"

"I was in hell and he made it more hellish. Which was perhaps what I wanted. I don't know. I've tried very hard not to think about it."

"Until you came back to Glensted."

"Until I came back to Glensted."

"What can I get you?" asked Victor.

He was wearing a shirt whose bright swirls of colour made Carrie's eyes hurt.

"Tomato juice, if you can make it really, really hot."

He laughed. "I can do that."

"And I'd like the spaghetti puttanesca."

"One spaghetti puttanesca, Poll," he called through to the kitchen. "When's it due?"

For a moment, Carrie thought he was talking about the spaghetti.

"Oh," she said. "Right. Soon."

"You're the friend of the detective, aren't you? I've seen you together."

Carrie made a non-committal noise.

"It took years for Glensted to get over Charlie and Duncan," said Victor. "Decades. So this is very painful."

"You knew Charlotte Salter well, didn't you?"

"I'd say I was one of the few people who understood her."

"I heard you say that on the podcast."

"She was a beautiful soul."

Carrie had heard him say that as well.

"Your place must be one of the hubs of the community," she said. "How long has it been here?"

"Thirty-four years," said Victor. "Who would have thought it possible? Time, eh?" And he shook his head wonderingly.

"So you must get a feel for everything that's going on."

"People tell me things," he said. "They know they can trust me."

"I'm sure."

"In that room there, for instance." He jerked his head backwards. "That's where the journalist interviewed

Etty, shortly after Charlie went missing. I heard her sobbing her heart out."

"What journalist?"

"Alice something-or-other. From *The Herald*. She's still around. She's been covering the latest tragedy."

"That's a long time to be on the same beat."

"I think she took a break and only recently returned."

"So what did Etty say in the interview?"

"I don't think it ever got published."

Waiting for her puttanesca, Carrie found Alice Clayton on Twitter and sent her a message. A few minutes later, a reply pinged on to her screen with a mobile number to call.

SEVENTY-TWO

Etty slowed as they approached the river.

"Are you OK?" Maud asked.

"Why shouldn't I be?"

"You found a body here. The dead body of someone you cared for. That must have been a terrible thing to cope with. And then a few days ago a woman died in your arms."

"Look," said Etty, "I'm sure that it's part of your new sensitive policing method to create some kind of emotional bond with people. But I'd really rather you just asked the questions you need to ask." She gestured around. "And what's all this? Is it to create the right atmosphere? I know I look a bit of a wreck and I probably am a bit of a wreck but I'd rather do this professionally. If you want to interview me, I'd prefer it was in an interview room, being recorded, if necessary with a lawyer present."

She stopped and looked at Maud, who was standing with her back to her, apparently just staring at the river.

"I'm sorry," Etty said. "Are you actually listening to what I'm saying?"

Maud turned.

"This isn't an interview," she said. "Anyway, we can't go back to the police station just yet. As I told you, we're meeting the Ackerleys."

"Are they going to interview you for their podcast?"

"I don't know. What do you think?"

"Are you serious?"

"I'm serious about asking what you think?"

"If you're asking, I'll tell you. I think it's completely inappropriate for a detective in an ongoing investigation to talk about it in public."

"Have you listened to the podcast?"

"Yes."

"What did you make of it?"

"Have you ever had someone read your diary without your permission?" Etty looked challengingly at Maud but the detective didn't reply. "Have you ever been burgled? It didn't just feel like a crime. It felt like being invaded and trampled over and violated."

"But if they solve the crimes," said Maud, "would that make you feel different about it?"

"You're a detective. Aren't you the one who's supposed to solve them?"

"I don't care who solves them. I want them to be solved."

"So where did you arrange to meet?"

"At the bridge, where Duncan Ackerley's glasses were found."

Etty glanced at the detective as they walked, a nimbus of fair curls around an alert, clever face, a slight figure, so young, so apparently self-assured.

"One of my team is going to be joining us as well," Maud said.

"Why do I need to know that?"

"It might not bring back happy memories. You probably met him when you were being questioned. Jack Lovell."

"I don't remember him. Not that it matters."

They saw the two brothers standing by the bridge, apparently in conversation. Lovell was standing to one side. Etty turned to Maud.

"Are we just chess pieces that you're pushing around, hoping that something will turn up?"

"Give me a chance," said Maud. "Something may come of this."

She was speaking in a soothing voice. Etty recognised it as the voice an adult might use in talking to a badly behaved child and she was about to say something, but she stopped herself. Maud wasn't the officer who had arrested her and put her in a cell. She suddenly thought about how she must seem: a distraught, damaged, middle-aged woman, behaving badly to anyone and everyone.

"I don't know what I can add," she said, in as calm a tone as she could manage. "It's been such a long time."

As they approached, the two brothers turned to them. Morgan looked sprightly and animated, Greg more solemn, his shoulders hunched.

"Etty!" said Morgan, and she could feel his eyes rest on her blistered cheek. "So good to see you. How are you? I wanted to come and visit you but Greg said we should let you rest up a bit first. What a terrible, terrible thing."

Greg came across and put out his hand.

"Are you all right?" he asked.

"Getting there," said Etty, briefly putting her hand into his. "Niall and Penny are looking after me. I'll be gone in a few days' time."

He nodded.

"It's all been so shit for you," he said. "Some home-coming. I'm really sorry."

"It's not my home," she said.

"No. Of course not."

"I'm not really sure why we're here," she said.

Greg shrugged. "She said she wants to get a clear picture in her mind."

"Do you have a clear picture in yours?"

Greg nodded.

"Actually, yes," he said. "I remember every minute of that day. You don't forget things like that, however old you get. There'll always be a before and an after."

Etty turned away. She too could feel the wind and the cold, and feel the terror in her chest as she and Greg pushed the boat over the mud and into the icy water. She could see the shape bobbing in the river. She could see Duncan's dead eyes staring at her.

Jack Lovell walked over towards Maud. He looked puzzled, wary.

"You asked me to be here," he said. "It's the weekend, and I've left the wife furious and the twins screaming, but here I am. Why?"

"You know what this is?" Maud gestured towards the bridge.

"It's where Duncan Ackerley left his glasses before he jumped." Maud didn't reply, so Lovell continued. "I thought this was the one bit of the case where everyone agreed."

"All right. Describe it to me: what everyone agrees on."

The two detectives walked out on to the bridge, curving upwards until they reached the middle. Maud looked around, up the river and then down towards the sea.

"So what happened?" she said.

"Duncan Ackerley is feeling remorseful so he—"

Maud interrupted him. "Don't talk about his state of mind. Just tell me what he did."

Jack Lovell clenched his jaw and flexed the muscles before replying.

"He comes to the middle of the bridge. He takes off his glasses and places them on the edge, round about here."

He tapped the barrier.

"Why?

"I thought you didn't want me to talk about his state of mind. But what else could he have done?"

"He could have left them on. He could have put them in his pocket."

"Does it really make a difference?"

"Maybe not."

"All right, he could have left them on or put them in his pocket but he didn't. Perhaps he didn't want to see where he was going. It's a long way down. He put them on the edge here and he climbed over and threw himself into the water."

"He had an injury on his head," said Maud. "About here." She gestured with one finger above her right ear.

"Perhaps on his way down to the water, he struck his head on one of the pillars. That meant he was unconscious or semi-conscious when he hit the water. It would have made things quicker, probably. Or perhaps he hit a boulder or some sharp object in the river." He looked at Maud, waiting for a response. "So what do we do now?"

Maud nodded at the group behind them.

"I thought we could all take a walk down the river."

"Is that really a profitable use of our time? Why waste time on the one bit of the case we're sure about?"

Maud shook her head slowly.

"I think this is the key," she said. "But I can't make sense of it."

"I've no idea what you're talking about."

They walked back to the bank of the river where Etty, Greg and Morgan were waiting. The brothers were deep in conversation and Etty was facing away from them, staring across the water.

"I wanted to talk about the events of Christmas Day, 1990," said Maud. "So I thought it might be helpful to do it here. This is where your father's glasses were found on 29th December and what led detectives to conclude he had taken his own life. Shall we head downriver to where his body was found?"

They set off in an awkward group. Maud walked in front with Etty, Greg and Morgan behind and then Jack Lovell taking the rear. Maud first spoke to Etty, but kept looking back at the Ackerleys.

"You arrived at the Ackerley house at about one, right?"

"That's right."

"Where were the rest of your family?"

Etty lit a cigarette, shielding the flame of her lighter with a hand. She took a deep drag before she spoke, staring straight in front of her.

"It hadn't been a good morning. Alec had gone out for a walk."

"With anyone?"

"He said he wanted to be alone. Paul was up in his room. He was in a bad way. I think Niall had gone out. I can't remember where Ollie was. He didn't come with me, anyway."

"And Duncan wasn't there when you arrived, is that right?"

"He'd gone out earlier," said Morgan, from behind.

"Who was there?"

"Frances was making Christmas dinner," said Etty. "And Greg was helping her."

"I had just got back from a walk," said Greg.

"Yes, I saw that in the file," said Maud. "Did you go with anyone?"

"No."

"Why?"

"Why what?"

"Why did you go for a walk on your own?"

"I don't know. I just wanted to clear my head. I went that way, towards the sea."

"You'll notice that nobody has an alibi," said Morgan, almost cheerfully. "We thought we might do a special episode on that. About alibis and lack of alibis."

A woman with a Dalmatian was approaching them and they had to stop and step apart to let her through. She looked at the group with obvious curiosity, and then jerked her head when she recognised Morgan. They didn't speak until she was some distance away.

"That's not quite true," said Maud. She looked at Etty. "You had an alibi. Your brother, Paul."

"Not for the walk over," said Etty. She remembered Paul's muddy shoes that morning, then pushed the memory away. Nobody really had an alibi, not even her.

"And Greg had an alibi," said Lovell. "I read it in the file. A family with a dog. Bowden was their name, I think."

"The Bowdens," said Greg. "I forgot."

Etty stopped, so suddenly that Morgan bumped into her from behind. She looked around and swallowed hard. She saw the little landing stage. It looked weather-beaten, parts of it had rotted away, but she had a flash of memory that was physical rather than visual. She

433

could feel what it was like to be there, the cold, the growing sense of recognition that was spreading in the stomach and the chest, that shape in the water.

All of them stepped down the bank on to the wooden platform.

"Careful," said Greg, "I'm not sure it's safe."

They all stood staring across the water.

"So this is where you saw the body?"

"We saw it—him, Duncan—from the bank," said Etty. "He was there." She pointed. "He'd been caught on the buoy. How weird: do you think that's the same buoy, after all these years? Same buoy, same river flowing out to sea."

"So tell me what you did when you saw the body."

"We didn't know it was a body at first," said Greg, glancing at Etty as he spoke. "Or we probably did."

"I thought it was Mum," said Etty. "I was sure."

"I guess I did too," said Greg. "I told Etty not to come with me but she insisted."

"I had to see. I had to know."

They were speaking in a kind of duet, passing from one to the other, both staring out at the sluggish tug of the water rippling past them.

"I rowed," said Greg. "And she looked out."

"Then I saw. I saw it wasn't Mum. For a moment . . ." Here Etty looked quickly at Greg, then back at the river. "For a moment, I felt this stab of utter relief. Then I saw it was Duncan. I saw his open eyes gazing at me."

Morgan was staring at them both, as if he had never heard the full story before.

"Greg was very calm," said Etty. "He made me take the oars and he tried to pull Duncan into the boat, but he was too heavy. So I tried to row while he held on to the body, but the boat was barely moving and we swapped. Greg rowed and I held on to it. On to Duncan."

"You're right, I was calm," said Greg. "I didn't feel it then. I just needed to get him to the shore."

"We dragged him up the mud."

"And we tried to bring him back."

"But he was dead."

They stopped. There was silence, the small waves slapping on the mud and the birds crying out.

"All right then," said Etty at last. "You brought us all to the place that's been haunting us for thirty years. It's one of the places I see behind my eyes when I can't sleep at night."

"You know what?" said Morgan, speaking at last and with no trace of his usual theatricality. "It's not just that our father died. Or Charlie went missing. It's that it destroyed all the happy things from before that. I used to love this river. We used to swim here." He nudged Greg. "We used to sit here with our fishing rods. Sometimes Dad used to join us, even though I don't think he enjoyed it that much."

Maud looked at him and smiled.

"I used to fish with my dad, too. What did you catch?"

"Crabs, mainly. But sometimes we'd get mackerel. We used to take them home and fry them."

435

Maud raised her eyebrows. "Mackerel? I didn't associate that with rivers."

"This isn't any old river. It's almost the sea here."

Maud knelt down, dipped her hand in the water and let the water flow against her fingers.

"It's cold," she said, and stood up and brought her fingers to her lips. She suddenly smiled. "It's salt."

Then her eyes narrowed. "Who's that staring at us?" she asked. "Is it another journalist?"

"No," said Etty after a pause. "That's Ollie. Why has he come back?"

SEVENTY-THREE

Maud was almost late. She ran up to her room in the Anchor, washed her face, changed into baggy jeans and a sleeveless T-shirt, untied her hair and shook it into its riot of curls. She put her head round Carrie's door and told her she was going for a walk with Silas and would be back later.

He called to say he was nearly there and she went on to the street to meet him. She saw him walking towards her and it was like seeing someone she barely knew: a broad-shouldered, good-looking man with a quick stride. He'd had his hair cut and she didn't recognise the damson-pink shirt he was wearing. Yet it had only been a few days.

She went towards him and he raised a hand and gave that lovely, easy smile. She could feel fear and desire deep in her stomach and she tried not to let them show in her face.

"Maud," he said, and kissed her.

A camera flashed.

"Fuck," she said, whirling around and seeing a small man with a big camera grinning at her.

"Come on." Silas took her arm and they walked rapidly out of Glensted. "Where shall we go?"

"How long have you got?" Maud asked.

"A couple of hours."

"You really couldn't stay the night? We could walk on the coastal path and then have dinner . . ."

He pulled a face. "Sorry," he said. "Things I can't rearrange. Work stuff."

"On a Sunday?"

"That's right."

She saw the stubborn set of his mouth.

"Let's go along the river for a bit then," she said. "There's a circular loop you can do."

They walked the way she had gone earlier with Etty, Morgan and Greg. The tide was higher, nearly to the path. Wind ruffled their hair, blew hers in a tangle over her face.

"How've you been?" he asked.

"I've been worried."

"I'm sorry about that."

"About us, Silas."

'I told you—"

"I know. You told me you were busy. So are you saying I'm just imagining things when I feel there's something badly wrong?"

"Things have been stressful at work," he said. "And I guess that makes me . . ." Then he stopped.

"Silas?"

"It's nothing."

"Silas, please, please tell me what you've been feeling. Nothing is as bad as being in the dark."

Though as she said this, she thought that perhaps there were things that were worse.

"I don't know, Maud."

"What don't you know?"

"I don't know."

"About us?" she made herself ask.

They stopped walking. He made a despairing gesture.

"I've just started this new work thing and it feels exciting but scary."

She waited.

"And we've bought a flat together. And then on top of that ..."

Again he stopped. She didn't speak.

"Then trying for a baby. Like, planning when to have sex. It just feels—well, you know."

"I don't. What does it feel?"

"Like everything's all happening at once, and maybe it's bad timing."

"So you're saying you want to hold off on the baby front?"

"I don't know."

"If we stopped trying for a few months, would that make a difference?"

"I don't know."

"What *do* you know?"

"I'm feeling pretty wretched."

"Why didn't you say any of this? Why did you just avoid it all?"

He thrust his hands into his pockets and stood staring out at the estuary, not looking at her. She watched his face, her chest aching.

"Because I'm saying maybe—maybe everything's been too fast, Maud."

"We've been together for four years."

"It's the timing."

"Do you mean it's not just the baby you're not sure about, Silas?"

"I don't know."

"Don't make me the one who has to say it." Maud pulled damp strands of hair from her cheek.

He turned to her then. She saw the effort it took for him to look her in the eyes and she gazed back, not flinching.

"I think we should press pause."

"On what?"

"I don't mean break up," he said. "I mean, just—have a little time on our own. Take stock." He saw her white face, and took her hand. "I do love you," he said. "Don't think I don't still love you."

Maud watched a small sailing boat out on the water, a figure at the helm like a cut-out in the glare of the sun. She thought of things she could say, but she didn't say them. What was the point? She wasn't going to plead with him.

"Maud?"

"Yes."

"I think I'll stay at my parents for a bit, to think things over."

"Right."

"Just a few weeks."

He let go of her hand.

"Maybe you should walk back the way you came," she said. "I'll go on a bit, do the loop."

"Are you all right?"

"Don't be so stupid, Silas. Just go."

SEVENTY-FOUR

"How was Silas?" Carrie asked as they sat in the bar, she with her spicy tomato juice and Maud with a large glass of red wine that she hoped would blur the edges of her pain, but it didn't.

"Busy with work," said Maud briskly.

Carrie glanced at her curiously, then looked away.

"Today," she said after a pause, "I went to Victor's."

"He's a creep," said Maud.

"What kind of creep?"

"A creep who was in love with Charlotte Salter and who, as soon as she disappeared, seduced her bereft teenage daughter."

"That's not good. Anyway, this creep told me about a journalist who'd interviewed Etty about her mother disappearing."

"You mean, when it was all going on?"

Carrie nodded. "So I met her—"

"You met her?"

"Alice Clayton."

"That name rings a bell."

"She's been covering the Bridget Wolfe murder."

Etty remembered a middle-aged woman with grey hair and an alert face, holding out her mike at that surprise press conference. She had asked about police incompetence.

"She never published the interview. She found out that Etty was a minor. It would have caused a ruckus."

"But?"

"But she gave me the recording. And a little machine to play it on."

"Wow."

"She's been thinking of going to see Etty again, to try and get another interview—but she's reluctant. She said it had been so rawly intimate that somehow it felt wrong to use it to get access now."

Maud drained her wine and stood up.

"Sounds like a nice woman. Let's go listen."

They sat in Carrie's room, Carrie in the soft chair by the window and Maud on her bed, her shoes off and knees drawn up. Carrie plugged in the machine and pressed "Play."

It was awkwardly constrained at first. Etty described her mother's family, her work, her interests, what she looked like. But something happened; the constraint fell away. Maud and Carrie listened to the young, ardent voice describing the woman who had gone missing over thirty years ago: in a yellow bikini in Cornwall; weeping every time she and her daughter watched *Dumbo*; playing football with her sons; holding Etty's forehead while she leaned over the toilet bowl and vomited the first time she had ever got drunk. Everyone liked her mother, she said, because she liked them. She made everyone feel special.

"Poor little thing," said Maud, as Etty's voice cracked.

Etty described the night of the party and the terrible days that followed, the police searching the house and dragging the pond, about finding Duncan's body on Christmas Day, about the case packed with Etty's clothes.

"I know she's still alive," she said. "I know she is. I know. If she was dead, I'd feel it."

But a few seconds later, she said she knew her mother was dead, because she would never have left without Etty.

"Shall I tell you the thing that would be most awful?" Her voice was ragged with emotion. "That Mum never gets found and I spend the next two years with Dad, me and him alone in the house. And we never get to know if she's alive or dead, and every day for the rest of my life I'll be missing her. I don't think I could bear it."

"Which is what happened," said Maud as Carrie turned off the machine.

"Have we learned anything?"

"We've learned that Charlotte Salter had a dangerous gift for making people feel special. And if we didn't know it already, we've learned we need to find out what happened to her."

The two women sat in silence for a while, then Maud spoke abruptly.

"I think Silas and I are breaking up."

"Oh, Maud."

"That is, I think he's breaking up with me."

Carrie heaved herself out of her chair and went to sit on the bed beside her friend.

"I am so sorry," she said. "I didn't know you were going through this."

"We were trying for a baby," said Maud drearily. "I think he got scared."

Carrie put her hand on Maud's shoulder but Maud was stiff and unyielding.

"Don't be nice to me," she said. "I'm going to solve this case before I collapse."

SEVENTY-FIVE

"Jack, you write," said Maud, gesturing to the flip chart. "Nobody can understand my handwriting. Let's start with Charlotte Salter. What have we got?"

That her marriage was unhappy and her husband unfaithful. That she had been planning to leave home, taking her daughter Etty with her, and had an interview for a job in London. That she had spent most of the day at home. That Gwyneth Mayhew had claimed to have seen her sometime between six and six-forty-five on the evening of the party.

"Ten minutes max from the barn," called an officer. "Probably six or seven. And yes, there were streetlamps back then: she certainly could have had a clear view."

"So it looks like Charlotte was headed to the party and would have got there by seven at the latest."

"So something happened between the old lady's house and the party?" asked Mason.

"You're forgetting the ladle. Al, did Frances Ackerley recognise it?"

"She thought it might have belonged to her," the officer said. "But on the other hand, as she said herself, it's just a ladle, nothing remarkable about it. And it was thirty years ago."

"Yes, but you'll see if you look at the timeline that Charlotte Salter went to the Ackerley house in the early afternoon of the day of the party, and borrowed a ladle from Duncan."

There was a silence.

"I don't get it," said Lovell slowly.

Maud gave him a grin. "You do though, Jack, don't you?"

"It doesn't make sense."

"Let's see about that. Now we know that almost nobody had watertight alibis. Almost everyone left the party at some point, even the birthday boy himself." She pushed her hair back from her face. "Let's leave Charlotte Salter for now and think about Duncan Ackerley—who was rumoured to be involved with Charlotte Salter; certainly they were friends. He went out on Christmas Day morning and wasn't seen again until Etty Salter and Greg Ackerley went out to look for him and saw his body in the river, tangled up in a buoy. Nobody had alibis for his death either, but in the end that didn't matter because the police concluded he had taken his own life in a fit of remorse.

"This morning"—she turned to Lovell—"you said the one thing we were certain about in all the uncertainty and chaos was the way in which he died: by jumping from the bridge. Why do we think that?"

447

"Why?"

"Yes."

He rubbed his nose. "Because his glasses were found there."

"When were they found?"

"On 29th December."

"Four days after he died. What did Frances Ackerley say about those glasses?"

"Al?" said Lovell. "You said you'd ask her when you were enquiring about the ladle."

Al shrugged. "She said they were just his old glasses."

"Did you ask her how often he wore them?"

"Yeah, but she was rather vague. She just said, every time he couldn't find his other pair."

"And where's the other pair?"

"I didn't ask. I mean, this was thirty years ago!"

"OK. Now let's turn to Bridget Wolfe, whose death comes thirty years later—at a time, let's be clear, when the Ackerley and the Salter families are all back in Glensted for the first time since the double tragedy. A podcast made by the Ackerley brothers goes live in the early hours of Sunday 29th May in which Bridget discloses—with some excitement—that she has found a diary belonging to Charlotte Salter. Later that day her house is set alight and she is burned to death. Heather and Frank, you've been working on alibis."

"The thing is," said DC Dillon, "it all seems a bit chaotic."

"Alec Salter ran off," added DC Mason. "His family was out looking for him."

"All of them?"

"So they say. Though Niall didn't know at first his father had gone AWOL."

"Morgan Ackerley says he went looking as well," said Dillon.

"And Greg?"

"Greg was at his mother's house with his wife and Frances. He'd been out earlier to collect champagne in Hemingford for a family do."

"Victor Pearce can't say where he was," said Dillon. "Although he remembers seeing the old man wander past his bar. He says that he went out to do some errands at about the time of the fire."

"That's a bit vague."

"And Gerry Thorne found him and lost him again."

"What did they all have to say about listening to the podcast?"

"The Ackerleys heard it all together as a family after Greg Ackerley returned from Hemingford. Elizabeth and Oliver Salter heard it in the morning; in fact they were listening to it when Alec Salter disappeared."

"And Elizabeth Salter says her father could plausibly have heard it. He was outside the kitchen when it was playing."

"I see."

"Niall was at home with his wife listening to it when his sister rang to say Alec had disappeared."

"And the Thornes both claim they haven't heard it," said Mason. "Even now."

"You sound like you don't believe them."

"They were both interviewed for it. I think it's plausible that they would have wanted to know how they came across—which wasn't well, by the way. And they were acting very strangely."

"What about Victor Pearce?"

"Pearce said he'd heard it that morning: he knows because he talked about it with the young woman who helps out in the bar."

"So apart from the Ackerleys—Morgan aside, of course, who made it, and the Thornes, who we are inclined not to believe—everyone had listened to it before Bridget died," said Maud.

"That's about it."

"Frank, come and find me after the meeting. I've a technical task for you."

She stood up, signalling the meeting was over.

"The other thing we need, of course," she said, pulling on her jacket, "is a body. We need to find Charlotte Salter."

Seventy-six

"Tell me it's good news," said Weller.

"It's not good news," said Maud. "But it's not bad news either."

"If it's not good news and it's not bad news, then what is it?"

"It's more like an alert."

"An alert? Why do I not like the sound of that?"

"You told me to keep you informed."

"Yes, and what I would really like you to inform me is that arrests have been made and charges have been brought."

"We're not at that stage yet."

Weller started to say something and then stopped.

"Sorry, sir, what were you going to say?"

"No, Maud, you were ringing to tell me something, to give me an alert, you'd better just do that."

"Please, what did you want to say?"

There was a pause and then Maud heard what sounded like a sigh.

"Maud," he said finally, "I'm not asking for sympathy.

It's my job to make decisions and to take responsibility for them. But do you know how big a decision it is to remove someone from running a murder inquiry? People in the force take umbrage at things like that."

"I can see that," said Maud. "But I'm not clear what I'm supposed to do with that information."

"There are people who want me to pay a price for what they see as disloyalty to their team. And one way of me paying that price is for you to fail. Look, Maud, I'm not going to be a backseat driver. I'm not going to second-guess your decisions. But is there anything I can tell people about how the investigation is going? Have you got a bone I can throw them?"

"Not just now," said Maud.

"Well, I can't accuse you of not being blunt. Give me something, Maud. Have you made any significant progress?"

"I have some thoughts."

"You have some thoughts? Would you care to share some of those thoughts with me?"

"I think it would be better to see what comes of them."

"I suppose there's no point asking you to say more?"

"I'm sorry. I know you're under pressure. But it won't be any help giving you partial information."

There was a pause. Maud knew she had failed to give Weller what he wanted.

"All right, Maud," he said, not sounding as if it were all right at all. "I'll just say that a result would benefit both of us."

"A correct result."

"That's obviously what I meant," he said in a sharper tone. "So if the case hasn't progressed, what was it you wanted to alert me about?"

"Do you remember that podcast about the murder? The one done by Duncan Ackerley's two sons."

"Of course, I do. I just read a piece about it in the *Daily Mail*. Apparently it's gone viral. There are people all round the world wondering why the British police haven't solved this murder yet. That's all we need."

"I've agreed to appear on it."

"What do you mean? In what way?"

"In the normal way. They'll ask me questions and I'll answer them, if I can and I think it's appropriate."

"Why on earth are you doing that? I can see why they'd want to interview the detective in charge. But what's in it for you?"

"I'm not exactly sure. But it might produce something. It's a bit like when detectives go on TV and ask for witnesses."

"Detectives who do that normally go through media training. Have you done that?"

"No."

"You need to be careful, Maud. What they want from it isn't the same as what you want from it."

"I think we all want the same thing: to find some kind of an answer to what happened."

"I'm not so sure," said Weller. "They also want to trap you into saying more than you're meant to."

"I haven't got much to give away," said Maud.

"Is that meant to make me feel better? Look, I'm tempted to say no to this. It's one thing to fail, it's quite another to fail with millions of people all round the world watching, or listening, or whatever it is they're doing."

"I'd like you to trust me on this one, sir."

"Just be careful. All it takes is just one careless word and you'll end up being one of those things that go all over the internet."

"There are people out there who know something. This might be a way of flushing them out."

"I don't know," said Weller. "A colleague of mine on a murder case once gave a five-second answer to a harmless young woman holding a microphone. The last I heard he was working in a call centre somewhere."

SEVENTY-SEVEN

Morgan and Greg were already in the graveyard of St. Peter's when Maud and Carrie arrived. The two detectives made their way through the gravestones, looking at the names as they went.

Carrie pointed at a clump of graves of Harcourts, going back to the early nineteenth century. In a separate section there were rows of identical white gravestones, all naval casualties from the Second World War, most of them teenagers.

Morgan and Greg looked up as they got closer.

"It's a beautiful spot," said Maud. "And a beautiful day. But why here?"

"We mustn't leave it in the dressing room," said Morgan.

"I don't know what you're talking about," said Maud.

"It's a rule I have when doing interviews. There's a risk that you have a conversation about all the things you're going to talk about in the interview and then when you start recording and say it all again, it sounds stale. What I'd like to do is to get you miked up and then we can talk as if we were just friends having a conversation."

Greg looked at Carrie, who was panting heavily.

"Would you like somewhere to sit?"

"I'm fine," said Carrie. "This is a baby, not an illness."

He flushed.

"I hear the podcast is doing even better than it was before," said Maud.

Morgan raised his palms in a gesture of helplessness.

"It's all gone a bit crazy," he said. "This company just got in touch. They want to take it over. We can be part of their empire. That's what they said. Part of their empire."

"Do you earn money from something like that?"

"I think that comes with the empire."

Maud laughed. "So you're going to be rich?"

The two brothers looked at each other.

"It would feel wrong," said Greg simply.

"What Greg means," said Morgan, "is that we've come back here and we're asking people to share their pain with us. We can't be earning ten grand an episode and advertising mattresses or whatever it would be from that pain."

Maud pulled a face. "Ten grand an episode?"

"I won't say we weren't tempted."

"Does it change things?" Maud asked. "Knowing that so many people are listening?"

"It's not such a big deal for Morgan," Greg said. "He's used to doing programmes watched by millions and being recognised in the supermarket."

"What about for you?"

Greg pondered this before answering.

"It's not like actually being famous," he said. "People aren't going to recognise me in the street."

"People might be misunderstanding what we're trying to do," said Morgan. "I think there's a danger that they're confusing us with Hercule Poirot and believe that we're marshalling the evidence and that we're going to have a brilliant solution in the final episode. That's not what it's about."

"Then what is it about?"

"It's hard to put into words." Morgan was speaking in an earnest tone. "You could say it's about the messiness of life. There isn't a plan. Things happen that aren't intended. In the end you don't find the answers and you have to find a way of living with that. But we need to start the conversation. Without that stuff about not finding an answer, of course." He attached a newly acquired microphone the size of a fingernail to the lapel of Maud's jacket. He and Greg both put headphones on.

"We'll just do a quick check for sound," Morgan said. "Why don't you tell us what you had for breakfast?"

"I had a cup of coffee," said Maud.

"And what else?"

"Nothing else. Maybe an apple. I don't remember."

Greg shook his head disapprovingly.

"It's the most important meal of the day."

"I've heard that."

"All right, we'll start now," Morgan said with a

reassuring smile. "Just treat it like a conversation. Don't worry about making mistakes, we can deal with it in the edit."

When Morgan started speaking, Maud noticed that he sounded very slightly different. This was his professional voice.

"I'm standing in St. Peter's churchyard, right next to my dad's grave."

Maud looked down and saw the simple grey slab: Duncan Ackerley, 1947–1990.

"I'm joined by Maud O'Connor," Morgan continued. "Or, to give her her full title: Detective Inspector Maud O'Connor. It's good to have you here, Maud."

Maud didn't reply. She suddenly felt unsure of the right tone. She didn't feel as if she could agree that it was, indeed, good to be there, as if she were appearing on a chat show.

"You were put in charge of the inquiry quite recently. Why was that?"

"I imagine they just wanted a pair of fresh eyes."

"I know that you must be limited in what you can say about the inquiry, but can you tell us how it's going?"

"There are interesting developments, but you're right, I can't be specific just at the moment."

Morgan gave a rueful smile. "As you know, we're not here as professional journalists. We're here as grieving sons. We've lived with this for more than half our lives. Do you understand that Greg and I and the people of this community might feel angry about how little the police have achieved over thirty years, that maybe 'interesting developments' sounds a little vague?"

"Could you describe this anger a little more precisely?" Maud said.

Morgan seemed surprised by the question and took a few seconds to consider his answer.

"You know, for me and my brother, this is about a place as well as about our family. When we do this podcast, we devote a lot of time to thinking where we should do it. We want our listeners to walk around Glensted and along the river with us. As soon as we knew we were going to talk to you, Greg said that it had to be here, in the churchyard, close to the victim. Our father is just a few feet from where we're standing and we thought that closeness might bring it home to you."

Maud realised that this was a kind of ambush. The idea was to spring this on her and the hope was that she might get upset or angry and say something she hadn't planned, something revealing, something that would make a good moment on the podcast.

She looked round at Greg and smiled slightly, and then back at Morgan.

"What do *you* think?" she said.

"What do you mean?"

"My job is to listen rather than to talk. You've been making this series. You've been talking to people around Glensted. Why do *you* think your father died?"

*

The interview didn't take long. Maud politely side-stepped Morgan's questions and Morgan, to compensate, increasingly addressed his dead father whose grave they stood beside. Every time he did this, Greg looked embarrassed.

"It's a wrap," said Morgan.

"I think it's going to rain," said Carrie. "It's so humid."

She was sitting on a slightly raised grave next to Duncan's plot, legs stretched out, hands on her belly.

"Are you all right?" Maud looked at her suspiciously. "You're not going to—?"

"No," said Carrie crossly. "I'm not. I'm just hot. There needs to be a proper storm."

"Can you take a photo of us for the Twitter feed?" Morgan asked her.

With difficulty, Carrie heaved herself to her feet, leaving the headstone for support.

"Doris Winters," she said with approval. "That's a name you don't hear much now. She was ninety-seven."

She took the camera and Maud stood between the brothers. Carrie took several photos and handed the camera back to Morgan.

"Can I ask a question?" Greg squatted to slide the recording equipment into a canvas holdall. "Are you making progress?"

Maud looked out across the graves, some grey and mossy, others shiny with newness.

"Maybe," she said.

"Maybe?"

"That's off the record and it's all you're getting."

Maud walked back into the centre of Glensted the long way, by the river. The tide was coming in rapidly. She suddenly came to a stop, staring at the eddying water, then gave a laugh of surprise.

She took out her mobile.

"Jack," she said. "I've been an idiot. I need to have the local tide times for December 1990. At once."

SEVENTY-EIGHT

"Why did you come back?"

Etty, Ollie, Niall and Penny were sitting in the garden with a lunch of bread and cheese and salad. Etty had a glass of white wine. Inside they could hear doors slamming loudly and then an angry shout.

"Mia's failed her driving test," said Niall glumly. "That means I have to go on putting my life in danger."

"I think I felt a drop of rain," said Penny, tipping her head up to look at the sky that had turned an eerie purple colour.

"We need rain," said Niall.

Mia stomped into the garden, her own little storm cloud.

"Why are you all looking so gloomy?" she asked, as she cut herself a giant slice of cheese and laid it over a piece of bread. "I'm the one who should be in a bad mood. Arsehole."

"Who?"

"The arsehole who failed me."

"Don't be ridiculous. You got three majors, so of course you failed," said Penny.

Mia glowered at her and left.

"Why, Ollie?" Etty said again. "Shouldn't you be at work?"

"I've taken some days off."

"What for?"

"I hate my job anyway."

"We haven't all been together for years," said Etty. "Decades. And now ..." She pushed her thin, ringless hand into her short hair. "It's like we can't keep away."

"I just thought ..." Ollie began, then stopped. "I won't stay for long," he said. "I can sleep on the sofa."

"It's fine," said Niall. "Stay for as long as you want. This brie is a bit too runny for my liking."

"I for one," said Penny, "am pleased you have all finally decided to spend time together."

"We haven't decided," said Etty. "We just are."

"You've been ill," said Niall. "That's why you're here. You're getting better, though, aren't you?"

"Yes," said Etty.

Though in truth she didn't know. The world she had lived in before seemed infinitely far off, a dream of a life she no longer inhabited, and she had the strangest feeling she was coming apart, bits of her that had been tightly knotted together fraying, her hold on herself loosening. It made her feel small and helpless. She kept thinking about Charlie and about Paul, and every time she thought of them she was pierced with sorrow.

"I have this sense," began Ollie. Then he stopped again and picked up a piece of bread, looking at it as if he didn't know what it was.

"Yes?"

"I have this sense of dread," Ollie said at last. "As if something very, very bad is about to happen."

"And that's why you've come back?"

"Yes."

"You wanted to be a family," said Penny.

Ollie looked at her wonderingly.

"Yes. Yes, I suppose I did. Funny old family we've been, though."

"What kind of bad thing?" Etty asked.

"I don't know. Don't you feel it?"

"No," said Niall. "It's probably because there's a storm on its way." He rose to his feet. "Well, I need to get back to work."

"Me too," said Penny. "I've those invoices to send off."

"We'll clear up," said Etty.

They watched Niall and Penny leave together.

"They're a nice couple really," said Ollie.

"Yes."

"I always thought Niall was a bit ridiculous, but he's done the best of any of us."

Etty nodded. Her head throbbed.

"I do feel it," she said. "I do feel something is about to happen."

SEVENTY-NINE

"Here you are. I printed them out for you."

Lovell put a sheet of paper in front of Maud and she looked at it, running her finger along the rows.

"I don't see why it's important," said Lovell. "But it looks like it was high tide at around half past eleven that day."

"I see."

"Is that any help?"

"Yes, Jack. It's exactly what I needed."

Jack Lovell stood for a few seconds, waiting for her to say more, but there was a rap at the door and Frank Mason put his head around it.

"You're busy," he said.

"We're done here."

"There's something I want you to see."

"You look pleased."

"I got that footage."

"You did? Brilliant." Maud rose swiftly to her feet and nodded at Jack. "I'll take you through it all shortly," she said to him.

"That would be nice," he said, "when you have a moment."

But she didn't seem to notice the sarcasm.

"I think you must be nearing the end," said Frances Ackerley to her sons as they sat together at the kitchen table, while the rain splattered down outside, drops bouncing like little bombs off the patio.

"What do you mean?"

Morgan was peeling a mango with great concentration, but he put it down and turned to her enquiringly.

"Lester and I were saying how it must be time for you to get back to your normal lives," she replied peaceably.

Greg smiled at Morgan, but there was a hint of bitterness in his voice when he said: "Mum's tired of having us here."

"I just mean you've been here a long time," she said. "Doing this podcast thing."

A shadow passed across Morgan's face.

"And there's Katherine waiting for you," she said to Greg.

"She's not waiting for me," said Greg. "She's working."

"Well, anyway."

"You're telling us to leave," said Morgan. He looked like his teenage self, resentful and pitiful.

"No, no. Just that you can't have much more to say. I mean, it seems to me that you've said everything there is to be said. And more."

"If you've got a grievance ..." began Morgan.

"No, Morgan. Not a grievance. I'm simply saying that you've talked to everyone, you've gone over and over the case and picked its bones dry, you've unearthed old secrets and opened old wounds."

"Mum," said Greg.

He leaned towards her, but she pulled back sharply. Her eyes glittered in a way that was horribly familiar from the old days.

"You've made intimate things public knowledge, trampled over our life as if it was just entertainment. Yesterday, a journalist came to see me and asked me to share my story. People ring me up wanting to interview me. When I go into Glensted now, I feel everyone staring at me and it's as if I'm back there. Do you know what that feels like?"

"You should have said if you didn't like what we were doing."

"I told you I wanted nothing to do with it."

"I think Mum's right," said Greg. "It's time to call it a day."

"Just stop, you mean?"

"Lester says we need to have our house to ourselves again," said Frances stubbornly.

"And I agree with Lester," said Greg. "We did that interview with the detective, and you can just put in a few of your grand thoughts to round it all off."

"Grand thoughts?"

"That came out wrong."

"Look," said Morgan, almost pleadingly. "We can't just stop. We're a phenomenon."

"Maybe I don't want to be a phenomenon," said Greg.

"Anyway," said Frances. "Isn't it all coming to a head?"

"What do you mean?"

"I just gathered that impression."

"Who from?" asked Greg. "Impression of what?"

"Don't get so heated. You boys always did get heated."

"Not that you ever noticed," said Greg in a low but carrying voice.

Frances looked at him. "I know you had a difficult time when you were young. I know I wasn't a proper mother to you. But you're adults now. Middle-aged adults. It's time to let go of everything and move on."

"Let go?" Morgan gave an incredulous laugh. "Move on?"

"Like you did, you mean," said Greg. "After Dad died."

"Yes. Like that, Greg. I will not be made to feel guilty for putting my life back together after Duncan killed himself. Would you have preferred me to have remained a grieving wreck?"

"You didn't just recover," said Morgan. "You became happier after he died. That was what was hard for us. It was like you were almost glad he was dead. But what about us?"

"You're talking as if you're still fifteen," said Frances.

"Well, when I was fifteen, we never talked about it. Because you were *ill*."

"You say that as if I was malingering."

"We needed a mother," said Morgan. "Instead, we had to look after you."

Greg got up and went to the window, where he stood looking out across the estuary and marshes dissolving in the rain.

"When I'm here," he said, "not an hour goes by that I don't think of him and miss him."

Morgan nodded. "I get that. But is it such a bad thing to remember?"

"I don't know."

"Perhaps we should have family therapy."

"That's a very bad idea," said Frances.

They fell silent. The rain came down, pattering off the leaves of the trees outside, splashing from the gutter. Morgan stood and joined his brother at the window.

'Do you think that detective knows something?" he asked, in a low voice, so that Frances couldn't hear.

"I don't know."

"Was doing the podcast wrong?" He spoke almost pleadingly. Greg didn't look at him, just went on staring out across the sodden landscape.

"At any rate, it's set something in motion," he said. "I don't you think you can stop it now."

EIGHTY

Maud was starting to think something had gone wrong. Maybe there had been a problem with her directions. But then a white van turned round the corner and pulled up beside her. The driver's door opened and a tall, rangy man got out. He had floppy brown hair, an oversized patterned jumper and jeans and trainers.

"Hey, Matt, was the traffic all right?"

Matthew Moran smiled and looked over Maud's shoulder.

"You sound like my dad," he said. "Whenever someone visits him, he never asks how they are. He just asks what the traffic was like, what route they took to get there."

"OK," said Maud. "How are you?"

"Puzzled," said Matt.

"What about?"

"You have crime scene investigators up here, no?"

"It's not entirely their fault, but the local force has been messing up crime scenes for more than thirty years. It seems to have become a tradition, like Morris dancing. Also, for some crazy reason, I have a particular regard for your talent. I think you might be able to find things that other people can't find."

Matt narrowed his eyes in suspicion.

"If I need a reference, then I know who to turn to, but I can't un-mess up a crime scene."

"We'll see about that."

"Anyway, wasn't the murder you're investigating in a burned-out house in a field somewhere?"

"That's only one of the murders I'm investigating. I want you to take a look at this."

The door of the barn was now fastened with a padlock. Maud took a bunch of keys from her pocket and tried them one by one until the padlock opened. She pulled the large door open enough so that they could step through.

Inside the air felt stale, dust hanging in the air. Matt looked around.

"What's all the building work?"

"They're converting it into a house. But it's on hold for the moment."

"So what am I looking at?" asked Matt.

There was a rough wooden table in the middle of the space. Maud took a collection of photos from her jacket pocket and laid them out. They were the Polaroids from the party. Matt looked down at them.

"Were these taken here?"

"December 1990," said Maud. "It was the fiftieth birthday party of Alec Salter. From the various accounts I've heard, there were around a hundred people here. But one person wasn't. Alec Salter was unhappily married to Charlotte Salter. She was meant to be at the party but she wasn't there and she hasn't been seen since."

She glanced across at Matt, who was standing with his hands in his pockets. He looked puzzled, almost bored.

"As you can see from the photos," she continued, "there was a long table along the wall here …" She gestured to the wall near the large door they had come in through. "It had drinks on it. From the photos you can make out the usual stuff. Bottles of wine, beer, water and a punchbowl." She gestured towards the other end of the space. "Over there was another table with food. Dips, crisps, that sort of thing. But this …" She gestured at the space where the drinks table had been. "I'm more interested in this."

"You know what I'm going to say."

Maud smiled. "I think I can imagine."

"The thing you said that particularly caught my attention was 'thirty years ago.' And what caught my attention after that was the talk of a party and a hundred people trooping through here." He shook his head. "And then you say it was a party that a woman didn't come to. As a crime scene investigator, I don't really know what I'm supposed to do with that."

"I didn't say that she didn't come."

"You literally did just say that."

"I didn't say that she didn't come. I said that she wasn't there."

Matt looked puzzled once more.

"I'm sorry. I don't understand the distinction. I'm just a poor, simple scientist who investigates crime scenes."

"I think this *is* a crime scene," said Maud.

"What?"

"And I think it might be the only crime scene in this whole case that hasn't been contaminated by people crawling all over it."

"Are you going to tell me what you mean?"

"The Salters had a terrible marriage." Maud stopped herself. "I'm not sure if that's the right way of describing it. Alec Salter was a bully to Charlotte Salter and he was unfaithful to her. That's more accurate. And there was evidence that she was planning to leave him. The police got hung up on that theory. But the evidence also suggests that she was coming to the party. She got dressed for it. She was seen by a witness walking in this direction. And then there's this."

Maud walked across to the table and tapped one of the photographs. "Look at this."

Matt leaned in more closely.

"What is it I'm supposed to be looking at?"

"This wasn't a fancy catered party. It was the sort of event where different people bring stuff to. And according to the files, Charlotte borrowed a ladle that she was going to bring for the drinks." She tapped the photography. "This ladle."

Matt looked doubtful. "Are you sure it's not just any old ladle?"

"Its owner thinks she recognises it."

"So you think she was killed here?"

"Yes."

"The ladle came here." Matt considered this for a moment. "I suppose it isn't possible that someone killed her on the way and then brought the ladle to make it look like she'd come."

Maud shook her head. "I think that's a bit too clever. Nobody would think, there's her ladle, she must be at the party, nothing to worry about. No. I'm sure that she arrived and didn't leave."

Matt pulled a face. "You mean you think her body's here?"

"I think it *was* here."

He gestured helplessly. "So what do you want from me?"

Maud frowned. "A person, or persons, unknown, encountered and killed Charlotte Salter in this barn. The dead body is here, there are partygoers about to arrive. Where do you hide the body?"

"How do you know the body was hidden here? They could have taken it outside somewhere. Hidden it in a bush or the boot of a car."

"It's possible," said Maud thoughtfully. "If the killer—or killers—managed that, then the whole thing's hopeless and I've been wasting my time and yours. But it might not have been possible. People were about to arrive. What do you do?"

Matt walked slowly around the building. He moved in a sort of slouch, but Maud recognised his casual demeanour. Beneath it he was concentrating hard.

"Stone walls all the way round," he said. "Was it

like this back in 1990? Could there have been a partition wall in front of the stone?"

"No. It was just like this."

"Was there any kind of stage or platform, something you could hide a body under?"

"There was only the table for the drink and the table for the food. And you couldn't hide anything under either of those. It would have been clearly visible."

Matt looked up towards the high ceiling, the beams.

"I thought about that," said Maud. "There's no way up there except using a ladder. You couldn't get a body up there and, if you did, there'd be nowhere to put it."

"Could there have been some box or packing case?" said Matt. "Something they might have used for delivering things for the party."

"If there are, then they don't show up in any of the photos."

He put his hands back in the pockets of his jeans and turned to Maud.

"Is this official?"

"What?"

"This. Me. Being here."

"I'm in charge of the inquiry. If I decide to authorise something, then it's official."

"Do the rest of your team know?"

"They'll know when they need to know."

Matt shook his head sadly. "I'm not here as your last, desperate throw of the dice, am I?"

"No," said Maud, smiling. "I've got a few more desperate throws of the dice in mind."

He looked down at the ground. "What's this?"

There was a narrow trough that ran the length of the floor.

"It was a cow shed," said Maud. "The cows were in stalls. They'd back on to this trough. It was to collect their dung."

"I don't remember seeing it in the photos. Could it have been built after 1990?"

"No, this is as old as the building."

The two of them walked back to the table and examined the photos more closely. Then Matt leaned right down and touched one of them with the tip of a finger.

"There's some kind of planking over the gap," he said. "It must have been to stop people falling into it."

The two of them looked at each other and a smile slowly appeared on Maud's face.

"It's not possible," Matt said. "They couldn't have." He looked more closely. "The space is big enough, I suppose. But right in the middle of the party. People standing on top of it. Walking on it. Dancing."

Maud looked at Matt more intently. "Could it have left a trace?"

"Everything leaves a trace. Of some kind. But it was thirty years ago. More than thirty. The chances are one in a hundred. One in a thousand." He kneeled down and looked into the trough then back up at Maud. "Have there been cows in here?"

"Not for fifty years. At least."

"What about other social events?"

"I checked. The building has been closed ever since that party. Until the construction work started a few weeks ago. There's probably dust from that."

Matt mumbled something, like he was talking to himself. He stood up. He looked dissatisfied. He was shaking his head slowly.

"I can't believe this," he said. "I really can't believe it."

"You're going to try, though, aren't you?"

"I'm probably just wasting your time. And mine as well. But I've driven all the way out to the back of beyond so I might as well give it a go."

Five minutes later he was standing in his full kit, all white, gloved, shoes covered. On the table he had laid out his tools, the scalpels, brushes, tweezers, torches, evidence bags.

"This will take a while," he said. "You might want to go somewhere. Have a coffee or do something that might actually have a chance of working."

"I'll wait," said Maud.

Matt looked along the length of the trough. "Is there any particular part of it that you think might be more likely?"

"Not that I can see."

He took a head torch from his canvas bag and adjusted the elastic strap around his scalp. He switched it on.

"Then it looks as if we might be here for some hours."

*

477

He worked in miniature and took his time, moving inch by inch along the trough with his small measuring wheel, his delicate brush, the tweezers that picked up apparently invisible items which he put into the evidence bags or polypropylene collection tubes. He made careful notes and took photos of everything he was collecting.

It was strangely consoling to watch his patient concentration. The air was warm and dry inside the barn. Outside, birds sang and from the distance came the rumble of traffic. After a few minutes of watching Matt work, Maud took off her denim jacket and laid it on the floor. She sat down cross-legged in the rectangle of sunlight that lay across the floor and took her notebook from her backpack. The pages were clotted with bullet points and timings, crossings out, arrows pointing in different directions and maps she had made of the area with comments beside them. There was Bridget's house beyond the church, among the doodles of trees. There was the river, the Salters' farmhouse, the Ackerleys' place, Victor's café.

Maud took the top off her pen and stared down at the scrawl. It felt to her that the case had been like a photograph developing in a darkroom: very slowly, the murky images had clarified and resolved. It had seemed at first like a violent mess, and now it had sharp outlines, and started to make sense. Horrible sense.

A fly buzzed. The sun went briefly behind a cloud and then emerged again. She could hear the tiny noises coming from Matt where he crouched over his work: the almost inaudible swish of the brush, the scrape of the scalpel, the sound of an evidence bag being sealed, the click of the camera.

She thought of the ladle that Charlie had borrowed from Duncan. Of the taste of salt from the river, and the tide times. Of the CCTV she and Frank Mason had watched together yesterday and the way that, instead of triumph, she had felt stern and sad. She thought of Charlotte Salter's beguiling face on the fraying poster, and of fifteen-year-old Etty's voice in the interview, her raw anguish.

She unscrewed the top from her pen and at last allowed herself to write down the name she had been holding in her mind for days now. She stared at it for several minutes, then closed the book.

"I think I'm done," said Matt, taking off the head torch and sliding pouches and tubes into his canvas bag.

"And?"

"I don't know. I have things I can work with."

"Things?"

He gestured at her to move in close.

"Fibres. Stains. I take it there are samples of Charlotte Salter's DNA?"

"There are."

"I will need that."

"Thank you, Matt."

"Don't get your hopes up."

EIGHTY-ONE

Maud stood in front of her team at their morning briefing. She waited for silence and then looked around the room, from face to face.

"You've worked hard," she said.

The silence thickened. Maud's throat felt suddenly dry, and she took a sip of water from the glass in front of her.

"Jack, Heather, are you ready?"

Lovell drove the three of them in his car, which, Maud saw with satisfaction, was now immaculately clean. They left Hemingford, passed over the bridge where Duncan Ackerley's glasses had been found, then followed the road towards Glensted.

"Left here," instructed Maud, and the car swung on to a narrow lane.

The tide was very low and long-legged birds picked their way over the mudflats, stepping delicately over the small rivulets and pools.

"Park here," said Maud, as they turned on to the track.

Lovell pulled over and parked. Dillon's forehead was gleaming with sweat, and she kept passing the back of her hand over it. No one spoke.

They walked up the track and came to the house. Maud stepped forward, gave her shoulders a small shake, then rapped on the door. Dillon and Lovell positioned themselves behind her. Maud heard Lovell give a short, hard cough. The door opened.

"Mrs. Ackerley," said Maud.

Frances stared at her. She suddenly looked her age: an eighty-year-old woman with a hard life behind her and dread in her eyes.

"What's happened?" she asked. "What do you want?"

"We're not here for you," said Maud. She sounded, thought Lovell, oddly tender.

"Who then?"

"I think you know."

Frances took a step back. Her body seemed disarticulated, like a puppet with its strings broken. She put a hand on the door jamb and said nothing.

"Mum?"

Frances turned and they could see Morgan behind her, the smile on his face fading as he noticed their expressions.

"Hello," he said. "Would you like to come in?"

"We'd like to see your brother," said Maud.

"Greg? He's down by the river." Morgan was trying to seem nonchalant. He fixed the jaunty smile back on his face. "He's trying a spot of fishing, after our conversation the other day."

"By the landing stage?"

"Yes. But can't I—?"

"Stay here, please," said Maud.

She and the two other detectives left the mother and son framed in the doorway. They made their way round the house, through the garden to the gate at the bottom. Maud pushed it open and they went single file along the little path towards the estuary. Now they could see a figure standing with his back to them, standing by the water. But he wasn't fishing. His hands were in his pockets and he was simply gazing out across the water.

Their footsteps were soft on the mud, but he must have heard them because he turned and watched them as they approached. He kept his hands in his pockets, and didn't appear surprised or dismayed. His eyes were very blue in the brightness of the day.

"Hello," he said.

"Mr. Ackerley," said Maud, stopping a few feet from him. "We'd like a word, please."

"We can talk here. I was going to try my hand with a rod. It's been years, decades."

"I think we'd better do this a little more officially," she said.

"The car's up on the road," said Lovell.

They turned and all walked back along the path,

Greg following Maud as she led the way through the gate, up the garden, round the house, past the door where Morgan and Frances still stood, slack-faced and motionless. Morgan took a couple of jerky steps forward, but Greg raised a hand.

"Don't worry," he said. "I'll be back soon."

"Gregory James Ackerley," said Maud, speaking slowly and clearly for the machine. "I'm interviewing you about your possible involvement in the deaths of Charlotte Salter, Duncan Ackerley and Bridget Wolfe. You do not have to say anything. But it may harm your defence if you do not mention when questioned something which you later rely on in court. Anything you do say may be given in evidence."

He looked at her as if he was concerned for her mental health, then slowly shook his head.

"I didn't think people really said that in real life."

"We do."

"This is crazy," he said.

"Do you want a lawyer?"

"Why would I want a lawyer? How could I have killed any of them? My father killed himself, and even if he didn't, I was nowhere near where he died. People saw me. A whole family. Bridget Wolfe died in a fire and, again, you know perfectly well that I wasn't even in Glensted when that happened. As for Charlie—you don't even know she's dead. There's no body."

"Let's take those things in order," said Maud, looking into his calm face. "At the time your father died, you were seen walking along the banks of the estuary where it widens towards the sea. Yes?"

"Exactly."

"The assumption has always been that he died by jumping—or falling, anyway—from the bridge where his glasses were later found."

"Right."

"His second pair of glasses. His spare pair."

"So?"

"Which were not found until several days after his death."

"Because no one looked."

"Or because they weren't actually there until later. The police took it for granted that his body was taken by the river towards the sea, because that's what rivers do—they flow towards the sea. They thought it got caught up in the chain attached to a buoy, near the landing stage by your house, and had it not been for that it would never have been found."

Greg shifted in his chair. Maud leaned forward slightly.

"The tide was high at eleven-thirty that day."

"I'll take your word for it."

"You must have been startled to see your father there," said Maud. "You and Etty. It must have been a bit like a nightmare for you."

"Of course I was shocked. Of course it was like a nightmare. He was my father."

"When I dipped my finger in the Heming the other day and licked it, I tasted salt. I'm a city girl. I'd never thought about a river flowing in two directions. I suppose I knew that the Thames was tidal but I'd never really thought about it that way."

Maud paused and waited. Greg said nothing. His face was puckered in apparent confusion.

"If your father had entered the river further downriver—say, approximately where you met the Bowden family that day—he could have been swept back upriver, towards the bridge, not out to sea."

"You're all wrong."

"That was quite clever of you," said Maud. "When the body was found, you realised that you had a perfect alibi if you could make it look like your father had entered the river upstream. Obviously that alibi doesn't work any more."

"This is stupid," he said.

"Do you want your lawyer yet?"

EIGHTY-TWO

Two hours later, Maud was back in the interview room. Greg and the duty lawyer, a young woman with a ponytail and a clever, freckled face called Tania Broughton, sat opposite her. Jack Lovell, sitting to one side, switched on the recording machine. Maud repeated her words of caution, stated they were continuing the interview, read out the time: 11.35 am.

"You said you weren't in Glensted when Bridget Wolfe died."

"That's right."

"You stick to that?"

"Because it's the truth."

"Would you like to tell me what you did on that morning, Mr. Ackerley?"

"I'm only going to repeat what I've already said. I got up quite early and had breakfast with my wife, my brother, my mother and Lester, and Lester's two grandchildren. We were planning the barbecue we were going to have later—it was a family reunion. I was telling everyone what I'd got for it the day before, and I suddenly remembered I hadn't collected the champagne I'd bought. So I had to drive into Hemingford to collect it."

"So that's what you did?"

"Yes."

"What was the name of the shop?"

"Sol and Fender."

"Go on."

Greg shrugged. "I drove there, got the champagne, drove back. Morgan was still there, and Mum and Lester. I don't know where the kids were; somewhere around. And then we all listened to the podcast, where Morgan interviewed Bridget Wolfe, and she claimed to have found Charlie's diary—"

"She did find it," said Maud.

"Well." Greg licked his lips, the first sign of nervousness Maud had seen in him. "It was the first I'd heard of a diary. I was a bit annoyed, as a matter of fact."

"Annoyed?"

"We were supposed to be working together."

"I see. And then?"

"Then Ollie called and said his father had gone missing. Morgan went to help look, and I stayed at home with Mum."

"Thank you," said Maud.

Greg sat back. "So you see," he said.

"You have nothing to add?"

Greg's eyes flickered between her and his lawyer.

"Not that I can think of."

"You claim that you collected the champagne that morning from Hemingford?"

"Morgan can corroborate it. And my wife."

Maud nodded towards Lovell, who got up and left the room, returning with a small computer that he put on the table.

"I want you to look at this," said Maud. "It's a bit blurry, I'm afraid, but you'll get the picture."

Jack pressed "Play" and a grainy black-and-white image appeared on the screen. It was a small car park with a few cars in it. A few seconds passed. A figure appeared carrying a box. Maud leaned forward and pressed "Pause."

"Do you recognise that person?"

Greg gave a small laugh. "Of course. It's me."

"Good."

She pressed "Play" again. The figure walked up to a hatch-back, rested the box on a raised knee while he searched for the key in his pocket, then opened the boot, slid the box inside and closed the boot. Then the figure climbed into the car, which after a few more seconds slid out of view.

"Well?" said Maud.

"Well?"

"This seems to confirm Mr. Ackerley's story," said Tania Broughton.

Maud put her finger on the small white numbers at the base of the screen.

"Can you read this for us?"

"Me?" Greg put a hand to his face, touched his cheek experimentally and then his temple.

"Can you read what it says at the bottom of the

screen? It reads 28-05-22. That's the date. And then: 15.37.21. That's the time. So Mr. Ackerley, you actually collected the champagne on Saturday 28th May, at just before twenty to four in the afternoon. Not on the morning of Sunday 29th May, as you claim. You have no alibi for the day that Bridget Wolfe was murdered, only a false alibi. What do you have to say to that?"

He didn't reply.

"What were you actually doing on that morning, Mr. Ackerley, when you left the house saying you had to collect the champagne that you had in fact already collected?"

Greg had dropped his gaze and was now staring fixedly at his hands that were plaited together and resting on the table.

"Why would you lie about your whereabouts—and lie to the police later?"

Greg lifted his head briefly but said nothing.

"We all know that you actually drove to Bridget's house and set it ablaze. With her inside."

"No."

"She died a terrible death," said Maud.

"You've got nothing, just a story you've made up," said Greg. "It's all supposition. The way the river was flowing, your imagined scenario at Bridget's house. Maybe I collected the champagne the day before—" He shook off his lawyer's warning hand. "Maybe I did and just forgot. But nothing places me at the woman's house with a can of petrol. Nothing says I killed my father, or that he didn't take his own life. And as for

Charlie, there's not even a body. You don't even know if she's dead."

Jack looked across at Maud. The CCTV footage of Greg was damaging. In front of a jury it would look very bad indeed. But was it enough? If Maud's strategy had been that Greg would break down and confess to everything, then it had failed. But Maud just looked thoughtful.

There was a knock at the door and before anyone replied it opened and a uniformed officer appeared.

"I'm noting that Constable Forest has entered the room," said Maud. "For some reason."

"I'm really sorry but there's a Dr. Matthew Moran to see you," said the young officer. "He said it was urgent. I said you couldn't be interrupted and he said to interrupt you anyway."

"I'm terminating this interview now," Maud said, leaning forward and switching off the machine.

"Is Greg Ackerley free to leave now?"

"He is not free to leave now." She looked at Lovell. "Get an officer in here to keep Greg company and then join me outside."

EIGHTY-THREE

As soon as she was out in the corridor Maud called Carrie and asked her to join them. Looking round, she saw Constable Forest standing so close to her that she had to take a step back.

"What?" she said.

"I put him in the store room," he said. "I thought you might want some privacy."

Maud laughed. "Yes, I suppose I do."

When Maud entered the room, Matt Moran was looking round at the detritus of office furniture and electrical equipment piled up along the far end.

"Nice office you've got here," he said.

"If you've come in person, then I'm thinking you've got something interesting to share."

"It's only preliminary," he said, shaking his head and smiling. "I couldn't believe it. I thought that being out here in the wilderness had driven you insane."

"Did you get a bloodstain?"

"Yes."

"Was there enough for identification?"

"Yes, that used to be a problem. Thirty years ago. Do you want me to give you my lecture about polymerase chain-reaction method?"

"You can save your lecture for your appearance in court. I just want to know whether Charlotte Salter's body was hidden in that barn."

Matt hesitated for a few seconds.

"What I can say is that the traces of blood that I retrieved belonged to Charlotte Salter. Or, to be more precise, the sample I retrieved from the barn is identical to the sample you gave me of Charlotte Salter's DNA."

As Maud started to say something, the door opened and Jack and Carrie came in. Maud introduced them to Matt.

"So?" said Carrie.

"She was there," said Maud. "All the time that party was going on, she was there, under people's feet."

A slow smile spread across Carrie's face, as if she'd seen a magic trick perfectly performed.

"Fuck," said Jack, and then looked around, blushing. "I mean: really?"

Nobody spoke for a full minute, each of them seemingly lost in their own thoughts.

"I just had to see all of your faces," said Matt. "I'd better be getting back."

"Not yet," said Maud.

"Is this a meeting?" said Carrie. "Because if it's a meeting can we go to a proper room with chairs so that I can sit down?"

"If we go to a proper room with chairs," said Maud,

"then people will start joining us and interrupting us and there'll be an agenda and we'll never get anything done. Let's find you something to sit on and then the four of us can have a conversation."

It took some effort from Matt and Jack to pull an office chair from behind a stack of desks so that Carrie could sit on it. The rest of them stood around the cramped office, finding somewhere to lean.

"So we know Charlotte Salter's body was hidden in the barn during the party," said Carrie. "What next?"

"That's exactly the right question," said Maud. "By the way ..." She turned to Jack. "Could you get the file of Polaroids of the party?"

He left the room. Matt took out his phone and looked at it.

"You're sure you really need me to be here?" he said.

"Just give me a few minutes," said Maud.

Jack came back into the room and handed Maud the file.

"People are wondering what's going on," he said. "I didn't know what to tell them."

Maud seemed not to hear what he was saying.

"You have a body that you need to hide quickly because people are about to arrive," she said. "You hide it under some boards. It's improvised and a bit desperate but it works. What then? What do you do with the body then?"

"Where do we even start?" said Cassie. "It was thirty years ago. So much of the evidence must have been lost or destroyed."

"I know," said Maud. "So why don't we try and work with the evidence that we actually have?"

"But this bit we know, don't we?" said Jack.

"Do we? What do we know?"

"They found Charlotte Salter's coat by the river and it makes sense. It's perfect. You throw the body in and the tide washes it out to sea."

"That's one theory," said Maud.

"What's wrong with it?"

"If you want to get rid of the body, why do you leave the coat on the bank to show that you've done it? Duncan Ackerley's glasses were placed on the bridge to mislead people about where he had entered the water. The coat was placed on the bank to make it look as if she had killed herself."

"Or the murderer might have dropped it," said Jack.

Maud didn't respond to this suggestion. She just ran her finger along the edge of the file.

"I think ..." she began, and then stopped. She was visibly thinking hard, muttering something to herself under her breath. "Yes, yes." She looked around at the other three, as if she were surprised they were still there.

"Have you got something to share with us?" Carrie asked.

"Where's the best place to hide a dead body?"

The other three exchanged puzzled looks.

"Is that a quiz question?" asked Matt. "Or just a general inquiry?"

"A general inquiry. Where, all things being equal, is the best place to hide a body?"

There was a battered old desk in one corner of the room. Maud walked across to it, opened the file and started to lay out the pictures on it.

"There were actually two dead bodies in Glensted on the day of the party."

"What do you mean?" said Carrie.

Maud picked up one of the Polaroids and handed it to her.

Cassie squinted at it.

"What am I looking at it?"

"Behind that couple, on the table you can see part of the flower arrangement for the party."

Carrie held the Polaroid up to her face, then closer.

"Is that a wreath?"

"Yes. Here it is again." She pushed another Polaroid across. "It must have been sent along to the party by mistake. I checked. It was intended for a funeral that was taking place on the afternoon of the day after the party. It was for a Glensted woman called Doris Winter."

"I sat on her grave," said Carrie.

"Yes." Maud looked round the group. "Does anybody remember Greg Ackerley's job that year, before he went to uni?"

"Don't look at me," said Matt.

"He worked for his father, chopping down dying trees, but also attending to things in the village, including the church," said Carrie. "Doing odd jobs, cutting the grass."

Jack looked puzzled. "Are you saying that Greg Ackerley swapped the bodies?"

Maud smiled. "That wouldn't be much help. Then you'd have to get rid of Doris Winter's body instead of Charlotte Salter's." She turned to Matt. "What do you think? Can you get a team together?"

Matt considered this.

"All right," he said. "So you'll need to get an exhumation order."

"I've never actually done that before."

"I have," said Matt. "It comes with the job."

"So who do I go to?"

"I think someone's going to need to write this down." He nodded at Jack, who took a notebook from his pocket and opened it. "For a start you'll need a licence from the Ministry of Justice. Your boss will be able to sort that out if you tell him what you've told us. You'll need some relative of that dead old woman to sign off on it. You should contact an undertaker to deal with the woman's coffin. And you said that this was in a churchyard?"

"That's right."

"You'll need permission from the church. There's some technical term for it that I've forgotten. They probably need to make sure you're not using the body for some satanic rite."

"Is that it?"

"No. You need to contact the local council. They'll almost certainly insist that someone from health and safety is present at the exhumation. Some local authorities also have an official who's specifically responsible for cemeteries and crematoriums in the area. They'll probably want to oversee the whole thing. You'll also need someone to obtain and set up screens for privacy. I'll arrange for the lighting. The authority might want to do it in the middle of the night. You know, for privacy."

"Bloody hell," said Maud. "It's going to be like a festival."

"It's a sensitive issue."

"I want to do it today," said Maud. "Or tonight, if that's what they want."

"Get on to your boss. If you can convince him, the MOJ will nod it through. And you need to find some next of kin. You're not moving the body to another site so it should be OK, but people are funny about these things."

"All right," said Maud, "I'll phone my boss. Jack, you find an undertaker and a relative."

EIGHTY-FOUR

It was like a party in a bad dream. It was one in the morning and there were vans parked along the wall of the churchyard. A group of young men expertly assembled metal tubes and suddenly there was a marquee over the area surrounding Doris Winter's grave. Local uniformed officers had created a cordon around the whole churchyard. Inside it, among the graves, people stood in groups. Maud moved between them making sure that no journalists or random members of the public had managed to sneak in.

A large, cheerful-looking woman in a sensible anorak introduced herself to Maud.

"We don't often have things like this to deal with here," she said. "In fact, never."

"And you are?"

"Terry Tofton," she said. "Environmental Health Officer. Acting, actually. The real EHO is on maternity leave. Normally I'm inspecting drainage facilities in schools and that sort of thing. I had to look this up, see what was needed."

"I think it'll be quite straightforward," said Maud.

"You've got to make sure it's the right grave. Or rather, *I've* got to make sure."

"We've done that."

"I've got to ensure maximum privacy. That's why we're doing it at this ungodly hour."

Maud looked round at the tent, which had an eerie glow now that the lights inside had been switched on. She felt that it must be far more visible now than if it had been done in the middle of the day.

"And I know you must all be used to this," Terry Tofton continued. "Dead bodies and murders and everything. I'm aware that a sort of gallows humour comes with the job. But it's my responsibility to make sure that the site and the body is treated with respect."

"We'll do our best."

"Though I must admit it feels rather like a horror film. I'm half expecting to see some zombies marching out of the darkness. It gives me a bit of a shiver." Tofton gave a little chuckle at that. "So what is it you're expecting to find here?"

"It's part of an ongoing inquiry," Maud said, as blandly as she could manage.

It was clear that Tofton had more questions to ask so Maud edged away from her, murmuring that she had matters to see to. She entered the tent and was briefly blinded by the lights. They were so harsh that they almost bleached the colour out of the grass and the shovelled soil.

It was a big job. Four gravediggers had been hired,

two from the next borough. Four of them on double time. Maud tried not to think about what that would do to her budget. She joined Matt Moran, who was standing at the edge of the excavation looking down. The shape of the coffin was clearly visible now, but the wood itself was badly cracked and decayed, and splitting apart.

"Any interest in the Doris Winter coffin?" Matt said.

"I just want it out of the way."

"This'll take a while. The Winter remains will be . . ." He hesitated and turned to her with a faint smile. "Fragile. Things might get a bit messy."

"I want what's underneath to be as undamaged as possible."

"We'll do our best." Matt looked around. "All right, everyone. Let's get kitted up."

Over the next half-hour, as she watched Matt and his team down in the hole with plastic sheets and a hoist and a body bag, she felt a pang on behalf of the body of Doris Winter. She hadn't asked for this. She had just wanted rest in the earth after a long life. It felt wrong exposing her remains to all of this. "We'll get you a proper burial," Maud murmured under her breath, feeling almost foolish.

"All right," said Matt finally, when Doris Winter's remains were bagged up and had been removed by the dark-suited undertakers. "We're clear."

The gravediggers had gone. It now looked more like an archaeological dig. Matt and his team were crouched at the bottom of the excavation working with trowels and spades that looked more like scientific instruments. It was very quiet. They all spoke in murmurs. The forms Maud had signed spoke of "due respect" and everyone seemed aware of this.

Maud was standing at the entrance of the tent feeling tense and exhausted and apprehensive when she heard a shout from behind, a shout that sounded shocking, like someone interrupting a religious ceremony. She turned and saw Matt. His surgical mask hid his expression but his eyes were flaming.

"Get over here," he said.

She walked over to him and looked down into the hole where he was gesturing. It was almost nothing really. In one patch at the end, the clay had been pushed back and exposed just an inch or so. It was dirty and decayed, but it was unmistakably a piece of cloth.

"You were right," said Matt. "A graveyard is the best place to hide a body."

Eighty-five

At twenty past seven on the morning of Thursday 9th June, Etty was in the shower. Ollie was still asleep on the sofa bed in the room that used to belong to Niall and Penny's eldest daughter and Niall was in the kitchen with his wife, emptying the dishwasher, when the doorbell rang.

"Who can that be?"

"Probably a delivery," said Penny.

Niall looked out of the window, a plate in his hand.

"It's not a delivery," he said. "It's that detective."

"Shall I go?"

"No, I will."

But he didn't move.

"Niall?"

Niall put the plate carefully on the side, then pushed his fingers through his hair.

"It's very early," he said. "I wonder why she's coming so early."

Penny looked across at him where he stood rooted to the spot, his pouchy morning face wearing an expression of almost comic bewilderment. He looked old and at the same time like a defenceless boy.

"There's one way of finding out," she said.

"Yes. Of course."

The doorbell rang again and Etty came downstairs in a towelling robe, her hair damp.

"I'll get it," she said as she went towards the door.

"It's the detective," said Niall.

She turned, her hand on the doorknob, and for a moment they stared at each other. She pulled open the door.

"Etty." Maud didn't smile. She was wearing jeans and a blue cotton shirt; her unruly hair was pulled tightly back from her face. She looked serious and tired. Behind her was DS Lovell. He was thinner and sharper than ever.

"You're early," said Etty.

"Can we come in?"

"Of course."

She stood back and the two detectives entered the house. Etty led them into the kitchen where Niall still stood by the dishwasher, his wife beside him.

"You've found something," he said.

"Is your brother here as well?"

"Ollie? I think he's—"

"I'm here."

Ollie's face was all stubble and creases. He had pulled on a pair of trousers and a T-shirt, but his feet were bare.

Penny put a cup of coffee on the table for him and he subsided into a chair.

"Do you want some?" she asked Maud and Jack.

"No, thank you."

"What have you found?" Niall asked.

Maud looked at the Salters; as she did so, Etty and Niall, as if by some unwritten agreement, moved together until they were standing on either side of Ollie.

"In the early hours of this morning," she said, "we found a body."

"Mum?" Ollie was holding his coffee in both hands, which shook so that the hot liquid trembled. His eyes looked red and sore. "You mean, Mum's body?"

"It's possible," said Maud. "We will need to check dental records to confirm it. But we have found various items with it that you might be able to identify."

None of the siblings spoke. The silence in the room was thick.

"I know this is hard," said Maud.

"What items?"

"Jack?"

Lovell stepped forward and laid a small transparent envelope on the table. Inside, among specks of earth, were pieces of jewellery. Maud laid a sheet of plastic on the table, and then very delicately, as if they might disintegrate, she slid them out. A diamond engagement ring, a plain gold wedding band, a badly tarnished pair of drop earrings, like silver tears, a tarnished silver necklace, its links clogged with dirt.

"Do any of you recognise these?"

"Oh dear," said Niall. "Oh gosh."

Penny, standing at the stove, put a hand to her chest and waited.

"I don't know," said Ollie. "I don't know."

But Etty knew.

She was a child again, sitting beside her mother at her dressing table, and watching her as she threaded the earrings into her lobes and then turned to smile at her daughter. She saw Charlie lift the blonde mass of her hair and pin it up with a tortoiseshell clasp, then fasten the necklace round her neck. Etty used to twist that wedding ring round and round on her mother's fingers when they talked.

She could smell her mother's perfume, and the aroma of freshly mown grass that came through the open window was from thirty years ago. The light that fell in a rich golden shaft through the window was light from her childhood.

"They're Mummy's," she said.

"You're sure?"

Etty lifted her eyes from the jewellery but Maud didn't think she was looking at her.

"Quite sure."

She laid a hand on Ollie's head as he bent forward and Niall put an arm round her waist.

"You've found her," Etty said. "After all these years, you've found our mother for us."

"I'm so sorry," said Maud.

Beside her, Lovell made a meaningless noise deep in his throat and shifted from foot to foot. Penny moved forward and stood beside Niall. She took his hand and raised it to her lips, holding it there.

"We knew she was dead," said Niall after a pause.

"Not really." Ollie's voice was hoarse and crumbly. "There was always a bit of me . . ."

"Where was she?" Etty's face was very pale and the scar on her cheek stood out in a livid welt.

"In the churchyard."

"So she was here all the time." Etty's voice was soft. "We looked and looked but she was always here."

"What do you mean, in the churchyard?" Penny asked.

"She was buried in the same grave as an old woman who died at the same time."

She waited for the question she knew must come. It was Penny who asked it.

"Do you know who killed her?"

"We are holding someone for questioning."

"Who?" Ollie stood up with a screech of his chair. He looked ghastly. "Who are you holding? Who killed our mother?"

"That is not information that we can—" began Lovell, but Maud cut in.

"Greg Ackerley," she said.

"Greg? *Greg.*"

"We haven't charged him," said Lovell.

"We believe he killed your mother, his own father, and also, thirty years later, Bridget Wolfe."

"Greg?" Ollie took a few tottering steps towards her. "Fucking fuck. Jesus Christ."

"Did she suffer?" asked Etty. She seemed not to have

taken in Maud's disclosure, but was still gazing at the rings and earrings and necklace, her eyes large and dark in a face that seemed to have shrunk.

"We don't think so," said Lovell.

"Greg?" Niall sat down heavily on the chair Ollie had leaped up from. "I don't believe it."

'We don't yet know how she died," Maud said to Etty. "There will be an autopsy to determine cause of death."

"I am going to kill him. I am going to strangle him with my bare hands."

"You have to understand," Lovell said, casting a disapproving look at Maud. "We haven't charged Mr. Ackerley; we are simply holding him for questioning."

"Can we see her?" Etty said to Maud.

"See the body?"

"See our mother. I want to see her."

Maud thought of Charlotte Salter's skeleton, the teeth intact in the skull, the bones dark under shreds of cloth: almost abstract now, a relic from long ago.

"I understand," she said.

"Why?" asked Niall. "Why did he do it? Three people. Greg. His own father. I don't quite ..." He rubbed his face with his hands as if trying to wipe away cobwebs. "I don't understand."

He turned to Penny, his face screwed up.

"I was sure it was Paul," he said, as if they were alone in the room. "I thought that was why he took his own life."

"I know," she said, bending down to him where he sat.

"I never told you. I never told anyone."

"But I knew."

She put a hand on his puckered face and he started to cry. With a thumb, she wiped away the tears.

"We have to see her," repeated Etty. "We've waited for her for so long. All our adult lives, we've been waiting for her to come home."

"Why did you do that?" Lovell asked Maud as they left the house.

"You mean, tell them we believe Greg Ackerley killed their mother?"

"Of course I mean that."

"They have to know. We will need to ask them about what they remember of him at the party, and then on Christmas Day."

"We don't have the evidence against him."

"He was at the party before anyone else, because he helped set up the barn. The only scenario that makes sense is that Charlotte Salter arrived early, otherwise people would have seen her."

"Scenario is the right word. It's just supposition."

"And he would have had a good reason to stay on after everyone left, to clear up."

"You're right, but it's still all circumstantial."

"He would have known about the grave for Doris Winter."

"It's nowhere near enough."

"And then, he was at the right place on the day his father was killed."

"You don't even know Duncan Ackerley was killed."

"Duncan must have discovered that his son killed his friend—"

"You certainly don't know that."

"And Greg would have had the opportunity to collect his father's spare pair of glasses and put it on the bridge—the bridge Duncan Ackerley did not jump from."

"You're just—"

"I know, it's not a smoking gun. But the circumstantial evidence all adds up, Jack—even before we come to the false alibi he created for himself on the day Bridget Wolfe was killed. He would have heard the podcast when it went live, thought she was a threat because of the diary, even though it turns out there's nothing in the diary to incriminate him, poor unlucky woman, and decided he needed to set fire to the house and her along the way."

"It's a pretty flimsy alibi."

"He didn't have time for anything cleverer. He must have been in a state of pure panic."

"I still say that it's not enough," Lovell said stubbornly.

"It's way more than your old boss had when he decided Etty Salter was the murderer."

"At least she was at the scene."

"It's him, Jack. I know it's him."

"The CPS won't buy it."

Maud sighed, the heat going out of her.

"We'll see about that," she said. "First, we need to go and talk to Greg Ackerley again, tell him that the body of the woman he killed all those years ago has been found."

EIGHTY-SIX

"Would you like to make a comment?" asked Maud.

Greg Ackerley's glance moved between the detective and his solicitor.

"I don't know what you mean. I can't just make comments. I'm really glad that . . ." He paused, like someone with a stammer, as if the words were hard to utter. "Her body was found. It will be good for her family to get, I don't know, some kind of . . ."

The sentence faded away.

"Closure," said Maud. "Is that the cliché you were reaching for?"

Tania Broughton leaned forward.

"What Greg is obviously trying to say is that if you ask specific questions, he will answer them. If they are appropriate."

"You know what would give the family closure? If you just put an end to all of this and just own up to what you did."

Both Maud and Broughton looked at Greg, who didn't speak but just shook his head.

"You were at the place where Charlotte Salter died and when she died. The body was found in a prepared grave where you worked and that you knew about."

"Anyone could have known that," said Greg, almost in a mumble.

"You were seen at, or near, the spot where your father's body must have been put in the river. A pair of his glasses was taken from your family house to make it look like the body had been put in the river upstream rather than downstream."

Greg just looked down at the table.

"And you were caught lying about your whereabouts at the moment when Bridget Wolfe was killed. It doesn't look good, does it?" Maud waited but still he didn't reply. "Don't you have anything to say?"

Greg turned to Broughton.

"That's not right, is it? Aren't you meant to be saying that I don't have to prove that I'm innocent? She actually has to prove that I'm guilty." He looked back at Maud. "And I'm not guilty, anyway."

Broughton seemed to take a hold of herself.

"Greg is right," she said, "as you must know. If you have specific evidence connecting him to the actual murder scenes, then you should reveal it. If you have specific questions, you should ask them. But really, we're getting to a point where you need to charge Greg or let him leave."

A crowd had gathered round the excavated grave, held back by police tapes. Journalists were there in force. It would be on the lunchtime news that day. In Victor's bar, it was all anyone talked about.

Frances and Morgan Ackerley had taken the phone off the hook. They had closed the curtains and did not answer the door when a man from the local news rang the bell.

"You know it's nonsense, right?" Morgan said to his mother.

Frances's eyes flickered round the room, unable to rest on anything, unable to meet the eyes of her son. She looked old and frail, and yet at the same time more like the mother Morgan remembered from his childhood: there was a furtive, hunted air to her.

"Mum," he said, more urgently, frightened now. "You know it's not true."

Eighty-seven

Alec Salter's room looked out across a large, well-kept lawn and mature oak trees. But he was looking straight ahead at nothing.

"Hello, Dad," said Niall.

Alec looked round, but his eyes remained cloudy. His left arm scratched at the arm of the chair.

"How are you?" asked Ollie.

"I want my lunch. You're late."

"It's not really time for lunch."

"How often do I have to tell you? I can't just sit here waiting."

The three Salters looked at each other, then Etty stepped forward. She looked down at the old man, his skin sagging on his face, his knuckly hands fluttering and scratching, his expression querulous. There were a few days of grey stubble on his face. He had crumbs of something white on the corners of his mouth. Her father.

"We've come to tell you something," she said.

He stared at her, unseeing.

"They've found Mum," she said. He didn't react. "Charlie," she added. "They found her at last."

"Charlie?"

"Yes," said Ollie. His voice was ragged; his eyes were still sore from weeping.

"Tell her I want lunch."

"Dad." Niall put a hand on his father's shoulder and then withdrew it. "Charlie is dead."

Alec stared back out of the window.

"I want my lunch," he said. "I want gammon and eggs."

"You're sure it was Greg?" Etty asked Maud. Niall and Ollie had gone back to Glensted, but Etty had remained in Hemingford and, after walking restlessly around the streets, had gone to the station and asked to see Maud.

"It doesn't quite work like that. I'm about to send a report off to the Crown Prosecution Service and if they think there is a reasonable chance of a conviction, then they will authorise me to charge him with murder."

"I wasn't asking how it works. I'm a lawyer. I know how it works and I don't care how it works. I want to know if you are sure it was Greg?"

Maud hesitated before answering. It wasn't really an appropriate question. But then she thought: *So what?*

"He did it. We've got him at the scene of the first two murders and he faked an alibi for the third." She took a deep breath. "But I want to be really honest with you, Etty, and I want you to prepare yourself. It's my opinion that there's enough to convict him but someone sitting behind a desk at the CPS may not agree. And if they do agree, the right defence lawyer might just sow enough doubt."

Etty looked at her shrewdly. "You haven't got it, have you? Not quite."

Maud hated to say the words out loud. "There's no actual physical evidence connecting him to the crime. It might not matter, but you never know."

Maud thought Etty might flare up or cry, but she just looked resigned.

"What does it matter? It's all too late anyway."

"You can't say that."

Etty walked towards the square window that looked out on to the high street and stood gazing out. Against the light, she was little more than a silhouette. When she spoke, she didn't turn round.

"Do you want to hear two terrible things?"

Maud didn't respond. It felt as if Etty was talking to herself.

"I was almost disappointed that it wasn't Alec. I think he wanted to. Probably more than Greg. Greg was probably just too adoring of her and it all went wrong. Alec really hated her. It would have been neater if it was Alec. It would have fitted better."

"What was the other thing?"

Now Etty did turn, but because of the light, Maud still couldn't make her expression out.

"I used to be angry with Mum. I was angry with

515

her for putting up with Dad. I was angry with her for disappearing. She was always so nice about everything. Why didn't she fight back?"

Maud felt awkward. It was time to leave. She had so much to do.

"Everyone has feelings like that," she said helplessly. "It just takes time."

Etty actually laughed at that. "Time? I think I've had plenty of time."

"Have you got someone you can talk to about this?"

"I was talking to you."

"I mean . . ." Before Maud could say what she meant, her phone rang. It was Matt Moran. She looked apologetically at Etty. "Can I?"

"Sure," said Etty.

As she listened to Matt Moran, Maud kept her face blank, not showing her emotion.

"You don't sound very excited," Matt said.

"I'm with Charlotte Salter's daughter," said Maud.

"I understand. Do you want to come over? Dr. Searle wants to show you himself."

"Any news?" asked Etty as Maud ended the call.

"We'll see. Maybe your mother did fight back after all."

Dr. Searle, Matt Moran and Maud stood contemplating the skeleton on the slab.

"Do you know how she died?"

Searle took a pen from his pocket and used it as a pointer.

"There was probably a short struggle. There are fractures on the fingers of the left hand, here. Defence injuries. Like this." He held his left hand up in front of his face, the palm outwards. "There's a cranial injury that would have been decisive. But it's the right hand that's really interesting. You'll see the clawed, curved fingers, like someone with severe arthritis. You sometimes get that after death. But not this time. In the last seconds of her life, she grabbed at anything she could get hold of. Her hand locked and stayed locked for thirty years." He gestured towards a table. "It's there in two evidence bags. Hair."

"I didn't know you could get DNA from hair," Maud said.

"It can be a problem," said Matt. "But not if you pull it from the roots."

"It must have hurt him," Searle said.

Maud made herself remember.

"Greg was wearing a cap at the party," she said.

"That makes sense."

"Now we just need to make sure that it matches. We'd better go and get a sample from Greg Ackerley."

Eighty-eight

"Gregory James Ackerley. I am charging you with the murders of Charlotte Salter, Duncan Ackerley and Bridget Wolfe. You do not have to say anything. But it may harm your defence if you do not mention when questioned something which you later rely on in court. Anything you do say may be given in evidence."

Greg lifted his head wearily and shook it.

"The DNA sample we took from you with your permission matched the sample from the hair roots we found in Charlotte Salter's hands."

"It's not right," he whispered.

"She struggled with you and ripped out your hair. It was her last act."

"No."

"You were wearing a cap to cover the wound and, as Ollie Salter said during the podcast, you were violently sick that evening. You must have been utterly terrified."

"I was drunk," he said. "Just drunk."

"You hid her in the cow trough and after the party ended, you buried her in the open grave waiting for Doris

Winter, covering it with a thin layer of earth and knowing that the following day another coffin would be placed on top. You took her coat and threw it in the river."

"No."

"Your father must have suspected. I imagine he followed you on the Christmas Day walk you took and told you he knew. You lashed out at him, maybe hit him with ... was it a stone? Then you tipped him into the river. Which took him back towards your house, rather than sweeping him out to sea."

"No."

It was the only word he seemed to be able to utter.

"But the police assumed he would have been swept downriver. You turned that to your benefit, claiming the Bowden family as your alibi and planting evidence on the bridge so the police would think your father took his own life. Which they duly did."

Greg shook his head again. The lawyer whispered something into his ear but he moved away from her.

"You thought you had got away with it, and you had, until the Salter family gathered to sort out the house, and Bridget Wolfe found a diary. She exaggerated its importance. You never needed to kill her. But you didn't know that—you gave yourself an alibi with that business with the champagne and on the morning of Sunday 29th May you doused her house and outbuildings with petrol and set fire to them. Not caring that Bridget Wolfe was inside."

"You've charged him," said Tania Broughton. "The interview has to stop."

Maud looked at Greg. His eyes were flickering between the two women. He became visibly more agitated as the silence went on and on.

"Let's just finish all of this," said Maud.

"Good," said Greg. "I want to finish this as well."

"I don't mean that. I want you to stop playing this game."

"I'm not playing a game."

Maud saw that his hands were resting on the table. She leaned across and put her hands over them, as if he were a child who needed calming.

"I wish I'd known Charlotte Salter," she said, in a softer tone, almost like she was talking to herself. "It sounds almost stupid to say, but she was just kind to people. She liked them and they liked her. Apart from her husband." Maud stopped and then seemed to remember something. "And you, of course."

"You don't understand anything." Greg was almost inaudible.

"What was that?"

"I said you don't understand anything. Of course, I liked her. Everyone loved Charlie. She smiled at everyone and she flirted with everyone and then when they . . ."

He stopped and looked at Tania Broughton. She shook her head vigorously.

Then Maud saw him take a decision. She watched his face twitch and then crumple, as if the last of his control was finally breaking up. She didn't move, waited. Then she heard him take a rasping breath.

'It doesn't matter any more." Greg looked Maud full in the face. "You want to know? All right then." His face was hardening now, his voice becoming louder and clearer; Maud could feel the self-righteous anger building in him. "She flirted with me. She smiled at me. She was touchy, feely, all over me, putting her arm round my shoulder, taking my hand. She knew what she was doing, all right. And on the night of the party, she arrived early and said she had something to say to me. That I had to stop being silly about her, that she was old enough to be my mother. She found it funny, like she'd set a trap for me. She laughed at me. *Laughed*."

"And you punished her for laughing?"

"I didn't punish her," he said angrily. "Everything went red, as if my eyes were full of blood. I couldn't see, I didn't know what was happening, and when it was over she was there on the ground, her eyes open, staring up at me. It wasn't me. It was like someone else had done it."

"And your father? Was it like someone else did that?"

"I felt like I was on fire, like my brain was burning, I was only just holding it together. But it would have been all right. But then he followed me that Christmas morning and started talking about it, about that bloody ladle, about how he knew she'd gone to the barn. On and on and looking at me like he could see through me. I just wanted him to stop, to shut up. I didn't mean it. He fell and hit his head."

"And what about Bridget Wolfe? Did you not mean that?"

Greg sat back in his chair. He looked tired. Infinitely tired.

"I just meant . . ." His voice faded away.

"You were just going to burn her house down, is that what you're going to say?"

"Yes."

"But she was there."

"Yes," said Greg. "She was there."

"Was it the red mist again?"

"I guess that's what my defence will be. That I lost control."

"Like you did with your father?"

There was a flash of anger in his eyes again. Maud saw the temper in him.

"If that bloody woman had just left well alone . . ." He was searching for the right way of putting it. "Everything wouldn't have got stirred up again. It just hurt people all over again."

"It's a bit late for your father. And Charlie. And Paul Salter. And Niall, Ollie and Etty Salter."

Greg looked at her with an almost pleading expression.

"You have to understand. None of this was meant to happen. It's not me. I'm not a bad person."

"All of this because thirty years ago you thought a woman laughed at you."

Maud watched his face turn ugly. She looked at her watch.

"This interview is now concluded," she said.

EIGHTY-NINE

Ollie and Niall had decided they didn't want to see Charlie's darkened bones lying on a slab, so Etty went to the morgue alone.

Maud accompanied her, but at the door Etty said, "If it's OK, I want to do this by myself."

"Of course."

She went into the cold, stark room where the skeleton lay, and a man in a white coat lifted off the sheet and withdrew.

She stared at the bones, at the grinning skull. This wasn't her mother. Her mother was somewhere else: in the memories and the hearts of her children, in the air they breathed.

Then she looked at the hand in its death grip. Very gently, she touched it.

"You caught him," she said. "You fought for your life, and you didn't get that, but you got the man who did it."

She put a small wild rose into the hand.

"Well done," she said. "You did well. You always did well. All your life. I'm so sorry."

Maud, watching through the square of glass in the door, saw Etty put the flower in the bones of her mother's hand and saw her lips moving. She put her hand to her throat and touched the little locket that hung there. Her face was bright with love and sadness.

Then she turned away and Maud opened the door for her and the two women walked back into the sunlight.

NINETY

On the day that she was to leave, Etty picked roses from Niall and Penny's garden and walked to the churchyard. She laid the flowers on Paul's grave and sat down beside it. She half wanted to say something to him, goodbye or sorry or something, but she didn't. He wasn't there; he couldn't hear. She would only be speaking to the wind. Soon enough, his mother would be lying beside him. Dearly beloved.

Maud sent a message to Silas. *Coming home. Will you be there?* He didn't reply.

She ignored the dozens of emails and messages that congratulated her, asked her for interviews and quotes for stories they were writing. She would deal with everything later.

She drove back to London with Carrie and dropped her off at her flat.

"Thanks for everything," she said as Carrie struggled out of the car, panting and cursing.

"Like you said, what else would I have wanted to do

with my maternity leave?" She gave Maud a smile that made her small face crinkle. "Well done. Your boss must be over the moon."

"More relieved than anything else."

Carrie patted her stomach. "I'll let you know."

"Do that. I'll come and visit."

It felt she had been away for months, but it had been less than two weeks. She slung her bag over her shoulder, opened the front door and then the door to their flat.

"Hello," she called as she mounted the stairs.

But as soon as she reached the top of the stairs, she knew he wasn't there. His coat and jackets were gone from the hooks in the hall, his shoes were missing from the shoe rack, apart from a tatty pair of summer sandals.

Maud put down her bag and went into the living room. There were gaps in the bookshelves; a painting and some photos had gone from the wall; the drinks cabinet he'd bought on eBay was no longer in the corner.

He had left the kitchen tidier than he usually did. The dishwasher had run its cycle and was ready to be unloaded. The stripy pink apron that he always wore to cook was no longer on its hook, and the favourite mug that he always had his morning tea from was gone.

Maud wandered into the bedroom. She didn't bother to open the wardrobe or the drawers in the chest, because she knew what she would find. She closed the curtains and lay down on her side of the big bed. Their sports arena, Silas had once called it. She put her face in the pillow. He was gone and it was over. Now she could cry.

But she didn't cry. She thought about the Salter children waiting for their mother to come home until waiting wore a groove into them and became part of who they were. She remembered how the three of them had drawn close together when she told them their mother's body had been found, making a tight group that looked at long last like a family. She thought of Charlotte Salter's fingers clutching at the hair of her murderer, not letting go for more than thirty years.

She got up from the bed, washed her face, pulled on a clean shirt and her scuffed boots, picked up her keys and left the flat. She walked swiftly to her local pub, where she ordered a packet of crisps and a half-pint and stood at the bar.

It was karaoke night. She wasn't going to weep. She was going to belt out a song until her throat hurt and her battered heart felt like it would burst.

NINETY-ONE

Etty opened the living room window and let the sounds of the night blow in. Cars revving at the bottom of the road; a couple arguing; doors slamming; somewhere music playing, the bass notes throbbing.

It had been raining and even here, in the heart of the city, she could smell autumn in the air. Leaves were drifting down from the plane trees that lined her street. They floated golden in the lamplight. Summer was over.

She took out her phone and laid it flat on the table at the ready, then poured herself a glass of red wine and took a sip. She was extraordinarily tired but it was a tiredness that gave clarity to her thoughts, as if everything was sharply outlined and backlit. Memories ran through her like a spool of film. The weeks she had just lived through, fire and tears and a pile of bones, the skeletal fingers still fastened in their death grip. A river that ebbed and flowed with the tide. A decaying house and a father reduced to his proper size: not a monster any more, but only a damaged and damaging man after all.

She pushed away all images of Greg and thought instead of his father, Duncan, who for so long she had only remembered as a drowned body twitching in the tide, his ghastly eyes staring at her. He had been a kind man. She thought of her brothers—the ones that lived and the one who had died. She thought of Charlie, and with such concentration that she almost felt that if she turned she would catch a last glimpse of her mother before she disappeared.

Then she thought of herself, Etty Salter, young and full of hope, and for the first time let herself feel compassion for that terrified, lonely girl.

Maybe at last she could learn how to forgive herself. Maybe it wasn't too late to begin again, do it better this time. At least she could try.

Reaching across to her phone, she pressed "Play." Morgan's soft voice filled the room.

Thirty years ago, in a village in East Anglia where the land is swallowed up by mudflats and marshes and a hard wind blows in from the sea, a woman went missing.

It was midwinter, sleety and dark, but Christmas was coming. There were festive lights in the high street, decorated trees in the windows, smoke curling from the chimneys of the houses. And in a barn on the edge of the village, people were gathering for a party.

But one person never arrived, and life was changed forever in that ordinary little village. Her disappearance was the start of a chain of terrible events that for more than three decades blighted the lives of two families.

This is a story of dark secrets that were buried a lifetime ago, but which never lost their power, and of the grip that the past has upon the present.

It is the story of the people whose lives unravelled from that winter day: sons and daughters, brothers and sisters, partners and friends.

It is the story of a woman. She is a wife, a mother, a confidante. She is impulsive and warm-hearted and full of life. When people describe her, they use words like "radiant," "vital," "generous," "optimistic." She is a woman of appetites: she loves food, red wine, long hot baths. She loves dancing. Walking in all weathers. Jigsaw puzzles. Gossip. Weepy films. Nice clothes. Crumpets. Marmalade. Chance encounters. Peonies and sweet peas. Candles. Mangy dogs. Lost causes.

She loves life. She loves people. Above all, she loves her four children.

Her name is Charlotte Salter.

ACKNOWLEDGEMENTS

It takes more than an author to build a book. In our case, it takes each other, and we also have so many brilliant people who have joined us in the process.

We are forever grateful to the wonderful agents who have been our champions and our rocks: Sarah Ballard and Eli Keren at United Agents, Sam Edenborough at Greyhound Literary, Joy Harris from the Joy Harris Literary Agency. Thank you.

We are happy to be part of the lovely Simon & Schuster family. The team there have watched over this book. In particular, we would like to thank Katherine Armstrong, Suzanne Baboneau, Ian Chapman, Jess Barratt, Hayley McMullan, Louise Davies and Genevieve Barratt.

In the US we have—as always—benefited from the kindness, support and skill of others.

Once again, we're grateful to our fabulous US agent, Joy Harris, who watches over us. And so many thanks to the wonderful team at HarperCollins: Emily

Krump, Tessa James, Danielle Bartlett and Christopher Connolly.

Booksellers work on the front line. We thank the ones we have met and the ones we haven't for their enthusiasm and energy, and for their commitment to books. Also, thanks go to the organisers of literary festivals around the country, and to libraries and book groups. Like most authors, we travel to small venues and to larger ones over the year, and we are bowled over by the unflagging optimism and passion we find. Books depend on their readers as well as their writers: this is the soil in which they grow.

Crime may be dark and misanthropic, but crime writers are a kind, generous, supportive and all-round lovely group of people. To you all, thank you!

And lastly another kind of family: our own rowdy tribe, who are our life's blood. Our children and their partners, our brothers and sisters, and our last remaining parent, have been ridiculously nice to us this year. Some of them have put us up in their homes, all of them have kept us going and given us joy. And our grandchildren have made us very, very happy.

Nicci French is the pseudonym for the writing partnership of journalists Nicci Gerrard and Sean French. The couple are married and live in London and Suffolk. They have written twenty-five books together.